SPELLBOUND TO THE FAE

FAE

JC COMPTON

CONTENTS

CHAPTER I

Outskirts of Antioch, Byzantine Empire, 1097.

YVAN KNEELED BEFORE THE small wooden table in his tent, his palms joined together, and pressing his rosary against his forehead.

"Eternal Father," he whispered. "Please hear my prayers and deliver my lord, Robert of Flanders, from his sins, so that the gates of Your realm may not be closed to him. Eternal Father, please hear my prayers..."

Aged twenty-two, Yvan De La Haye-Thompson was a pious knight, descended from an Anglo-Norman family. As the oldest son in his family, he was not allowed to join a religious order like he wanted to and was expected to marry and carry out the lineage. But because he could not bring himself to marry, he had instead joined Robert II, Count of Flanders, Stephen of Blois, Robert Curthose, Hugh of Vermandois, and the French and Flemish forces on the first crusade, answering the call of Pope Urban II. Filled with admiration at first for Robert of Flanders, the man who knighted him, Yvan embarked on this journey like any young man, filled with hope and dreams of glory in the name of God and his lord. He took the teachings of Jesus to heart, and he devoted his life to his lord like he devoted his heart to Christ. He saw the handsome young lord, clad in a white tunic with a red cross over his golden armor, like a messenger from Heaven, one who should remain pure and untainted—crusade or not. But, to his great disappointment, he found that the lords he followed and their armies were not messengers from Heaven, far from that. If any of them had faith at all—and he often doubted it—it melted like snow in the sun the moment they saw a woman, and now the soldiers spent more time busy with prostitutes underneath their tents than sleeping or praying at night. This crusade was no spiritual journey for them, just another opportunity to get away from their castles, their homes, and their wives, and behave worse than Pagan idol-worshippers, all while earning their forgiveness in the eyes of God. It deeply troubled Yvan, who fought so hard against his own desires, and he often wrote his spiritual father Anselm of Canterbury, a holy man who did not hesitate to stand up to the king of England in the name of Christ and true faith. Anselm, who knew of Yvan's sins, always reminded him to keep on praying and never give in to the flesh, for the Lord saw who among His children were true to Him in their hearts, and they would be rewarded in the end. Anselm's letters were Yvan's only light of hope as he sat in this debauchery camp while the city of Antioch remained under siege.

After he thought he had prayed enough, he got up and left his tent and went to his lord's, where he found him, again, in good company. The young woman sitting on his lap was fully dressed, but her cheeks were flushed, and so were Robert's. They were both drinking wine and laughing. Two soldiers stood quietly nearby, guarding their lord.

"Yvan? What's going on?" Robert asked, finishing his glass of wine.

"My Lord, may I please talk to you privately?" Yvan said, pursing his lips with displeasure at the scene before him.

Robert scowled. He was weary of his knight's sermons, and certainly did not want to hear another one tonight.

"Is it about my faith again?" he asked.

"Yes, my Lord," Yvan said.

"I don't have time for that," Robert replied angrily.

Yvan suddenly threw himself on his knees before him and brought his hands together.

"My Lord, I implore you," he said. "Please give up this lifestyle and repent for your sins! I know our Eternal Father will forgive you! Jesus, the shepherd would never let a single lamb go astray!"

Robert brought his hand to his forehead, looking annoyed.

"Listen, Yvan," he said. "I know I'm a sinner. But right now I'm at war. Do you know how difficult it is to lead an army, risking my life every day? How can a man survive without a little comfort?"

He pulled the beauty on his lap closer to him and she smiled.

"But the Lord is..." Yvan started, but Robert dismissed him with a gesture of his hand.

"I'm a weak man, and I'm tired. Why don't you just pray for me, and I will confess when I return home?" he said.

"Do you swear you will confess your sins?" Yvan asked him.

"Yes, yes," Robert said hastily. "Now go to bed."

Yvan, in the great naivety of his youth, believed him, and so he left him that night, assured that he would send the young woman away and go to bed. He ignored the soldiers laughing as he walked past them in the camp, and returned to his tent, where a surprise awaited him. He stopped in his tracks and stared at the young man in heavy chain mail and armor covered by a long purple and red tunic. He had removed his helmet, and his long blond hair fell upon his shoulders like an angelic crown. He turned his gray eyes to Yvan and smiled.

"My Lord! Finally!" he said, falling to his knees before him.

"F-Florian?" Yvan said, astounded. "Had I not asked you to wait for me in Canterbury?"

Though he shared a deep and pious bond with his servant, the young man was also one of the reasons Yvan had wanted to leave his castle, and why he had asked him to remain by his mother's side.

"Please don't tell me that you come with bad news!" he said, immediately falling to his knees with him. "Is my mother...?"

"No, my Lord, your family is doing fine," Florian said, turning his gaze up to him, and his eyes were filled with both relief and guilt. "Oh, please forgive me, my Lord, but I just couldn't let you go to war alone when I have devoted my life to you!" he said.

He looked tired and weary, and Yvan could tell he had come on foot, carrying only little food, and braving every danger to come to him. How could his heart not be partial to such a courageous young man? Yvan ran his fingers through his dirty blond hair and embraced him and kissed his forehead.

"You are forgiven. I'm just glad you made it here alive," he whispered.

He did not want Florian to be here, when he had come all this way to escape him and the sinful feelings he inspired him. He had gone on this crusade to cleanse his soul and his body, but now that Florian was here, in his arms, he knew he was doomed.

"My Lord..." Florian whispered.

Yvan could feel his heart beating as fast as his. He was becoming weak again, and he could not let himself be weak.

"Come, you need a bath and some food," he said, getting up.

He took Florian's hands and helped him up. Because the camp could be ambushed anytime, soldiers were discouraged from bathing in the nearby river, so Yvan had a wooden tub brought to his tent, and he filled it with water. He then ordered Florian to undress and get inside, and insisted on washing him himself, perhaps the way he wanted to cleanse his own body of sin.

"My Lord, this is embarrassing. I should be the one washing you," Florian gently protested as his master's large hands roughly scrubbed him with a brush and soap.

"Nonsense. Jesus would certainly do the same for you," Yvan said with a smile.

Florian laughed, then said: "There's enough room for two in the tub. Please let me wash you too, my Lord."

Yvan stopped scrubbing his back and looked into his eyes, wondering if he was thinking about the same things he thought every time he saw him. But Florian's eyes were so pure, so innocent, that he could not refuse him.

"Alright," he said.

He got up, removed his armor and clothes, and slowly got into the tub with him.

While the tub would be large enough for two short men, it really was not for anyone as tall as Yvan even by himself. He brought his knees up to his chin, embarrassed, but Florian laughed.

"I guess I miscalculated," he said, making Yvan more comfortable. "Well then, let's take care of your beautiful hair, my Lord."

Yvan's hair was long and black, and Florian loved washing and combing it for him. He was simply trying to make him feel at home, even so far from home. So he let Florian wash and untangle his hair, which needed it, in the quiet of the tent. Only a small candle burned on the table nearby, its flickering light dancing on their naked bodies.

After combing his master's hair, Florian proceeded to wash him, except he did not use the harsh brush on his skin, but his hands. Slowly, he spread soap on Yvan's hairy chest and arms, his long fingers gliding ever so gently on his skin. Yvan closed his eyes, trying not to look at him, not to think of anything, but the young man's tender touch only awakened his sinful nature more and more.

"My Lord, would you please stand so I can wash your legs now?" Florian asked in what sounded to Yvan's cursed mind as a hot whisper. He shook that thought away and stood before him, knowing that his servant would see what troubled him so much right now. He looked away and tried to remember a prayer, or even a single line of a prayer, but he couldn't, so he closed his eyes. Florian noticed his struggle.

"Oh, my Lord, it must be so hard, being around all these loose women!" he said.

"I have sworn that I would never marry or lay with a woman, like Christ," Yvan said in a solemn voice.

"But you are a man of flesh," Florian said. "If you have no one to help you remain chaste, I fear that you may someday give in to temptation."

Yvan opened his eyes and looked at his servant kneeling in the tub before him and gazing upon him with the same adoration as a devout to God. Florian was too good-natured. He was willing to do something unnatural only to help rid him of his sin, so that his thoughts could remain pure on this crusade.

"Florian, you don't have to. I can pray more," he said softly.

But Florian shook his head.

"Let me be soiled. I don't matter, I am but your servant. And through your prayers, I too will be forgiven for my own sins..." he whispered, and for the first time, Yvan realized that the young man probably shared the same sin as him. And in that moment, his mind was defeated.

He let the young man take care of his needs and soiled his mouth under the disguise of preserving his chastity with women, but in his heart, Yvan knew he was sinning, and he blamed it on women. If not for all these Jezebels running from tent to tent half-naked, would he even have such thoughts? Surely, his body had been poisoned by these witches and their craft. So he decided to pray more and cleanse himself, and now the poor Florian, whom he was taking to Hell with him.

After the crusade was over, he received land near Calais in France, and moved there with Florian and only a few other servants. Despite his family's pleas, he still refused to marry and dedicated his life to God, praying incessantly for the forgiveness of the one sin he could not rid himself of.

Florian was self-sacrificial, and after letting his master soil his mouth, he told him he could soil his body as well, if it prevented him from breaking his chastity vows. But when they lay together like man and woman, were they not doing just that? Florian said they were not, for they were simply fighting the Devil's attempts to make Yvan give up on his vows, and that it did not matter that his body was soiled in the process. At first, Yvan felt sorry for him, but as the years went by, as he heard the eagerness, the lust in the soft moans of his servant as he used his body to relieve himself from his desires, Yvan began to understand that the Devil was not only in women, but also in this beautiful man, with his angelic blond hair and beard, the one man he could never refuse.

The thought tormented him day and night, and the more he tried to keep Florian away from him, the more he longed for him. But one day, after a week of fasting and prayer, he finally found the courage to send him away. Florian stood before him, shaking, as he listened to him. They were alone in Yvan's bedroom.

"My Lord... no!" Florian said.

"You heard me. You must go," Yvan said, refusing to look at him.

Florian fell to his knees beside him and took his hand. They were not young anymore. Yvan was forty-five and Florian forty-one, but the blond angel had lost nothing of his beauty or his love for his master.

"My Lord, I have no one but you! I am nothing without you!" he pleaded, and Yvan could hear the tears in his voice.

"Florian..." he said, troubled. "We can't continue like this. You want to help rid me of my sins, but *you* are my sin. As long as you remain by my side, this poison will never go away."

He turned to Florian, who looked up to him with his tear-filled eyes.

"If you feel as I do, then our only sin is love!" Florian said. "Did you not say you had for me the purest, untainted love?"

"I do, but..." Yvan said.

His heart was breaking. He knew that the only way to be at peace with God would be to chase Florian away and never see him again, but how could he live on this Earth without the man who had been by his side for over twenty years of his life?

"My Lord, my Master, I beg you!" Florian said, clinging to his hand. "Punish me if you want, strike me, starve me, but please don't send me away! I shall die if I cannot be by your side!"

Yvan could no longer hold back his tears, and they rolled quietly down his cheeks. So many tears, for all the words he could not tell his beloved servant.

"My Lord, if you still have tears to cry for me, then you must know that I need you!" Florian insisted, wetting his large hand with his tears.

Yvan once again felt weak and fell to his knees and embraced him. No, he could never live without him, much less fight the sin in his heart. But he knew that God was watching him and frowning upon him, for he was soon after killed in battle. A spear through the heart. He died in a few minutes, and in the confusion of the battlefield, he was not even granted his last wish: to see Florian's face once again—or so he thought. For he did not quite die.

The light came for him, but it did not take him to Heaven, as he still vaguely hoped. It took him instead to a battlefield, except the soldiers were nothing like those he had ever seen. They wore no armor, but uniforms, some blue and white, some green. Some wore pointed black feathered hats, some hard green helmets, their swords shot fire from their tips, and thousands of bizarre catapults spat out boulders with the sound of thunder. They came crashing all around him, and he fell to the ground, covering his head with his hands, and begging God to hear his pleas and forgive him. But God did not answer him. No one did. Now he was sure he had gone to Hell, and Hell was not made of fire, but of endless battles and death.

But he opened his eyes again under a tent. He blinked several times, wondering what had happened, or whether he had been dreaming, and then he heard someone crying by his side and turned to him. It was Florian. They were in his tent, and his servant, thinking he was dead, was crying by his side.

"Florian..." he whispered.

Florian opened his eyes and stared at him, and his face first turned pale, but color soon returned to his cheeks. He rushed over to his lord and examined his chest, then touched his face and his hands, and cried even more.

"Oh, Eternal Father," he said, turning his eyes up to the divine being he hoped was watching over them, "This is a miracle! Thank you for listening to my prayers! Thank you!"

If Yvan had been himself, he would have joined him in prayer, but he was not quite himself anymore. The moment his servant turned his head up and exposed his neck to him, a new, primal, almost savage desire to bite it rushed through him, and he grabbed him and began to drink his blood. The poor man did not understand, but he was not afraid. He knew that something magical had happened to his master, for he was alive after being dead for days, and so he let him do what his body apparently needed to do now. He moaned softly as his master drank him, as though it was a pleasurable experience for him.

After feeding on him for a few seconds, Yvan realized what he was doing and backed away from him, horrified.

"What... what am I?" he said.

He looked at his hands, and they were pale... and he thirsted for blood? Yvan knew the name of the creature that drank human blood: a vampire. And now, as he saw the man responsible for his sins in his human life sitting beside him, a small, indecent stream of blood pouring out of the wound he left on his neck, and gazing upon him with loving eyes, eyes that begged for more, he knew that Florian was the one responsible for this.

"Does it matter what you are? You are alive; it's all I could ever wish for!" Florian said, throwing himself in his arms.

Yvan tried to keep him away, but his servant would not let go.

"Florian... I am dead! I am a monster!" he protested.

"But you're here with me! Your heart is beating, and I can hold you in my arms again and talk to you!" Florian said, gazing into his eyes with emotion. "Yvan... Oh, Yvan, I love you! When you were found on the battlefield, lying in your own blood, I... I..."

He wiped away a tear, and Yvan stared at him, trembling with fear and confusion.

"Florian... We're... brothers in arms, shield mates, aren't we?" he said.

Florian's beautiful gray eyes suddenly clouded, and he frowned.

"No, Yvan, you know we're not."

"We are," Yvan insisted, and since he would not listen to him, Florian pressed himself against him, burying his head in his neck.

"Yvan, you died," he whispered. "I saw you die and come back to life. So if you're no longer a creature of God, then what difference does it make what we are?"

"Florian!" Yvan said.

He tried removing his arms from him, but Florian would not let go.

"Yvan, I love you and this time I won't let you go!" he repeated. "Oh, why... Why can't you just say the obvious? But you won't say it, so I will show you. I will become like you and be with you forever, as we were meant to be!"

And with this, he bit Yvan's neck as hard as he could - which barely scratched Yvan's now undead skin - and then he began to lick the little blood coming out of the wound. And as he did, Yvan felt waves of pleasure crashing through his body, waves stronger and more sinful even than those he experienced when he lay with him. He had become a demon, a fiend, and all because of Florian, the beautiful young man who had tempted him all these years and tricked him into becoming his lover. Yes, he had been tricked, and he was being tricked again into indulging in whatever new sins he could indulge in in this new form. So, gathering all his strength, he pushed him away and struck him across the face. Florian fell to the ground and let out a loud cry of pain and terror. Yvan sat there, on the bed where he had been lying, his entire body shaking as he listened to Florian's cries, until he realized why he was crying: with his new strength, he had torn off his face.

"Florian! No!" he cried.

He rolled off the bed and tried to reach him, but Florian, who could no longer see anything, waved his hands desperately to keep him away.

This could not be real, Yvan thought. It had to be a nightmare. Or was this God's punishment for his sins, for their sins?

After a few minutes in agony, Florian stopped struggling, and then he stopped breathing, and he lay there, pieces of his face splattered all over the floor, the bed, the blankets, and a large puddle of blood underneath him. Yvan curled up in a ball on the floor, crying desperately.

Soldiers soon came, alerted by their cries, and found them. They immediately knew what Yvan was and tried to kill him. He killed them instead—all of them. He massacred the entire camp that night with his bare hands, swords, hatchets, anything he could find. He needed to kill them to appease the excruciating pain in his heart, the pain of having killed Florian. But Florian, also, did not die.

Days, years, and eventually centuries passed, and Yvan learned to live on as what he now was: an almost immortal creature. There were others like him, and when he came across them, they were interested in his Herculean strength. But he wanted nothing of this life, so he remained alone in his castle, killing any human who came near, and soon he became a legend, the 'Monster of Calais'. This monster lived a life of seclusion and repentance for his crimes, and though he still believed Florian had been tempted by the Devil to seduce him, just like Eve was tempted to make Adam eat the forbidden fruit, what he had done to him was far worse. Not only had he condemned his immortal soul to Hell by soiling his body like he would a woman's, but he had also stolen his life. Even Hell was too sweet for what he was, and he thought perhaps making him live forever as a monster in this world was God's punishment. But, even in his bottomless despair, Yvan's heart never changed. Centuries after Florian's death, it still yearned for him, and though he had stopped counting the days since his faithful servant left this world, he could never erase him from his mind. Night after night, he prayed in the small chapel of his castle for God to forgive Florian and accept him in His realm, and to punish him instead for his servant's sins.

It was one such night, as he kneeled in front of his altar, barefoot in his brown monastic robe, that an angel appeared to him—or rather a seraph. The man appeared out of thin air and seemed to be walking down an invisible staircase. He was a tall Norse, and he was clad in a pure white robe, his long blond hair braided close to his head. His face bore intricate tattoos, and he had the build of a warrior. At first, Yvan thought Jesus Christ had appeared before him, but he remembered that Jesus was not Norse and would not tattoo the skin God gave him.

"Who... Who are you?" he asked, turning his black eyes up to him.

"I'm Erik... What exactly are you doing, brother?" Erik asked, curious.

"Praying," Yvan said.

"For what?" Erik asked, quite confused.

"I am a sinner," Yvan said solemnly, returning his gaze to the altar. "Because I was weak, my servant was possessed by the Devil and in turn seduced me, and I murdered him. We both were defeated by Satan."

"Then why do you need God to forgive you? Wasn't it Satan's doing?" Erik said as he reached the ground.

. He stood beside him and the altar and gazed at the large Jesus on the cross hanging above it. Unlike Yvan, he had lost his faith in God when he learned that he was in fact a half-angel. God was basically his grandfather, not some almighty creature who would ever do anything for him.

"God hates Satan, but he hates sinners too," Yvan muttered.

Erik sighed.

"What if I told you that God really doesn't care that much about humans, and not at all about creatures like us?" he said.

"Lies," Yvan said.

"No, brother, it's the reality of this world. We are alone in it," Erik said. "No amount of prayer will ever make you feel better, but you can atone for your 'sins' through your actions. You can make this godless world we live in better by punishing criminals of the underworld. How about it? We could certainly use your legendary strength."

Yvan gazed at him, perplexed. The idea of doing good deeds to repent for his sins had never crossed his mind now that he was a monster.

It was that night he decided to follow this curious young man, this half-angel from the North, and become a seraph. And as a seraph, he found that he could use his monstrous strength to destroy the seeds of evil, not only in the underworld but also in the world of humans, and thus serve God in the only way he now could. He was powerful, more so than he had ever been, and now he had a license to kill—granted by God himself to the mysterious order of the seraphim and the angels. But he soon found out that power came with other temptations, and the greatest of them was to expand one's power and control over others, and so he did during the Inquisition.

During the twelfth century, the Church went on another crusade, this time against heresy within the Kingdom of France, where many of these new religions had emerged. One of them was Catharism. Originated in southern France, the Cathars called themselves devout Christians but refused to obey the Church, and it was

said that among their ranks were many witches, practicing their craft under the disguise of piety.

Yvan still blamed women for his sins and what had
happened to him and Florian, and he was eager to join
the Inquisition and rid the world of humans of these
Jezebels and harlots who seduced men with their potions and charms. For if women were chaste and modest,
if they covered their hair, stayed at home, and obeyed
their husbands like the Bible told them, he thought,
none of these heresies would have appeared in the first
place. Women were the temptresses who had brought
sin and evil into this world. Erik, on the other hand, did
not need an excuse to burn witches; it was something
he enjoyed because it made him feel powerful, and he
did not see why he should be ashamed of it. He was
a half-angel by blood and had been appointed to the
position of seraph, which meant he could do anything
he wanted in this world. So, they traveled together to
the South of France along with human clergy members
affiliated with their order.

As creatures of the underworld in the service of God,
Yvan and Erik were expected to be able to better identify those men and women who had made a pact with
the Devil, and they indeed identified a few vampires,
shapeshifters, and werewolves, but most of the people
brought to trial were just mediocre humans. But the
clergy wanted confessions, so they were tortured until
they admitted to flying on a broomstick at night, or kissing the devil's ass in a ritual, and then they were burned
at the stake. And while Erik found Yvan awfully naïve for
believing any of the things they confessed to, the former
crusader firmly believed them, and was now convinced

that the forces of the Devil were at work everywhere, now more than ever, in an attempt to eradicate the power of God from this world.

One of the fiercest group of witches he ever encountered was a Cathar sisterhood in the mountainous region of Gevaudan, which fell under the jurisdiction of the Bishop of Mende. Yvan would always remember that particular witch hunt, for it was the first in which he encountered witches who did not fear him, and women who did not fear men.

The leader of the sisterhood was Aurelia Escobar, a Spaniard of Moorish descent. Though she claimed her family had converted to Christianity, the locals naturally suspected her of being a heretic, or perhaps even a secret Muslim. But the moment Yvan looked into her burning black eyes, he knew that she was like him. She was still a human, but something in her proud stance, her fierceness, triggered his instincts as a vampire. If they simply hung her, she would awaken again in her true form, so she would have to be burned alive, for fire was one of the safest ways to eliminate a future vampire. But in order to burn her, he first had to obtain a confession from her.

"I will repeat the question one last time," Bishop Barnard, the primary inquisitor, said. "What were you and the five other women we captured doing alone, at night, in the ruins of the old abbey?"

Aurelia, who had been tied to the rack for hours, naked in the cold dark room, showed impressive resilience, but even her strong will was beginning to falter.

"Chanting hymns..." she repeated, breathing heavily.

The torturer tightened the ropes and she screamed. Yvan watched her body quiver with pain without any emotion.

"But a book was found... a book with blank pages. What was it for? Was it a grimoire to write down your spells?" Bishop Barnard insisted, leaning over her.

She spat in his face.

"You'll never know," she said, and for him it was enough of a confession.

"We have a confession. Burn her tomorrow with her sisters," he told the other clergy members and inquisitors present.

Aurelia never flinched when she heard her sentence. Instead, she let out a sigh of relief.

Yvan walked over to her and leaned over her.

"Are you not afraid?" he asked, looking into her eyes.

She ought to be, for she would become an example for all the other harlots and witches like herself, but, unashamed of her nudity and her position, she gazed into his eyes defiantly in response.

"We know of the spells to destroy your kind, and someday, my great-great-great-granddaughter will kill you!" she said, spitting in his face.

Yvan wiped his face and took a step back, glaring at her with utter fury. He could smash her skull to pieces right here and there, but that would be too easy. She who thought herself a witch and pretended to curse him should die a slow and painful death instead.

"Burn her slowly. I want to hear her scream and beg for God's mercy," he told the inquisitors, before walking away.

But no matter how many witches and heretics he burned, there were always new groups emerging, because evil was deeply rooted in the world of humans. Satan spoke to them and seduced them, through women and sinners like himself, and every time those sinful thoughts that had plagued him as a human returned to his mind, he punished himself by isolating and praying. And so he did that night again, in a small crypt near the village of Javols, where the interrogations took place.

There, he sat on the ground, his head leaning against the cold stones of the wall, and his eyes lost in the darkness. In his mind, he was reliving his last day as a mortal, his first night as a vampire, and how he had mutilated and murdered the poor Florian. He closed his eyes in pain. Florian said he *loved* him. Love was good, it was something that came from God. But what their bodies wanted came from Satan. How could someone as pure and honest as Florian carry inside him both the will of God and that of Satan? Even as the years passed, it still did not make any more sense to Yvan. Florian's death still did not make any sense. The only thing he knew was that it was all his fault. He could have said 'no' when Florian tempted him, he could have refused to let them both become sinners. But because he was weak, they both fell together, and he ended up murdering him and becoming a monster. And he had lost more than a faithful servant, a friend. He had lost the one that meant everything to him.

A man then entered the crypt, and from his light footsteps and his floral scent, Yvan knew that he was a vampire, probably come to test his strength against a giant.

It didn't matter. He could easily kill him. He outpowered most of them.

"I'm not in the mood for a duel," he said in a low sigh.

"Really? I had something else in mind," the man said, and Yvan suddenly turned around, horrified, as he recognized his voice.

"F-Florian?" he gasped.

The man standing before him, clad in a black hooded cloak, still had beautiful, long blond hair, but no face. In its place was a black hole filled with smoke. Yvan got up, shaking, and he was not sure whether it was with fear, joy, guilt, or all at the same time. He could not believe it. Was the man before him real or a ghost? But he clearly had the scent of a vampire, and he was there, after being dead for centuries.

"How is this possible? I saw you die..." Yvan whispered in shock.

"That's right, because you killed me..." Florian said in a less-than-friendly voice that seemed to echo all around them from the walls.

He began to pace slowly across the crypt.

"Do you know what it feels like to have your face torn off? And by the one who has all your heart and trust?" he asked.

Yvan couldn't answer him. He lowered his eyes in shame.

"It hurts," Florian said, turning back to him. "But something happened inside my body, perhaps as a result of drinking your blood, and I couldn't die. I became stuck in this world, without a face."

Yvan shrunk even more before him. He did not know whether Florian had come to simply face his killer or murder him, but whatever he did to him, Yvan knew he deserved it.

"Why won't you look at me?" Florian then snapped at him.

"Because... it's my fault. I did this to you," Yvan said.

"And do you know what I want? What I've been tracking you down all these years for?" Florian said, coming closer.

"Answers?" Yvan said softly. "I have none for you. I'm a monster, and I did what monsters do."

Florian suddenly raised his hand and Yvan was hurled against the wall with incredible strength. Though the faceless man's hands never touched him, he could feel them around his throat, his arms, his hands, and even inside him. They were going to rip him open.

Florian slowly walked up to him, maintaining his invisible grip on him.

"You took my face, but you left me with a few other gifts... Master," he said in a cold, almost sadistic voice.

Yvan could hardly breathe, and now he could sense just how powerful Florian was, but he had no fear, only guilt... and love.

"Florian... I'm so sorry for what I did to you. You can kill me now. I deserve it," he said softly, as tears poured down his cheeks.

Florian seemed to hesitate.

"What are you waiting for? Do it," Yvan urged him.

But Florian let go of him instead and turned around.

"I can't kill you," he whispered. "I should not have drunk your blood after you drank mine."

"I don't understand..." Yvan said.

"Surely you know what it means in our world," Florian said.

Yes, Yvan knew now. He had learned it from the few peers he encountered over the years. The vampire who bit someone and then let them drink their blood became their blood master for all eternity, and the poor human or vampire who became their eternal blood servant was bound to obey them.

"Then I order you to kill me," Yvan said. "Please, do what is right and kill me now."

Florian turned his faceless head to him again.

"I should kill you..." he said.

"Then what are you waiting for?" Yvan said.

But Florian did not budge. Long minutes passed, and Yvan was the first to break down in tears and fall to his knees before the one he still loved so much.

"Please, Florian! End this nightmare for both of us and kill me!" he said.

He wanted to turn back time and undo what he had done and give him back his life and his face. He wanted to embrace him again like he used to at night, to kiss him, to feel him in his arms, but he couldn't. He had no right to even think about these things after what he had done. And yet his lips trembled, desperate to tell him what his heart had been hiding for so many years.

"I wish you would not cry and just say it," Florian said in a trembling voice. "Why was it so hard for you to admit that we were not just doing those things to rid you of your lustful thoughts about women? Yvan, you never even looked at women! How many years can you go on deceiving yourself? But even now, after what you've done to me, you won't say it. You'd rather let me live on like this, wondering why I gave myself to you, my heart, my soul, my very life, all for nothing... You're nothing but a coward!"

Florian no longer had eyes to cry, but the voice that echoed around him was filled with the tears he could not shed, and it only broke Yvan's heart more. Yes, he was both a sinner and a coward, torn between the desire to be one again in the underworld with the man who had been more than his lover as a human and who seemed like he still wanted that flame to live on, and the knowledge it would only make the horror of his actions worse. It was better for Florian to never know and hate him. If only he could rid himself of the last of his feelings for his former master, then, Yvan thought, perhaps he would be able to kill him the next time they met, like he deserved.

"Florian..." he sobbed, covering his face.

"I don't have a name or a face. You took both from me, along with my life," Florian said, and he walked away, leaving Yvan alone.

CHAPTER 2

Eve was born in France in the year 1749, near a small village named Javols in the Gevaudan region. Deep in the heart of the Massif Central mountains, with its bone-chilling, snowy winters and mild summers, it was an isolated region in which most people spoke Occitan or *Langue d'Oc*, and, despite years of persecution during the Inquisition, the local Christians still firmly believed in magic and folktales. A legend said the giant Gargantua came through the region and his strides were so big that he dropped his two clogs miles apart and they turned into rocks that could still be seen by the locals. Others spoke of a sunken city in the Thau Basin, of which the church bells would sometimes ring underwater. There were legends about fairies, rocks that would curse those who tried to move them, magical wells, and, later, that of the frightening *bèstia de Gavaudan*, the Beast of Gevaudan. Until the eighteenth century, the region was also a stronghold of Protestant dissidents like the Huguenots and the Camisards, and often saw the king's legions marching through its muddy paths on campaigns to tame the rebellious spirit of the locals.

Eve was a child of Gevaudan, and she, too, was a rebel, though her family were not Protestants. She was a rebel because, when she was born, they said she was a boy and named her 'Paul', and as she grew up, she knew she was not. The earliest conversation she remembered having with her sweet mother Maryse on the matter was just after she turned five. Maryse was a beautiful young woman, smart, creative, and also a child of this land of mountains and magic. She took Eve on her lap in the soothing darkness of their little farmhouse and listened to her. Not like an adult listened to the sweet chatter of a five-year-old, but like a free soul would listen to another free soul, only one a little younger. Eve knew and understood what the adults said, and she knew her body was not made like her mother's, but she knew she was a girl, and, because she loved and trusted her mother, she told her. And Maryse simply smiled and said: "You know what? I think I've always known that you were a girl."

"You're not angry, *Maman*?" Eve asked her. She had not expected to be scolded, but she did not really know how her mother would react.

"I'm not angry; I just feel sad that we never realized. My poor baby..." Maryse said, holding her tightly against her chest.

Her curly black hair fell all around Eve's small shoulders like a soft curtain, protecting her from the outside world. She smelled like kitchen herbs and sometimes flowers, more often like woodfire smoke, though. They were simple people.

"Do you think *Papa* would let me change my name?" Eve asked, clinging to her.

"I don't know, sweetheart. But do we need a man's permission to do what we want?" Maryse then said, pulling away to look into her eyes. She smiled and her brown eyes shone like the sparkling water of the river near their home.

"So, what shall I call you from now on?" she asked her.

"I don't know," Eve said.

"Well, when I was pregnant with you, if you were a girl, I wanted to name you Eve," Maryse said.

"I like it," Eve said with a smile. "And…"

"Yes?"

"Can I wear a dress like you now?" Eve asked.

She wished she was old enough to sew her own clothes – her mother had enough work around the farm - but she wasn't. Maryse lowered her eyes sadly. They were too poor to buy fabric to make her a new dress, and she already knew she would face her husband's disapproval, but she was creative and talented and could make things out of nothing.

"I could cut you a new dress out of my old blue skirt!" she suddenly said. "There are holes in it, but I could patch them up with scraps of the lace I used to make my Sunday dress."

"Like Cinderella?" Eve asked, excited.

"Better than Cinderella! Your mother is the best seamstress in town," Maryse proudly said.

So, the Cinderella dress was made from an old skirt and adorned with lace. Maryse's magical fingers worked all day and all night, skillfully turning a hole into folds here and covering up a discolored patch there, and when Eve was finally able to try it on, she truly felt as though her fairy godmother had dressed her in gossamer and silk. All she was missing were glass slippers and a prince. For the first time, when Eve looked at her reflection in the old, cracked mirror in her parents' bedroom, she saw herself, her true self. But her father suddenly walked in on them and shouted: "What the hell is this masquerade?"

Eve took a step back and hid behind her mother's skirts, who stood defiantly in front of her husband.

"I made a dress for Eve," she said.

"You mean Paul? Have you lost your mind, woman?" he said.

He was more annoyed than angry because he thought this was just dressing up, and that his wife and son were wasting time instead of working on the farm.

"Paul, take that costume off and go take care of the pigs. They won't feed themselves," he then said roughly, turning around.

He went into their small living room, which was only separated from the bedroom by a patchwork curtain, muttering about this 'nonsense' and asking himself why he had married a lunatic. But Maryse was not a lunatic; she was far from being insane. In fact, she was one of the wisest people Eve ever encountered in her life. She kneeled beside her child and smiled, hiding the anger and hurt her husband's words had caused her.

"*Maman*, I don't want to wear boys' clothes again," Eve whispered, her eyes filling with tears.

"Don't worry. We don't care what men tell us to do, do we?" Maryse said.

"But he'll beat us if we don't obey him…" Eve said.

"We'll see about that," Maryse said with a wink.

But Eve was right to worry. When her father understood that this was more than her putting on a costume for play, that this was who she truly was, he beat her, and he beat her mother too, but she continued to stand up for her daughter. Luckily, none of this lasted very long. Eve's father had an accident while working in the barn one day. The wound got infected and he died soon after, and Eve always thought her mother had summoned some sort of magic to protect them – perhaps a fairy spirit, who had made this accident happen. She was not sad when they buried her father, who was only a source of danger in her world.

After his death, the farm was peaceful for the first time. There was no drinking, no cussing, no yelling, and no beatings – only the love of a mother and daughter. Maryse was widowed and had no other children, but she did her best to keep the farm running. They could no longer sow and reap large crops, but with the milk from the cows they made cheese, cream, and butter to sell. They also sold their pigs' meat and for some time they were alright. But several years of bad crops made the price of grain skyrocket, and they had to sell most of their livestock to buy flour. They sold their pigs first, then their cows, keeping only a few chickens. Like nearly all the peasants living in the mountains, they often faced famine in the winter when the fruit and vegetable preserves they had made over the summer ran out and the chickens stopped laying eggs, but they learned how to make meager rations last. Stale bread was never thrown away but added to soups. Beans provided the protein they needed, and with potatoes they could make bread, potato cakes, and stews. And because Maryse knew the herblore and how to harvest wild herbs in the forest, there were always delicious herbal teas and remedies for everything in their home. They were poor and hungry, but not miserable. The walls of their little stone house were full of cracks, but they filled them with mud and twigs, and they had kept bags of duck feathers from betters days which they used to fill their eiderdown quilts and pillows. Shawls with too many holes were disassembled and the wool used to knit new ones or woven into warm skirts for the winter, and as they huddled close to the fireplace, knitting, mending clothes, or making patchwork quilts from those that could not be salvaged, Maryse told her daughter of ancient folktales while sipping on hot herbal tea. Even when she was cold and hungry, those were magical days for Eve, and she pictured herself as Cinderella, living by the hearth, and Maryse was her fairy godmother.

In the village, they were shunned, and the local vicar, who was the only schoolteacher, would not allow Eve to come to school in a dress, so Maryse stopped sending her to school and taught her how to read and write as best she could at home instead. Despite the pressure she faced to remarry, she never did, saying she would rather go hungry than take another beating from an angry husband, and it also angered the vicar. But Maryse was a servant to no man, and she taught Eve to be the same.

"Never expect a man to give you what you can get yourself," she always reminded her. "We are daughters of this land. We are healers, keepers of the ancient herblore. We obey no man."

"Yes, *Maman*," the now thirteen-year-old Eve answered with a smile, before returning to the savory potato stew she was cooking.

Eve was never a very talkative child, she was a listener, and even more so as she grew up and her voice deepened. She hated her voice, so she listened and learned quietly. She was a dreamer and she was sensitive; she did not know how well she would fare in the outside world, in the village, if her mother ever died. Sometimes she felt like she was too fragile for this world. Maryse probably knew - she knew her so well - and that was why she tried so hard to instill confidence in her. But, at the time, Eve did not see herself ever standing up to the villagers like Maryse did when they called her a witch, or telling the vicar to get off her property or she would put a pitchfork through him when he tried to pay her a visit to tell her about all her sins. Eve did not put pitchforks through people; she made stews. She made different potato stews every day with the herbs that grew in their garden, sometimes adding other vegetables as well. The village could hate them, but they had each other and they were happy, and that was the only thing in this world that truly mattered—Maryse often reminded her of it.

In the year 1764, just as Eve turned fifteen, a series of gruesome deaths terrified all of Gevaudan. The victims, mostly teenage girls tending to their herds, were left dismembered, mutilated in horrific ways. The locals were quick to blame the murders on the Beast of Gevaudan. Some less superstitious city folk thought it was the work of a giant wolf and went on hunting expeditions to kill it. But no one was able to capture the monster or wolf behind the murders, and the King of France eventually heard of the story. He had his own suspicions about a reclusive aristocrat who lived in an old castle deep in the mountains, but nobody knew why or how any man could be behind such horrific crimes. Eve only heard of the stories through her mother, whose neighbors, despite hating her, still came to warn her. She asked Eve to stay indoors after dark and said she would reinforce the fence around the property to protect their chickens. As a child of this land of magic and mystery, Eve did not fear supernatural creatures, she was intrigued by them, but she obviously did not want to die, so she obeyed her mother and remained in their small house after the sun set.

November came and the frequency of the attacks only increased, just as the King's troops arrived from Paris to hunt the beast on horseback with rifles. Eve watched them at a distance, a long line of horses and soldiers in blue uniforms and wide black hats. They looked handsome and strong, and like they could possibly kill the beast, but she did not want it to die. Something in her longed for everything dark and misunderstood, and she thought this beast was no savage killer, but a hungry creature, just like she, a poor peasant, was hungry. And like she and her mother were hated and shunned, perhaps this beast had also been shunned by its pack, and perhaps it, too, was alone. She leaned against the fence that separated her family's property from the Dupuys, their closest neighbors. Their oldest daughter Bernadette, who was tending to the chickens, noticed her and walked up to her. They were not exactly friends, and the girl did not really understand why 'Paul' wore dresses, but all people had in mind at the time was to protect each other from the monster.

"You should make sure to finish your chores before dark. The beast kills people very close to their homes," she said in an anxious voice.

"Really? I thought it had only attacked children up in the mountains with their herds," Eve said, keeping her voice as quiet as possible. The neighbors didn't like to see their children talking to her.

Bernadette came closer.

"A woman was devoured *on her doorstep*," she said, gazing around her as though the beast could hear them.

"That beast must be really hungry to attack humans so close to their homes," Eve said.

"It's hungry and it's *hunting*," Bernadette said. "Oh, and they say most of the attacks were carried out on full moon nights."

"Full moon nights?" Eve repeated.

The story was getting more and more intriguing.

"You know what the villagers say about your mother. They won't protect you. Save yourself. Stay home," Bernadette said, before returning to her work.

Eve did not understand why Bernadette took the time to warn her, since she, too, thought her and her mother were witches and lunatics. The cold breeze on her cheek came to remind her that the sun was setting behind the heavy, dark gray clouds. A thin layer of frost already covered the ground, and the air was humid. It would snow that night. Eve liked the cold and the snow and didn't mind the long winters of Gevaudan. She loved the pure crispness of the air and the smells of the pine trees and smoke from her home's fireplace. She thought about Christmas and the present she would give her mother. A few months back, an elderly neighbor was very sick and Eve made a tincture with herbs to treat her. Though the woman was reluctant at first to try this 'potion' from the daughter of the local witch, her granddaughter eventually convinced her and the tincture cured her. Eve did not ask her for any kind of payment, but the woman insisted on giving her wool from her sheep, so Eve took it and spun it herself in the barn, and now she was making a brand-new woolen skirt for Maryse. There would not be much on the table that year for their Christmas dinner, but Maryse had promised they would have potato cakes, pickled onions, and perhaps even some salted pork – something they rarely ever had anymore. They would be happy in their little house filled with love. Eve sighed and pulled her shawl tighter around her shoulders as she remembered she still had to lock the chickens in the coop and get some dried herbs from the shed before dinner. Her mother had a bad cough; she needed a thyme infusion. So Eve left the fence and her dreams and returned to her chickens. As always, she counted them. One was missing. It had to be Margot. The adventurous little hen had a habit of getting through the fence and wandering into the woods. Eve turned to the dark woods beyond the property fence and then to the sky. The full moon was already visible between the clouds, but the sun had not quite set yet. The beast did not attack until dark; she still had time to go find Margot. They couldn't afford to lose a hen; they needed to sell her eggs to sustain themselves. So, she climbed over the fence and marched quickly toward the woods, calling out softly to the hen. She would usually come on her own: she was not eager to spend the night out in the cold when she could sleep in the warmth of the coop. But, this time, she did not come. Just as Eve was wondering whether she should give up, she heard paws crushing twigs behind her – paws way too heavy to be those of a fox. It had to be a wolf. They were common in the mountains. So, she did what peasant children were taught to do when they encountered one: scare it away with noise. She removed her wooden clogs and struck them together loudly, shouting: "Wolf! Wolf!"

Rather than frighten the beast, though, it only seemed to intrigue it. She heard it circling around her in the shadows of the bushes and she knew that she had to run – now. So she darted off barefoot in the direction of her home, running as fast as she could, and the beast gave chase. It was faster than her. It eventually caught up to her and knocked her down with a heavy blow to the back of her head. Eve fell, stunned and dizzy, and rolled over, only to be pinned to the ground firmly, but not by a wolf, nor a beast. A man was towering over her, and he was the one pinning her to the ground. A man... well, not quite. He had long black hair and the clothing of an aristocrat, and his face was that of a man, except it was covered with brown and black fur. And his eyes... his eyes were blood-red. He hovered over her, baring sharp fangs and snarling, but seemed to hesitate as she stopped struggling. There was no point in struggling: he had her. If he wanted to devour her, then he would. He was a supernatural creature, one that belonged in the darkness of the forest and the folktales of peasants. She was not surprised to encounter a supernatural being in this land of magic, only sad that she had to leave this world that night, and so young. She turned her eyes to the now dark sky and breathed in the cool, crisp air one last time. Despite her and her mother being shunned, despite the poverty and hunger, she still loved this land she was born in and would miss it on the other side. But the beast did not kill her. He spoke to her instead.

"Who are you?"

His voice was deep and ethereal. She turned her eyes to him and gazed into his blood-red eyes. They were slowly changing to a greenish, yellow color, and the fur on his face retreated until forming a beard. He was a man now, a rather handsome one too, if one liked men in their mid-thirties.

"What are you?" she asked him, still frightened, but also excited.

He let go of her and rose to his feet.

"What are you doing alone in the woods? Aren't you afraid?" he asked.

"I'm a child of the mountains, sir," she replied, and he smirked when he heard her voice.

She lowered her eyes, but his fingers cupped her chin and made her look into his. She held her breath, her heart beating fast under his dominating yet gentle touch.

"Go home now, child of the mountains, or I might devour you," he said.

"Then why didn't you tonight?" she asked, looking into his beautiful yellow eyes.

He let go of her and turned around.

"This is my territory. The next time you step into it, I will show no mercy," he said.

"Wait! Are you that reclusive aristocrat the villagers talk about?" she asked him as he began to walk away. He stopped and briefly turned to her.

"My name is Nicolas," he simply said, before leaving.

Nicolas. No, she was not afraid of him. He had her heart racing for other reasons. From her youngest age, her mother had warned her to stay away from bad men, and he was obviously one of them since he wanted to devour her, but the way he towered over her, the way he touched her and looked into her eyes, all made her feel things she had never felt before.

Before she met Nicolas on that cold November night when the natural and supernatural worlds came together, Eve had barely ever talked to a man, apart from her father and a few villagers now and then. The boys in the village teased her and tried to lift her skirts when she went there to sell eggs, and she ran from them. But this man, who had actually said he might kill her, somehow did not frighten her, not as much as he ought to. Now she thought he might actually be the 'Beast of Gevaudan', but there was clearly a supernatural explanation behind it. Perhaps he was cursed and now forced to feed on human blood on full moon nights, and if that was the case, then he probably felt very lonely and sad. She stepped inside her home, barefoot and disheveled, and her mother rose from her chair with wide eyes.

"Where were you? What happened?" she asked, terrified.

"Nothing happened to me, *Maman*. We just lost Margot again. She wandered off into the woods. I searched for her, but I fell and lost my clogs," Eve said, trying to hide the turmoil in her young heart.

Maryse rushed over to her and pulled her into a tight embrace.

"Eve, you must never, never go out into the woods after dark. That beast is out there!" she told her, and then she coughed.

"*Maman*, you need to sit down," Eve said, guiding her back to her chair.

She sat her in the chair and went to the kitchen to make her a hot herbal tea. She gazed at the laundry awaiting her tomorrow in the laundry basket, and the blood-soaked towels left by her mother. Maryse was bleeding way too much for this to be a period, and she had lost weight. She knew something was wrong with her, something more than just a cough, but they could not afford to call a doctor. Few of the locals could. All they had were herbs, so Eve made her a thyme infusion to at least relieve her cough.

"Here, *Maman*, you drink this. I still have to lock up the chickens," she said after bringing her the infusion.

"No! No!" her mother protested, clinging to her.

"I'll be fine. The fence is strong. If I see that beast coming, I have plenty of time to get into the house," Eve assured her. "But if we leave the chickens out, not only a wolf, but a fox might also get one. We've lost one already."

Maryse reluctantly let her go out again and lock up the chickens where they would be safe for the night, and as she did, Eve gazed at the woods, hoping that the man would return. She wanted to know who he was, and why he turned into a beast. Perhaps she truly was a lunatic, like the villagers said. Yes, it had to be madness that made her feel attracted to this dangerous man.

Now with the exciting knowledge that she had met the 'beast', and that he would not harm her – at least she thought so – Eve no longer hesitated to leave the safety of her home to go out and perform her daily chores. In fact, she tried to be outside as much as possible to catch one of the neighbors and question them. Soon enough, Bernadette noticed her leaning over the fence between their properties and walked over to her.

"Any news?" Eve asked her.

"Two children taken. They were six and eight," the girl said sadly.

"That is so sad," Eve said, lowering her gaze.

"Is your mother safe?" the girl then asked.

"Yes, we're fine. We only lost one hen."

The girl's eyes opened wide with terror.

"It means the beast is getting closer to our homes!"

"No!" Eve immediately said. "I mean… I don't know. The hen just wandered off into the woods. Any animal could have taken it."

"Well, we should still report it to the king's soldiers. They are scouting the forests day and night."

Eve tensed. What if they found Nicolas and accidentally killed him?

"Have you heard about an aristocrat named Nicolas?" she asked.

"You mean Count Nicolas de Castelcombe? He's the owner of the castle beyond the peak," Bernadette said, frowning.

"Why does he never come to the village?" Eve asked.

"He's probably too old. If he's still alive, he has to be now. He hasn't been seen in decades, some people think he's already dead," Bernadette said.

"Oh…" Eve said, disappointed. "Does he have any sons?"

"No. He never married," the girl said. "What's your interest in him?"

"I was just curious, that's all," Eve said.

There was no way the man she had seen could be this Nicolas de Castelcombe, unless his supernatural transformation somehow granted him eternal youth as well.

"Do you think the beast could actually be a man?" she asked.

"Like a werewolf?" Bernadette said, frowning. "I suppose anything is possible. When I hear the stories about the bodies and the condition they were found in, I'm ready to believe anything."

Their conversation died out, but Bernadette lingered near the fence, picking at the frozen wood with her fingers.

"Why do you wear a dress?" she then asked Eve.

"What would I wear apart from dresses? I can't just go naked," Eve said, laughing.

"I mean… you're a boy. You can go out and do what you want in the world. Why would you choose to be a girl and have no freedom? I would kill to be a boy," Bernadette said.

"But I'm not a boy. I'm a girl," Eve simply said. "What's the point of living at all if it is to be unhappy? And I could never be happy if I had to pretend I was a boy every day to please the villagers. Besides, nature doesn't care what we are or what clothes we wear."

"But don't you want to be free? I would much rather pretend to be a boy, go to the city and live on my own than marry one of the boys from the village and end up pregnant at fifteen."

"I am free," Eve said with a smile. "And my mother doesn't remarry because she is also free. We define freedom and happiness by our own standards, and it upsets people like the vicar."

Bernadette broke into a smile for the first time.

"Is that why she said she would put a pitchfork through him?" she laughed.

"Probably," Eve said.

"You know, I would be friends with you if my parents let me. I don't mind what clothing you wear or what you want to be called," Bernadette said, surprising Eve. She was not aware that anyone wanted to be friends with her. "I wish I was as brave as you are…" the girl then added.

No one had ever called Eve 'brave', but perhaps she was, after all. She had survived an eerie encounter with a supernatural being, and she and her mother had survived all these years without anyone's help.

"Well, I should go now," Bernadette said.

"You could come over to our farm sometime. I will make you some herbal tea," Eve offered.

"Oh, I couldn't. My parents would kill me. They say you're witches…" Bernadette said, looking over her shoulder.

Eve laughed. She didn't mind being called a witch; she was proud of the ancient knowledge her mother had passed on to her, even if it was misunderstood. But, no, she did not cast spells on people. She made them herbal teas and tinctures to treat their colds and other ailments.

Bernadette was the first friend Eve remembered having as a human. She was somewhat shy, and her bravery only extended to talking with the shunned neighbor over the fence, but still it was more than any of the other villagers. Eve sometimes brought her lavender and chamomile infusions thereafter, which she left on the fence for her, and Bernadette would come up and talk to her while doing her chores. And through her, Eve heard more about the king's campaign to catch the 'beast'.

For three years, the king's best hunters and marksmen scouted the woods and they caught and killed several large wolves, but the carnage continued. And as all human means failed to catch what was actually a supernatural being, people began to turn to religion to save them, and the vicar was quick to accuse the two suspected 'witches' of having conjured some demonic entity. Soldiers, of course, had little interest in these fantastic theories, but the villagers began to visit Eve's farm at night and leave amulets and other items meant to banish them if they were demons. Eve and Maryse laughed at them and ignored them, but what Eve could no longer ignore was her mother's health. Now she was not only bleeding, but she was still losing weight and often threw up after eating. She complained of intense pain in her abdomen that no herbs seemed to make better. Eve begged her to let her go fetch a doctor, but Maryse refused. Perhaps she knew, like Eve knew, that she had cancer, and that nothing could be done for her. And when her condition deteriorated to the point she was bedridden, Eve sat by her side most of the day, only going out to tend to the chickens. At eighteen, she was old enough to be married, and her neighbor Bernadette had just got married and was pregnant with her first child, but Eve still felt like a child. She did not know what she would do without her mother.

"*Maman*, you must get better," she told her in a tearful voice while holding her hand.

"Oh, I'll be better in no time," Maryse lied, trying to bring her comfort.

"What will I do in this world without you? Everyone hates me!" Eve said as tears streamed down her cheeks.

"You will be brave, as you have always been. And if someone tries to hurt you, you grab that pitchfork and kill them!" Maryse told her in a very serious voice.

"I can't do that, I'm not strong enough!" Eve said.

"You have to be. We have no one but ourselves in this world," Maryse said, holding her hand firmly. "We are fighters, you know it!"

"I'm not a fighter. Not without you…" Eve whispered.

"Why should you ever be without me?" Maryse said. "My body will die someday, but my spirit will not. It will always be with you. Always."

Eve lay her head on her chest and cried, and Maryse wrapped her arms tenderly around her. She did not feel strong enough to be on her own in this place where everyone hated her. She climbed onto the bed and fell asleep beside her mother, listening to her breathing, and in her dreams that night she remembered all the happy times of her childhood. She remembered the Cinderella dress, the warm spring and summer days when she and Maryse would tend to the garden together, Maryse's smile and her laughter, her scent, the fragrance of herbs drying in the shed and the herbal teas they drank together by the fireplace. Everything in the world she loved and needed was here, in this small farmhouse, with her mother. But when she opened her eyes the next morning, the room was cold. It was always cold on winter mornings. That was no surprise; the fire always died out during the night. But it was a different sort of cold that had fallen upon their home. It was chilling, empty, and eerie. Eve could sense that something had happened, or that something was about to happen, like the veil between the natural and supernatural worlds was lifting once more. She turned to her mother. She was very pale and barely breathing.

"*Maman! Maman!*" she cried, shaking her, but Maryse never opened her eyes.

Instead, her breathing weakened more and more until it eventually stopped. Eve lay her head on her chest and listened to her heartbeat slow down until it, too, stopped. And then she felt her limbs slowly turning cold, as cold as the air around them. First her fingertips, then her wrist, her arm, her chest and her face. Everything seemed unreal. It was too sudden; she was not ready to lose her and be forever alone in this world.

"*Maman! Maman*, where are you?" she cried. "Don't leave me alone! Don't leave me!"

But her sweet mother could no longer hear her, or if she could, she could no longer reply. She was in a different world now, and Eve was in the real world, and alone.

She lay by her side for hours, not knowing what to do. All she wanted was to turn back time and bring her back, or, if this was a nightmare, to wake up from it. But the realization that Maryse was gone, that she was no longer inside the cold body beside her, eventually sunk in. A great peace settled around the house, as though Maryse still lived within its walls and protected her beloved daughter. But the noise Eve heard outside was not peaceful. She got up, startled, and ran over to the dirty old window. In the distance, she could see a large crowd, perhaps twenty or more villagers, walking toward the farm. They were carrying torches and shouting: "Burn the witches! Burn them!"

Eve turned to her mother, terrified, and cried: "*Maman!*"

Her mother did not answer her, but she thought she clearly heard the voice of a woman in her head telling her: "*Run!*"

It was almost like her mother's voice, but somewhat different. It was supernatural, but Eve trusted her senses and what she saw enough to obey it. There was no way she could move her mother's body, but she needed to take her with her—even just a little piece of her, so she ran up to her, grabbed the brown shawl she had covered her with that night, and ran out the back door.

"Over there!" she heard men shout as she climbed over the back fence and made for the woods.

She did not even turn around; she knew they were chasing her. She heard the barking of dogs: they would be able to follow her tracks unless she could get to the river, but the water was frozen at this time of the year. There seemed to be no escape, no safe place to run to, but still she could not give up. Maryse gave her freedom, and she would die of exhaustion before she surrendered to these people and let them kill her! She ran as fast as she could, tripping now and then and tearing her dress on branches and stones. Her bare feet were bleeding and frozen from running in the snow, but her spirit was strong. Yes, she was strong, so much stronger than she had thought!

As she passed the mountain peak, she saw the old castle she had heard of in the distance, the one where Nicolas de Castelcombe probably lived. It was the only place where she could hide because there lived the only monster capable of warding off the monsters following her. Nicolas could have killed her that night, but he didn't; he even told her his name. Did he want her to find him and come to him someday? Either way, there was no time to think. She ran down the mountain slopes and into the valley, and finally got to the castle's old, fortified walls. They were partly destroyed on one side of the property. Without any hesitation, she climbed the wall and entered it, throwing just one glance toward the mountain slopes. The villagers, with their dogs and their torches, were still giving chase. Would they dare to trespass on the old aristocrat's property? She looked for a door, a window through which she could get in, and finally found a hole at the bottom of a wall. The bricks had partly collapsed, and an animal had dug its way inside. So she slipped inside and fell onto a cold stone floor. She lay there for some time, breathless and sore. Her lungs were hurting, her feet burning from the cold and the pain, but still she needed to run, to find a place to hide. She looked around her: she appeared to be in an old kitchen that had not been used for years. There was a heavy wooden door open a crack. It led to stairs. So, she crawled to the door and painfully got back up on her feet. She slowly climbed the dark spiral staircase, feeling the moist stones of the walls on either side with her hands, until she bumped into another door. She slowly pulled it open and emerged into a hallway. Outside, she could hear the dogs barking. They were encircling the property, but not entering it. Perhaps they were afraid of the old aristocrat. She walked slowly down the dark hallway and let herself into a room at the end of it. There was light inside, but not daylight: the windows had been boarded shut and a single candle had been left burning on the table. It appeared to be a dining room. The furniture was dusty and did not appear to be used any more often than the kitchen downstairs. On the table was a bowl filled with porridge. Would the master of the place be very angry if Eve sat down in a chair? She was exhausted and there was no one there, so she walked up to the table and sat on one of the chairs. She gazed at the bowl of porridge on the table. She was hungry, as always, but she was not a thief. But there was something else in the bowl. She reached for the spoon and stirred it and blood came up to the surface. She let go of the spoon with a startled cry then covered her mouth, terrified. Nicolas or whoever lived here had certainly heard her and the dogs barking outside. What would happen to her? She wrapped her shawl tightly around her shoulders and sat shaking on the chair, her eyes lowered, until she heard heavy footsteps in the hallway. They stopped for a moment in front of the door, then the man entered the room, saying: "What on earth is going on?"

His voice was angry. Eve closed her eyes and held herself tighter.

"Please don't kill me!" she whispered.

The man grew quiet. He seemed to be listening to the men and the barking dogs outside.

"They want to burn me alive. They say I'm a witch!" Eve said.

She was shaking so hard now she could hardly sit on the chair, and tears streamed down her cheeks. She could no longer speak, terrified as she was. He was going to kill her, she was sure of it now, but at least it wouldn't be as painful as being burned alive.

She heard him walk up to her and stop. He then walked away… to get a knife or weapon? He didn't seem like he needed one in order to kill on the night they first met. But, to her surprise, he returned with a bucket of water, soap, and scraps of fabric. He was as she remembered him: tall, strong-built, dark, and handsome, except he looked a little sweeter that day. His eyes were not hungry and feral. His long black hair was clean and combed and he was clean-shaven. He was wearing only a partly buttoned white shirt and breeches, as though he had been resting or sleeping until he heard the commotion. He kneeled beside her and took her wounded feet and placed them in the ice-cold water. She let out another cry.

"Don't move," he told her.

His voice was cold and irritated, but he held her feet delicately, and he began to wash them with soap and water. Her body still shook, but not only with fear. This dangerous man's gentle touch, the way he caressed her feet as he washed them, once again awakened the same feelings inside her as the night they first met. She held her breath as though it could help her stop shaking.

"I… I can do that myself, sir," she told him in a shy whisper.

He lifted his gaze to her and smirked. He then took her foot and kissed it. If he had told her now that he wanted to devour her, starting with her feet, she would have said 'yes', if only to feel those burning lips upon her skin again, lips that lit fires in her heart.

The man then dried her feet with a towel and carefully wrapped the scraps of fabric around them.

"T-Thank you Sir, you are too kind…" she said.

"I'm not kind. And you will have to clean those blood-stains on my rug," he then said, getting up.

"I'm so sorry!" she immediately said. "I will do anything you ask me, but please don't send me out there to those men!"

She tried to get up, but her sore feet would not support her, and she fell forward. He caught her in his arms. It was the first time a man ever held her, even though it was not his intention. But he did more than that. He scooped her up in his arms as though she were as light as a feather.

"Sir!" she vaguely protested, but he ignored her.

He took her upstairs to his bedroom and lay her on the bed among the wrinkled sheets. Her heart was racing again, and her cheeks were flushed. She was scared, confused. She did not know what to expect next. Too much had happened in her simple life in just one day. So she began to cry. He sat beside her on the bed.

"Why these tears? Are you scared of me now?" he asked her in a calm voice.

"M–My mother… my mother died this morning… and these men… they came to our farm with torches. They say we are witches who conjured the beast that has been attacking the villagers!" she said in a trembling voice.

"I see," he said. "So you came straight to that beast. Why?"

"You're… you're not a beast," she said softly.

"I am a beast, you saw me. Why aren't you asking what I am?"

"Because I saw what you are."

"And you came because I can see what *you* are," he then said.

At the time, she did not know that she was a supernatural creature like him, so she did not understand his words. She shook her head, confused.

"I could devour you," he then told her, and his eyes began to glow again like they did that night.

"Well… I trespassed on your property. If that is what you want to do, then do it," she said sadly. She lay her head on the pillow and gazed at him. Yes, he could devour her, and she would join her mother before their souls were so far apart they could never be reunited. But he smiled and began to crawl over her. She quivered as she felt the heat of his skin underneath his clothes brushing against her. He towered over her now, surrounding her with his manly scent, and the closer his lips came to her skin, the more she wanted them to lay another kiss - this time on her lips. But he did not kiss her. He lowered his head over her chest, near her neck. She had a small cut there, from a branch or thorns. His lips parted and a long red tongue came out and licked her skin slowly there, tasting the blood from her wound and sending chills down her spine. And for the first time, she experienced the longing for a man, underneath her clothes, in her chest, and down in her loins. Her skin longed to be touched and caressed by this man's giant hands, her chest swelled under the sweet teasing of his tongue, and she unwillingly let out a low moan, then covered her mouth, embarrassed. He removed his tongue from her skin, a satisfied grin on his lips.

"You're too willing to be devoured. Don't tempt me," he said.

He then got up and walked away, leaving her alone in the room. She did not know what to do. She did not understand his intentions. Did he want to devour her or… something else? Did she want him to do something else to her? And what? She was just a girl with a teenage infatuation for an older man because he looked noble and dangerous. But he had kissed her foot and licked her skin… She curled up into a ball and pulled the blankets over herself, and she felt strangely safe, surrounded by his scent. It was but an illusion, even she was aware of it at the time. Her mother had warned her against bad men. But could he be called a bad man just because he was a supernatural creature who ate… whatever was natural for his kind to eat? He had not eaten her yet. She closed her eyes and fell into a deep sleep.

CHAPTER 3

"ARE YOU READY YET?" Nicolas asked in his usual semi-annoyed voice.

"In a minute!" Eve said as she gazed at her reflection in the mirror.

Her straight black hair was quite long now and usually tied up in a bun, and she had taught herself to curl the front with a curling iron to create the 'sheep's head' hairstyle she had seen on the few wealthy women who crossed Javols before she moved in with Nicolas. All the new trends and hairstyles, of course, originated in Paris and slowly trickled down to the countryside, but she liked to think that she was fashionable. The richest women had wigs and did not have to bother doing their hair; they had a professional perruquier take care of it. But Eve was proud to have inherited Maryse's clever fingers. Unlike them, she was self-sufficient. Her dress and petticoats were also handmade.

Eve had been living with Nicolas for two years now, since that first night when she ran into his castle to escape the villagers. He told her she could stay with him and she insisted on becoming his maid to pay for her keep, but he told her she did not need to pay for her keep since she was going to take care of herself—and he meant it. He let her choose between the old kitchen through which she had first entered his home and the attic as her room, and she chose the kitchen, where she could sleep by a warm fire in the hearth. She was allowed to resize and wear any of the former servants' clothing she could find in the attic, to clean up the vegetable garden and cook with whatever she could find there, as well as with the flour and salted meat and fish he kept in barrels in the pantry. He only occasionally ate human food and preferred to feed on humans on full moon nights, when he became a werewolf. He often said that he might eat her too, but she did not believe him.

The 'Beast of Gevaudan' was a man, after all, who was once an ordinary aristocrat. Only on full moon night he suddenly began to grow fur all over his body and transform into a wolf. He never knew why or what had cursed him, not even if it ran in his bloodline. He was left as a monster in this world, without answers, so he had retreated in his castle and only left it to satisfy the urge to feed on human flesh. But Eve did not see him as a monster. He was just a man with a unique body, like she was a woman with a unique body, although he did not know at first. Because she feared his reaction, she did not tell him, and he did not ask questions, only hinting now and then that he would like her to sit on his lap, but she just laughed and ignored him. One day, however, he had apparently had enough of the hinting and decided to make a move on her, but not as she had expected. She was cleaning his room while he sat in a chair quietly observing her, when he suddenly got up, grabbed her by the waist, and threw her on the bed.

"Nicolas!" she protested, thinking he was teasing her again, but he was not.

There was sorrow in his eyes as they plunged into hers. He lay atop her and brought his fingers to her chin and caressed it.

"Eve, why will you no longer talk to me?" he asked her.

She would not talk to him because, as she grew older, so did her voice deepen and it embarrassed her. Not only that, but new things were happening to her body, things she had never experienced before, like sexual desire and soiling herself at night when she dreamed of him. Having grown up mostly around women, she knew nothing about her body and what to expect from it, only that it kept growing further and further away from how she saw herself. She did not picture herself as a princess, she would only ever be Cinderella, living in her old kitchen by the hearth, but Cinderella didn't have to worry about facial hair and her voice deepening, did she? She removed her eyes from his.

"Is it something I did? Do I frighten you?" he insisted.

A brute like him would have frightened any other woman, but, unfortunately, not her.

"No," she said shyly.

He let his head fall against her chest and breathed in her scent like the famished beast he was.

"Nicolas…" she whispered, and only then realized that her voice betrayed her own desire for him.

"Eve, I want you! I've wanted you since I first saw you," he whispered. "But now you hate me… why?"

"You're wrong… I also want you," she whispered, breathing hard.

"Oh, Eve…" he said in a low and sensuous snarl that sent shivers throughout her entire body. And when he started kissing and licking her neck, she knew she was lost.

His hands moved down her waist, her legs, and she did not want him to stop, until they slipped underneath her skirts and he found what was between her legs.

"Nicolas, I'm…" she tried to say, but he gazed at her and grinned.

"You think I don't know that you're a man in a dress?" he said.

"I'm not a man, I'm a woman!" she protested.

"You have a cock, honey, you're a man," he said, moving his lips over hers. "But I wouldn't want it any other way," he whispered before kissing her.

She was angry and hurt by his words. She wanted to protest, but the sweetness of his kiss, and the way everything in her body longed for him, quickly made her give in.

She let him kiss her, and then remove her clothes and make love to her for the first time. She did not even know she could use her body in that way. It hurt at first, then it felt so good she forgot all about the pain, and, because he was her first, she thought that his desire to pleasure her meant that he loved her. She was not his prisoner, she was always free to walk away, but he kept her captive with the burning desire he inspired her, with his wild kisses, his rough caresses, and his massive shaft. He was her count in the daytime and her werewolf at night, between the sheets, and she was contented with their relationship.

But Nicolas was not only a beast in bed, he was also in everyday life. Though he had received a fine education, he was rather clueless, perhaps even naïve, and he never could guess why the woman who now shared his bed got upset every time he called her a 'man in a dress', because he thought he was just stating the obvious, just like the fact he was a werewolf. There weren't any other words to describe what he was, and he could not comprehend what difference it made what one called someone else. Still, he seemed to genuinely suffer when he made Eve cry and always tried to make things right in his own awkward way. When she refused to sleep in his bed and returned to her kitchen and the hearth to spend the night, she would sometimes find a rose by her straw mat in the morning, and when she asked him about it and he simply grunted in response, she knew – or thought - it meant that he loved her. She had come into his house like Cinderella, but now they were more like Beauty and the Beast, or rather Beauty and the Oaf. But she loved him, with all her young heart.

She had no women around her anymore, but her mother had taught her how to make her own skincare products and makeup, and so she learned to wax every unsightly hair on her body, circle her eyes with a charcoal crayon, and tint her lips with a rouge she made from beet root powder, beeswax, and oil. Her naturally pale complexion and dry skin saved her from pimples and required no powder; she only added a little touch of rouge to her cheeks. And though her hair was not very thick, it could be styled in a way to look thicker. Nicolas said all this makeup and hairstyles were silly and he liked her better without anything on her face, but he let her do as she pleased because it made her happy, and he did not like to see her cry.

She finished touching up her makeup, arranged her blue handsewn dress one more time and checked herself in the mirror of the bedroom. They were going out for the first time that night - meaning outside of Gevaudan, to a big city, and she wanted to look perfect.

When she was ready, she rushed down the stairs and joined Nicolas in the great hall. He was elegant that night too in his dark crimson justaucorps coat, breeches, and matching hat. He had even bathed and washed and combed his hair, for once. Since they were traveling far and he no longer owned horses, he had rented them, along with a coachman from Javols. They would be riding in his personal carriage, though—a luxury in Eve's dazzled peasant eyes.

He offered her his arm, and they left the castle. It was a two-day journey to Montpellier, and they would be traveling by night because werewolves were not very fond of the sunlight. This was before trains, and traveling North to Paris would have been a much longer journey. But Eve's knowledge of the world was so limited that even an average-sized city like Montpellier could just as well have been Paris to her. Furthermore, she would get to see the Mediterranean Sea. She had never seen the ocean in her short life.

They planned on reaching the city before dawn on the second night and retreating to a hotel, and he would not emerge again until the next evening. Eve was, of course, free to go out into the city in the daytime, and he preferred to let her shop for feminine things alone anyway, but he had promised to take her to the theater in the evening, and she was excited about it. She still thought of him as the love of her life, her only love, and now she was finally doing something fun and exciting with him, just like any other couple. Because they were an ordinary couple, only they couldn't be married.

"Am I your wife?" she asked him as they rode silently in the carriage.

He turned puzzled eyes to her.

"I can't marry you. It would be illegal," he said.

He had that very depressing, down-to-earth vision of the world that always saddened her. He was a stern man with no imagination whatsoever.

"But if my birth records were amended to say I was a woman, would you marry me?" she asked him, hopeful.

He stared at her.

"Not unless you can also amend my death certificate. I'm supposed to have died at thirty-six. That's when I retreated from the world after becoming a werewolf," he reminded her.

Again, that dreadful lack of imagination. She sighed. They exchanged no other words during the rest of the trip.

They didn't see much of the city when they arrived just before dawn because it was still dark and raining, so they settled in a comfortable hotel in the Ecusson, the historic center of the city, in a room with thick curtains over the windows, and Nicolas went to bed, but Eve was too excited to sleep much. She awakened around ten o'clock and immediately got out of bed. She dressed quickly, did her hair and makeup, and went to Nicolas before she left.

"Nicolas, I'm going out to buy a few things," she whispered, placing a hand on his shoulder.

He muttered something and pulled the covers over his head. He did not like to be awakened in his sleep, but she was in a good mood that day and would not let his sourness spoil her fun. So, she left the hotel quietly, greeting the boy at the front desk on her way.

"Enjoy your day, *Madame*," he told her, bringing a bright smile to her lips.

Filled with renewed confidence from this simple encounter, she walked proudly down the crowded paved streets of the downtown area, gazing with wonder at all the tall buildings around her.

With a population of about thirty thousand, Montpellier was not even comparable to a city like Paris and its six hundred thousand inhabitants, but it was the largest city Eve had ever seen, and her young eyes simply could not stop feasting on the beauty of the buildings, the shops, the majestic Arc de Triomphe, as well as the Faculty of Medicine, the oldest medical school in western Europe, and the botanical garden. There were several modern castles around the city belonging to wealthy families, such as the Château d'O, the Château de la

Mogère, and the Château D'Alco, all testimonies of the city's merchant wealth. There were market stalls everywhere selling lavender and herbs, olives and olive oil, Espelette peppers from the Basque Country, dried figs, dates, and apricots, and even spiced orange preserves. Eve couldn't resist the enticing smell of the fruits she never got to eat in her childhood and bought a pound of them, which she immediately started eating as she walked down the streets. She closed her eyes with delight as she tasted the sweetness of the dried fruit, and she thought this place might be Heaven.

The streets were bustling with people, with sounds and scents from the markets, and the nearby ocean brought to the city its warm and salty breeze. There was just so much to see and do Eve did not know what to do next. But she and Nicolas would not be staying there very long, so she knew she ought to at least get herself some new clothes and other items she needed.

Back in those days, of course, the paved streets were covered with horse manure and trash, but the smells were no different from those on a farm and did not inconvenience her any more than that. She made sure to stay out of the mud and the filth as to not soil her worn-out shoes. She would need a new pair of those too, and some knitting needles and yarn. If she could buy colorful yarn, she could crochet lovely shawls and blankets. As she was walking down Rue Saint-Pierre toward the Saint-Pierre Cathedral and making a list in her head of all the things she wanted to buy, she did not notice a group of young men who had begun following her until they apprehended her rather roughly. One of them grabbed her arm, forcing her to turn around. She gazed at him with angry eyes.

"Hey, what's that look for, darling? Don't you want to keep us company?" the young man said with lustful eyes and a grin.

She was surrounded by four men now, and people around them on the street just walked by, unconcerned. They probably assumed that, since she was alone, she was a prostitute and not worth helping.

"Let go of me!" she cried, trying to free herself from the man's strong grip.

"Relax, we just want to show you a good time. How much do you charge?" he asked her.

"How dare you?" she said, furious. "My man will *kill* you all!"

"Your *man*?" they laughed. "Is that your pimp or your husband?"

"Hey!" a loud voice shouted near them.

Eve turned around and she saw another woman—one like herself. She was almost six feet tall and wore an even taller powdered white wig and a very nice gold and white silk pannier dress. She was strong-built and imposing enough to make the young men let go of Eve's arm and run away.

"Are you okay, honey?" she then asked her, placing a friendly hand on her shoulder.

"Uh… yes, I guess I should be more careful," Eve said, as she watched the men run down the street.

"The streets of Montpellier are fairly safe during the daytime, but a pretty girl like you should be careful. Men are… beasts."

Her comment made Eve laugh because her man was actually a beast.

"I'm not a prostitute, by the way. I was just shopping for some clothing and a few other things," she said.

"Well, you've come to the right street, and I own a shop. I'm a seamstress. Perhaps I can interest you in some models," the tall woman said.

"Oh, that would be amazing!" Eve said. "And thank you," she then said as they began walking together.

"First time in the city?" the other asked her with a smile.

"Yes."

"Well, my name is Faustine, and you can come to me anytime for help. Sisters support each other."

"I'm Eve, and… how did you know?" Eve asked her.

"Don't worry honey, you pass a lot better than I do. I just… sensed it," Faustine said.

The moment they started talking, Eve and Faustine had a sort of *coup de foudre* as friends, and they both felt like they had known each other forever, like true sisters. Faustine took her to her small but elegant boutique in which she sold not only ready-made pieces, but also fabrics, and everything a woman with clever fingers like Eve needed to make her own dresses.

"What is your favorite color? Let me guess… lavender," Faustine said, leaning over the counter.

"Yes… how did you know that?" Eve asked her.

"With your black hair and sky-blue eyes, lavender is your color," Faustine said. "And what's your budget?"

"Oh, there is no budget. It's on my man's account," Eve said.

"Oh, sure. What's his name?" Faustine said, grabbing her book of accounts.

"Count Nicolas de Castelcombe," Eve proudly said.

"Oh, so you've got yourself a count! Are you an actress?" Faustine asked with interest.

"No, I… I'm nobody really," Eve said shyly. "I just ran into his castle one night and he fell in love with me, I guess. We've been living together for two years."

"Oh, I love it! I want to hear your story!" Faustine said. "But first, let's get you styled up for your prince!"

They tried on different styles of dresses, and Eve selected four: three for everyday wear and one for going out. Nicolas would surely tell her if she needed other dresses, for other occasions. The dresses she had made for herself were all based on outdated patterns. The robe à la française, with its loose pleats in the back, was definitely out, and the more formal robe à l'anglaise, or fitted gown, like the one Faustine wore, had replaced it. Sleeves were still worn elbow-length, with discreet gauze or muslin cuffs around the elbows, and the back of the skirt could be gathered up, à la polonaise, or left as it was. Panniers, or side hoops, could be added underneath to widen the skirts near the waist and make you look slenderer, or if on the contrary you were too skinny like Eve, they made you look like you actually had some curves.

"How do you like it, honey?" Faustine asked Eve after they fitted her in a cream-colored dress with a discreet floral print. "Do you want to try on bigger panniers?"

"Oh, I couldn't," the very modest Eve said, who already felt shy looking like such an elegant lady. "Do I need them? Am I too skinny?"

"The problem is not how skinny you are, it's that you don't have a butt, sweetie," Faustine said. "So how about we add this?"

She lifted her skirts and slipped a small cushion underneath, tying it around her waist, and suddenly Eve had her dream silhouette.

"Oh Faustine! You're amazing!" she said, delighted.

"Making women look perfect is my trade," Faustine proudly said. "Now, let's take care of your hair."

"Oh, my hair is so thin… I don't know how to give it any volume except by curling it," Eve said with a deep sigh.

"Not a problem. I have plenty of wigs," Faustine said. "Do you want thicker black hair, extensions, or a powdered white wig? I've got what you need."

They went to the front of the shop and Faustine sat her in front of a large mirror, and they tried on multiple wigs and hair extension pieces until Eve found just what she liked. She clipped on hair extensions which Faustine curled for her, and on the top of her head she put on a tall, curly black hair wig. Faustine decorated it with pink ribbons and fresh flowers, and Eve felt like she truly looked like a princess now.

"There you go, beautiful, all you need now if some jewelry and you would certainly be invited at the court of Versailles!" Faustine said when they were done.

"Me? At court? Oh no, that's not possible," Eve said, but now she could picture herself riding in a beautiful carriage pulled by four white horses, going to Versailles with Nicolas, and dancing at a ball.

Three other women then entered the shop and kissed Faustine's cheeks.

"Bonjour Faustine," they said.

"Bonjour," Faustine said, "Oh, my darlings, you need to meet Eve!"

She gestured for Eve to come over and the young women also kissed her cheeks. Unlike her and Faustine, they were women with the right bodies, who could marry and have children, but they had not come with any husbands - and they didn't have any.

The five of them sat down around two small tables and chatted around a cup of tea and some delicate pastries sweeter than anything Eve had ever tasted before. She listened to their stories as she stuffed herself with these sweets from another world.

The three young women, Lucie, Maude, and Leontine - 'Titine'—were femmes galantes, or coquettes, courtesans who slept with rich men who doted on them. They were not quite like prostitutes in that many of them selected their next catch for his money and titles, but they did have pimps - libertines like themselves who helped them connect with rich men. They all admired a certain Jeanne Bécu, now known as the Countess du Barry, who had risen from the filthiest Parisian brothels to the coveted place of official mistress of King Louis XV, and if they were provincials and could probably not have a king, they could at least hope to find a count or a duke.

"Do you think she will last?" Titine asked the others.

"They say she's pretty good in bed," Maude said.

"And the old king surely doesn't go to the brothels. He doesn't know any of the things the girls do there," Lucie said, laughing. "But I know what to do, and tonight I am meeting my new lover, Count Montmorency."

"Oh! How exciting!" Titine said. "How rich is he?"

"Eve's got herself a count too. She's been living with him for two years," Faustine said, smiling, and Eve blushed.

"Two years? Lucky you!" Maude said. "I'm about to leave Bertrand…"

"After only three months? What happened?" Faustine asked.

"He's too old, there's nothing going on down there anymore. I have to ask the stableman to take me for a ride - if you know what I mean," Maude said, and they all laughed.

"So, what did you do for a living before meeting your count?" Titine asked Eve, who felt shy again.

"Oh, I didn't do anything really," she said.

"That's not good. You sound like you've become dependent on him," Maude warned her. "Don't do that, sweetie. Men either marry you or let you go, and when they let you go, you need to have some form of income."

"Do you sing? You have such a beautiful mezzo voice," Lucie said.

"Oh no, I couldn't possibly sing… I can make cosmetics and lotions, though," Eve said.

"Really? Do you have one for pimples? I'm so tired of sticking mouches on my skin every time I break out," Maude said.

"Can I touch your skin?" Eve asked.

"Sure," Maude said.

Since she wore powder and makeup over her face, Eve felt her temples and her neck, then said: "You have oily skin, you need to apply a green clay facial mask once a week, followed by an astringent like witch hazel, and then a non-greasy moisturizer. Hazelnut oil diluted with a little bit of water would be ideal."

The girls all looked at each other, amazed, then at Faustine.

"Where did you find this girl?" they said. "Are you selling beauty products? All of us would definitely buy them!" they then told Eve. She lowered her eyes and blushed again.

"I… I only learned those things from my mother," she said.

"Well honey, if you ever need work, you just make those cosmetics and I can sell them," Faustine told her.

"You should really learn how to sing too. I know a Madame who can teach you," Lucie said, who was also a singer.

"Yes… Yes, I would love to sing," Eve said, not really sure what a 'Madame' was in this context.

None of these women knew her, but they had already adopted her as one of their own, just like Faustine. They didn't ask Faustine any questions and just accepted her like an older sister. Eve liked them. She had so much fun with them, in fact, that she stayed at the shop, talking with them, until it was time for Faustine to close. She quickly ushered them out at seven o'clock, then noticed a man waiting on the street.

"Oh, Eve, do you know this man?" she asked, turning to her.

Eve looked out the window and recognized Nicolas. He looked angry, but he was often in a bad mood when he woke up. She laughed.

"Yes, that's Nicolas," she said. "Well, thank you for having me today. I had so much fun!" she then said, turning to Faustine, who gazed at her with concern.

"Eve, I don't like the look in that man's eyes. Has he ever been violent with you?" Faustine whispered, taking her hands, but Eve laughed again.

"No, not with me, don't worry," she said.

"Do you mean he can be violent with others?" Faustine asked, her eyes widening.

"N-No, I mean... don't worry about it," Eve said, smiling.

She stepped out of the shop and waved goodbye to Faustine, then turned to Nicolas, who grunted and began to walk. She followed him back to their hotel, and only once they were inside did he begin to interrogate her.

"Who were those women? Prostitutes?" he asked, furious.

"They are singers, actresses, and Faustine is a seamstress," Eve replied.

"And what were you doing with them? Thinking about a new trade?"

He walked over to her and she backed up against the wall, frightened for the first time.

"No! What are you insinuating?" she replied.

He took her hair extensions in his hand and looked at them with a disgusted frown.

"Then why do you need this... costume?" he said.

"Costume? Well, excuse me for trying to look beautiful for you!" she snapped, and she slipped away from him and sat on the bed and crossed her arms.

"Why do you need a wig? You have hair," he said like the oaf he was.

"Thank goodness I still have my own hair, like most young people!" she said, her eyes filling with tears. She covered her face with her hands and began to cry.

Nicolas observed her for a moment, then came to sit beside her and tried to embrace her, but she wouldn't let him.

"Faustine is my friend!" she said. "She's like me, and she protected me against a group of men trying to…"

She couldn't bring herself to say the word 'rape', but that was clearly their intention. This time he forced her into his embrace and she could hear his heart beating faster. A low snarl was forming in the back of his throat, and she could feel fur growing on his cheeks. He was going to transform soon, but she knew he would never hurt her.

"I should never have let you go out alone," he said. "From now on, you're not allowed to go out without me. Is that clear?"

She did not answer.

"Eve!" he said, grabbing her face and forcing her to look at him.

He was no longer Nicolas, but something in between him and the Beast of Gevaudan, but still in his eyes she could see the pain, the worry, and the love he had for her, and she felt guilty for endangering herself like that.

"Eve, I don't want to lose you," he said. "If something happened to you…"

"Well, nothing will ever happen to me," she said sadly.

She lowered her eyes, removed her wig and her hair extensions, and looked at him again, and he seemed to calm down.

"I'm just Eve, the peasant girl in clogs," she said.

"Eve…" he whispered, cupping her face. "I can't marry you, but I'd rather you be the Countess of Castelcombe and be safe with me, than you be a prostitute. These women will only get you in trouble!"

Her eyes filled with tears again and she began to cry. For the first time in her life, she had found a group of women who accepted her, but Nicolas was asking her to choose between them and him, between behaving like a proper wife or a harlot, and he knew that, presented in that way, it was an easy choice to make. But for her, it was not.

They returned home to the castle, but things were no longer the same. Now, Nicolas criticized Eve's dresses and her makeup, he called her a coquette and said that if she wanted to be a woman, she ought to behave like a respectable one. After all, she was almost a countess now. She pointed out to him that even the Dauphine Marie-Antoinette, the future Queen of France, wore makeup and taller wigs than anyone else in the kingdom, but it only infuriated him. They argued often, and she permanently moved back to the kitchen, where she could at least wear her makeup and wigs and not be bothered. He ignored her for several days, but, as always, he eventually came knocking on her door. He did not have to; it was not locked. But he was respectful of her moods.

"Are you done sulking?" he asked behind the door.

"Go away!" she said.

That night, she wore the dress Faustine had picked for her. Faustine had excellent taste, and she looked very beautiful, like a princess, only she had no other prince than Nicolas. But what could she hope for, anyway? Would any other man accept her? And she knew Nicolas loved her, in his own, awkward way. She heard his heavy footsteps go up the stairs again. He would return to his room and wait for her to be ready to talk to him, as always.

A cold breeze suddenly came into the kitchen through the cracks between the bricks in the wall, where she had fixed the hole through which she had first entered the castle. She got up and looked around the kitchen for her mother's shawl. It was not in the chest where she usually kept it and she did not remember washing it recently. A terrible thought then crossed her mind: could Nicolas have taken it to hurt her? She rushed up the stairs to the dining room and checked the fireplace. A warm fire burned in it, but she did not see anything that looked like her shawl.

"Nicolas!" she called out anxiously, but of course, he did not answer.

She went up the stairs to the next floor and opened the door to their former room. He was sitting in a chair at his desk, reading the chronicles of the Castelcombe family—a collection of hunting stories and who married their first or second cousin. Even his interests did not extend past the walls of his castle. He turned weary eyes to her.

"Are you talking to me now?" he asked.

"Where's my shawl?" she asked him.

"What shawl? You have dozens," he said, frowning.

"My mother's," she said.

He looked befuddled.

"The brown one!" she insisted, leaning against the desk.

"The one with holes in it?" he said.

"Yes!"

"I threw it away," he said.

"You what?" she said, horrified.

"It was full of holes. I thought it was a rag," he shrugged.

Her eyes filled with tears, and she backed away slowly.

"But I showed it to you so many times! I told you it was all I had left of my mother!" she cried.

"I didn't know it was important. I'll buy you a new one," he said, getting up.

He looked uncomfortable and confused, as though he did not understand how he had once again hurt her feelings.

"You can't replace it! Do you even understand how precious it was to me?" she said.

She was crying now, and he tried to go to her, but she pushed him away.

"I'm done with you!" she cried. "I can't live with a man who disrespects everything about me!"

And, without thinking any further, she ran back to the kitchen and began to throw her dresses and wigs into a carpet bag. Nicolas slowly came down the stairs and observed her from the door.

"Eve, what are you doing?" he asked.

"I'm leaving you, that's what I'm doing!" she said.

All of her dresses wouldn't fit in the bag, so she dug through it again, pulling out the ones she did not need.

"And then what? You're going to return to your farm? The villagers burned it to the ground," he said in a calm voice, as though he did not truly believe she intended to leave.

"Then I'll walk to the city," she said.

"Everyone in Javols thinks your mother cast a spell on you to transform you into a girl, and the next big city is Montpellier. Do you really think you can walk all the way there?" he said.

"I will if I have to. I have good legs," she said.

"Eve, stay here, with the man who loves you," he then said, in a softer voice.

"Who loves me? You don't even see me as I am!" she said, turning to him in tears.

"I let you wear the clothes you want and go by the name you want. I protect you, I buy you everything you could possibly want..." he said, again not understanding.

"But you see me as a man in a dress!" she snapped.

"Because that's what you are!" he retorted, raising his voice. "Why in the world should I not state the obvious? And what difference does it make, anyway?"

"It makes a difference!" she said. "I love you as a man, and I want you to love me as a woman, but that's not what you see in me!"

He rolled his eyes and let out an exasperated sigh.

"But I see you as you are!" he said. "Listen, I'll buy you a new shawl and wigs, and call you my wife if that's what you want. Will you stop throwing these hysterical fits, then?"

"Oh, I'm hysterical now?" she retorted.

He sighed again and leaned against the wall as though he did not know what to do with her anymore.

"I did everything for you!" she said, bursting into tears again. "I took care of myself and you. I cleaned for you, cooked for you, slept with you, and you still can't have the most basic respect for me!"

"I don't remember forcing you to do any of it," he pointed out. "You're the one who came into my castle. The doors are not locked, Eve."

"Then watch me leave now!" she said.

She grabbed the last of her toiletries, a kitchen knife, which she wrapped in a piece of leather, and stuffed them in the bag, then closed it.

"Eve, you need me," he tried telling her, but she pushed him aside and walked past him with her bag, up the stairs, and out the front door of the castle this time.

The sky was dark outside and the air was unusually cold and damp for September. Winter always came to the mountains sooner than the coast, but it was not quite there yet. Nicolas came out and stood on the steps near the great wooden doors, looking both angry and distraught, but he again made no move to stop her. He called out to her instead.

"You will come back, Eve! You will because you're a supernatural creature like me, and only I can understand you!"

She stopped and turned around for a second, then shrugged and walked away. She had walked into his castle like a thief, but she was going to leave like a queen, with her dignity at least.

"Eve!" he called out to her again as she walked down the path to the front gates of the property with her little bag. It was nighttime and she was alone, but she was a child of the mountains, and she feared neither the wolves nor the werewolves.

CHAPTER 4

WHEN EVE WAS ANGRY, her anger could last for days, and it was a good thing. For if she had stopped to think, she might have turned around and returned to Nicolas that night. After all, she knew nothing of the outside world, except that it was dangerous for women alone. She was on her way to a faraway city, to the only friend she had, and having no clue what she would do next. But, energized by her rage, she kept on walking.

She walked long hours through the forest and mountain paths until she came to the main road. She knew where it led: back to Javols. She would have to cross the village, but she no longer cared. The villagers could try to burn her if they wanted, and she would stab them. She would *kill* anyone who tried to hurt her. But the village was empty at this hour, except for an officer who passed her on his horse. She did not pay any attention to him and continued walking on the muddy path, but he stopped his horse and turned around.

"Are you alone, *Mademoiselle*?" he asked.

She stopped and looked up at him. He was a young man, about her age or a little older but with a baby face, and he wore his hair tied back in a ponytail and curled on the sides, like many a nobleman. He was rather dashing in his blue and red military tailed coat with shining golden buttons, his white breeches and black boots, and his black cocked hat contrasted beautifully with his strawberry blond hair. With his bright blue eyes and the few freckles on his nose, he looked like an adolescent, and his smile had the same candor. He carried a sword on his side.

"Don't be afraid, I'm an officer in the army," he said as she failed to respond to him. "Where are you going?"

"Montpellier," she simply said.

"On foot? Aren't you going to wait for the stagecoach to come to the village?"

"I can't stay in this village," she said, lowering her eyes – not because she felt shy with him, but because she did not really want to make conversation.

"I don't need to know your reasons, but I can't let you walk alone," he said. "That beast is still out there killing people."

"Oh, I can take care of myself, thank you," she said, and she began to walk again.

He followed her on his horse.

"*Mademoiselle…*" he insisted. French men were so persistent.

"Listen," she said, turning around. "I don't know what you want from me, but you're not going to get it. I'm a free human being and I have legs, and I'll walk all the way to Montpellier if I want to."

He smiled because she had answered him. She made a mental note never to engage in conversation with a stalker again, or they never let go. This one certainly didn't. He brought his horse up to her again as she was walking.

"Am I at least allowed to tell you how beautiful you are?" he said pleasantly.

"Yes, you are allowed to," she said, looking straight ahead.

"If you want, I can take you to Montpellier on horseback. It's on my way," he said.

"No thanks."

Seeing no reaction on her part, he got off his horse and began to walk by her side.

"You look like you've been crying," he said, now with concern.

"So what? Everyone cries," she said.

"My name is Clement Darrieussecq, and what's your name?" he asked.

His name was so curious she couldn't help but smile, and eventually started giggling.

"What is it?" he asked, not understanding.

"Your name... even I don't think I can pronounce it," she said, turning to him.

His eyes lit up at once.

"Ah, it's so much better when you smile," he said. "And my name is Basque in origin."

"So you're from the Basque Country?"

"I certainly am," he proudly said. "Are you from here?"

"Yes, I'm from Javols," she said, losing her smile. "I need to go now."

"Wait, please. Let me take you on horseback," he pleaded again. "I can tell you don't want to be here, and you'll be safe with me, I promise."

She hesitated for a moment, then looked at the distant horizon, beyond the mountains. The sun would rise soon and the villagers would come out and see her.

"Alright," she said, "But only until the next village."

"Of course," he said with a bright smile.

Eve was still young, but she was no longer naïve. She knew exactly what he wanted, and therefore she was not surprised when they made a halt in an abandoned barn the next evening and he threw himself on her in the hay like a famished wolf, kissing her neck and caressing her skin.

"Clement!" she gently protested, but his kisses were so passionate she did not really want him to stop. He was starved for her in every way, and the hard bulge in his breeches left no doubt as to his level of arousal. But she knew he was not trying to rape her. He did not look like he had it in him. He finally pulled away from her lips to gaze into her eyes.

"*Mademoiselle*, your charms have bewitched me," he said, breathless and rosy-cheeked. "But I am a gentleman, and I do not want to force you if you don't want me."

She gazed into his eyes, unsure. Her body was certainly responding to his, but he was not Nicolas, and she did not know whether he would understand what she was.

"I do, but…" she said in a whisper.

"Oh, *Mademoiselle*!" he said, delighted, and waiting no further, he began to lift her skirts and caress her legs until he found what was between them and said: "Oh…"

She gazed at him, waiting to see his reaction, but apparently it was not much of a problem for him. He threw himself on her again and kissed her passionately.

"Clement!" she protested, but he was too sweet to resist, so she finally gave in to him that night and let him make love to her as long and as hard as his young body permitted it. It was a new, strange yet exciting feeling to let a stranger inside her, to let him suck on her and tease her, to surrender to him without any commitment or concern, free to experience the pleasure without the pain of being in love. But perhaps he did not understand what they were doing as she did, for as she lay in his arms afterwards, beginning to fall asleep, she thought she heard him whisper: "Eve, I think I'm in love with you…"

Clement was a kind young man who did not abandon her on the side of the road as she had expected at first. He took her all the way to Montpellier on horseback and once there, he begged her for her address so he could see her again.

"I don't have an address yet," she told him after getting off his horse.

"But you'll be staying somewhere, right?" he said.

"Yes, at a friend's place, hopefully."

"Please tell me your friend's name," he begged her again.

"Clement, you need to go now," she told him.

She walked away, and he watched her in awe, as though he had just found the muse of his dreams and lost her. But she was not ready to fall in love with another man. Right now, she needed friends, so she went to Faustine's shop on Rue Saint-Pierre.

It was a beautiful, sunny day, and the air was moist and smelled like the ocean. Seagulls flew over the city and she loved listening to their songs as she walked down the paved streets. It was not the first time she saw the city, but she felt like a new person now, free from her tormented love for her reclusive werewolf. She was a free woman, and if all she could be in this world was a coquette, then she would embrace that lifestyle fully and make the most of it.

As she had hoped, Faustine remembered her and was overjoyed to see her again. Lucie and Maude were in her shop, enjoying some tea with a distinguished, older woman whom they introduced as Madame de Guigne. Aged forty-two but still beautiful, she was a courtesan who had 'made it', marrying a rich widower who owned castles and land, and adored her.

Faustine and the other girls wanted to know everything about Eve's story, but, like the last time, the pastries caught her attention first, and the girls laughed as she stuffed herself, closing her eyes in ecstasy.

"She is so cute," Madame de Guigne said, eyeing her with shining eyes. She did not only like men but also bedded some of the coquettes now and then, sometimes with her husband too, and while Eve finished the last coffee cake, she listened to her and Lucie talking about some orgy they had taken part in.

"And the best part is that my husband is never jealous," Madame de Guigne said. "He just said: 'When you're done, ladies, come and sit on Daddy's lap'."

Lucie, Maude, and Faustine all laughed.

"And what about you?" Faustine then asked Eve. "Are you still with your count?"

"Oh, no. I left him," Eve said, pretending like she didn't care.

Her throat was tight and her heart heavy, but these girls were right: no man was worth her tears, and certainly not him. She told them what an oaf he was, always reading his hunting chronicles and living like a recluse, and how she left the castle and intended to walk all the way to Montpellier but met a handsome officer and ended up rolling in the hay with him in an abandoned barn.

"And then, in the middle of the act, he said: 'By the way, what's your name?'" she said, and all of them laughed with her.

"Oh my goodness, Eve, where do you find these men?" Maude said.

She was laughing so hard she almost cried.

"So, are you still interested in becoming a singer?" Lucie asked Eve.

"I don't know. Maybe," Eve said.

"You can take singing lessons at my place. I have a pianoforte," Madame de Guigne said.

"But I have no money to pay you…" Eve said.

"Oh darling," Madame de Guigne said. "You pay me later, when you get a castle of your own."

"Madame de Guigne will teach you everything you need to know to catch another rich man – this time not on the side of the road," Lucie said.

"I'm not sure Eve is ready for that. She's never even lived in the city," Faustine said.

"Well, it's up to you," Lucie told Eve directly.

Madame de Guigne pulled out a small card from her purse with an address written on it and handed it to her.

"This is our home in Montpellier. We hold a salon there on Thursday nights. Come," she said.

Eve took the card and smiled.

"Thank you," she said.

Faustine was right: she had never lived even in an average-sized city like Montpellier and she did not know exactly what a 'salon' was. She knew absolutely nothing of the world of the coquettes, except that it was probably more glamorous than her life with Nicolas. That night, she stayed with Faustine, who did not have much room in her small home but tried to make her comfortable. After changing into a nightgown, Eve lay in the one bed while Faustine removed her wig and makeup in front of the vanity. Faustine was very much older than her, and she was already losing her thin, blond hair, but she still took care of the hair she had left because it was precious to her.

"Faustine, are you also a coquette?" Eve asked her, rolling over in the bed.

"No," Faustine replied.

"Then how did you find the money to open your own shop?" Eve asked.

Now she also wondered how come she never got bothered about wearing dresses in the streets. Unlike Eve, she did not pass at all, but still she tried to be herself.

"I am the Viscount of Chambery," Faustine replied with some sadness. "I was chased away by my father but not disinherited. He still sends me money, but I am not allowed to return home unless I wear men's clothes."

"I'm so sorry... That must be very hard," Eve said. "I guess I was lucky, my mother always accepted ."

Faustine removed her dress, petticoat, panniers, and corset, and slipped on her nightgown before joining her in the bed.

"Eve, sweetheart, there are some things you need to know before you go out into this world and choose your path," she told her in a serious voice. "Do you know anything about the laws in this kingdom?"

"Not really," Eve admitted.

Of course she knew that criminals were arrested and prosecuted, and that women were the legal property of men, but that was about it. Faustine gazed at her, her eyes filled with motherly compassion.

"Our very existence is illegal," she explained. "Under French law, the penalty for biological men caught wearing women's clothes is death. Biological women caught wearing men's clothes are usually not put to death, but they can face incarceration and public beatings."

Eve stared at her with surprise. She thought her village was an isolated case of bigots still living in the witch trials era. Because of her father, she knew she had to be careful around men, but she never imagined that people like her and Faustine faced the death penalty simply for existing.

"Of course, they can't arrest and put to death everyone who crossdresses, so women like us are usually just added to the registry of prostitutes and fined," Faustine continued. "But in the eyes of society, we are extremely dangerous individuals."

"Because we wear dresses?" Eve asked.

"It has to do with patriarchy and the order it imposes," Faustine said. "In this order, biological women are inferior human beings, and biological men superior. For the 'superior' to choose to live as the 'inferior' is considered a much greater transgression than the opposite. Men caught sleeping with us quickly turn around and accuse us of having tricked them so they can avoid prosecution."

"That's ridiculous!" Eve said, shocked. "I've never been dishonest with my lovers. They knew what I was and they had no problem with it!"

"People will become liars to save themselves," Faustine said. "And I'm not trying to frighten you, on the contrary. You need to know that women like us are like the coquettes: we are at the very bottom of the social hierarchy. No one protects us, we have only each other."

Eve sighed and lowered her eyes.

"Perhaps my mother did the wrong thing by allowing me to be myself and protecting me from this world. Because I was safe with her, I never really learned how to fight for myself," she said.

"On the contrary, your mother did the right thing: she loved you as you are," Faustine said. "You can learn how to fight, but you cannot learn how to love and respect yourself when even your parents despised you. That confidence your mother put inside you is like a magical shield that will protect you in this world. I don't have a shield like that."

Eve gazed at her and smiled.

"You are strong, Eve, but you must be wary of men - especially those you will fall in love with," Faustine then warned her.

"Well, after my experience with Nicolas, I'm not sure I want to love again…" Eve said sadly.

"Did he hurt you? Is that why you left?" Faustine asked.

"No, never."

"Are you sure?"

"Yes, why?"

"I just… I have a bad feeling about that man. The way he was waiting for you that night and talked to you… Please, don't agree to see him again," Faustine said.

"Why would I ever see him again?" Eve said, forcing herself to smile.

"Because you're in love with him, and he will come looking for you," Faustine said.

Eve pursed her lips. Faustine could see right through her and the act she was trying to put on to hide the fact that she was heartbroken. She tried and tried to hold back but was unable to and burst into tears.

"Oh, Faustine… what will I do now?" she sobbed like a child.

Faustine pulled her into her embrace and kissed her hair.

"Sweetheart, you will be just fine without him, I promise," she told her in a soothing voice. "It's not Nicolas you miss, it's the feeling of having someone. You think you need it to feel validated because you are young, but as you grow older, you will remember that you don't need anyone to validate you."

"But what will I do until then?" Eve said.

"Until then, I and the other girls will be there for you, and we will always remind you how beautiful and essential you are."

Eve pulled back to look into her eyes.

"I think I will take singing lessons with Lucie and Madame de Guigne," she said. "If I have a trade of some kind, then I will never need to return to Nicolas."

"If you become a singer, your trade will be prostitution," Faustine warned her. "Are you ready to make your body available to all the men they choose for you?"

"But they would not pick bad men for me, right?"

"No, we care about each other's safety," Faustine said. "But if someday you fall in love again, that man will not forgive you for having been with others."

"Well, it's a little too late for that already, since I've had two lovers," Eve said sadly. "Why are men allowed to sleep with whoever they want and not us?"

"Because they are the ones who make the rules."

"A neighbor, a girl, once asked me why I didn't live as a man since I would have more rights," Eve said. "But if society is so cruel and unfair to women, then it is society that needs to change, not me."

Faustine listened to her and smiled.

"You have something I don't: your beauty," she said. "Beauty is the most powerful weapon for a woman in this world. So, perhaps your voice will be heard."

"Then I definitely ought to sing and make my voice be heard - loudly," Eve said, and they laughed together.

Since Eve had decided to go to Madame de Guigne's salon, Faustine dressed her up like a princess, in a beautiful red damask pannier dress - colorful but tasteful - and put on her head the tallest wig Eve had ever seen, then sent her on her way like a fairy godmother. But this salon was not, as Eve had imagined, a ball. It was a gathering of rich people and nobles, mostly men, who enjoyed polite and witty conversation in the company of coquettes and libertine noblewomen with the prospect of sex afterwards. Being a simple farm girl, Eve had no idea how to mingle with people there, and when men approached her to make conversation, she knew very little about the things they were talking about. Still, many of them wanted to know her, and she unwillingly ended up sitting on a sofa with four of them around her, refilling her glass of champagne. She had also never drank alcohol before.

"And what's your name, you sweet thing?" one of them asked.

"Eve," she said.

"Oh no, I don't like Eve, it's too serious," he said. "How about *Nenette*?"

It was a slang word for 'girl', and so dehumanizing. She hated it.

"Yes, Nenette suits you better," another said.

She was about to respond, but they did not want to hear what she had to say.

"So, Nenette, have you heard about the great Count Everolles?" another yet said. "He married that little co-quette... what was her name? Oh, yes, Fanfan. So he married her because she had good legs and spirit, and not a month later, he found her fucking the vicar."

Eve was shocked at the vulgarity of these men and how they referred to her sisters, but they thought they were funny and all laughed. If she wanted to be a part of that world and be able to support herself, she had to be nice to them—to some extent, at least.

"Well, if one fucks a girl for her spirit, he should not be surprised that she also gets fucked - spiritually," she commented, and they loved her wit.

Madame de Guigne then joined them, dressed in a luxurious purple pannier dress, a tall powdered white wig on her head and a smile on her heavily powdered face.

"Is everyone enjoying themselves?" she asked.

"Oh yes," one of the men said. "We were just getting to know Nenette."

"Yes, I was just teaching them a lesson in the art of handling one's affairs with spirit," Eve said with a polite smile.

"She is amazing!" another man said.

"She is, isn't she?" Madame de Guigne said. "And she sings too. She will be performing in my castle next month."

Eve gave her a look that meant: *"What?"*

She had not yet taken any singing lessons and was not ready to perform, but Madame de Guigne gave her an accomplice smile before leaving her with her small crowd of admirers.

Despite the vulgarity of the men, Eve quite liked the salon and decided to stay with Monsieur and Madame de Guigne for some time. Lucie also stayed with them, supposedly for her singing lessons, but singing was not all the libertine couple taught the two young women. They were always upfront and straightforward about what they did: they were pimps. They prepared the girls, educated them, bought their dresses, and found them rich lovers. The girls were then encouraged to ask the men for as many dresses and jewelry as they could because, as Madame de Guigne said, hard times could always come and diamonds were a girl's best friend.

The first thing Eve had to give up to mingle with rich men was her accent. Like the peasant girl she was, used to speaking Occitan, she spoke proper French with a strong accent that might charm local men but would never get her anywhere in society. So, she practiced her accent with the help of the Guignes until it was almost right, and when she could speak properly, she also learned to read properly, and was encouraged to read books. Whether she learned something from them or not mattered very little, she just needed to know what people read and talked about. But reading came easily for her, and she greatly enjoyed learning new things from books. And, along with completing her education, the Guignes taught her how to play the pianoforte enough to entertain a crowd, and sing. The couple was much older than Eve and Lucie, but they were young at heart, and the singing lessons often ended with laughter, the lessons of etiquette with a game of tag across the many rooms of the mansion and a stolen kiss here and there. Eve truly had with them all the fun she never had as a child, growing up on a farm and working all the time, and even when they first took off her clothes to train her in sexual matters, she felt comfortable. They were surprised, at first, to discover a male body underneath her dress, but Madame de Guigne said that there were men with 'special interests' who wanted a girl just like her, and Monsieur de Guigne, who went both ways, showed her how gentle and sweet sex with an experienced man could be. She was never asked to do anything she did not want to do, and they assured her she never would be. That was the difference between courtesans and the prostitutes in brothels, and because of her beauty, Eve could be a courtesan and choose her men.

She was a mediocre singer, like Lucie, but the voice training lessons helped her achieve an even higher pitch that sounded much more feminine, and they gave her an official trade in case she was ever arrested: she could pretend that she was a performer and only wore dresses for her show. But her real trade would be prostitution. She was aware of it, and she treated it just like any other job. A client was soon presented to her. He was clean, well educated, polite, and not too demanding, and he liked her so much he asked to see her again. So, as she had been taught, she did not answer him and let him wait and long for her, and soon came presents for her. And after he sent her dozens of flower bouquets and jewelry, she agreed to see him again. It was an easy profession if she could just put up with being denigrated by men a little. She felt safe and carefree with the Guignes, but she missed Faustine, so after a few weeks she returned to her.

Faustine was not surprised to see her friend enter her shop one sunny morning, and there was even a surprise waiting for her: more flowers from an admirer.

"Who?" Eve asked, gazing at the large bouquet of roses on the shop's counter.

"A young man named Clement," Faustine told her with a grin.

"Oh, that one," Eve said.

"Do you want to see him again?" Faustine asked as she brought out tea and pastries for them.

"No, I don't need him. I've got a new, rich man now."

They sat together at a table in the shop. There were two more cups for the other coquettes who might drop by.

"How did you like staying with the Guignes?" Faustine asked.

"I liked it," Eve said. "I met some interesting people."

"And how are the singing lessons going?"

"Fabulous."

Faustine put down her cup and took her friend's hand. Eve no longer looked like the country girl she had met on the streets, all sweet and innocent. Now, with her thick makeup and pearl earrings and rings on nearly every finger, she looked like someone else, and spoke like someone else too.

"Eve, I can tell you're not happy. Don't force yourself to do something you don't want for the money. It's not worth it," she told her in a firm but compassionate voice.

Eve let her eyes wander aimlessly around the shop, its sweet pink wallpaper, the fabrics, the dresses and hats and wigs.

"The men at Madame de Guigne's salon immediately gave me a nickname, 'Nenette'," she then said, pursing her lips.

"Oh, honey…" Faustine said.

"Leontine has an unflattering nickname, too," Eve said. "I guess it's just the way women are treated in our world."

"It is, but you don't have to accept it," Faustine reminded her. "You can always do something else, like sell cosmetics."

"How much would it cost to launch my own brand?" Eve asked, returning her eyes to her.

"It's expensive," Faustine agreed. "You could work here with me, making dresses, and we could save up to start your own brand."

Eve smiled and shook her head.

"I don't want to be a burden for you," she said. "A girl can only be two things in this world: one man's wife or every man's whore. I can't be a wife, so that leaves me only the other option."

Faustine pursed her lips and lowered her eyes.

"Madame de Guigne has a count for me. I am to meet him next week. She said he is very excited," Eve said with a smile.

"Will he treat you kindly?" Faustine asked.

"He isn't violent with women. For the rest, men are all the same," Eve said.

Faustine looked worried, but she forced herself to smile anyhow.

"Well, perhaps he will be better than the others."

Eve shrugged. She no longer believed in her prince charming. There was only one thing men wanted from her: sex. She was what Madame de Guigne called a 'special interest', for men like Nicolas. And the only thing she wanted from them anymore was money and jewelry, so she would never have to live with a man or depend on him again.

As promised, a count was found for Eve, and then another, a few barons and even a duke, who, after dancing with her once at a masquerade ball, inquired about her. All she had to do was visit them or receive them at the Guignes' castle just outside the city, make conversation, sleep with them, and collect the money and jewelry. She did not have to make much effort to be polite, graceful, and polished; those things came to her naturally and Madame de Guigne already saw her as the next Countess du Barry.

"Who knows, perhaps you really will make it to Versailles," Aisha said one sunny afternoon, as they both relaxed in one of the rooms of the Guignes' castle.

Formerly known as 'Julie Duval', Aisha, the young coquette with tan skin and a thick mane of black hair, looked like a typical southern French girl to Eve, but the men in Paris did not know that. And because she did palm and tarot readings, and that everything esoteric and exotic was fashionable, Madame de Guigne had renamed her 'Aisha' and told her circles she had Moorish origins and was raised by Gypsies. As such, she had been taught some belly dancing and sometimes performed scantily clad at salons, after which everyone got a tarot reading, whether they wanted it or not. While she was not a skilled dancer, her readings were very accurate and everyone loved her, especially Eve, to whom she had also taught how to read the cards. But that day, Aisha was more interested in the pastries on the table beside her, and Eve was absorbed in a book.

Eve loved reading above all things. Now that she could actually read at the same level as the people in the salons, she could have an intellectual conversation with Plato or Aristotle in Ancient Greece through the pages of a book, but she also liked reading contemporary authors like Voltaire. Knowledge, she thought, was power, not beauty. But the men in the salons thought otherwise, and if they enjoyed her wit and conversation at first, when it came down to business, they preferred for her to shut up and spread her legs, like that imbecile, François, who once told her: "I'm sorry sweetheart, but when you run your mouth all the time you kind of ruin the mood."

"If I make it to Versailles, I won't need the Duke anymore, I'll get into the King's bed," Eve nonchalantly said, turning the page of her book.

"Oh, ambitious!" Aisha laughed.

Madame de Guigne then entered the room, an alarmed look on her face. She was holding a letter in her hand.

"What's the matter?" Aisha asked, sitting up, and Eve put down her book.

Madame de Guigne came to sit beside both of them on the sofa and slipped her arms around them.

"Maude… got sick," she said with a deep sigh.

They both knew what it meant. With all the diseases carried by men who frequented the brothels, they were all in danger of contracting something someday.

"It's the pox," Madame de Guigne said. "She didn't make it…"

Eve and Aisha sat quietly by her side, stunned. Death was very real in their world, even at such a young age, and the pox not only disfigured people but also made them die in terrible pain. The sweet and sassy Maude, with her curly red hair and her innocent smile, would never liven up their conversations, she would never sing with them, or laugh, or hold their hands again. Eve covered her face and began to cry.

"It's life, sweetheart. None of us are eternal," Madame de Guigne told her in a soft voice, but she was also heartbroken. She cared about each of her girls and watched over them like an older sister or perhaps a mother, but sometimes one of them just ran out of luck.

"Was there someone by her side?" Aisha asked in a small voice.

"Yes, Faustine. She nursed her until the very last moment," Madame de Guigne said.

"Oh, I must go to her!" Eve immediately said.

"Eve, the pox is very contagious. It would be best for you to stay away from her until we are sure she's not sick," Madame de Guigne said, but Eve shook her head.

"I know tinctures I can take to prevent illness, and I could make some for Faustine, too. Please, let me go to her. I have to be there for her!"

Madame de Guigne stroked her back softly.

"I don't want to lose you too."

"You won't, I promise," Eve said.

CHAPTER 5

Madame de Guigne knew there was little she could do to stop Eve. Had she known Maude was sick, she would have gone to her immediately, despite the risk of getting sick herself, but she was already gone and now Faustine needed her. So, Eve returned to Montpellier, where she found Faustine's shop closed. It was late in the night, but there was a candle at the window of her bedroom upstairs, so she knew she was awake. She began pounding on the door and calling her name until Faustine opened it. She looked ghastly, tired, and weary in her long white nightgown, her unruly hair barely tucked under her nightcap.

"You?" she said, surprised, but Eve threw herself in her arms.

"Oh, Faustine! Madame de Guigne told me what happened!" she said, her eyes filling with tears.

"Eve, sweetheart, you shouldn't be here. I might be contagious," Faustine told her while gently trying to push her away, but Eve would not let go.

"I know of a tincture that will keep us safe," she said. "Please, let me see her. Is she still here?" she begged her.

Faustine shook her head.

"The police came and said she had to be buried immediately and her bedding burned. My shop is also to remain closed for a month."

"What? But it's the pox, not the plague!" Eve said, shocked.

Faustine smiled sadly.

"To them, *we* are the pestilence... The harlots, the prostitutes, the women like you and me," she said. "They said my shop was a brothel, and the only reason they couldn't arrest me was because I have a title. A brothel...! Is it a crime to offer my friendship and comfort to women who were left no other choice by society than to sell themselves?"

She burst into tears and covered her face.

"Oh, Faustine, come, let's go inside," Eve said.

They went inside and closed and locked the door. She sat her friend down at one of the tables and lit a candle, then went into the kitchen in the back and lit a fire in the chimney and put a kettle of water to boil. She rummaged through the cabinets and found a few herbs and spices, as well as honey. Many of them could be used to help protect oneself against sickness, and Faustine had a small amount of powdered ginger. That would be perfect until Eve could make her a stronger tincture. So, she prepared ginger tea for both of them, and added some honey, and brought it to Faustine.

"Here, drink this. It will warm you up and make you feel better," she said.

Faustine took a sip and smiled through her tears.

"You are an angel, Eve," she said.

Eve took her hand and gazed into her eyes. She knew how cruel and unforgiving this world was to her and her sisters, but she still could not understand why. Men were no better than courtesans. All of them cheated on their wives, and none got arrested for it. It was unfair.

"I see anger and passion in your eyes," Faustine said. "But please don't do anything stupid."

"I won't," Eve said, who was already imagining what she would do to the police constables if she had a pitchfork right now.

She gazed sadly around the once lively shop. Now, in the darkness, it looked like a whole other world. It was the flip side of the coin for them, what awaited them after the glitter, the music and dances. It was the reality of their condition, as unmarried women or women who could not legally marry.

"Would you like to see her grave?" Faustine asked softly.

"Yes, please," Eve said, her eyes tearing up again. "Did she get a decent grave at least?"

Faustine shook her head and began to cry again, and Eve also burst into tears. Of course, the city of Montpellier would never let a prostitute have a grave with her name on it. She was probably buried in a mass unmarked grave.

"I made a little stone cross in the dirt, so we would know where she was buried," Faustine said.

"Can I go see her now?" Eve said.

"In the middle of the night?"

"Yes, I need to. I can go alone," Eve insisted.

Faustine was too distraught and tired to go with her, she could see it. So, she put her to bed and kissed her goodnight on the forehead and promised her she would be back before dawn. She then left the, making sure to lock the door behind her, and headed to the *cimetière de la Blanquerie*, the largest in Montpellier. She did not have a black dress, nor any time to change, so she was still wearing the blue pannier dress with a floral print she had been wearing when she heard of Maude's passing. She had only covered herself in a long, purple hooded cloak she borrowed from Faustine, and because she was so short, it dragged on the ground behind her.

She found the small stone cross easily at the foot of an old oak tree, and let herself fall to her knees and cried. She cried with anger and pain because of what they had done to the poor Maude, but she knew no one would hear her, no one would care. This was their message to her in death: "We hate you."

Feeling the need to be closer to her, she plunged her fingertips into the dirt. It was cold and soothing, and she let herself fall upon it, spread out her arms, closed her eyes, and she thought she could hear the ground softly humming underneath her. Something was moving inside her body again, like the morning her mother died, but this time it was like a warm wave throughout her entire body, and she could not tell whether it was pouring into her from the earth, or pouring out of her body into it, but it filled her with a great sense of peace. And then, as in a dream or perhaps a vision, she saw women from the past. Like her, they were hidden under long, hooded cloaks, and they seemed afraid. They were gathered in what appeared to be the ruins of an old castle or abbey at night, and one of them was carrying a grimoire, which she hid in the wall behind a loose stone.

Eve then saw the women hurrying through the forested mountain paths under the great pine trees, and as then ran away from their pursuers, hundreds of small green lights rose from the ground, the stones, and the trees. They moved roots here and closed the path with branches there, helping them escape, and Eve felt like she was each one of them, and each of the spirits, flying free among the trees. But the women were eventually caught and tied to wooden poles on pyres. As the fires that would claim their lives were lit, they chanted prayers in Spanish. They were not witches; they were women who had crossed the Pyrenees mountains, probably fleeing war, and had settled in France.

Eve saw their leader again as she was about to be burned alive, and she suddenly knew her name: Aurelia. She was the matriarch of the Escobar clan, from which Maryse was descended. She was a fierce Spaniard who fought against the inquisitors, and whose knowledge was passed down the generations from mother to daughter. It was because of her Eve now knew the herb lore. But the woman in her vision turned her eyes to her now, as though she could see her. Eve could not understand the words of the prayer she was chanting, but she knew it was for her, and then she felt something entering her body. It was a piece of Aurelia's spirit, and her daughters and granddaughters. They would now live inside Eve, like a piece of Maryse did, to protect her in this dangerous world.

The flames crept higher, the women's clothes caught on fire, and so did their legs. They cried out in agony as the flames engulfed them and the spirits watched, helpless before the senseless cruelty of humans upon each other.

Eve opened her eyes again and she was still laying in the dirt. She slowly sat up and felt the now warm earth between her fingers, and she realized that, while trying to shun her, they had in fact given Maude the best burial place: in the warm arms of Mother Earth, She who welcomed all her children, judging none of them, and now Maude would be protected by the spirits of the earth and the women like Aurelia, who died to be free. She was just another martyr of this world. And now the stone graves and crosses around her no longer looked like the trophies earned by good Christians after they died, but like emblems of the suffering the Church imposed upon people throughout the ages. To be returned to Mother Earth was to be freed from the chains of Christianity.

The sudden sound of footsteps in the grass behind her startled her, and she turned around. A man stood behind her, near the trees, clad in a long red cloak. She knew him only too well.

"Nicolas…" she whispered.

"Who died?" he asked in his deep voice.

"A friend," she said, lowering her gaze.

"A prostitute?" he asked. His voice was filled with reproach.

"A free woman," she said, looking into his yellow eyes again.

He stepped closer and she rose to her feet. She was not afraid of him, and nothing he could say about her friend would change her mind about her or the path she had chosen. But he was not there to talk about Maude.

"I've missed you," he said, and his eyes filled with a great sadness.

"That's your own fault. Blame yourself," she said coldly.

"Come home," he said.

"Home? You mean to *your* home? When was it ever a home for me?"

"Eve…" he said, taking her hand.

She did not want him to hold her again, to touch her, because she knew her heart was still weak with him. He was her first love, and she would never quite be over him. And now he was trying to rekindle those dark flames inside her in a moment of vulnerability, except she knew that he was not lying when he said he missed her, because, like her, he was very lonely in this world.

"I need you," he said, towering over her, and as his comforting, manly scent surrounded her, she felt herself weakening even more.

"Please, let go of me," she said in a whisper, avoiding his gaze.

"Have you found another man, one who loves you as you are?" he asked her, and he sounded like he would fall apart if she said she had.

"No. Men are worthless," she said.

"Eve, the men you sleep with are only interested in your body," he said. "I *love* you."

Tears welled up in her eyes as she listened to him, because she knew his words were true. None of her lovers cared about her. She was only a toy for them, a fetish, and, clueless and stupid as he was, she knew Nicolas had truly loved her. He probably still did because she was the one woman who did not fear him, who had walked into his castle and stayed with him, knowing he was the 'Beast of Gevaudan'.

"Nicolas, stop. We've had this conversation before," she said.

But she looked up at him and, for the first time, saw tears rolling down his cheeks. The sorrow in his eyes was heart-breaking, and his lips trembled.

"Eve, I have no one but you in this world. You were the only light in my world," he said. "Without you, life has been miserable. It was miserable before, except I had never known the sweetness of having you, of hearing your voice, of holding you in my arms. I may be only a stupid old man, but I love you with all my heart. Please... come home with me."

Now she was crying too, but she refused to let herself be swayed, so she turned away from him and removed her hand from his.

"Nicolas, please go now. Leave me alone," she whispered.

He took a step back and gazed at her quietly, but she would not look at him again, so he eventually ran away, and, in the distance, she heard the long, desperate howl of a wolf.

She returned to Faustine's shop and remained there, shedding the tall wigs and jewelry for a simpler dress, and when the shop was finally allowed to reopen, she began making and selling cosmetics to women, and, secretly, herbal remedies. She no longer wanted to be 'Nenette', the plaything of men, but Eve. And she did not need to advertise her products: word of mouth worked much better with her feminine clientele, and they flocked to Faustine's shop to procure themselves herb blends to ease menstrual cramps, to prevent pregnancy, or to end it sometimes. She was aware of the risks she was taking, but so were these women, and they were desperate to have some control over the main problem in their lives: back-to-back pregnancies and the fear of dying from one of them. They did not care who or what Faustine and Eve were; they were all the victims of men and their cruel laws. They were all sisters.

But not everyone was happy about Eve's change of career, and soon Madame de Guigne paid them a visit. She came alone and seated herself at one of the tables in the shop. As usual, Faustine brought her some tea. Eve was in the kitchen, working on a new batch of scented soaps to sell in the shop.

"Is Eve here?" she heard Madame de Guigne ask.

"Yes, I'll go get her," Faustine said.

She soon appeared in the kitchen and Eve turned to her.

"I'm coming," she said.

"Eve… you don't have to talk to her," Faustine told her in a low voice.

"Well, I live here now. She's going to see me anyway," Eve said.

She rinsed her hands at the water pump and dried them in her apron, then went to the front of the shop. Madame de Guigne seemed surprised to see her in a plain mauve dress. No panniers, no wig, only a corset to give it a little shape, and a large stained apron.

"Were you cooking?" she asked.

"No, I was making scented soaps," Eve replied with a polite smile.

"Is this a new hobby?" Madame de Guigne asked, somewhat amused. "Do sit down, honey."

Eve sat in a chair facing her and waited to hear what she had to say.

"So, when are you coming back to my place?" she asked.

Eve lowered her eyes.

"I don't know. I don't think that life is for me. I'm tired of being disrespected by men," she said.

The old Madame chuckled softly.

"Sweetheart, the world is full of men, and trust me, not one of them is different from your former lovers," she said. "They fuck you, belittle you, cuss at you, and fuck you again. What more do you think you will find here, toiling for your keep?"

"I'm not working to pay rent, but to help other women," Eve said. "I don't care whether I sleep with a thousand men or never lay in a man's bed again. I have a mind, and I can't shut it down to be pleasant to men."

"Nobody is asking you to be stupid. Just pretend to be around rich men and let them dote on you. Is that so hard?" Madame de Guigne asked her.

"Yes, it is," Eve said, moving her eyes back to her. "I don't want to be called 'Nenette' and pretend that I am stupid, or that I am anything other than what I am."

"You know, you're one of the lucky ones," Madame de Guigne said, throwing a glance in Faustine's direction, and now her voice was cold. "There's a niche market for people like you, but only a handful are pretty enough to be courtesans. The ugly ones end up in filthy brothels. But I see potential in you. I had a duke for you, and possibly some future clients at court. The gates of Versailles are just a few lovers away from you, Eve. And you're going to throw it all away to sit here in a pauper's dress, making potions and soaps in the kitchen. Do you have any idea where you would be if not for Faustine's rank and protection?"

"On the streets… or in a brothel," Eve said softly.

"With me, you could have everything," Madame de Guigne pressed her.

"But it's not what I want anymore," Eve told her honestly, because she had always been a good friend to her. It was a mistake.

"Fine then, but you owe me money," Madame de Guigne said in an angry but restrained voice.

"Martine!" Faustine said, but Madame de Guigne silenced her with a dangerous look.

"Money?" Eve said, not understanding.

"What? You think the voice training, the singing and etiquette lessons, and the dresses were all free gifts?" Madame de Guigne said. "You owe me forty thousand pounds, and I already deducted the diamond necklace your count just sent from it. So, how are you going to pay me?"

"I… I'll work," Eve said, knowing there was no way she could earn such a sum even if she worked an entire lifetime.

"I'll pay off her debt," Faustine said, stepping forth.

"No, Faustine," Madame de Guigne said. "Eve got herself in debt on her own. Now she must pay me back on her own."

"And I will, just give me some time," Eve said.

"I don't have time. Bring me all your jewelry," Madame de Guigne ordered.

Eve pursed her lips, got up, and went upstairs to the bedroom. She soon returned with all her jewelry. She was not a thief, nor would she run from her debts. She set the small jewelry box on the table. Madame de Guigne opened it and examined the pearl necklaces and earrings, the rings, the bracelets, then closed it, looking barely satisfied.

"It's not enough?" Eve naively asked.

"That won't even cover a third of your debt, honey," Madame de Guigne said. She got up and took the jewelry box, then said: "Pack up all your ball gowns and shoes, your fur capes, your gloves, and anything I can potentially sell. My servant will pick them up tomorrow. I will see how much I can get out of them and tell you how much you still owe me, then we can work out weekly payments."

"Y-Yes," Eve said, still in shock.

Even as a courtesan, she had remained so innocent it never occurred to her that a friend could turn against her, or that a woman's friendship could be a lie. Now she was left with an enormous debt to pay and hardly any money to live on, let alone make monthly payments on it. She did not know what to do, only that now the gilded days were over.

Madame de Guigne turned around once more before leaving the shop and said: "I'm not your enemy, Eve. I really wanted you to succeed, and I did everything in my power to help you. You're the one who threw it all away."

She then left and closed the door, and Eve let herself fall back into the chair, crying, but not over the loss of her jewelry and dresses, it was over the loss of her friendship with Madame de Guigne and the fact that now she would probably not be allowed to see her other friends anymore. Faustine sat beside her and wrapped her arm around her.

"Don't worry, Eve. We'll find a way to repay her," she said.

"Why… Why am I so stupid?" Eve sobbed. "I could just have continued working for her and paid her off…"

"I don't think so," Faustine said. "Madame de Guigne wanted to put you in a prince or a king's bed. How much do you think she would have had to invest to do that? I will tell you the truth: your dresses are country girl dresses, honey. No monarch would have touched you dressed like that. To even set foot at court, you need several court dresses, and the cheapest ones cost about ten thousand pounds. You would also need jewelry and wigs, and a proper carriage with horses. You would never have been able to repay her all that money."

Eve turned to her with wide eyes. She had never imagined that dresses could be that expensive, nor that some people earned and spent that much money. But that was the world Faustine came from and had left behind. Eve could not blame her for anything: she had tried to dissuade her from entering that world, but Eve thought she would be free if she did. As it turned out, no woman was ever free in this world. Either she belonged to a man, or to a pimp, or to someone like Madame de Guigne.

She wrapped her arms around Faustine and cried, and Faustine stroked her back and kissed her hair. Perhaps she was old and not so beautiful, but she was the kindest and most loyal friend to Eve, and Eve loved her dearly. They would find a way to survive together, somehow.

After losing her place among the coquettes of Montpellier, Eve truly realized how hard life could be. She did not mind being poor. In fact, she was better off with Faustine than she had been when she lived with her mother. The money Faustine earned with her shop was barely enough for one, and she'd had to rely on the money her father still sent her for all additional expenses, such as the doctor. She never did get the pox, but her health was not good. There was a lot Eve still did not know about her, but unlike Madame de Guigne, Faustine only hid from her the things that might make her sad, such as the fact that her heart was weak. She was almost fifty years old now, and she'd had a hard life, so Eve worked even harder so she could rest. Apart from making soaps and herbal blends, she worked on the dress orders until late at night, until her fingers were red and swollen and her eyes tired.

As her focus shifted from herself and her beauty to earning money for herself and Faustine, Eve lost the habit of doing her hair and makeup, and eventually of wearing a corset at all, and that was how, one day, she got picked up by the police while going to the market.

"*Monsieur*," a man in a blue and white uniform said, dropping a firm hand on her shoulder.

"It's '*Mademoiselle*'," she said, turning to him, but he shook his head like the headmaster of a school before a disobedient child, then grabbed her arm.

"Wait! I didn't do anything! Let me go!" she cried.

"Come with me," he said firmly.

Not understanding what she had done, she was dragged to the neighborhood prison, where she was taken to a cell. There, without any respect for her privacy, two officers frisked her and then, after confirming that she was not female underneath her clothes, they stripped her, beat her, and cut off her precious hair ear-length. They left her lying on the ground naked and bruised and crying. So this was what Faustine had warned her about; this was how they treated women like her. Her long, beautiful hair she had worked so hard to grow out... The bruises on her body would disappear in a few weeks, but it would take her years to grow out her hair again. They did it to hurt her and dissuade her from even trying to appear as a woman in public again. She covered her face and wept louder.

"Shut up, you degenerate!" the last of the men yelled at her before slamming the door of the cell shut and locking it.

She remained in the cell for hours, shivering in the cold. She needed her clothes, her dress, and not only to protect her from the elements. It was the shield that hid the parts of her body that made her uncomfortable. And now they wanted to force her to look at herself and be ashamed. But she once again heard that feminine voice in her head like the day her mother died. It said: *"Fight!"*

Fight. Yes, she could, if they did not sentence her to death. She prayed and prayed that Faustine would notice her absence and come looking for her. She prayed her mother and all her ancestors to protect her, and they did. The men finally returned and brought her some clothes—men's clothes. She picked them up, looking confused, but they simply told her: "Get dressed and follow us."

She had no idea how to wear men's clothes; she had not worn them since she was five years old, so she tried as best she could to put them on. They roughly finished dressing her, then pulled her into an interrogation room where a man sat at a table, a piece of paper, a quill, and a bottle of ink before him. She was made to stand before him, bruised and humiliated. The sun was setting already and the light coming in through the small, barred window was dim.

"Name please," the man at the table said without even looking at her.

"Eve… Chauvin," she said slowly.

"*Legal* name," he said, annoyed.

She lowered her eyes.

"Paul…" she whispered, and her eyes filled with tears.

The man wrote down her name.

"Date and place of birth?" he then asked.

She provided him the information, as well as her address.

"And what were you doing at the market today? Looking for company?" he questioned her.

"No, Sir. I was buying vegetables," she said.

"Buying vegetables?" he said, smirking.

"Yes, Sir."

He wrote everything down, then read to her the charges.

"*Monsieur* Paul Chauvin, in case you were not aware, you are a man. It is illegal in the Kingdom of France for a man to wear women's clothes. Do you understand this?"

"Yes, sir," Eve said, keeping her eyes lowered.

"You are hereby fined the sum of one thousand pounds for the crime of masquerading in women's clothes in public, and you shall serve three months in prison," he continued.

Eve's knees suddenly felt weak and her legs gave way underneath her, but two police constables grabbed her arms firmly and held her up. Prison? With men? What were they going to do to her? And what about Faustine?

"Three months! But Faustine needs me!" she said, desperate.

"However," the man continued, still in a reproachful tone, "The Viscount of Chambery told us you are his servant and due to his health issues, he cannot be without you. The sentence will therefore be postponed until Monsieur de Chambery either recovers or leaves this world. He has also paid your bail bond."

Eve stopped breathing for a moment, not understanding. And then she realized that Faustine had again used her privilege as a noble to get her out of this mess. What a joke the French judicial system was. They both had to pretend to be men—a master and servant—to prevent her from going to jail for simply wearing a dress.

"Be sure to thank your master. Not many people would tolerate your deviance," the man then said before gesturing to the others to release her.

They opened a door and pushed her out into the hallway where Faustine awaited her. This time, she wore men's clothes and a man's wig, and stood before them with the air of authority of the noble she was.

"He's all yours!" one of the officers said in a mocking tone, and he pushed Eve to her.

Faustine glared at them, then took Eve's arm and said: "Come."

They walked quietly down the now empty streets of Montpellier in what Eve would remember all her life as the 'walk of shame'. Few people saw them at this hour, but the humiliation of having to walk through the streets of the city with her bruised face, her hair cut short, and these clothes almost broke her. But they finally reached Faustine's shop, where they could be themselves again. Once inside, Faustine immediately drew her friend in her arms and kissed her.

"Oh, my poor Eve! What did they do to you?" she said.

But Eve, still in shock, slowly walked over to a mirror and stood in front of it. She brought her hand up to her short hair.

"My hair…" she whispered as tears of pain and anger rolled down her bruised cheeks.

Faustine came up behind her and embraced her like a mother.

"Oh, sweetheart, it will grow back. We'll put some extensions on you and you'll look great again!" she promised her.

"Why… Why do they do this to people like us? Why is it a crime to wear a dress? Who am I hurting?" Eve sobbed.

Faustine kissed her hair and held her tightly.

"No one… We just live in a cruel world," she said.

"I don't want to live in this world, I don't!" Eve said.

But Faustine would not let her talk that way. She forced her to turn around and look into her eyes.

"Eve, if you give up and do as they say or take your own life, then they will win, and our other sisters will continue to suffer," she told her firmly.

"But what can I do? The only reason they let me out was because of your title!" Eve said.

"I don't know what we can do, but giving up is not an option," Faustine said. "You taught me to be strong and bold. Now I want you to be strong and bold. I won't always be there to save you, and perhaps you will have to save others. I know you can do it. You have it in you!"

But Eve did not feel like she did. So she let herself collapse in her friend's strong arms and cried like she had never cried before.

CHAPTER 6

DAYS GOT COLDER, AND by the end of January, Montpellier even got some snow. The bruises on Eve's face and body had healed, but not those in her heart, and though her hair was slowly growing back, she felt like something had been broken inside her. It was her trust in this world and her future. It was then that she truly realized she would always be in danger in this world and that, if dying was not an option, then she would have to fight. She would have no choice but to become stronger, like her mother always told her.

It was on one of those snowy days, at the beginning of the year 1771, that she suddenly became very ill. She was about to turn twenty-two. It came upon her all of a sudden, as she was walking down the snow-covered paved street, now always on the lookout for any police constables and ready to run from them. The feeling hit her like a strong blow to her chest, like all the air left her lungs for a second and her vision went blurry. She staggered and leaned against the wall of a house and drew in a deep breath. After a few seconds, her vision was clear again and she could breathe normally. Her shoulders and arms felt a little sore and she was developing a headache - it was just the onset of a cold. It was inconvenient because she still had a lot of work to do at the shop, but she would make herself an herbal tincture that night and feel better in the morning.

She returned to the shop and went to the kitchen to start preparing a soup for dinner. She added some extra wood to the fire in the kitchen as it seemed unusually cold. It was always a little drafty there, after all. She checked the window: the cold air was coming in through the cracks in the wall around it, and even the dim sunlight that day seemed awfully bright to her tired eyes, so she covered the whole window with an old blanket. She then sat by the fire to peel potatoes and carrots and pulled her shawl tighter around her. Faustine then walked into the kitchen, looking startled.

"Eve, are you alright?" she asked.

"Yes, I'm fine. Why?" Eve said, turning to her, and once again her vision got blurry.

She shook her head then gazed at her shaking hands, and before she knew it, she had dropped the potato and the knife she was holding and was clinging to her chair. Faustine rushed over to her and immediately put her hand on her forehead.

"Oh, don't worry. I think I'm getting a cold. I'll be fine tomorrow," Eve assured her.

"Well, you don't have a fever, in fact, you're a bit cold. But your face is awfully pale. You need to get to bed and rest," Faustine told her.

"But your dinner…"

"Eve," Faustine said, serious. "I want you to go to bed, now. I will make dinner and bring it to you."

Eve wanted to protest, but she felt so weak and tired now she simply nodded. She let Faustine help her stand up and take her to the bedroom. She was too cold to want to undress, so she simply removed her shoes and slipped into the bed. There was a fireplace in the small bedroom as well, though they rarely used it, but Faustine brought some wood and started a fire for her, then she covered her with all the blankets she could find, but Eve's entire body was shaking now.

"You'll be warm soon," Faustine promised, and she nodded.

"It's nothing, really. I just need to rest a little," Eve said.

"You rest here, I will go make some soup for you. Call me if you need me," Faustine said.

She smiled and kissed her forehead, then returned downstairs, and Eve wanted to ask her to stay. Not knowing why, she didn't want to be left alone, but if she didn't work, then Faustine had to or they wouldn't eat that night. She rolled over to the side Faustine usually slept on and pulled the blankets up to her neck, still shivering. But, after some time, as Faustine had promised, she began to feel warmer and even discarded some of the blankets, and when her friend returned with some hot soup, she was able to sit in the bed.

"Your face looks a lot better already," Faustine said with a smile as she spoon-fed her.

"I'm sorry to burden you with more work," Eve said.

Faustine shook her head.

"You've been working so hard for me lately. I'm the one who should apologize to you."

"Working for you is a lot easier than working with men," Eve joked. "Men are so utterly stupid."

Faustine laughed and said: "Well, most of them, but not all."

Eve gazed at her with sparkling eyes and smiled.

"Not all? Have you been hiding something from me? A secret lover?" she said.

Faustine lowered her eyes and smiled, but somewhat sadly.

"A long time ago, I loved a man and he loved me," she said.

"What? And you never told me about him?"

"It was many years ago…"

"Now you have to tell me!" Eve said, taking her hands.

"Oh, I was so young back then…" Faustine said. "He was a nobleman like me, but of course, our love was forbidden. We both risked being disinherited by our fathers if they found out about us. This was before I started wearing women's clothes in public, but Hubert, my lover, knew. He was a shy, quiet man, and he adored me. The love we had was like a miracle I never hoped for in my life…"

"So… what happened?" Eve asked, holding her breath.

Unlike Madame de Guigne, she did not believe that one needed to be young and petite in order to be beautiful; beauty was what was in a person's heart. And with her kindness, her compassion, and her discreet presence, always protecting others in every way she could, Faustine was much more beautiful than Madame de Guigne.

"Well, we were careless, I guess," Faustine said sadly. "His father was the one who found us lying in each other's arms in the stables one day, when we were supposed to be out hunting."

"And what happened after that?" Eve asked.

Faustine pursed her lips and wiped away a tear.

"Our fathers found us brides and ordered us to marry. I refused, but Hubert was not so strong. He eventually gave in and married, and he had a child."

"What? But how could he if he truly loved you?" Eve said.

"We all live in prisons – some of them made of marble and gold. But not everyone is ready to leave their prison and go out into the unknown," Faustine said. "We're not the only couple whose parents were opposed to and eventually won. It happens all the time."

"And where is he now?" Eve asked, stroking her hand softly.

Now tears rolled down Faustine's cheeks and she wiped them away.

"Hubert died about ten years ago," she said. "Before he died, in a letter, he begged me to look after his child, and I send him money now and then."

Eve frowned.

"How cruel of him! After he abandons you and marries another, he asks you to look after his child? I would never have accepted!"

"No, Eve, it's not like that," Faustine told her. "If he'd had a choice, Hubert would have married me, but he married a woman instead, and she died a few years later. He raised his son alone, but Frederic was a rebellious child, always getting himself in trouble. Hubert was so worried for him, especially when he realized his days were counted, so he asked the only other person he could trust, me, to be like a mother to his son. And I felt compassion for this young man who didn't identify with the society he grew up in and preferred to live away from them, among the poor and the prostitutes, drinking and gambling away his life."

"Why did he choose such a life?" Eve wondered.

"Because he is a free soul, an artist. He wanted to be a musician, but his grandfather destroyed all his musical instruments. Noblemen can only work in the military. It is a matter of honor. No one would let their son work as a low-paid musician in the courts. It's just not done. You can imagine that my father doesn't tell anyone what I do for a living…"

"I'm glad he ran away then," Eve said.

Faustine smiled at her.

"Sweet Eve, I knew you would understand," she said. "I don't have to teach you anything. You already know that a family is much more than blood ties: it is the people we choose to have in our lives, and those who choose to love us and watch over us. Hatred isolates us, but love multiplies. The unconditional love we give a lost stranger or someone who has chosen a different path may sometimes be wasted, but for others, it will multiply, and they, too, will be able to love others in return."

Eve smiled and leaned against her large hand.

"If Frederic ever comes here, I will also treat him with love and compassion," she promised.

"I already know that you will," Faustine said. "But first, I need you to get well. So please get some sleep tonight."

"I will," Eve said. "But before that, there is something I want you to have, just in case something happens to me."

Faustine smiled.

"Nothing will happen to you. You are young and strong," she said.

"I know, but… would you please bring me that brown shawl I have been knitting?"

Faustine looked around the room and saw it, folded on a chair. She got up, went to get it, and brought it back to Eve, who wrapped it around her friend's shoulders.

"For me?" Faustine said, surprised.

"This is a replica of my mother's shawl, the one that brought me comfort after she died," Eve said. "If you think I'm brave, you have no idea how much braver my mother was. And she put love in my heart so that I could give it to others. Now you have my love and my mother's love to keep you warm at all times."

Faustine burst into tears and stretched out her arms to her and embrace her.

"Eve, you truly are an angel, and I do believe this , I can already feel your love through it."

Eve did not sleep very much that night, and her dreams were filled with soothing images of the pine forests, of the mountains and spirits, of her mother, but also terrifying images of fire and witches burning at the stake. She awakened, feeling sorer and heavier than the previous day, to the point she could not get out of bed. Faustine kept her warm and checked on her throughout the day, but she never developed a fever. Still, she sent for her personal physician, someone who would safely examine Eve without reporting her to the authorities. He examined her but was not able to determine the cause of her sudden illness and attributed it to exhaustion. He recommended rest and said she would get better soon, but she didn't. Her condition deteriorated quickly and after a week she was no longer able to feed herself. Sunlight hurt her eyes so badly that Faustine had to cover up the window and keep the shutters closed day and night.

"Am I going to die?" Eve asked her one night.

Faustine sat on the bed beside her, and the look in her eyes answered her question. Tears welled up in her eyes, and Eve also began to cry.

"I don't want to die," she whispered in a weak voice. "Who will protect you if I'm gone?"

Faustine kissed her forehead and caressed her cheek with her warm hand.

"You are a magical being, and I believe God himself sent you to me. But you are so pure He already wants you back," she said in a choked voice.

"I don't want to be with God, I want to be here with you…" Eve said, clinging to her.

"Whatever happens, you will continue to live within me," Faustine promised her. "And if I ever fall into despair, I will wrap your magical shawl around me and feel your love and your mother's love, and I will remember that I, too, can be strong. And in no time we will be reunited, in a beautiful place like your mountains."

Eve smiled through her tears.

"Yes, I will show you the mountains and the spirits of the forest," she said, and then she suddenly felt very tired.

She struggled to keep her eyes open, as though if she closed them she would never see her friend's face again, but Faustine gently lay her back in the bed and tucked her underneath the blankets.

"I'm right here, Eve. You can fall asleep," she said.

Eve tried to resist, but her eyes unwillingly closed, and she thought the last words she heard her friend say were: "Don't worry about me, sweet angel, you have the right to go."

Eve had what seemed like the longest dream ever that night. In this dream, she again saw generations of women passing down their ancient knowledge to their daughters. They gathered naked around bonfires, their skin painted, and danced to the sound of sacred drums under the moonlight. They summoned an ancient goddess and the spirits of nature to protect them, they cast spells, and Eve was a little girl among them, holding in her hands a book of which the blank pages slowly filled with words. And then, on the other side of the fire, she saw her adult self, hidden under a long, dark cloak. She was herself but also a little different, more beautiful, stronger, and her eyes were ruby-red. She stepped forward among the dancers and raised her hand above the fire, and from the dancing flames emerged the silhouettes of dozens, hundreds of spirits. They came out of the fire dancing with the joy of life, then disappeared into the shadows, and Eve somehow knew they were going to conquer the world. It was her legacy to this world, to the women who accepted her and loved her, and she gave the gift of love to others in return, so that they too could pass it on. Of course there were monsters in the darkness too. She could see them lurking around the dancers with their glowing eyes, but they all joined hands and cast a protective spell around the fire. Eve understood that the fire they were protecting was the light of hope. As long as the magic of hope and love burned in their hearts, they would be safe from the monsters in the darkness, and so would they protect others. She relaxed and closed her eyes, feeling reassured, and when she reopened them she was laying under a white sheet.

She blinked several times, wondering what was going on, but under the sheet she could not breathe, so she pulled it off her face. She was still lying in the bedroom, only it was cold and dark. The fire had died out in the chimney. Her first thought was that something had happened to Faustine, and then as she saw her body covered with the white sheet, and the flowers that had been placed beside the bed, she understood what had happened: because she was so cold, Faustine probably thought she was dead. She needed to let her know she was alive and well, so she got out of bed, feeling stronger than ever, and looked around her. The window was covered up and the shutters closed, but she could tell it was dark outside.

"Faustine?" she said, but no answer came.

She looked at her clothes: she was no longer wearing her nightgown but her favorite lavender dress, and Faustine had even curled her hair and slipped her dancing shoes on her feet. She wanted her to look beautiful on her deathbed.

Unsure why Faustine was not responding, she opened the bedroom door and slowly went down the stairs to the kitchen. She found her there, alone, sitting by the fireplace, her face covered with her hands.

"Faustine?" she said, and Faustine all but jumped out of her chair.

She stared at her with wide eyes as though she had just seen a ghost.

"Faustine, I'm feeling much better now. I'm not dead!" Eve told her with a smile.

She walked over to her but Faustine screamed and backed up against the wall, then fell to the floor and curled up in a ball, shaking with fear.

"Faustine?" Eve said, stopping.

"Stay away from me, whatever you are!" Faustine begged in a tear-filled voice.

"But it's me, Eve. Don't you recognize me?" Eve said, confused.

Faustine uncovered her face for a second and looked at her, then covered her face and screamed again.

"Faustine…" Eve said.

"Oh, Lord, please save me! Please!" Faustine repeated.

Eve tried to reach out to her but she pushed her away, screaming again, and Eve stood there, confused for some time. She thought Faustine was her friend, and she loved and trusted her with all her heart, but now she no longer wanted her there. So, even though she did not understand why she was suddenly so scared of her, she grabbed her cloak and left the shop.

The streets were dark and mostly empty. She began to walk aimlessly until she stopped in front of the window of a shop and gazed at herself. She was still the same, but her face had changed somewhat. It was still skinny, but her cheeks had filled in a little. But the most surprising thing about her face was that her eyes were no longer blue like a clear sky, but ruby-red. She then looked down at her dress and her thin dance shoes, now wet from the snow. It was cold outside, but she was not as cold as she should have been.

Having no clue what had happened to her, she began to walk again, and the few people she came across also screamed and ran away when they saw her, and she ran from them, frightened, until she reached the outskirts of the village. The forested paths and the distant mountains were before her, and behind her the small port town and the ocean, and her happiness. She was alone in this world again, like the night she ran away from her home, fleeing the villagers who wanted to burn her alive. Was she truly a monster, something so dark and frightening even Faustine no longer recognized her? She began to wonder whether she had truly died and come back to life through some sort of magic. If so, then no one in this world could tell her what she was. So, once again, she entrusted herself to the earth and the trees and began to walk toward the forest.

Eve would always remember the first night of her undead life as the loneliest, most frightening she had ever experienced. That night, for hours, she walked aimlessly down the snowy forest paths, lost in a sort of dark dream. As each and every footstep took her further away from Faustine, her only true friend in this world, the one who gave her a home, so did her heart break more and more. Where would she go now? Who could she turn to? Everything pointed to the same truth: she had died and somehow come back to life… as a ghost? There could be no other explanation. And if she was still here and not on the other side, it meant that she was trapped. Her throat tight at the thought she had just lost everything she had only to face an eternity stuck in between worlds. She began to run and tripped and fell. Her lavender dress was torn and dirty now, her hair a mess, and her cheeks wet with tears.

"*Maman! Maman!*" she cried out desperately, as though her mother's spirit could still hear her after all these years, but no one answered her but the distant cries of animals. She rolled over on her back and turned her eyes to the black sky.

"Faustine…" she wept.

A brown cat slowly emerged from the bushes and observed her for some time. It then walked up to her and licked her fingers, but, in her great despair, Eve wanted no creature's pity or compassion.

"Go away! Leave me alone!" she snapped, but immediately regretted it.

The cat hissed, scratched her, and ran back into the hole in the bushes it had come from.

"Wait!" she said, sitting up, but it, too, was gone, and she was left alone.

She lay back on the soft bed of snow and fallen leaves and contemplated the great darkness around her. Her dress was thoroughly wet now, and she was cold. Nothing. There was absolutely nothing left of her life and dreams.

She lay there for hours, determined not to move until this world gave her a reason to, and it eventually did. The moment the sky's colors began to change, a sudden fear gripped her heart. She again had no idea what it meant. She wanted to watch the sun rise and listen to the songs of the birds as they awakened, to feel like a normal day was beginning and chasing away this cold and dark nightmare, and yet some new instinct told her that if the sun rays touched her she would burn. So, like a frightened animal, she got up in a panic and began to run again. And because it was the darkest place near her, she got down on her hands and knees and crawled into the hole in the bushes where the brown cat had disappeared a few hours prior. And it was not just a hole, but a long tunnel underneath the thorn bushes and shrubs.

She followed it, having no idea where she was headed, until she emerged in what appeared to be the ruins of an old building. She stepped out of the tunnel, confused, and gazed around her. She was in a small room with a stone floor and partly collapsed walls. The roof and ceiling were gone, and the vegetation had grown over them so dense no light could enter. She was in the darkness, and she was safe. Was the brown cat a messenger sent by her mother to take her to this safe place, after all?

"Kitty, kitty, are you here?" she called out, but it did not come.

As her eyes got used to the darkness, she then noticed an old book that had been thrown onto the ground as though someone had dropped it in a hurry. She picked it up and suddenly remembered the vision she had had on Maude's grave. This was the same place and the same book she had seen. The image of Aurelia's eyes upon her in her dream also came back to her. Aurelia wanted her to find this book. Why? And wasn't it a little too late now that she had died? She opened the book and turned its pages. They were all blank. Not like time had erased the ink on them, rather like nothing was ever written on them. She frowned, closed the book, and set it on a stone. And then, tired and weary, she lay on the ground, wrapping herself in her cloak, and closed her eyes.

Ghosts—or whatever she was—slept. At least she did, and she awakened after many hours, feeling a little better except for her throat being so very dry. She was hungry, too. She got up and dusted off her dress and looked at her hands again sadly. Whatever she was, she was here and now, and she needed water. The song of an owl nearby alerted her that the sun had set already, so she cautiously crawled out of the tunnel and listened until she heard water. She followed the sound and found a natural spring from which she drank, but it did little to appease her thirst. As for her stomach, she thought about catching a rabbit or a squirrel—she knew how to do that—but the moment she imagined herself building a fire she shuddered with fear. Like the sun, she did not want to be anywhere near fire.

She got up and started walking again because there was nothing else to do. If she was a wandering ghost now, she thought, perhaps she would finally get to see the world. She could walk down every path in every forest, up every mountain, and across every desert, except she would have to do it all alone. Her eyes once again filled with tears and she wiped them away. And then she heard the distant voice of a human, a man whistling as he walked down the path to his village. Hiding in the shadows, she snuck up on him and observed him. He was in his thirties, a robust man carrying an axe. But as he made his way down the snowy path, unaware of her presence, all her ears could hear was the sound of his heartbeat and the blood pulsing through his jugular vein.

It took less than a second, less than the time to even think about it. She came down upon him with a loud shriek, pinned him to the ground, and was biting his neck. The poor man struggled and cried out for help, but she gorged herself on his fresh, hot blood until his heartbeat weakened and eventually stopped. Only then did she let go of him and moved away. She stared at his dead body for a few minutes, her mouth filled with the taste of blood, until she realized what she had done—and what she probably was. She cried out in terror, scrambled to her feet, and ran away again.

"No! No! No!" she repeated as she ran, wiping the blood off her lips and smearing it all over her cheeks as she tried to wipe away her tears.

There were monsters who fed on humans, some on little children, and there was a kind of monster that drank blood—one that usually rose from the grave. She was a vampire.

Why her? What had she done to God or anyone to deserve this? Who would ever answer her?

On the fifth night of this nightmare, hiding all day and walking aimlessly at night, her footsteps guided her back to the place where her old home used to be. In place of the little farm filled with the warmth and love of Maryse were only its foundations, debris, soot, and ashes. Small snowflakes spiraling down from the sky landed on Eve's cold cheeks as she gazed at what was left of her and Maryse in this world: nothing. They had been hated when alive, and in death even their memory had been erased.

"*Maman*… I'm sorry," she whispered. "You worked so hard and sacrificed so much for me, all for nothing… nothing!"

Her tear-filled eyes then moved away from the remains of her home to the dark forest path up the mountain, and she remembered that fateful night when she first encountered Nicolas – a werewolf. Nicolas… Had he not warned her, before she left him, that she, too, was a supernatural creature? Could he sense it back then already? But if he knew, perhaps he would not be afraid of her. Yes, there was one person left in this world who could give her answers and, perhaps, once more, accept her.

Before she could even think, her feet were already running up that path, up to the peak, and then she crossed it and ran down to the valley, tearing her dress on rocks and branches along the way, until she finally reached the old castle where she had once lived with him. She remained for a moment before its heavy wooden doors, hesitating as she tried to catch her breath, but the sky was already turning blue behind the mountains, and she needed to take shelter somewhere. With timid hands, she knocked on the doors, but Nicolas did not answer. So she opened the doors and let herself into the great hall.

"Nicolas… Nicolas!" she cried out, desperate.

This time, he heard her. He came rushing down the great staircase before her and stopped when he saw her. He was still unchanged, in his crimson justaucorps and white shirt, his long black hair falling over his broad shoulders. He looked like he needed a bath and a good shave.

"Nicolas…! I… I'm scared!" she said, bursting into tears.

He cautiously walked down the rest of the stairs and closed the distance between them. He, too, noticed something different about her, but there was no fear in his yellow eyes.

"What happened?" he asked her, gently cupping her face with his large hand.

"I… I don't know! I think I died, but I'm here! And I've killed people and drunk their blood, like you!" she said, turning her sad eyes to him.

He pulled her into his arms and embraced her, and she clung to him desperately and cried more as he stroked her hair. And she realized how much she had missed him and being loved even a little by this big oaf of a man. She had left him on a whim, thinking she could find something more in the outside world, but what had she found in the end? Men who disrespected her intelligence and treated her like a fetish, pimps who pretended to be her friends in order to traffic her and force her to work for them forever, and a friend who rejected her in the end when she changed. There was nothing for her out there, and Nicolas knew it all along; that was why he had tried to keep her away from that world and its frivolousness.

"Your place is here with me. I told you so," he said.

"You're not afraid of me?" she asked in a small voice.

"No."

"What am I going to do now?" she sobbed. "I don't know who I am anymore. I don't know why I'm still alive and what my place in this world is…"

"The first thing you need is to rest," he said, kissing her hair.

"Will you let me stay here?" she asked.

She looked into his eyes and saw there nothing but love and compassion. He caressed her cold cheek and kissed her forehead.

"This is your home," he said.

"My home?"

As she let his burning eyes gaze into her soul and his lips adorn her quivering skin with kisses, she understood there was something more between them than there was before, or perhaps she just did not see it until now. Their encounter was not a coincidence, and she believed the spirits of the forest and mountains had guided him to her and her to him because they knew that, in the near future, she would need his protection, and now all she wanted was to feel safe and protected again.

Like a defenseless child, she let him scoop her up in his strong arms and carry her to his bedroom—the one they used to share. Because he hated sunlight, the windows were boarded up. She could rest there without fear. And, like a prince, he lay her on the bed and covered her with the blankets. Then he sat on the side of the bed and gazed at her with shining eyes.

"I'm scared…" she said again in a weak voice, and he understood what she needed from him. So he lay beside her and pulled her into his embrace.

"I was also scared when I awakened as a werewolf," he told her. "There was no one to explain to me why this happened or how I would live thereafter. I had to find the answers on my own. But when I found you, I knew that you and I were similar. All I ever wanted was to protect you, to make sure you were not alone like I was when your transformation would take place. But I was not able to keep you here."

"I'm sorry, I didn't understand," she said, burying her face against his chest.

She breathed in his comforting scent and, surrounded by his warmth, she felt a little better.

"I know I'm not the prince of your dreams. I'm old and boring," he said close to her ear. "But, Eve, I love you. More than anything in this world, I love you."

She looked into his eyes again and let him move closer and kiss her. And thus began her second captivity with him.

CHAPTER 7

EVE SAT ALONE IN the attic, as she often did at night, gazing at the dark sky through the broken window. She sat on an old chest, surrounded by old things left by those who had passed when she might live forever. She did not count the days after she moved back in with Nicolas in his castle, but she saw more than ten summers and winters come and go. Sometimes, she wondered what happened in the outside world, but that world had rejected her. So, she remained here, in this castle frozen in time, where nothing would ever change, especially not her. She had to be at least thirty now, but her face never aged. Never a wrinkle, never an imperfection on it. Her hair still grew, but slower. She was glad her facial hair grew so slowly: she never had much of it, but it was much easier to manage now. It took a long time for her to grow out her hair again, but now it fell almost down to her waist and she cherished it. Since there was little else for her to do during her waking hours, she combed and braided it, sometimes picturing herself as Rapunzel in her tower, except she never thought about leaving it. She had her castle and her prince, even if they were not those of a fairy tale, and that was all she would ever have in this world.

Nicolas did not want her to leave the castle now, for her own safety, so he went hunting for both of them. He killed and devoured humans outside and brought back frightened villagers for her to feed on. One of them was the vicar who used to say she and her mother were witches, and she felt no compassion for him as she drank all his blood. When she was done with him, she dropped his lifeless body on the ground and said: "Go to hell."

There was nothing wrong with what she was. Nicolas' complete lack of imagination, which she found so dreadful a few years back, meant that he did not waste time thinking about what he could have been in some fantasy life. He lived here and now, as he was, and he considered feeding on humans the most natural thing in the world. Wolves fed on flesh and blood, and he was part-wolf, so he fed on flesh and blood, and she, as a vampire, was meant to feed on blood only. In his own way, he helped her feel more at ease with herself. They were not quite the same: she noticed that he did age, but very slowly, while she did not age at all, and he was obviously a lot hairier than she would ever be, but they were both supernatural creatures with similar lifestyles. They still had little in common as people, but she needed someone to love and protect her. He needed her in his life, and she needed the heat of his body.

Though she could see the desire in his eyes, he did not rush her to become his lover again. He waited, and after several months, she came to him of her own will, and in his arms she discovered that her body could still feel things, and that she needed to feel those things again. He was still a rough, clueless lover, but now she knew her body better she was able to guide his lips and hands to pleasure her as he pleasured himself with her, and he even held her in his arms afterwards and told her he loved her and would never let her go. Those were the moments she preferred, those that still brought some joy to her life, and she felt love for him again. No, she never truly stopped loving him because he was her first.

But even his love could not lift the dark clouds on her mind. The little girl filled with dreams of fairy tales who had come to the beast's castle one night, hoping to find shelter, had died, and Eve was a broken woman without a purpose in this world. And though Nicolas sometimes went to the city alone and brought back presents for her—dresses, jewelry, and even the wigs he so hated on her, she had lost interest in those things. But that night, he brought her something else.

She barely noticed him when he pushed open the creaking door of the attic. That night, he carried the scent of humans, but not blood. He had not fed.

"I'm home," he simply said.

She slowly turned her absent gaze to him. Her eyes were usually black now, unless she was very hungry. Only then did they turn that ruby-red color she so hated, the one that reminded her of her first night in this new life.

He walked over to her and kissed her forehead.

"Where were you?" she asked with as little emotion as always.

"I went to Montpellier. I brought back a new dress for you. Would you like to try it on?" he said with a faint smile.

"I suppose," she said.

He brought an old, dusty chair near her and sat on it.

"I have other news that concerns you," he then said.

She could tell he was trying to be tactful about what he was about to tell her, but at this point, nothing mattered.

"What could possibly concern me? I have lost everything," she said sadly.

"I went to the shop where your friend used to live. It was closed," he said.

She raised her shoulders. It didn't matter anymore.

"Did Faustine move away?" she asked.

"I assumed so, but when I inquired about the shop owner, I was told that the Viscount of Chambery—I suppose that would be 'Faustine'—had died."

She stared at him for a moment, stunned. He took her hand.

"Died… from what?" she asked in a trembling voice.

"The Viscount died seven years ago of a stroke," he said, caressing her hand softly.

Three years after she left.

"H-How…?" she asked, confused.

"Time passes, people age and die," he reminded her, and she knew he was right, yet for the first time in years, she felt something move in her heart and tears welled up in her eyes.

"Was someone by her side? Was she alone?" she asked, leaning over to him.

"I don't know," he said.

"I want to go see her grave!" she said.

He suddenly let go of her hand and his eyes were angry.

"Why? What difference would it make?" he asked.

"Why would I not go see her grave?" she insisted.

But he rose to his feet and turned around.

"No," he said in a firm voice.

"Why?" she said, also getting up.

"I'm not taking you to Montpellier, where your former lovers live!" he snapped at her.

She stared at him, speechless. She could not believe the man before her, who had been so quiet and eager to win her heart again, was still thinking about what happened over a decade ago.

"Why on earth would I ever see them again? Have you forgotten that I'm dead in their world?" she said.

"But you still think about them, I know it!" he said, turning back to her.

His breathing was hard, his fists clenched, and hair was beginning to grow on his face again.

"So, all these years, when I thought you cared about me and respected my grief, all you were thinking about were the other men I slept with? I can't believe it!" she said, and she did what she used to do when he upset her: she walked right past him and ran down the stairs. And he followed her.

"Eve, where are you going?" he shouted in a thunderous voice behind her.

"Leave me alone!" she said.

He tried to grab her arm, but she snatched it away from him and ran down to the kitchen, where she closed and locked the door.

She looked around her: the old kitchen was just as she had left it, except dustier. So, she was back to Cinderella's quarters, near the hearth. Nothing had changed between them after all… She remembered once dreaming she was a fairytale princess and trying to turn her fate into some beautiful story with a happy ending. But, alive or dead, there seemed to be no happy ending for her. She walked over to the straw mat near the hearth on which she used to sleep and lay on it and began to cry.

"Faustine…!" she sobbed helplessly, burying her head in the feather pillow.

Nicolas knocked loudly on the door.

"Eve, open the door!" he ordered.

She grabbed a kettle nearby and hurled it at the door.

"Can't I even cry for the loss of my friend in peace? Leave me alone!" she shouted.

"I can't leave you alone when you're crying!" he said.

"You have no compassion whatsoever for me, just like before I left you!" she said in response. "I just learned that my only friend in this world is dead, and all you can think of are the men I slept with years ago!"

She heard him sigh loudly and seemingly retreat, but he suddenly kicked the door open, knocking it right off its hinges, and came into the kitchen. She sat up on the mat, frightened. She knew he was strong and prone to outbursts of anger, but it was the first time this anger was directed at her. Or was it? Now she remembered the first time he got so angry with her, when they traveled to Montpellier. She backed up against the wall of the hearth as he approached her, her eyes wide with fear. But he kneeled beside her and reached out to her.

"Eve, I'm sorry. I'm just a stupid, jealous man," he said in a softer voice, but as his large hand approached her, she remembered the men who had arrested and beaten her and covered herself with her arms.

"Don't touch me!" she said.

He ignored her and caressed her hand softly, then her hair, but she did not want his caresses now, she did not want him to touch her. She had no words to describe that insidious feeling of aggression from his simple gesture, only that it meant he would not respect her boundaries. She was his, and he could do what he wanted with her.

"You see? This is why I don't want you to return there," he said in a soothing voice. "They trafficked you, they abused you, beat you, incarcerated you... I don't want you to ever face that again."

"Take your hands off me, you're scaring me!" she said, and this time he removed his hands from her.

"I'm sorry..." he said, and she could hear the sorrow in his voice.

Without another word, he got up and left her, and she cried for a long time, upset and confused. But, as she lay there alone in the cold darkness, she began to miss him and regret yelling at him. After all, he had never hurt her. Was she simply projecting her fear of men on him because he broke down the door? Granted, it was not what normal men did, but he was a werewolf. Perhaps he only wanted to push it open, but his supernatural strength made it seem like he was breaking it down. She got up and wiped away her tears and returned to him.

As she had expected, she found him in their bedroom. He was sitting at his desk, holding his head in his hands, but immediately got up when she entered. She looked up to him. His face was miserable and his cheeks wet with tears.

"Eve!" he whispered before embracing her.

She timidly wrapped her arms around his large back.

"Oh Eve, I thought you were going to leave me again!" he said, pressing her against his chest.

"Where would I go?" she said softly.

He moved back slightly to look into her eyes and cupped her face with his hand.

"But I don't want you to stay here only because you have nowhere to go. I want you to tell me you love me again. Eve, you never said it once since you returned..." he said.

His words were true. She had not realized that all this time she never told him, not even once. Could she blame it only on her grief over losing her life as a human? She lowered her eyes and pressed herself against his chest again.

"I'm sorry..." she whispered. "It's not that I don't love you, it's just that I forgot how to let anyone inside my heart."

His arms tightened around her and he kissed her hair.

"What should I do? Please tell me what I need to do to have a place in your heart again," he said.

"I want you to be with me, not to be my enemy. I need you to trust me," she said.

"I trust you… I'm just not good at showing it," he said.

She pulled back and looked into his eyes again, a faint smile on her lips. His lips then came down upon hers in a slow, romantic kiss, but this time she was the one seeking passion. She needed to feel his true love in every way. So she pushed him down on the bed and crawled atop him. His eyes opened wide with surprise, but he liked it. But more than sex, she wanted to bite him and drink his blood—not to kill him, but to feel the pleasure of drinking the blood of the man she loved. It made no sense, even to her, but she figured it was probably some vampire instinct.

"I want… I want to drink your blood," she whispered, looking into his shining yellow eyes.

"Please, do it," he said without any hesitation.

As a werewolf, he loved anything that would give him a rush of adrenaline, and when she fell upon him and bit his neck hard, it was not only adrenaline that flowed through his body. He pulled her tighter in his arms and moaned, and the bulge in his breeches tightened as she drank him. She never knew how erotic a vampire's bite could be. But she removed herself quickly, afraid of hurting him, and he gazed at her with wonder, his yellow eyes glowing and his cheeks flushed with desire.

"Oh, Eve!" he said.

In a swift move, he pushed her down on the bed and rolled over her, and she let out a surprised cry. Now he towered over her, hair growing on his cheeks and all over his body, but only from the intense arousal she had given him. He removed the jacket of his justaucorps and tore apart his shirt, exposing his masculine, hairy chest to her.

"My dress is in the way…" she told him in a hot whisper, and he understood.

With a wicked grin on his lips and a low and hungry snarl, he tore her dress and corset open and fell upon her chest, covering it with burning kisses. She rolled her head back and let out a soft moan of delight as his lips trailed down her skin to her loins. She needed this. She needed this now to feel alive, and like there was some meaning to her curse. She wanted passion to chase away all the darkness and sorrow, and that night, he made love to her with the passion of a beast again, pounding her in long, hard thrusts, crushing her in his strong arms. She was his and she felt alive again in his arms, and she thought she could live on it.

Time passed and winter returned, and it brought Eve that dream or vision again. In her sleep, she saw women standing in a circle around a fire. One of them was Aurelia, and she wore a hooded crimson cloak over her dress. Another was Maryse, her mother, and she wore a purple cloak, and by her side was Faustine, wearing a light blue cloak. Eve stood before them, the fire burning between her and them, and she was a young girl again in her patched-up peasant dress and clogs.

"What are you doing, Eve?" Maryse asked her.

Her voice was compassionate but firm, as though she were angry.

"I… I'm dead," Eve replied, not understanding.

"But you exist in that world. You can stand, walk, and talk in it," Aurelia told her, also in a firm voice.

"I don't understand…" Eve said.

Maryse stepped forward.

"Eve, when you told me you were a girl, I knew that your life would be hard—harder than even that of women born in the right body," she said. "That's why I taught you to fight! I wanted you to be able to take care of yourself after I was gone."

"I'm safe… now," Eve said in a small voice.

She knew she had failed her mother by letting others trick her and abuse her, and she felt so ashamed about it she only wanted to hide. But her mother would not let her.

"You made mistakes and you were hurt," she said in a warm voice. "But you must rise again and stand on your own. We died so that you could live on. The knowledge of the Escobar women must not disappear!"

What she meant was 'witches', and for the first time Eve realized there was perhaps more her mother had tried to teach her than how to make herbal teas. Indeed, she knew of tinctures and teas to cure illness, to rid women of their unwanted babies, to make them beautiful. The only thing she did not know yet was how to cast a spell on someone. But the one wanting to teach her that craft was not Maryse, it was Aurelia. She stepped forward and pointed her finger at the fire, and, untouched by the flames, in its center, was the book Eve had once found and discarded.

"Take it," Aurelia ordered.

In normal times, Eve would have feared the flames, but not in this dream. She bent over and picked up the book, and underneath it was a letter. She stared at it, surprised, but Faustine then stepped forward and spoke:

"Eve, I left something for you with the treasurer of Saint-Pierre Cathedral in Montpellier," she said in her habitual, soft voice.

"Your life has only just begun, and so has your destiny," Maryse said.

Before Eve could respond or take the letter, it vanished, and so did the women. In their place was the dark forest, and Eve noticed that a golden thread was tied to the ring finger on her left hand. It seemed tied to something else and disappeared into the darkness. She followed it down the winding paths between the trees, and as she went deeper into the darkness, so could she hear the 'tick tock' of a clock all around her. But she was not frightened, like she never feared the darkness or its mysteries, it intrigued her instead.

Suddenly, she all but bumped into a young man. He was barely taller than her and was dressed in a fashion she had never seen before. In his black suit with long pants and a funny, tall hat, he looked like he was attending a funeral. His brown hair was short, unlike the men in those days, and he wore a mask over his face.

"*S-Sorry,*" he immediately said in English, backing away from her.

The pitch of his voice immediately made her wonder if he was someone like her, born in the wrong body, and if their destinies were somehow connected. They gazed at each other with curious eyes. Eve was used to the way most men looked at her, to the lust or love in their eyes, but their feelings were always selfish. Even Nicolas' love for her was selfish. None of them wanted her to grow and thrive on her own, they wanted to *own* her like a trophy. But this young man expected nothing from her. His presence was calming and sweet, like a precious friend she could confide in and trust.

"Who are you?" she asked him in French because she spoke no English, and he did not seem to understand.

The sudden cracking sound of a branch alerted her that a large animal was lurking nearby, and they both heard the low, angry snarl of a wolf.

"Oh no, it's Nicolas!" she said.

She did not know why she should fear him—after all, she was not doing anything wrong—but still she began to back away. The mysterious young man fearlessly stepped in front of her.

"Don't worry, I won't let him hurt you," he said, but she did not understand his words.

But before anything happened, the loud chime of a clock resounded all around them and everything disappeared.

She opened her eyes beside Nicolas and sat up in the bed. She was still in the castle, in the safety of the bedroom with the boarded windows, with her werewolf by her side. But something had changed inside her. She had spent a decade asleep, it seemed, and now she was awake again. Perhaps she had officially 'died', but, like the women in her life reminded her, she was still there when they were not, and she had to carry out their will. There were still things she could—and had to do in this world, people she had yet to meet, and things she needed to find out about herself and her clan. And for that, she had to first go to Montpellier, whether Nicolas liked it or not.

Careful not to make too much noise, she slipped out of the bed and arranged the blue dress she had slept in, then went to the mirror to fix her hair. And the woman she saw in the mirror was the same as she saw only the night before, except she was also different. A young girl had gone to bed, thinking she had died and therefore everything was over for her, and she had awakened with the knowledge that this was just the beginning of a new life for her, as a grown-up woman, and in her features she could see the faces of her mother, her grandmother, and all her female ancestors down to Aurelia.

Nicolas opened his eyes and lazily rolled over in the bed. He had returned from a night of hunting in the early hours of morning and fallen asleep in his breeches and white shirt.

"Eve? Come here," he said.

"I can't. I must go to Montpellier," she replied after applying her lipstick.

She had no intention of being dishonest with him or sneaking out while he was asleep. In fact, she hoped that he would accompany her to Montpellier and be there for her. She was wrong.

"No, you're not!" he immediately said, getting out of bed.

He posted himself before the door and crossed his arms, a frown on his brow.

"Don't be silly, Nicolas," she said, already irritated by his behavior. "Faustine left a letter for me with the treasurer of the cathedral. I have to get it."

"And then... what?" he said.

"Then..." she started, but she realized she could not tell him what was on her mind.

What Aurelia and Maryse wanted her to do was to go out into this world and protect women, and Nicolas did not want her to leave the castle.

"I knew it!" he said.

He turned his head away, agitated, and ran his fingers through his long black hair.

"Nicolas, I'm not leaving you. You can come with me," she tried saying, but he shook his head.

"I 'can' come with you? What if I don't want to?"

"Then you can stay here," she said. "I will come back."

"I don't believe you," he said. "You have that look in your eyes, like the night you left me!"

"Nicolas!"

"I won't let you leave me again!" he suddenly stormed at her.

He grabbed both her arms so strongly she cried out in pain and pinned her against the vanity.

"Nicolas, stop!" she said, trying to free herself from his grip.

"I love you, but you don't love me! You're always thinking about other things and people!" he screamed in her face. "And now you want to wander again in the world that hates you and will only hurt you! When will you understand? You're not like those people and they don't want you among them. They don't even want you alive!"

"Well I'm dead anyway, so what difference does it make?" she shouted.

"Exactly! You died in that world because I was not there to protect you!" he shouted in response. "If you had been safely here and not living in a cold, drafty home, toiling all day, you would not have gotten sick and you would still be alive!"

"Let me go!" she cried, and she finally managed to free herself from his grip, but as she made for the door he grabbed her long hair and pulled her back to him and slapped her so hard she fell onto the vanity and cracked the glass. She stared at him in shock. His eyes were glowing red and hair was growing on his face again. He was transforming before her.

"You will not leave this room!" he shouted.

He turned around and left, slamming the door behind him and locking it. Eve immediately rushed to the door and began pounding on it.

"Nicolas! Let me out! Let me out, you monster!" she cried.

"No!" he said, and she heard his footsteps leaving.

She let herself fall to her knees, her head still dizzy. A few drops of blood rolled down the side of her face from a wound that had healed as quickly as it had formed. She wiped them off and looked at her red fingers. This was what happened to her mother when she disobeyed her father, and in the world of mortals, the Law said a man could beat his wife and children. Still, it did not mean Eve would settle for it. Nicolas had betrayed her trust—again. He said he loved her, but violence was an act of hatred.

"*Maman…* Aurelia… Faustine!" she whispered, in tears.

And the voice inside her she had not heard in so many years resurfaced and said: *"Fight!"*

It filled her body with warmth and her limbs with strength, the strength of all the women in her clan, and as she let love leave her heart and anger fill it instead, she felt more powerful, powerful enough to escape.

She rose to her feet with this new power and let it come out of her body in the shape of a fairy-like woman, whose long, flowing hair danced around her. And, her eyes focused on the door, she let out a loud shriek, so piercing it shattered the glass of the mirror and the boarded windows. The ethereal woman crashed into the door, destroying it. Eve then marched out of the room surrounded by the green halo of this creature. She found Nicolas at the bottom of the great staircase, in the main hall. His body had almost completely morphed into that of a wolf and he crouched, waiting for her, but now she had no fear of him.

"Out of the way!" she ordered.

He refused to move and let out a low and painful snarl, as though he were trying to refrain from attacking her, but she marched on forward. When she came too close, he lunged at her, but she launched her spirit at him and sent him flying across the hall. He rolled on the floor with a cry of pain, but she ignored him. She opened the heavy wooden doors and began to run, and the ethereal force retreated inside her body.

She ran up the snowy mountain path and into the woods, hearing the distant howl of a wolf. Nicolas was following her, and she did not know what he was capable of if he found her. She did not know if she could summon that spirit again or how to. So, she ran faster, tripping and falling along the way. But just as she wondered how she would ever make it, she saw the brown cat appear again before her. It observed her for a few seconds, then took off. As a child of the mountains, Eve was superstitious, and if the same creature appeared before her twice, she believed it was for a reason, so she followed it. It ran ahead of her in the bushes, through paths only a cat could see, and she struggled to follow it in her human form. It took her to the darkest part of the forest—in fact, Eve was not sure she was still in the same forest at all. She was still surrounded by tall pine trees, but instead of the shrubs around her were thorn bushes, and she was no longer stepping in snow but in a cold, muddy swamp of which the stench was nauseating. There were no swamps in the area, she was sure of it…

"Little cat! Help me!" she whispered in a panic.

The trees and thorn bushes were so thick she could barely see anything, but she could hear the splashing of a large animal somewhere behind her. Nicolas. She began to run again, until she saw a small figure, like that of a child, hopping from one stone to another like a frog. It had messy brown hair and wore old, patched-up brown and blue clothes. At some point, it stopped and turned to her, gazing at her with its feline eyes, and grinned, and she somehow knew this magical creature was the cat she had been following.

"I need to get to the village! Please, spirit of the forest, guide me there!" she begged it in a whisper.

The child spirit continued hopping from one stone to another until they came to what appeared to be the end of the swamp. It then morphed into a cat again and led her into even thicker thorn bushes, and she struggled to follow, scratching her arms, legs and face, but they eventually came out on the flanks of the mountain, and now Eve knew where she was. The river that led to Javols was below her and, if the stench of the swamp was not enough, she knew at least the water of the river would cover up her scent and Nicolas would no longer be able to follow her. She ran down the slopes of the mountain and immediately threw herself in the river. It was not frozen but ice cold. The brown cat followed her on the river banks, and its simple presence gave her the courage she needed right now. Had she still been human, Eve would probably have frozen to death in the cold water, but in her vampire form, it affected her less. Still, she could barely feel her legs by the time she got out of the water, near the village.

There were not many places where she could hide, but she knew of an abandoned farm not too far away. With the last of her strength, she walked there in the cold wind, wrapping her arms around herself. Vampires could get cold. She would remember that next time.

The farm was still empty and covered with ivy and moss. It would make a perfect hiding place until the next evening. She entered it and turned back to see if the brown cat had followed her, and it had. Kneeling by the entrance, she reached out to the magical creature, and it slowly came forth.

"Thank you, spirit of the forest, and I'm sorry for yelling at you," she said.

The cat purred happily, then suddenly scratched her hand and retreated a few paces away.

"Ouch!" she cried, pulling her hand away.

The cat then morphed into its childlike form again and rubbed its face with its little hands.

"Sorry!" it said.

"Why did you scratch me?" she asked.

"My name is Chapalu, and I'm a scratching cat," it said.

"Well, that explains it…" she sighed.

"Are you safe from the big bad wolf now?" it asked in a purring voice.

"I don't know," she said, lowering her eyes.

"What can the spirits do for you?" Chapalu asked.

Eve remembered how nature and its creatures were not her enemies. They were benevolent and desired only peace. Well, most creatures.

"Give me strength," she said, bursting into tears.

Chapalu resumed its cat form and came up to her and rubbed against her legs. She needed to take shelter now, for if Nicolas was still following her, or if he thought about coming down to the village, she might end up dismembered or worse. She shut the door and blocked it with the old table and chairs inside the farmhouse, and then she filled in the cracks with twigs and dirt, until no light entered the home anymore. Then, she lay on the ground in the darkest corner and curled into a ball, and Chapalu lay beside her to keep her warm. Perhaps reacting to the supernatural creature beside her, Eve's own ethereal spirit, the fairy that seemed to live inside her to protect her, came out and covered both of them. Because it felt like part of her but also not part of her, she decided to call it 'the Fae'. Warm and protected now, and confident that she would somehow make it, she closed her eyes.

The next evening, after sunset, Eve awakened alone, and it was just like that cold morning when she awakened by her mother's side—that same sense of loneliness and fear of the unknown. She was more alone than she had ever been in this world, but she remembered that, in the spiritual realm, she was not. Aurelia, Maryse, Faustine, and all the other women who loved her were watching over her, and so were the spirits of the forest like Chapalu. She sat up and shook her dress that had frozen overnight. At least, now that she was dead, she couldn't freeze to death.

Montpellier. She had to get there, and for that, she needed a horse. So she left her hiding place and ran to the village, hiding whenever she came across a human. She had not fed in days, but right now it was the last thing on her mind. She found a horse in another inhabited farm and took it. She had barely ridden on horseback once in her life, but she somehow managed to hang on without a saddle and, traveling two nights and taking shelter during the day, she finally reached Montpellier. She left her horse outside of the city and headed to Faustine's shop on Rue Saint-Pierre. She found it closed and abandoned. No one had wanted to buy it, perhaps because of her reputation. Good. She quickly found the spare key Faustine kept hidden under a stone near the back door and let herself into the pantry. Little had changed inside, except the building was dark and dusty.

She went into the kitchen first and lit a candle, then went into the shop and gazed at all the dresses and wigs, thinking about her friends. What had become of them? How many were dead now? She walked slowly through the shop, remembering the first time she met Faustine, on a sunny afternoon. She was her first true friend in this world, someone like her and who accepted her as she was. She had tried to protect her but, because Eve was young and stupid, she did not listen to her advice. But Faustine was always right, from the first day they met. She should never have returned with Nicolas. She should have run away as far as she could from him. Her throat suddenly felt tight at the thought of him alone. She had left him, this time for good, and he knew it – he, who loved her in his own, dark way. He would be desperate without her. She wiped away a tear and shook her head. Now was not the time to turn around and run back to him. She had to be strong.

She then went up to the bedroom where she and Faustine used to sleep. There, she set the candle on a side table and checked the window. The shutters were closed and a thick curtain covered it. She would be safe here during the day. She noticed a shawl on the bed—the one she had made for Faustine. It was folded neatly. She was probably wearing it when she died. Eve took it in her hands and held it against her heart. This shawl was supposed to protect Faustine and make her feel her and her mother's love, and now she was the one needing this love, so she wrapped it around her shoulders and lay on the bed and slept a little.

The next evening, as soon as the sun set, she got up, feeling stronger. Perhaps that shawl truly was magical, after all.

She changed into one of the dresses from the shop, making sure to put on a corset and wig—mostly so the police would not recognize her—and wrapped the shawl around herself. She then left the shop through the back door and went to the Saint-Pierre Cathedral. In those days, most people were Christians socially rather than spiritually, and the churches struggled to keep their parishioners interested in Mass. Most barely showed up on religious holidays, so the cathedral was empty except for a few devout worshippers and a man wearing a robe standing in a corner. Why did he legally get to wear a dress and not Eve? Human laws made no sense. She frowned as she entered the tall cathedral. Like her mother, she hated churches and what they represented. But she went to the man and spoke to him anyhow.

"Are you the treasurer?" she asked.

He frowned and gazed at her tall, white powdered wig, then her golden silk dress.

"I'm Reverend Canon Francis," he said. "I haven't seen you at church before. Are you from Montpellier?"

"No, I live far away," she said. "I need to see the treasurer, please."

"Do you have an appointment?" he asked.

"It's about the Viscount of Chambery. Tell him I'm... the Countess of Castelcombe," she said, as though a title might help her.

He frowned again but said: "Follow me."

He took her through a side door and up a narrow staircase to the church offices, where the clergy kept records and religious books. He knocked on the door and an elderly man's voice said: "Come in."

He let himself in and invited Eve to follow him. The old man in a white robe sitting at a wooden desk nonchalantly looked up from the book he was reading. All around him, the furniture, the bookshelves, the carpet, everything cost a fortune, and he looked quite well-fed. No need to wonder what he did with the parishioners' money he collected every Sunday.

"The Countess of Castelcombe. It's about the Viscount of Chambery," the canon said, before excusing himself.

The treasurer's expression immediately changed when he heard of Eve's title. He got up and smiled.

"I am Thomas of Mende, treasurer of the parish, and how may I help you, *Madame*?" he asked.

"My relative, the Viscount of Chambery, left something with you, for Eve Chauvin," she said, hoping her story matched whatever Faustine had told him.

"The Viscount... Oh, of course!" he said. "Why didn't he tell me you were a countess? I could have sent it all to you!"

"All?" she said, perplexed.

The man went to one of the bookshelves and pulled out a book. The shelf moved, and behind it was a safe, from which he took a letter and a small, ornate box and key and brought them to her. The box had been sealed with wax.

"What is in this box?" she asked.

"I do not know. As you can see, it has remained sealed ever since the Viscount's death," he said.

She took it, thanked him, and returned to Faustine's shop, where she would not be in any danger. There, she sat on the bed and took the letter first. She wanted to know what Faustine had written her. She opened it in haste and read:

'My dearest Eve,

If you ever read this letter, it will mean that you are alive and that I broke your heart. I still cannot explain to myself what happened. You were dead for two days. Your body was cold and your heart had stopped. And yet you rose again. I was so scared, I did not know what to do. I thought you were a ghost—and perhaps you are. And I chased you away… I immediately regretted it. I searched for you everywhere in town. I'm not even sure what I was looking for. All I know is that you are still here, in some form, and I, who had vowed to love you and look after you, chased you away.

My health is declining rapidly and I can no longer go out and look for you. Today, my physician told me I will probably die in the next few months. So, I will call upon the bishop to confess for my sins, and also leave instructions with the treasurer regarding my estate. My father is still alive, so all I have to give away is my jewelry. Half of it will be sent to Frederic, and I am leaving the other half to you. If, by some miracle, you are still alive, you will need it to live on your own. If you still love me, even a little, I hope you will find it in your heart to forgive my old, superstitious self. I am also leaving the shawl in the bedroom. If you ever come home, know that it has protected me and kept me strong on the nights when I felt alone and scared. I don't have magical powers like you, but I hope that when you wrap it around you, you will feel my love, like I always felt yours.

Your sister forever,
Faustine'

Eve held the letter to her heart and burst into tears.

"Yes, Faustine, I feel your love!" she wept.

She then took the small jewelry box and broke the wax seal on it and opened it. It contained valuable antique jewelry, probably heirlooms, worth thousands of pounds. She could not possibly accept such a gift, much less sell it, but Faustine clearly saw the practical use of it rather than the sentimental value. She knew that, if Eve was still alive, she would be alone in this world and in danger of being used and abused again. This jewelry would be her safety net.

Eve knew she could not stay very long at the shop. The locals would soon realize that someone was living there and notify the landlord, who would chase her away. So, she packed up two large carpet bags: one with dresses and other clothing, and the other with some of the soaps she had made, dry herbs, essential oils, Faustine's seamstress patterns and tools, and other things she might need to find work or even start a business. She was about to leave the shop when she heard noise outside. She moved closer to the shop's boarded up windows and listened.

"They killed it! Finally!" a man joyfully told another.

"What?" the other said.

"They got the Beast of Gevaudan! It was not a beast but a man – a werewolf!"

"Are you serious?"

"I am! His body is exposed on the town plaza before being burned!"

Eve dropped her bags and she thought her heart stopped. It was not possible… it couldn't be Nicolas.

She rushed outside and ran to the plaza where a large crowd had gathered to see the 'beast'. She pushed her way through them until she could see, and then she saw him. Nicolas lay dead on a pile of wood that would soon become his pyre. He had multiple gunshot wounds through the heart, the chest, and the head. She stood there, frozen in stupor before his body – the body of the man she had loved.

"If the beast was a man all along, how come they never caught him?" a woman wondered.

"He was very smart. But this time, the soldiers said it was almost like he wanted to be caught," a man beside her replied. "They said he stood up on his hind legs, his body covered in fur, and he let them shoot him. Only when he fell did he turn back into a man!"

Eve felt all the blood leaving her head as she listened to them, and when the clergy came and lit the pyre, she fainted.

It was the end of her life in the South of France and the love she had shared with Nicolas for so many years, and she knew she would never love again – not like she had loved him.

CHAPTER 8

As MUCH AS SHE hated and feared Nicolas, Eve spent years mourning him. Because she could not quite let go of his memory, she returned to his castle once. It had been only a few years, but an entire lifespan seemed to have passed since she last walked through the dark, empty great hall, the corridors. Her mind empty and numb, she walked through the rooms like one walked through time, and in the silence around her, the stone walls, she could still feel something of his presence.

As she entered the dining room, she remembered how it all started, how she had run to his castle, fleeing the humans who wanted to kill her. She had come instead to a beast who could be as loving as he could be cruel. If she was a princess, it was in a cruel fairy tale, in which her prince was not charming at all, but deadly. And yet, terrible as he was, she could not honestly accuse him of having ever lied to her, about his love for her or the rest. He had loved - to the point of wanting to die when she left him. She covered her face and wept again as she remembered his body, the shots through it he could easily have avoided. Why? She fell to her knees and found herself praying to go back in time, to do things differently, even picturing herself enduring more abuse if only he could live. She knew it was not reasonable but love often wasn't.

"Nicolas… Nicolas!" she whispered, curled up in a ball.

She needed his strong arms to protect her, his burning gaze upon her to make her feel alive. But they were both dead – except that for her it meant she would live on eternally.

And then, when she had cried enough, she rose to her feet slowly. Nicolas was gone. She repeated it to herself one last time, wondering where inside her she could find the courage to walk away from this place and from him once and for all. She needed a purpose, a dream, and she had one: to protect women. Not only women like herself, but all women. She remembered the old book left by Aurelia, so she searched for the old building where she had found it – if it was even real and not a dream. And it was very real: it was a twelfth century abbey called 'Notre Dame du Bonheur', Our Lady of Happiness. It had certainly not brought happiness to Aurelia and her sisters, Eve thought, as she walked through its, but as her fingers brushed against the cold stones, almost like they could hear their voices, echoes of the past trapped between these walls, as she sensed the profound, magical aura of the place, she once again felt the urge to *feel* this place with her entire being. She searched for the book in every crack, behind every stone, but she never found it. Was it just a dream after all? Her memories from that time were so dark and confused, she could not tell for sure. But even dreams had a profound meaning. Following her intuition, she closed her eyes and *felt*… this place, the forest and mountains, the air, the spirits and creatures of the forest, and as she acknowledged each one of them, they connected with her and poured their knowledge into her, and once again the Fae came out of her body. And, through its ethereal eyes, she saw what even her vampire eyes could not see: the book was just an image. Its contents were engraved on the walls of the old abbey, with some magic that made them invisible to the eyes of most. She walked around the ruins, letting the Fae absorb all this ancient knowledge. There were hymns of ancient times telling of the creation of this world, and stories of wars and carnage. There were warnings to the humans of the future to not let anger and hatred drive them to the excesses of the ancient people of the Earth. There were also formulas – not the recipes for tinctures and remedies Eve always thought Aurelia had passed on to her female descendants, but real, dangerous formulas, spells to kill a person at a distance or curse them, to lift the veils of this world, to summon and seal demons. Eve's ancestors were real witches, and this was their legacy to her, a secret so well kept she would never have found it as a human. Did they foresee what she would become?

She could not do anything with those spells, but she let the Fae memorize them, and then she thanked Aurelia and all her ancestors, and let the Fae return inside her.

With the jewelry Faustine had left her, she decided to travel to Paris, where she found nighttime work in the always busy dressmaker shops of the capital, and because she proved talented, she soon joined the prestigious house of Rose Bertin, Queen Marie-Antoinette's favorite fashion designer. As such, on some evenings, she was invited to Versailles even though she held no title, and because the Queen loved her voice, she often asked her to sing while she looked at new dress patterns with Rose. While Eve had directly witnessed the injustice of the world she grew up in, where people with a title like Faustine could do whatever they wanted and face almost no consequences while the poor did not even have the right to decide their own destiny, it was impossible not to love the young queen. The public wanted her to be a cold-hearted, selfish traitor, always conspiring with her native Austria, but none of the rumors were true. She was very much like a little bird in a cage, who had never even seen the misery her subjects lived in. She was a simple woman, aspiring only to live a quiet life with her children, but that was not allowed at court. Every moment of her day, from the time she woke up to the time she went to bed, was codified, and surrounded with long and unnecessary court rituals. As for her children, she barely ever saw them. She was bored so she spent money on lavish dresses and jewelry, but what she really craved were real human relationships.

"Eve, what does the world look like outside?" she once asked Eve as she fitted a new dress on her with Rose.

The court etiquette dictated that no one could address the queen unless she addressed them first, so Eve usually remained quiet unless asked to speak.

"I have never left the kingdom, Your Majesty," she politely replied.

"I meant outside of Versailles," Marie-Antoinette said in a sad voice. "Have you ever seen the ocean?"

"Yes, I have, in Montpellier," Eve said with a smile. "It's so vast... like an endless canvass of blue across the horizon. Seagulls fly in the sky above, sometimes diving into the water to catch fish. The air is pure and salty and carries the scent of freedom."

"I wish I could see it someday..." Marie-Antoinette sighed.

Eve noticed Rose frowning at her. There was no point in putting ideas of freedom in the mind of a bird in a cage, even if this little bird was an ordinary woman like them, with the same thoughts and feelings.

"The world is too great for any of us to see all we would want to see. But we can dream," Eve told the queen.

But the young queen's dreams and life ended shortly afterwards. After several years of bad crops and famine, the French Revolution broke out in 1789. It was the most violent time Eve lived through, and for months the paved streets of Paris were soaked in blood. Suddenly, those with privilege were the hunted ones, and those without, like her, were left alone. The one the court nicknamed 'the blue Cinderella' because she only appeared at night, always in her blue and lavender dresses, and disappeared before dawn, was an ordinary seamstress, but one with great dreams: she wanted to make a fortune and use it to build shelters for battered women and children. It was a new dream, inspired to her by a woman named Olympe de Gouges, who also recruited her in her suffragette circles.

The Revolution went on for years, and the King and Queen were both beheaded, as well as the Dark Lord of France, their vampire equivalent. For there was a whole vampire society, one with its own rulers and rules. Eve came across them now and then while hunting for her survival, but she did not like mingling with them. Their world was not based on money or privilege, like that of humans, but on dominance, just like a pack of wolves, and Eve had had enough of wolves.

Then came the nineteenth century, and France had a new ruler: Napoleon Bonaparte. He established an empire and, if people were not all happy, at least the streets of Paris were no longer smeared in blood. Empire, monarchy, the people of France just couldn't seem to decide how they wanted to be governed, and Eve, as always, followed her own ambitions. She was a quiet figure, almost a shadow, working behind the scenes for women, at first in France, then all over Europe. But her project required much more money than she could earn as a seamstress, more than the donations of the few sponsors she found. So, for a few decades, she returned to her old trade, as a 'special interest' courtesan. The world had changed and entered an era in which the differences between the sexes were accentuated in their clothing and behavior. Fragility was pre-ferred in women, who were encouraged to behave like damsels in distress – at least in front of men. After the loose-fitting, often sheer Empire dresses, corsets made their comeback and they were tightened until suffocation ensued, while hats and bonnets became dramatic arrangements of flowers and ribbons. Eve liked to have a nice waistline, but she refused to behave like a damsel in distress. As for men, they cut their beautiful, long hair short, and gave up flower-prints, damask, and lace for sober, usually brown or black suits, and, though a loophole in the new French Constitution technically decriminalized acts of sodomy, being even remotely thought of as homosexual or lesbian was seen as one of the worst crimes. Libertines were out, and society focused on the – idolized – image of the nuclear family, clean-shaven, tightly corseted, and pure in thoughts and behavior. And for all those who could not adhere to this model, there were brothels and salons where you could meet courtesans like Eve.

Rodrigue, David, Maximilien, Jules were some of the men who made her rich. Like her former clients, they were mostly homosexuals who did not see her as a woman but as a man in a dress, but all she cared about now was the money they could give her, which she could then use for her sisters in need. She was disillusioned about love and men. Nobody would ever see her as a woman, not the humans she slept with for money nor the supernatural creatures she slept with for pleasure – like Mehmet the Djinn, a fabulous catch in bed, but otherwise as dull as her werewolf had been. Some of her lovers were sweet and funny, and even talked her into posing almost nude for them. These were the early days of photography, and it intrigued her. She was not shy about herself, but now only she decided how her body was being used and marketed. She removed the bottom if they wanted, but never her corset, her garter belt, or her stockings. And because she was so beautiful, she fixed the price, and they paid it.

Because she never aged though, she had to 'vanish', move, and change professions every twenty years or so to not awaken any suspicion about what she was. So, in the late 1870s she retired from her glamorous life again, and in 1884 she opened her first herbalist shop on Rue Berthe in Paris, and simultaneously published her 'Kitchen Witch's Guide to the Supernatural World', which was soon translated into other languages. She continued her education, learning English and Italian, and began to give feminist lectures, often met with fierce opposition by the men who feared losing their privilege. Her life was busier than ever, between managing her shop, soliciting donations from rich sponsors for her shelters, writing books, giving lectures, and even doing a few tarot readings for her feminine clientele. She was a successful businesswoman, writer, and public speaker, and yet she felt lonelier than ever.

Often, during the winter months, as she walked down the snow-covered paved streets in the darkness, she remembered her home, her mother, Montpellier, Faustine, and, invariably, Nicolas, whose death had left an open wound in her heart. There was no happy ending for them, and yet, year after year, season after season, it was his face and his deep voice that haunted her. She never loved any man after him, he remained . Her employees often told her that it was not good to dwell on the past, and that, at her age, she should seriously think about finding a husband. If only they knew that she was *forever* twenty-two, she thought...

It was on one of her many nights roaming the streets of Paris alone that she first met Emily.

That night, as so often, she walked down the picturesque banks of the Seine River. Though her dresses remained in blue and lavender tones, she had traded her tall wigs for nat-ural-looking clip-on hair extensions and partial wigs, and modest, elegant, bustle dresses had replaced the wide pan-nier dresses and the high-waist Empire dresses. Even on the days when she saw no one but her employees, Eve made it a point to curl her hair, do her makeup, and dress nicely, because it made her feel alive. The corset that corrected her shapeless waist and hips, and the extensions that thickened her fine hair were her shield against the world and its cruelty, but she acknowledged that, for other women, they were instruments of oppression instead. Many women who came to her feminist lectures wore men's suits, and they were their shield. There was not just one way to be a man or a woman, but as many as there were people on Earth.

Even though it was not raining nor snowing that night, she carried an umbrella, as a habit and a weapon in the event of a bad encounter. They happened now and then – either hungry ghouls or vampire hunters – and she had the Fae to defend herself, but she preferred not to use it unless it was necessary. But that night, she noticed another solitary figure in the distance, a short, curvy young woman in a romantic white bustle dress with a cute polka dot print. She wore her blond hair curled and gathered in a bun under a small, elegant hat, and she, too, carried an umbrella. They stopped and stared at each other. They were the same, in every way. Not only was the stranger also a supernatural creature, but she was like Eve, one of those women not born in a female body, she could somehow sense it. She knew they existed, she had just never met any other than Faustine. The stranger was the first to make a move. Her black eyes filled with compassion, she walked over to Eve and asked: "Why are you crying, sister?"

Eve brought her fingers to her cheek and felt the moisture. She had not realized she had been crying.

"It's nothing… just thinking about the past," she said, lowering her eyes.

She really had no intention of starting a conversation, but the stranger immediately took her hand like a friend would.

"There is the past, but also the present, and the future," she said. "My name is Emily, and I have a flower shop nearby. Would you like to come over for some midnight tea?"

Eve stared at her, surprised. She had been invited to vampire salons and vampire's chambers for pleasure, but never to have tea. But Emily was determined to become her friend, and so Eve somehow ended up following her back to her small shop, called 'Mille Fleurs'.

"A thousand flowers?" Eve said as she read the sign.

"I love flowers," Emily said with a bright smile, and as they entered her shop, Eve understood why.

Emily sold not only fresh flowers, but also expensive tea sets, hairbrushes and mirrors, embroidered cushions, and all sorts of flower-themed collectibles. There were so many flowers in her shop it almost made Eve dizzy.

"How do you like it?" she asked.

"It's very… floral," Eve said.

Emily laughed and invited her upstairs, where they sat down around a cup of tea, as promised.

"Thank you for having me. I don't socialize very much with our kind," Eve politely told her.

"Oh, I was so happy to run into a sister… You know, not only because we're vampires," Emily said.

Eve smiled, aware that her smile might be somewhat sad.

"I had a 'sister' like you once, but she passed away. So forgive me if I get a little emotional," she said.

"Oh, sweetheart, I know how you feel. I, too, lost sisters and friends," Emily said, taking her hands.

"How old are you?" Eve asked her.

"Seventy-two, and you?" Emily said.

Eve smiled.

"A hundred and thirty-five. I'm old."

"Not so. We're like… good wine. The older the better," Emily said, making her laugh.

"Emily, you are very sweet. But I can't help but wonder what you want from an old vampire like me…" she said.

"Your friendship," Emily said. "There are few of us vampires, and even fewer of us are transgender."

"Transgender?" Eve repeated, confused. She had never heard the word before.

"Medical science is talking about us," Emily proudly said. "They finally have another word for us than 'freaks' and 'transvestites'. But my friend Hans could tell you ; he was a medical school student before awakening as a vampire."

"Is he like us?" Eve asked, taking another sip of her tea.

"He is," Emily said, her cheeks suddenly glowing.

"Is he your sweetheart?" Eve asked her with a grin.

"Oh… Oh, no," Emily said, positively blushing now. "I'm too ordinary for someone like him. I'm too ordinary for anyone in fact."

Emily was not what people at the time would have called a 'beautiful' woman. Whilst men liked a curvaceous figure, they wanted it to be hourglass-shaped, not pear-shaped like hers despite her corset. The natural rounded contours of her face, her small teeth and soft features allowed to pass, but her nose was rather flat at a time when people liked aquiline noses like Eve's. But when she talked and smiled, there was a charming youthfulness and candor to her that was irresistible.

"Will you be my friend, sister?" Emily asked, and she was too sweet to refuse.

"Sure… if you can put up with my moods," Eve said, and Emily smiled, delighted.

"Do you live in Paris?" she asked.

"Yes, I have an herbalist shop on Rue Berthe. I make tinctures, cosmetics, potions, and I can even calculate your natal chart or do a tarot reading for you."

"Oh, I would love that!" Emily said.

And thus they became friends, and later close friends. They visited each other's shops in the evening, before closing time, and the flower shop started selling cosmetics and the herbalist shop flower-themed collectibles. Life was a little better for Eve, in the great loneliness of Time, after she met Emily. They were opposites in their characters and tastes, even in their natal charts – Eve was a Pisces and Emily a Libra – but they somehow completed each other, though in a different way than Faustine completed Eve.

"So that's how my first time was – horrible," Emily said, laughing, as they were having tea together one night in her apartment above the flower shop.

"Oh dear, he only lasted five minutes? Even old Nicolas lasted about ten," Eve said.

"I was so sore the next day, too," Emily said, blushing.

"It's not just about spreading your ass. You need moisture down there, honey," Eve said, and Emily laughed again.

"Eve, you are so…"

"Vulgar? My lovers often said so," Eve said, unconcerned.

"Straightforward," Emily said, smiling. "But I love it!"

"I do have a lotion you can use the next time you have a man. Women over forty love it, too," Eve said.

"Oh, I don't think there will be another. Eric was the only man I ever loved and who loved me," Emily said, losing her smile.

She did not have much of a romantic life, much like Eve. Apart from her Eric who abandoned her when she became a vampire, she had never been loved, nor even wanted by anyone.

"Oh, Eve, won't you come to our meetings?" Emily then said.

She had that childish, puppy look on her face, like every time she wanted her friend to give in to her. Eve sighed, uncomfortable. While she was all for Emily's initiative to gather transgender people from the underworld, she herself was not that sociable as to want to partake in it. And, perhaps, like Emily said, she was afraid of meeting someone there and possibly becoming friends, or more. One friend was enough for her. But Emily absolutely believed that she should come.

"I don't know. I'm rather busy this month," she said.

"Next month then?" Emily insisted.

"Maybe."

Emily noticed a letter on her desk. The handwriting was terrible, so she figured it was probably from a man.

"What's that? Is it from a lover?" she asked.

"Oh, that?" Eve said, turning to her desk. "An Englishman who read my book wrote me last winter. I wrote him back and he only just replied."

"Well, who knows? This might just be the beginning of a great romance!" Emily said, excited.

For some reason, she was always convinced that Eve was on the verge of meeting her one true love even though Eve told her she was not looking for love.

"Is he handsome?" Emily then asked.

"He lives in England," Eve pointed out.

"Long-distance love is not such a problem these days," Emily said.

Eve rolled her eyes.

"We just happened to have a similar dream, nothing more. He's a paranormal investigator and I was trying to help him solve a murder mystery," she said.

"Oh, a psychic just like you! Meeting in your dreams sounds awfully romantic!" Emily said.

"Emily, just because I do tarot readings and have intuitions through my dreams does not make me a psychic. Besides, in that dream I was the murder victim and he put a pitchfork through my throat," Eve said.

While she liked the idea of them meeting through a murder dream, Emily found it a little disturbing and lost her smile.

"Anyhow, what's his name?" she asked.

"Ernest," Eve said.

This Ernest intrigued her for sure. For one thing, he had the handwriting of a seven-year-old but the vocabulary of an old man. But he was a Sagittarius, and they were full of contradictions. He was a human, to the best of her knowledge, but he could see and talk to ghosts, and he lived with three of them. He, too, had just gone through some rough times in his life and he was sick. It was not love she felt for him, but compassion, as a once-human who had suffered her share of losses, and she wanted to protect him from further suffering, if she could.

Because Emily was irresistible, Eve eventually let her talk her into attending one of her meetings. They were held in the luxurious apartment of a certain 'Madame de Sangue', also known as the 'Blood Countess' in the vampire circles. Despite her name, Emily assured her, Madame de Sangue was very sweet and just a bit eccentric. So, that night, Eve put on her most elegant purple bustle dress and hat, and presented herself at the address she was given, and knocked on the door. A six-foot-tall with a bright red long hair wig, red lips and an equally colorful dress opened the door.

"Well, hello there, darling," she said.

"Are you Madame de Sangue?" Eve politely asked her.

"I certainly am, and what's your name, honey?"

"Oh, Eve!" Emily hollered from inside the apartment.

"Oh, you must be Emily's friend! Come on in, darling!" Madame de Sangue said.

She ushered her in and closed the door, and immediately left her to go attend to other guests, but Emily came to greet her, kissing her on the cheeks.

"I'm so glad you finally came!" she said. "It's mostly girls tonight, but Hans is here and I am told Julien might come, too."

Eve offered her a polite smile, but she did not feel comfortable in this apartment decorated in the same gaudy fashion as Madame de Guigne's home. But Madame de Sangue was not a pimp, she just liked to wear and surround herself with flamboyant colors and things.

"Emily, do you have our calendar? It's for Sabine," she asked across the room.

"Oh, right here!" Emily said.

She left Eve to join her, and they both seemed busy, so Eve grabbed a glass of wine on the table and sat down on a sofa, where she was soon joined by a young man with short, blond hair and a foreign accent, who introduced himself as 'Hans'. Emily had not described him, but he was quite handsome, even for someone like Eve, who was used to dating only biological males, and there was a friendly aura about him.

"Might I keep you company? You look lonely," he said in a friendly voice.

"I don't mind," she replied.

"Emily has been telling us about you. She said you're a feminist speaker."

"Oh, I give a few lectures," Eve said. "I heard you study medical science?"

He lost his smile.

"'Studied' would be a better word. I had to quit when I became… well, a vampire," he said.

"Did you specialize in anything?"

"Not really, I liked everything," he said. "I'm that guy who talks a lot about science. Oh, by the way, I brought some pamphlets."

He reached into his vest pocket and pulled out some small flyers advertising an upcoming lecture by a human professor about gender.

"Would you like to go with me?" he asked, smiling.

"Sure, why not?" she said.

It had the looks of a romantic invitation at first, but as they were joined by the others, he began to give out flyers to all the girls and also invited them. Eve was just a little miffed, but she smiled politely anyhow.

The meeting began with the guests – all girls except Hans – introducing themselves and talking about their long journeys. None of them came from accepting families, and most had been thrown out on the streets when their parents found them cross-dressing. Some ended up dressing as men again and occupying men's professions, while others went 'stealth' and worked as dressmakers and shopkeepers, like Emily and Eve. All had been arrested and beaten up by the police at least once, and Eve could guess behind their reserved words, some had been raped as well. Unlike them, Hans came from an upper middle-class German family, and his parents thought of his crossdressing as a cute 'phase'. When they realized it was not, he said, his father brought out a wooden plank and beat him like never before. He told him: "If you want to be a man, then you must be able to take a beating!"

And so Hans did, again and again, until his father got tired of beating him and finally let him do as he pleased. He tried to enter medical school under his legal, female name, but they would not let him. So he chose to go stealth and enrolled as 'Hans'. Unfortunately, he died a few months later and awakened in his new life as a vampire.

All these heartbreaking stories made Eve feel somewhat out of place. Her story was sad, and she had been the victim of violence, but not on the same scale as any of the guests present, but it only reaffirmed her desire to fight against the injustice they all faced in society.

When came her turn, she told the group about her father not accepting her, but that he died when she was very young, and how she was raised by her mother who loved her and accepted her and had even chosen her name for her. She told them how coming from a clan of strong women had empowered her to fight to be herself in this world. She told them about her work as an herbalist and dressmaker when she was younger, but she did not feel like elaborating about her other activities as a courtesan. The girls listened to her with mostly appalled faces.

"Why are you even here?" one of the girls asked when she was done. "You've had no trauma in your life. You don't need anyone's help or protection."

"That's not true!" Emily said, standing up for her friend.

"Really? Look at her!" another girl said in a spiteful voice. "She's so petite and slender, she barely grows any facial hair, and she admitted how easily she passes as a woman. How do we know she's not a biological woman?"

"I am not!" Eve said.

"Prove it!"

"I don't have to prove anything to you!" Eve retorted.

"Now now, girls!" Madame de Sangue said, standing up.

But Eve also stood, furious, and glared at them.

"I'm so 'petite' because I went through famine nearly every year of my life as a child!" she told them. "And I wasn't lucky enough to find a regular job when I was on my own. Like the whole lot of you, I was trafficked by a couple of pimps. I was a prostitute who spread her legs on demand, and when I left them and changed into a vampire, I had no choice but to return to an abusive man who kept me prisoner and eventually became violent. Is that what you wanted to hear?"

Silence fell upon the group, and several lowered their eyes. Some turned up their posh noses, and others cringed, but no one had anything to say.

"I'm leaving," she said, grabbing her purse.

She walked out hastily, holding back her tears, until she was out in the hallway. There, she leaned against the wall and covered her face with her hand. What was she even thinking, going to a meeting full of young vampires from this century who had not known the famines, the Revolution, and knew nothing about the cruel and violent world she came from?

But Emily soon joined her and slipped her arm around her waist.

"I'm sorry, Eve. I didn't expect them to react like that to you," she whispered.

"They're right. I suppose I had an easier life than them as a child, but they've had an easier life than me, growing up in a time and place when food was always available and people's heads weren't being chopped off every day all over Paris," Eve said. "I will never fit in with this group…"

"We all have different pasts and trauma, but even if we didn't, we can still share our experiences," Emily said. "I hate it when some try to compare themselves to others. We're all here because we're transgender, not to determine who is more or less traumatized than the others."

"This is why I don't socialize," Eve said. "I'm done trying. I'll just go back to my shop and my herbs and books, and everyone will be happy."

Hans then came out of the apartment and walked over to them.

"Everything alright?" he asked, as though he had no clue why Eve left. "Eve! You're crying!" he then said.

A typical, clueless man, she thought.

"It's nothing," she politely replied.

He looked troubled.

"If you're leaving, at least let me walk you back to your place," he offered.

Eve turned to Emily, whom she was sure would have pre-ferred Hans to ask her, but she lowered her eyes and said: "You should go with him, Eve."

"Are you sure?" Eve asked her.

"Yes. Besides, I'll be back in your shop tomorrow night, as always," Emily said with a forced smile.

Eve reluctantly took Hans' arm and let him walk her back to her shop. She did not know whether he was clueless, not paying attention, or just tactful and not wanting to bring up her past, but he immediately engaged in conversation about other subjects. As it turned out, they had a lot in common. Her interest in nature and her knowledge of the herblore fascinated him, and she enjoyed listening to him talk about the different

subjects he liked to study, from psychiatry to otorhinolaryn-
gology, which was a long Latin word for anything related to
the ears, nose, and throat. He told her gruesome stories about
all the different things doctors found in people's ears and even
made her laugh.

"Back in the libertine days, men put a few other things in
people's ears," she then commented, and he immediately lost
his smile and cleared his throat. She did not understand why, at
the time, but she later realized that penis jokes were probably
not very funny for someone who suffered from not having one.
But it was only her first time meeting a transgender man, how
could she have known?

"Shall we take a detour by the graveyard?" she asked, trying
to cheer him up.

She liked walking through graveyards at night because they
were the quietest places in a busy city like Paris, but apparently
Hans did not care for them so much, or perhaps he no longer
wanted to accompany her but preferred not to say it.

"Sure," he said, forcing himself to smile.

From then on, the stroll became very unpleasant. Hans was
quiet, Eve felt like she was annoying him, and all she wanted
was to roll back time and never make that bad joke in the first
place, but it was too late.

He walked her back to her shop, tipped his hat like a proper
gentleman, then left. She sent him a note the next evening
through Emily asking him if he still wanted to go to that lecture
with her, but he responded that something had come up and
he would not be able to go. So, she returned to her usual
occupations, not really heartbroken, just a little pissed that such
a handsome, intelligent young man would give up on her after
one bad joke. With time, though, the whole incident made her
laugh. She was not ready to love again, but Emily was right:

perhaps she kept herself so busy as a way to avoid getting into a relationship and risk being hurt again, and perhaps she ought to think about her happiness too, not just that of others. But she was anything but lonely, especially with someone like Emily in her life. There were also the—human - women who worked in her shop, Cecile and Florentine, always eager to hear the latest gossip about the men Eve met, or more often did not meet.

"Any news from your German?" Cecile asked her one night, as she returned to her shop after running some quick errands.

"No, and I don't care," Eve said as she removed her hat and gloves.

"Good, because there's a letter for you," Cecile said, waving an envelope.

"A letter? From whom?" Eve asked.

She took it.

"Ernest," Cecile said, gazing upon her with mischievous eyes.

"And?" Eve said, pretending not to care.

She slipped the letter in her purse to read it later.

"They're writing each other every week now," Florentine commented behind the counter she was supposed to be dusting.

"If you don't have any work to do, I can give you some," Eve said in a mildly irritated voice, but her employees were like friends to her, and they simply giggled and returned to their work.

Emily then entered the shop to sit around and chat as usual, and she immediately rushed over to Eve.

"A letter? Is it from Ernest? Can I read it with you?" she asked, taking her arm.

Eve sighed. There was no such thing as privacy when one had friends.

"I will read it later and alone," she said, and Emily looked disappointed.

"But you'll tell me if it's good news, right?"

"Yes, I promise you will know if I have a man in my life, but, at the moment, I don't," Eve said.

"That's what people say when they're trying to hide their blooming feelings for a handsome, mysterious, romantic foreign pen friend," Cecile said in a melodramatic voice that made both Eve and Emily laugh.

"Or not," Eve said.

She left them, went up to her room, and shut the door. Only then did she pull the letter out of her purse and sat down to read it. She had a new life now, in the nineteenth century. She had friends, a long-distance friendship with an , and was even somewhat courted, even if it was awkward. Her life was moving forward again, and she thought her mother and Faustine would be proud of her. To any modern woman, she would have seemed very successful, but she remained unhappy, still mourning all she had lost. She was moving forward with her eyes closed, thinking only about the past.

She read Ernest's letter quietly, trying her best to decipher all the words. She was getting used to his handwriting, but some words and letters still required a certain degree of imagination to be understood. Their correspondence was polite and intellectual, and she appreciated it. She let him know whenever she had a dream that might concern him and, now and then, even did a tarot reading for him. And, because he lived with a child ghost, she also included small presents for the little Cornelius, hoping to keep him entertained in the afterlife. Receiving his letters was the most relaxing part of her life, and though she never truly opened up to him about being a vampire and a crossdresser, she felt like, at least, he understood her sense of humor and her perspective on things—unlike some others. But that night, she was just stuck in her habitual melancholy. Ernest did not seem in a much better mood, as he reminisced in his letter about the time he spent in Edinburgh, the place where his dreams were born and died, and how he had since grown up and lived mostly without a dream. How well she could relate to him. So she went to her desk, took a sheet of paper and a pen, and wrote to him about her own bitter-sweet memories in the South. She then paused, wondering if she was sharing too much information with him. But he already had her address and he had never showed up at her door. He mentioned an illness that often kept him at home. Tuberculosis? She did not want to become too attached to him if he was just going to die on her, but she couldn't help but feel compassion for this young man forced to live like an elderly because of a physical ailment. But the response she received changed everything.

In his next letter, Ernest told her about a dream he'd had, in which he was in a pine forest, with a golden thread tied to his finger. And when he followed it, he ran into a young girl in peasants' clothes wearing a mask. They had, once again, had the same dream, years apart, and this time one of which the meaning was obvious: their destinies were linked in some way. She sat down on her bed, confused, as she read his words, and, for the first time in ages, her heartbeat quickened. The date was May 6th, 1890. Why did she remember that day? Perhaps because it was the first day she truly felt like herself again – the Eve that lived before becoming a vampire. She felt young and hopeful again that this world had something waiting for her, that magic was still at work in her life somehow. Was there something more between her and Ernest, something that had brought them together, even at a distance? Now she wanted to find out. So she wrote him again, and he responded just a few days later.

In her letter, she told him about her dream. It was her cautious way of opening up to him, to see what he thought about it. Little did she know she was opening a floodgate. The response she received was unexpected, but it actually made her *happy*.

'Dearest Eve,

I read your letter over and over and held it to my heart. Yes, you and I are the same, and the golden thread of fate led us to each other. I had never met someone who understands me and the world I live in like you do, a woman not afraid to hear my stories of hauntings, a woman who would guide me through the pine forests of Gevaudan and tell me what the spirits there whisper, a woman who can see the essence of my soul, and never judges me, but embraces what is unique about me. All the kindness and magic of the spirits seem to flow through your golden heart, and I am in awe before you. You are so much more than all the other women I have met… I have framed a photograph of you I found in the newspaper and placed it beside my bed, so that I may always see you when I wake up and imagine that you are there with me. Your presence in my life brings me comfort and joy, and I would love to meet you if my work did not keep me away from home so often…

Do write me again, sweet angel,

Your Ernest'

Between May and June that year, they corresponded every few days, and the tone of their letters became increasingly romantic. Romance was something Eve had dreamed of but that she had never experienced with any man, between the stern Nicolas and her downright vulgar clients as a courtesan. But Ernest was a kind, mature, understanding man who knew how to touch her heart with his words, to make her feel like he understood her on a deeper level than any other man in her life, and through the words they exchanged her heart felt naked before him. He confessed to her that he was like Hans, a man born in a female body, and she dared to tell him that she was the same, a woman born in a male body. He had seen not only ghosts and spirits of nature in his life, but also vampires, so she hoped he would not fear her when—if—they met in person. For he still seemed shy about the prospect of them meeting in real life, and she did not understand why. He was healthy enough to work, after all. Cecile thought he had a secret—perhaps that he was already married. Florentine thought he was a fugitive, hiding from the Law, and the romantic Emily simply imagined that he was shy and awkward, like her dream man. Eve only shared with them that Ernest seemed to like her and she liked him, but they were not going to meet yet. The rest was none of their business. But she was both excited and thrilled. Now, this stranger, whose face she had never even seen, was on her mind all the time. She was distracted, daydreaming about showing up one day at his front door and finally discovering his face, and what would happen next. What was it like to be in love and be loved in return by someone just like her? Wouldn't they make the most perfect couple?

"It seems to me like a bad case of the love bug," Cecile commented one rainy evening in the shop as Eve stared at the wall, smiling like a teenager in love.

"I wish a man wrote me letters that made me blush like that," Florentine sighed.

"Oh, hush!" Eve said, aware that the smile on her lips and the redness of her cheeks betrayed her.

But her heart fluttered all day, every day, just thinking about the next letter she would receive in the mail. She had decided to be bold and confessed her feelings to Ernest in a letter rather than in person to avoid any bad surprises such as a secret wife opening the door instead of him. If he responded positively, she thought, she would then tell him about the fact she was a vampire, and if they decided to take it further, they could probably figure things out from there.

She was expecting a response the day before, but it did not come. So, she waited for Emily, who was going to pick up the mail that night before she came over. As she waited, she paced around the shop as nervously as a young princess waiting for her prince to come and rescue her. She had truly lost her mind over this long-distance relationship. What was wrong with her?

Emily finally walked in, carrying in with her some of the wind and rain. A passing summer rain.

"Anything for me?" Eve immediately said, rushing over to her.

Emily smiled and giggled and pulled out a letter from her purse.

"He replied!" she said, excited for her friend. "Oh, Eve, this means he loves you too! I'm so happy for you!"

Because she had no romance in her life, she projected herself on her friend and lived that romance through her, and she was always eager to hear about their progress on what she called 'the path to true love'.

"Did you read it?" Eve asked, frowning.

"No, of course not. But he replied quickly, it's a good sign!" Emily said.

Cecile and Florentine joined them and all wanted to know what he had written in the letter, but Eve ushered them away.

"I will read it alone," she said.

Her cheeks flushed and her heart racing, she retreated to her room upstairs. She drew in a deep breath and gazed at her reflection in the mirror. Yes, she absolutely looked like a teenager in love, but it was the first time she truly experienced such feelings in her life. A new and all-encompassing joy filled her old heart and brought it back to life, and the world around her no longer mattered. But she did not want to get her hopes up. After all, her bold attitude sometimes perplexed men. So she opened the letter and read it slowly:

'Dearest Eve,

I am not sure how to respond to your letter. I read it a thousand times, wondering what I should say, how to express my feelings with words. I think of you as a dear friend, and I never imagined anything more. I only shared my secret with you because I thought you would understand. I have recently met someone and we are now living together. I was going to announce it to you in this letter and I hoped you would be happy for us, but now I realize I may have only hurt your feelings. I am so sorry for any misunderstanding I may have created.

Ernest'

Her heartbeat slowed down as she read his words, and all excitement left her. So that was it? After leading her on with his passionate words, he just announced to her that he had met someone else? She couldn't believe she had fallen for this lying flapdoodle. At her age, didn't she know any better? Men were all the same. She got up and paced across the room. Anger, pain, sadness, embarrassment, so many feelings rushed through her at the same time, but the worst of them was knowing that the one to whom she had finally decided to give her heart, after so many years, was already taken. Worse, he was never even interested. And, like teenagers with a broken heart, she covered her face with her hands and began to cry.

She cried for a long time as the reality slowly sunk in, but she still refused to believe it. So, she walked over to her desk and took her tarot deck, hoping to find in the cards some clue about Ernest's feelings for her, or that he would soon break up with the new person in his life. Holding her breath, she asked the cards what Ernest was feeling right now and drew a card. The Lovers. Of course, since he was in love with someone else. More tears rolled down her cheeks. She asked the cards what the future of their relationship would be and felt like drawing two cards this time. The first one that came out was The Devil. A shady deal, lies. The second card was The Hierophant, which represented a union or marriage. Why? It did not make any sense. Obviously he was a liar and he was with someone else. Perhaps the cards were simply warning her to give up on this shady character, and she did not even need fortunetelling to know that.

After some time, having not heard from her, Emily knocked on her door, but Eve did not want to talk.

"Leave me alone, please," she said softly.

"Eve... you're crying! What happened?" Emily asked in a panic.

Eve sighed, got up, and opened the door.

"Eve?" Emily said.

"I'm going for a walk," Eve said.

She walked past her and went down the stairs to the shop, and Emily followed her.

"What happened? Did you get bad news from Ernest?" she asked, not understanding.

"I don't want to talk about him anymore," Eve said as she put on her hat and grabbed her purse and her umbrella near the front door.

"I'm coming with you!" Emily said, but Eve turned around and took her hands.

"Thank you, Emily, but sometimes I just need to be alone."

She kissed her on the cheek and left, and Emily stood in the shop for some time with Cecile and Florentine, both staring at the door with puzzled eyes. She then turned around, crossed the shop, and headed upstairs to Eve's bedroom. Since they were close friends, they went into each other's apartments all the time and Eve's employees were used to her. There, Emily picked up the letter Eve had left on the bed. She read it, then grinned.

Eve had only just stepped out of her shop when she realized she had left the letter on her bed, and she didn't want anyone to find it. She was sure none of her friends would read it, but still she preferred to get rid of it. It was too painful and embarrassing. So, she spun around and returned to the shop and rushed upstairs. And she found Emily holding the letter in her hands, looking surprised.

"Emily? What are you doing in my room?" she asked her, frowning.

"I… I just wanted to know what happened," Emily said.

She dropped the letter and tried to embrace her friend, but Eve would not let her.

"I didn't give you permission to read my mail, did I?"

"But I want to be there for you, as your sister!" Emily pleaded. "We'll get over this together! I can stay here and sleep by your side, like Faustine did. I'll be there for you until you're no longer sad!"

She grabbed Eve's arm and pressed herself against her. Now she was becoming intrusive.

"Let go of me!" Eve said.

"But we're sisters, aren't we?" Emily said.

Eve finally managed to disengage herself from her strong grip and forced her out the door.

"No, Emily, we're not sisters, and you're not Faustine!" she said, furious. "Faustine would never have crept into my room to read my private mail. You're a sick woman, and I don't want you here anymore!"

"But…" Emily said, her eyes filling with tears.

"Did you not hear me? Go! Now!" Eve shouted, and the poor Emily ran down the stairs, crying, and left her shop and never returned.

Eve was upset that night, both because of Ernest's letter and Emily, and she cried for a long time, but after a few days, she realized that she had overreacted with Emily and sent her a letter apologizing. Emily sent her a polite response, saying that she always remained in her thoughts, but that she would no longer come to her shop. And thus their friendship ended at the same time her relationship with Ernest did.

CHAPTER 9

EMILY SAT IN FRONT of the mirror, combing her long blond hair before she went for a walk that night. She was wearing her white polka dot dress, her 'lucky dress' because it was the one that made her happy, the one she was never allowed to have in her life as a human. She still remembered the look of horror on her mother's face when she walked in on her one sunny afternoon in their home in Chantilly, stealing her dresses and trying them on in her room. She was a minor at the time and she had not committed any crime under the current French Law, but still her parents sent her to a correctional home—for boys. The children, aged eight to sixteen like her, were stripped of their clothes and their heads were shaved, and they were made to attend classes in the morning and work in the afternoon. Most of the work required physical strength Emily did not have, and she was bullied by the boys. It did not take long for one of them to start sexually assaulting her. They took everything from her: her beautiful hair, her body, her dignity as a human being, all for the 'crime' of being a girl stuck in the wrong body.

By the time she was released, at the age of sixteen, she was broken, and so damaged inside she could never be fixed. She was brought home by her cold-faced, silent parents in a carriage, and they had supper quietly that evening before going to bed. But Emily did not go to bed. She waited until they were asleep, then quietly went down to the laundry room where her mother's polka dot dress was hanging, waiting to be dry-cleaned. With a smile on her face, she touched it with her scar-covered hands as though it were a magical item that could erase her from this world and bring her back as the young woman she ought to be.

"You ought to wear that dress," a voice said in the darkness behind her.

She removed it from the clothesline and changed into it, then ran her hand through the short, blond curls on her head.

"You ought to have long hair," the voice then said.

"That's right. I ought to take back the hair they stole from me," Emily said, gazing into the emptiness of the room.

So she stepped outside, in their small backyard, and picked up the hatchet her father used to cut wood for the fireplace. She then quietly crept up the stairs, as in a dream, confident she would not be heard, and opened the door to her parents' room.

How did she make it to their bed? She did not remember - only that some supernatural force helped her lift the heavy hatchet over their sleeping faces. There was blood, a lot of blood, and she remembered holding in her hands her mother's blond hair and her scalp with it and putting it on her head. It was a strange, uncanny memory, like an out-of-body experience.

She lowered her eyes as she walked down the rainy streets of Paris, hiding under her umbrella as though the few people walking by were all watching and judging her.

"It wasn't my fault… he made me do it," she whispered to herself.

But she was not going to let anything dampen her mood, not even the passing squall outside. It would end soon and the night sky would clear up. When she wore her polka dot dress, only good things could happen, like meeting the demon who introduced her to the other transgender creatures of the underworld.

It was a long time ago, after she died in a carriage accident and awakened as 'something else'. She was not sure what she was, only that now she had to hide from the sunlight. She returned to the small flat she rented with Eric, the only man who had ever loved her, and seeing her alive frightened him so much he tried to run away. But even in her blood-stained polka dot dress after her accident, nothing bad could happen to her, so she could not let him leave her.

"It's not fair, only your clothes are red. His should be too," the voice told her this time, and so she reached for the kitchen knife and put it through his belly once, twice, and many more times until his clothes were red like hers. But after falling to the ground, he did not rise again like her. She sat beside him and shook him and called his name, but he had stopped breathing and no longer moved. She began to cry and curse the prankster voice in her head that had tricked her. Then, when she realized Eric was truly gone from this world, she grabbed the knife and returned it against herself. It hurt, but she did not stop breathing like him. She was stuck here, in this world, and she cried even more until she heard footsteps beside her. She looked up and saw the most beautiful man she had ever seen: tall, dark-skinned, with long black hair and a thin mustache and beard. He was wearing a purple and green suit and kneeled beside her. A kind smile on his lips, he removed the knife from her bloody hands and cupped her face.

"Don't be a bad girl and hurt yourself now," he told her.

Then, with the gentleness of a prince, he scooped her up in his arms and took her away to his realm – or rather his apartment. She let him undress her and bathe her in a tub filled with rose petals. Never losing his tender smile for her, he washed away all the dry blood from her skin and the wounds that had already closed up. He then dried her and bandaged her remaining wounds and dressed her in another dress, just like the one she had soiled.

"Sir, who are you and why are you doing this for me?" she asked him in a whisper.

His smile widened.

"You are one of us, the ones nobody wants, those too strange to ever find a place in this world," he said. "And I am your prince."

Her prince… did it mean he saw her as a princess?

That night, he took her to his bed and made love to her, and she thought she could forget everything, all the sadness and sorrow, and start anew. He told her she was a supernatural creature, a vampire, and that she would only ever live at night now. But if she was a sweetheart and obeyed him, she could be much more in this world. She did not aspire to be more, only to be loved by him, so she did everything he told her to do, whether she understood his intent or not, and at first he rewarded her with his love. But that, too, ended.

She began questioning the things he told her when she met other vampires—real vampires—and she found out that they drank blood to survive, and she did not. They saw her as one of them. They said she smelled like one, but they wondered how she could survive without doing the most basic thing they did: hunting and killing humans. She did not know, but Astaroth assured her that everything would be alright. There was another woman like her, also a vampire, who was special, and she would be her friend. He told her when and where she would meet her, and, indeed, that night she met her and they became best friends... until she got angry and chased her out of her home. Did she know that Astaroth had made her intercept Ernest's letter and give it to him? He read it, frowned, and threw it away. He then provided her with another letter to deliver to Eve in its place, and she did as she was told, asking no questions. She did not know the contents of the letter until she read it in Eve's room. It was a breakup letter. Finally. She wanted to keep her new friend all to herself and this pen friend was getting in the way. Now she could console her and be her one and only support. But things did not go quite as she had planned, and Eve caught her and chased her away. Broken once more, Emily retreated to her apartment where she cried for days and nights. She called her sweet demon, who usually appeared to comfort her when she needed it, and he did, but his demeanor had changed.

"I only asked you to do one thing for me, and you couldn't even do that," he said in a cold voice.

"But I did! I became her friend, her true friend!" she sobbed. "Oh, please, you must help me mend our friendship! I can't live without her, I can't!"

He shrugged and turned his back to her.

"If you want to have friends and keep them, stop acting like some freak," he said before disappearing.

"No! Wait!" she cried, but he was already gone. "I'm not a freak, I'm not..." she repeated.

"How cruel of him to abandon you like this..." the voice in her head said. *"It looks like no one will ever love you, Emily."*

"Shut up! That's not true!" she said, shaking her head. "You're just an illusion. You don't exist!"

"Are you sure I don't exist?" it said. *"Or could it be that none of this does?"*

Emily lifted her gaze and she was no longer in the bedroom of her apartment but in her parents' bedroom in her old house. They lay on the bed, covered in blood, the hatchet beside them.

"No... No!" she cried.

She ran out into the hallway and pushed the door to another room, but only ended up in the same bedroom again.

"This is not real... You're not real..." she repeated as she ran across the house, trying every door.

She finally got to the front door and opened it, but had to stop herself. Before her, instead of the street, was a great, dark hole with clouds floating in it. The sky? Why was the world suddenly upside down? She shut the door and ran upstairs to the attic, hoping to find there the exit. But when she opened the door, she found herself in a room she did not know. It was an attic, but not hers. It was filled with dusty boxes and toys scattered all around. She took a step forward, then another, and tripped on an invisible string and fell. She hit the floor hard and when she looked up again, all the toys were converging upon her: china dolls with broken faces and missing eyes, jack-in-the-boxes jumping in their boxes, puppets, and toy soldiers marching in perfect ranks. And then she heard that same voice again, the child-like voice she had been hearing for years:

"Bun venit acasa, moroi..." it said, and she screamed with terror.

Stanley got off the train in Paris Gare Du Nord station and looked around him. It was his first time in France and he spoke very little French. Belial had provided him with a map of the railroads and Paris, since he insisted on stopping there, but it was all in French. The demon also left him directions on how to get to—what was the name of that city?—'Rouen', where he was to meet up with him. Cornelius stood by his side, gazing at the busy crowd around them.

"Well, here we are," Stanley told his ghost friend. "Aren't you glad you got to see France, thanks to me?"

"But where do we go now?" Cornelius asked, looking up at him.

Stanley pulled out another piece of paper from his pocket and unfolded it.

"Her address is '38 Rue Berthe'. That's Berthe Street, right?" he said.

Cornelius raised his shoulders. He didn't more French than Stanley did.

"Anyhow, let's call a cab," Stanley said.

The ex-demonic and ex-angelic hitman, also a necromancer vampire who could see and talk to spirits and travel through time after swallowing the Time Key, had traveled to France after being recruited on a very special mission by the demon Belial. But before that, he had a special mission of his own: finding Eve and explaining to her what had happened—if she would even listen to him.

They called a cab and got into it. Stanley showed the coachman the address and the man had no problem taking him there and dropping him off, ghost and all. The young man then stood before the cute little shop with the words 'Eve's Herbal Remedies' elegantly carved on a sign and painted on the window. It was a little after seven in the evening, and the shop was still open and packed with women. Stanley's heart was racing at the thought he would finally see her again, but all this feminine energy inside the shop made him uncomfortable.

"Are we going in?" Cornelius asked by his side.

"Uh… How about we go get her a gift or something first?" Stanley said.

"A gift?"

"Well, she's a woman, and she's probably angry. Women like to receive a gift as an apology."

"Like flowers?"

"Yes, great idea. Flowers," Stanley said.

Cornelius followed him quietly down the dark paved streets, but he knew his friend was only trying to buy time because he was nervous. But, because he was frozen forever as a seven-year-old child, he did not always understand the complexity of adult relationships. In his humble ghostly opinion, 'sorry' was enough of an apology.

Stanley's eyes moved from one side of the busy street to another, checking out shops, until he thought he sensed something, or rather someone, following him. As a former hitman, he immediately slipped into a dark alleyway and made himself invisible. He watched the street for some time, but saw no one, yet he still had that odd feeling, the same as he'd had on the night he encountered that shapeshifter who murdered Aleksandra.

"Who is it?" Cornelius whispered by his side.

"I'm not sure, but I don't like this…" Stanley whispered. "Whoever it is, I can no longer sense them. They seem to be gone."

It made sense. His pursuer would not attack him on a crowded street, but he would have to remain vigilant. But for now, he resumed his visible form and crossed the street like any other gentleman out that night. There was a shop on the other side of the street, called 'Mille Fleurs', and it appeared to sell flowers. It was still open, so he pushed the door and immediately froze, and not only because the shopkeeper turned out to be a vampire, but because he felt that presence again.

The short woman with curly blond hair and a floral print dress behind the counter stared at him for some time, looking terrified at first. When a vampire stepped into another's territory, the most powerful one could claim it or even kill the other, and Stanley was clearly more powerful than her, but he did not want to frighten her.

"Uh… It's not what you think, I just came to buy flowers," he said in English, before remembering that he was in France now, but she apparently spoke it too and understood him. She let out a sigh of relief and laughed.

"Oh, my goodness, you scared me," she said. "Yes, of course, you can buy flowers here."

"I'm so sorry for scaring you. It wasn't my intention," he said as she came over to him.

"So, are we buying flowers for a special someone tonight?" she asked with a smile.

"Yes, I… There was a misunderstanding, and I just wanted to buy her some flowers," he said awkwardly, more because of the situation he was caught up in than because of her. She seemed like a very sweet person and, listening to her mezzo voice, he wondered if she might even be like him.

"Ah, but those can always be fixed," she said. "What sort of flowers does she like?"

"I'm not sure. I don't even know that she likes flowers…"

"A strong, independent woman, then? Orchids will certainly win her heart."

She spoke confidently and he could tell that she knew her trade well. The presence he sensed in her shop was not hers.

"Is there anyone else here?" he asked, looking beyond the counter.

"No, my employee is off tonight," she said.

"Your employee, are they… human?" he asked.

She seemed confused by his question and returned behind her counter to wrap the orchids for him.

"I don't eat my employees," she said, sounding a little offended.

"Oh no, I didn't mean that," he immediately said. "I… Uh…"

"Here are your flowers. That will be one franc please," she said.

He placed the money on the counter and took the flowers.

"I do apologize if I offended you, madam," he reiterated.

He turned around and was about to leave when she called out to him.

"Wait, Sir."

He turned around and she walked over to him, wringing her hands.

"You didn't offend me… Well, yes, you did, a little, but not to the point of making me angry. I mean…"

He smiled. She was just as awkward as him, at least when interacting with other vampires.

"Would you think it rude of me to offer you one of these flowers as an apology then?" he said, pulling out one of the orchids from the bouquet. He handed it to her. She smiled and took it, her eyes beaming with joy.

"Thank you," she said. "My name is Emilienne but everyone calls me 'Emily' because I love English literature."

"Really? I do too. I'm Stanley," he said, tipping his hat. "I'm glad you speak English because I don't speak any French except 'bonjour'."

She laughed softly when she heard his accent, but her black eyes sparkled.

"Stanley, it's my turn to be rude now," she then said, and she took his hand. "I have a feeling… You're like me, aren't you?"

"Yes, I believe we are the same," he said.

He did not know the French laws regarding crossdressing, but he was sure they were not very different from the British laws, and speaking about it openly could get them both in trouble.

"There is a group of people like us, and all are creatures of the underworld. Would you like to come to our next meeting?" she asked him.

Oh great, another one who thought he needed more friends. Socializing was a pain in the ass, and he would rather have met her again in a quiet setting, but he did not want to risk offending her again.

"I am on a tight schedule, but if can make it I will," he promised.

"Good! The next meeting will be in an apartment I own in Rouen, and after that we have one at Madame de Sangue's address here in Paris. I will write down both for you," she said.

She went over to the counter and wrote down the dates, times, and places on a piece of paper.

"Uh, you said Rouen? That's actually where I'm headed after Paris," he said.

"Oh! Then it's meant to be!"

She handed him the piece of paper.

"Thank you. Well, good night then," he said, tipping his hat again.

He left the shop, and she stepped outside and watched him walk away with regret, then she returned inside like an automaton and the moment she closed the door, the shop became dark. It was no longer filled with fresh, fragrant flowers and beautiful objects, but with the scent of decay from rotting flower buds and dust and spiderwebs. She began to hum to herself and, taking a pair of scissors, she cut off the rotting flower buds, leaving only the stems. Then she whispered: "Stanley..."

Stanley returned to the herbalist shop, and it was less crowded now. So, armed with his flower bouquet, he pushed the door open and stepped inside.

"*Bonsoir,*" a lovely human in a pink dress said behind the counter. Not the lovely he was looking for, unfortunately.

"*Bonsoir,*" he said hesitantly, "Uh, do you speak English?"

"A little," she replied with a thick accent. "How can I help you?"

"I would like to see Mademoiselle Chauvin, please."

"She's not here at the moment," the employee replied. "Are these flowers for her?"

"Yes," he said. "Do you know when I might be able to see her?"

The young woman looked annoyed, as though she often got such demands.

"Mademoiselle Chauvin is very busy, but I can give her your flowers. What's your name?" she asked, grabbing a notepad and a pencil.

"It's... Ernest," he said.

Her faced shifted into a frown.

"I don't think she wants your flowers, sir," she said.

She had apparently been talking with Eve, and Eve was very upset. He set the flowers on the counter anyhow.

"Could you please tell her that there has been a misunderstanding and that I need to talk to her?"

"I will tell her, but I doubt she will want to talk to you," she said.

"Thanks," he said, tipping his hat.

"Just so you know, she's got herself a man," the young woman told him as he was leaving.

"Good night," he replied, before walking out.

Cecile took the flowers, and she was about to throw them away when Eve came down the stairs. She was dressed in a new, white bustle dress with black trims, complete with a matching hat, gloves, and umbrella. She was going out.

"It's closing time, Cecile," she said. "Can you take care of the bookkeeping tonight?"

"Of course," Cecile said.

"Flowers? From whom?" Eve then said, noticing the bouquet.

"The man said his name was 'Ernest' and he wanted to talk to you," Cecile said.

Eve froze for a second, then pursed her lips.

"I told him you were not interested," Cecile added.

"You did well. I don't want to see him or talk to him," Eve said. "Throw those flowers away and if he comes back, tell him to leave or we'll call the police."

"Yes, Mademoiselle Eve," Cecile said.

"Good night Cecile. When you're done closing, you take a cab home. I don't want you walking alone in the dark," Eve said, placing her hand on her shoulder.

She was very protective of her employees, many of whom had fled abusive marriages or violent homes, and she would not let another potential stalker near them.

She left the shop and walked briskly down the street. She was heading south, to one of the luxurious apartment buildings on Place Vendome, but slowed down as she walked past Emily's 'Mille Fleurs' shop. It was late and she was closing. Behind the window, she noticed Eve on the street, but immediately turned away from her as though she would not even look at her. It saddened Eve, but she had tried to make peace with her.

The loss of her and Ernest at the same time was brutal, but it was just another hardship, and she had been through many. The fact she could get angry and chase away a friend who only wanted to be there for her frustrated her, but it was quite like her. What she could not forgive herself was letting herself fall in love like some stupid teenager, when she knew exactly what sort of wolves men were—not to mention the actual werewolves. She had slept with so many men - man-children, narcissistic manipulators, abusers, sex addicts - without ever opening her heart to any of them, and when she finally thought she had found someone different, she fell head-over-heels for him only to find out he was already taken and either completely clueless about her feelings or just a liar who derived pleasure from leading her on. It hurt her because her feelings were genuine, but the more she thought about it, the more she felt relieved. After all, even if he accepted her as a transgender woman and a vampire, would he have accepted her past as a courtesan? What if they ended up living together and ran into one of the men she had slept with? Faustine had warned her: men were territorial and did not want the 'damaged goods' left by another. Sleeping around was their prerogative, and they did not want women who did the same. So, she locked away her heart once more and settled for what she could have, and what she wanted now.

She opened the door to a certain apartment building and went up the stairs, then stopped in front of an apartment and knocked on the door.

"Astaroth? It's me," she said.

The door opened slowly and she let herself inside. The apartment was lit with candles, creating a romantic atmosphere.

This one was trying hard to win her heart. She smiled to herself and closed the door.

She had met the demon during one of her long night strolls on the banks of the Seine River. Just another lonely night, walking aimlessly on the wet pavement and contemplating the dream she had to give up. Ernest belonged to someone else, and he had not been truthful about it, so why was she still thinking about him at all? Because she missed his awkward sweetness, his impassioned words for her, his dry humor. And now someone else was embraced by his awkward arms and heard his sweet words. She wiped away a tear—when would she ever stop crying? - and noticed a man sitting on a bench with an air of melancholy. He was not a vampire, but, like her, he was a creature of the underworld. He was by far one of the most handsome men she had ever seen: tall, broad-shouldered but slender, masculine, long black hair tied back in a ponytail, tan skin, and sharp but beautiful Middle Eastern features. He wore a purple suit and hat with a contrasting green tie but looked more like a foreign prince than a Parisian dandy.

She stopped and observed him until he noticed her. He got up, looking worried, and walked over to her.

"Mademoiselle…" he said in a deep, sensuous voice. "Why are you crying?"

She wiped away another tear and shook her head.

"It's nothing," she said.

"In my experience, when a woman says 'nothing', it means there is something, but she is afraid that expressing it will attract the scorn of those around her," he said, and his lips parted into a kind smile. He was a gentleman.

"It's a heartbreak. There, are you satisfied?" she replied.

She had not meant to sound as angry as she did, but he was not offended.

"No, I am sad for you," he replied. "Tell me, who broke your heart?"

"Just a man… a pen friend," she shrugged.

"May I walk with you?" he offered. "You look like you need company."

"I don't mind," she said. "Are you a vampire?"

"No, I am a demon," he said. "And what is your name, beautiful?"

She stared at him with suspicion.

"You won't get anywhere with me with flattery," she warned him.

"I apologize," he said with a smile. "In my culture, we always praise a woman's beauty."

"And what if she isn't beautiful?"

He laughed.

"All women are beautiful to me," he said.

She finally broke into a smile.

"My name is Eve. Are you Ottoman? What's your name?"

"The place where I was born was not a kingdom nor an empire," he replied. "The world changed, and so has my name. People have called me Ishtar, Ashtart, Astarte, and now they call me Astaroth."

She turned to him, surprised.

"Those are the names of female deities."

He grinned and said: "I changed, through magic."

So, he was like her, except he had been able to transform his body through some powerful magic.

"Would you like to ask me something?" he said.

"Oh… no. I mean, of course I am curious, but your transition is a personal thing. It would be rude of me to ask," she replied, blushing slightly.

"I don't mind telling you more. Would you like to come to my apartment?" he said.

She hesitated for a second, then nodded. She followed him to his apartment that night and they talked and became lovers, not because she was in love, but because he was kind to her, and she wanted to forget Ernest. And when he made love to her, it was all about her pleasure, not his. He worshipped her body with his lips, his tongue, and his fingers, showing her new pleasures none of her former lovers could give her. He knew exactly what a woman like her needed and how to give it to her, and she willingly surrendered to him and let him love her body. And that night, again, she had come to let herself be worshipped. If her heart could not be contented, at least her body could.

She removed her hat and gloves and set them on a side table, along with her purse, and walked over to the bedroom where she was sure to find him. And he awaited here there, with his insane demonic charm, lying on the only clad in a bathrobe. She smiled as she saw him.

"I've been waiting for you…" he said languidly, gazing into her eyes.

They were not in love, no. This was purely a pleasurable affair between two consenting adults. Astaroth was not a liar at least: he was openly polyamorous, but when he praised her beauty, when he told her how he longed for her, she could see in his deep black eyes that she was the one he desired above all. He was her instrument of pleasure and love, and all she had to do with him was surrender and let herself be treated like a queen.

Looking into his eyes, she slowly unbuttoned and removed her dress and petticoat, and went to him.

CHAPTER 10

Stanley presented himself at the address Belial had given him in Rouen. He had to agree that it was a charming little town, with its half-timbered houses and medieval street layout – so different from Paris and its wide boulevards - its secret passages between the houses like the Scottish *closes*, its gothic cathedral, and even the tower where Joan of Arc had been imprisoned before being burned at the stake. All the historical names in the brochure Belial left with him were in French, and they were long and complicated, so he had given up on trying to pronounce them. It was a beautiful place, but it did not have the almost mystical charm of Edinburgh. Also, the city belonged to demons. He noticed many of them roaming the streets, mingling with ghosts from every century, humans, as well as a few vampires and vampire hunters. He cringed at the thought of all the demons here, but Belial had not been bad to him. He had even let him make a halt in Paris on the way, even if that turned out to be a waste of time.

Stanley read the names of the building's residents printed on golden plaques near the heavy wooden doors with sculpted handles. All were blank or crossed out except one: 'L. Baille'. So he did live here, in apartment four. He pushed the heavy doors open and went upstairs and knocked on his door. The demon soon opened the door, a smile on his face.

"Well, it looks like you made it after all," he said.

"Am I late?" Stanley asked as he stepped inside.

"No, you're just in time," Belial said,

He invited him to sit on one of the sofas and Stanley gazed around him. The decor was all in crimson tones, with the sort of lavish furniture he thought only royalty owned, sculptures of naked Antiquity demigods and goddesses, and grotesque paintings representing macabre scenes and scenes of Hell and the Apocalypse.

"Do you like the paintings?" Belial asked, taking a seat.

That night he was wearing what were apparently his colors: a crimson sack suit and a yellow vest and tie over a black shirt. He was quite the dandy and looked much more like what he truly was: a demon.

"I'm not really into art. So, what did you want to talk about?" Stanley asked.

"Your mission," Belial said. "But first, were you able to get your business taken care of in Paris?"

"Does it matter?" Stanley asked.

He was in a bad mood and did not want to talk about it, and certainly not with the demon who would probably try to propose a solution to his problem, and his problem was no longer the fact that Eve was angry, but that she had someone else.

"You're in a terrible mood. I can sense it," Belial said with a grin. "What happened? Heartbreak?"

Stanley leaned back in his chair and crossed his arms.

"If you have nothing important to say, I ought to leave," he warned him.

"Dear Stanley, don't be like that. I promised you happiness," Belial said in what seemed either like a concerned or a condescending voice, or both.

"I'm leaving," Stanley said, exasperated, but the moment he rose from his seat, the demon disappeared and reappeared behind him. He grabbed both his arms firmly and forced him to sit down, then reappeared on his seat, his legs crossed.

"What now? Are you going to detain me here until we have a therapy session?" Stanley snapped at him.

"Maybe," Belial said without losing his smile.

Stanley grunted and crossed his arms again. He looked away from the demon's piercing green eyes. He had made a pact with him, and that meant that the demon could subordinate him if he so wanted, but he seemed to prefer persuasion rather than brute force – most of the time.

"Alright, so let's start by closing our eyes and taking a deep breath," he said.

"Are you serious?" Stanley said, rolling his eyes.

"Absolutely. In order for you to do your job, I first need you to be thinking about that job," Belial said. "I will even perform the exercise with you."

Stanley sighed and reluctantly closed his eyes as the demon did the same.

"Now, let's breathe in deeply... inhale, exhale," Belial said.

Stanley followed his instructions and he did find that it helped clear his mind, at least enough to focus. He opened his eyes and found the demon sitting on a table by his side.

"How did you get there? I didn't hear or feel you move," he said.

"The demon you are to follow and observe can do the exact same thing," Belial said. "You should never let your guard down, even for a second."

"So this was just a trick? I thought you really cared about my mood," Stanley said, somewhat disappointed.

Belial laughed and stroked his shoulder. It was just a little too pleasant.

"It was a lesson, and yes, I do care about your mood," he said.

He disappeared again and reappeared in his seat.

"I'm sending you to a meeting of transgender creatures of the underworld. A certain 'Emily' is holding it at her place tomorrow night," he said.

Stanley smirked.

"Are you kidding me?"

"I know you hate socializing, I get it…" Belial said, but Stanley cut him.

"She already invited me."

Belial suddenly lost his smile and leaned forward.

"When and how did you meet her?" he asked.

"In Paris. She runs a flower shop. Why?" he asked, frowning.

"Was anyone with her?"

"No, but I did feel a presence similar to that of that child who murdered Aleksandra."

Belial got up and crossed the room. He grabbed a rolled sheet of paper in a drawer and brought it back, then sat beside Stanley on the sofa. On the sheet of paper, which he laid out before them, were names and lines connecting them. Some of them had question marks beside them. Yvan Thompson's name was connected to the candyman and Belphegor. The candyman and Beelzebub were connected to the and Astaroth. And Astaroth was connected to several names. Separate from the others was a question mark, and underneath it the words 'puppet master'.

"Puppet master?" Stanley said.

"I don't know his or her identity yet, only that they are the person who ordered the murder of Aleksandra," Belial said.

He then wrote down Emily's name and drew a line connecting her to the puppet master with a question mark.

"Really? You think Emily is part of some conspiracy?" Stanley said.

"We can't rule out anything," Belial said.

As a major demon, he had seen it all before and trusted no one.

"So all I need to do is go to the meetings and report to you?" Stanley asked.

"For now, yes. Observe my associate, Astaroth. Tell me who he talks to, and what he does."

"Easy," Stanley said. "And how will I recognize him?"

Belial smiled.

"In the event that an expert hitman like you would not recognize a demon, I am sure there will be introductions during the meeting," he said. "Do you think you will survive socializing for a few evenings?"

Stanley rolled his eyes again.

He returned to his lodgings that night—a small hotel room in the poorer parts of town. Because of the nature of his mission, Stanley could not stay in any of the numerous hotels owned by demons, and he could not meet twice with Belial in the same place. While it was not uncommon for the demon to receive visits from members of his 'harem', his associate would quickly become suspicious if he heard that a certain vampire visited him more frequently than the others, and demons had ears and eyes everywhere. But Stanley was used to working in the shadows.

The next evening, dressed in his usual black suit and equipped with his French-English dictionary, he headed over to Emily's apartment. He left Cornelius at the hotel, just in case this Astaroth could sense his presence and become suspicious of him. That night, he was there only as Stanley, the random transgender man invited by Emily in her flower shop.

Emily owned an apartment in the western part of town, near the Seine River, in a lovely neighborhood where people had the time and money to hang flower pots on every windowsill and balcony. All this posh stuff made Stanley sick. He grunted his disapproval of all this frivolousness, slipped his hands in his pockets, and entered the apartment building and went up the stairs, but he came to a sudden halt on the second floor. On the third floor, he could hear Eve talking with someone. He looked around him to make sure he was alone then made himself invisible, climbed the stairs and posted himself where he could observe her at a distance. Callie was right, he really had stalker tendencies.

Eve was having a conversation with a good-looking young man—a vampire with short, neatly combed blond hair and a trendy gray and brown pinstripe suit. His style could be described as: 'I come from such a posh family that even when I pretend like I don't pay attention to my clothes, they end up looking fashionable'. Stanley wanted to puke. He could not see his love's face, only her long black hair that fell in perfect curls over her shoulders under her purple hat, but just being so close to her at last made his heart race and flutter. She was so petite yet so imposing with her charisma, and her voice was strong yet melodious. She and the young man spoke in English, both with what sounded like the same accent to Stanley, but the young man was obviously a foreigner, or they would be speaking French.

"The least you could do is say 'hi', Hans," she told the young man.

She sounded upset, and he looked embarrassed and like he did not really want to be there, talking with her.

"Good evening," he said, slipping his hands in his pockets. "Listen, about that time…"

"What time?" she said, lifting her chin defiantly.

"Eve…" he said with a sigh. "I know I invited you to that lecture, but something just came up."

"No need to make up excuses. You could just tell me you were no longer interested," she said. "Even though you're the one who invited me out, a little honesty never killed anyone."

"Eve… It would not have worked out anyway," Hans said, and he looked like he would make himself invisible like Stanley if he could to escape her.

Typical player, Stanley thought. He could not stand weak men like him, who led women on and then ran away the moment they realized the woman was not as they expected, or when she was getting serious about them. Still, he would not suffer to see him talking to her so close, so he made himself visible and quickly moved beside her.

"Is there a problem?" he asked, and both of them jumped with surprise.

"Oh, hello there. I didn't even see you coming. No, everything is fine," Hans replied with an uncomfortable smile.

He offered him his hand to shake, but Stanley glared at him angrily, and the blond understood and left.

"Who the hell are you?" Eve then asked him, frowning.

"Apologies, *Mademoiselle*, my name is Stanley," Stanley said, turning to her and tipping his hat, but politeness would apparently not win her heart.

"Who do you think you are? I'm not some damsel in distress in need of your help, you patronizing ass!" she snapped at him before walking away.

"It's pronounced 'arse' in proper English," he remarked.

She turned around and said: "Get lost! Is that proper English?"

She was indeed the love of his life, down to their shared vulgarity. He sighed and leaned against the wall as she entered the apartment and shut the door behind her. This was going to be more difficult than he had anticipated. He had not planned on her being there, nor her being in such a bad mood. Was it because of Hans? Was he her 'man' and they had just broken up? Not only was she going to be difficult to approach, but it saddened him that she did not even remember his face. Perhaps he was too ordinary compared to Mister Perfect in his expensive suit. He closed his eyes and drew in a deep breath, but Emily then came out and noticed him.

"Oh, Stanley!" she said, and she rushed over to him.

"Oh, hello Emily," he said, trying to regain his composure.

"Did something happen?" she asked.

"No, nothing," he said.

"Come, let's go inside!" she said happily, and she took his arm and led him into the small but already crowded apartment. Eve shot him a dangerous look as he walked in and turned away, as though he was not worthy of her attention.

That night, there were not only vampires but also demons—all transgender—and a few androgynous individuals, like the tall brunette Hans gazed at with shining eyes. Stanley had been worried about finding himself alone among a group of French speakers, but the guests appeared to be from all over Europe and perhaps further, and in order to understand each other they all communicated in English.

Emily took him to a sofa and sat with him.

"You look intimidated," she remarked.

"I was a little worried about not being able to communicate with people here," he admitted.

"Oh, you must be a young vampire," she said. "Most vampires my age or older have traveled and speak several languages."

Her comment made him feel even more out of place, especially since Eve and that pretty boy were both multilingual.

"But you don't need to speak many languages," she immediately added as she noticed his discomfort.

He shifted on his seat, mostly to move away from Emily who seemed to be inching closer to him, but his eyes remained fixed on Eve. She was not socializing with the others. She stood alone, a glass of wine in her hand, now shooting spiteful glances at Hans and some of the other girls.

"Do you know her?" Emily suddenly asked.

"Huh? Who?" Stanley asked, startled.

"Eve."

"No. I just went to one of her lectures, but there's no way she would remember me. I'm nobody," he joked. He had expected her to laugh with him, but instead her eyes filled with sadness.

"I'm also nobody," she said. "I introduce myself to people, but they forget me. And when they show up again, they ask me who Emily is…"

She lowered her eyes and seemed about to cry. Stanley turned to her on the sofa and smiled.

"I remember you, the girl from the flower shop," he said.

He was not trying to flirt with her; he just had a soft spot for some women, especially when they were crying or about to. He liked all women, even if he had a preference for brunettes, and Emily was sweet and easy-going. She did not judge people at a glance, and she was not opinionated like Eve. She had many qualities, but unfortunately Stanley's heart still belonged to Eve. Even when she ignored him, when she rejected his attempts to talk to her and insulted him, he could not forget the words they had exchanged in their letters and the dreams they had shared.

"You do?" Emily said, hopeful, and he smiled in response.

He thought he would be able to spend a mostly quiet evening in a corner with her, but soon they were surrounded by a crowd of women. He and Hans were the only men in the group, and that apparently made them very popular with the ladies. Keeping a low profile was not going to be an option, and Stanley was beginning to feel nervous with all these eyes on him. But the one they were apparently all waiting for then entered and all eyes turned to him: a tall, handsome demon with long black hair and a purple and green suit. Astaroth.

They all sat around him, and he introduced himself as a transgender demon, one who had obtained his full male body through the magic of a demon above him in the hierarchy. He told them he used to be a goddess and people called him Astarte, but in order to live as his true self, he had had to give up on his role and become a demon instead. Like them, he felt like he had to lose everything he had in order to live as his true self, and many in his audience could relate to him. Stanley did not know whether his story was true or not. With his experiences, he was reluctant to trust a demon, but he certainly described the feelings of transgender people with great accuracy, to the point even Stanley agreed that he had probably, at some point, been changed by another demon.

Emily, who led the meeting, then invited everyone to introduce themselves. There was Hans, the know-it-all medical school student who was in all other aspects rather clueless, Charlotte, the harpy painter with sapphic inspiration, Monica, just your average, middle-aged shapeshifter and occasional journalist, Mischa, the quiet and standoffish intersex vampire who liked photography, and Eve, who introduced herself as an author and feminist speaker. But when came Stanley's turn, he lowered his eyes and wrung his hands nervously. He couldn't help tapping his foot on the floor and felt completely over-whelmed. He knew if he opened his mouth now, he would start stuttering.

"Stanley?" Emily asked by his side.

"Uh, can I just skip the introduction?" he asked in a low voice.

He needed people to stop staring at him, and right now. Belial was right to ask him whether he would survive this meeting: now he was not sure of it.

"Of course, dear," Emily immediately said. "Well, friends, how about we split up and enjoy some refreshments? Vampire snacks are on the first table, demon snacks on the next."

She was really thoughtful about the diversity of the guests, and they appreciated it. There were red meat snacks for the vampires—sandwiches and cold meats - and raw meat for the demons, and Stanley preferred not to know *what* kind of meat they were made from. All left their seats and headed to the food, and Stanley got up and retreated to a corner. Not far from him, Hans was apparently trying to flirt with Mischa—and failing.

"So… Uh, what sort of photography do you do?" he asked, standing side by side with the tall brunette, who seemed com-pletely uninterested.

"Candids," Mischa replied.

"Oh. And what is that?" Hans asked.

Mischa turned to him with curious eyes.

"It's a portrait taken when the subject is not posing. I set up my camera on the banks of the Seine River at night and capture passersby."

"Nice," Hans said, smiling. "So, are you trying to capture certain moods or feelings?"

"No, just people," Mischa replied in the same monotonous voice.

"People are interesting," Hans said.

"People are strange," Mischa replied.

"Also," Hans said, who was struggling to keep up.

Stanley smirked. Hans was never going to get anywhere with that one. Emily then noticed the young necromancer alone and joined him.

"Was it too much for you? Do you need some fresh air?" she asked him.

"I'm fine, I just... I just don't like being looked at. Not by you like this, but by crowds," Stanley said, wiping the sweat off his face.

"Oh, I'm so sorry, I had no idea," she said. She took his arm again as though she was his sweetheart. He did not want her to, but she had that coercive friendliness, and he feared that he might break her heart if he asked her to let go of him. They both then overheard some of the girls talking about Eve.

"It's her, I know it..." Charlotte said.

"Rivoltin's nude model? The *cocotte*?" Monica said.

"Absolutely!" Charlotte said. "I'm surprised she came in a dress tonight, she seemed to enjoy exposing herself to the camera."

They both giggled and Eve, who had heard them, walked over to Astaroth and sat beside him, Hans, and Mischa, whom he was entertaining.

"What's a 'cocotte'?" Stanley asked Emily in a whisper.

"It's... nothing," she said, looking embarrassed for Eve.

"I don't speak French," he reminded her. "Is it the French word for a model?"

Emily looked at him and sighed as though she needed to look like she felt guilty about telling him, even though she really wanted to.

"Well… *coquette* and *cocotte* mean a courtesan, a high-class prostitute. You don't usually find them in brothels, but in the theaters, the private salons. They only prey on rich men they select."

Stanley sensed some rivalry between the two women, and that Emily did not like Eve as much as he had previously thought. And yet she did not seem the kind of person to invite someone only in order to humiliate her.

"Anyhow, how about we go sit with Astaroth?" Stanley said.

"Oh, but it's quieter here. Over there, people will be staring at you," she said, caressing his arm softly.

He was stuck now because he had made the mistake of telling her about his fear of being looked at. So he was forced to spend the evening with her, listening to her talk about her flower shop and all the flower-themed objects she collected, made, or sold. He tried to take an interest in her conversation, but it was just so far from the world he lived in that he struggled. She noticed his discomfort again.

"Am I boring you?" she asked him in a small voice.

"N-No, not at all," he said.

"I'm sorry. You don't have to sit here and listen to me," she said, and she looked about to cry again.

"You're not forcing me…" he tried saying, but she shook her head.

"I'll just go and fill up the snack trays for everyone," she said, and with this she got up and retreated to the kitchen in the back of the apartment.

Stanley felt bad. He had not meant to hurt her feelings by not listening to her, even though he couldn't care less about flowers and pretty things. He then noticed Eve about to leave with Astaroth. She was holding his arm and he did not like that. He got up and went over to her and this time grabbed her arm to get her attention. She turned around, looking furious.

"You again?"

"Uh, Miss Eve, I am truly sorry for interrupting you earlier. Might I have a word with you before you leave?" he asked.

"Didn't I already tell you to get lost?" she retorted, but the demon by her side smiled at Stanley. He dropped his hand on his shoulder and stroked it in a way that made him uncomfortable.

"We'll talk next time, dear Stanley," he said.

"Keep your filthy hands off me, you pervert!" Stanley said, moving back.

The demon seemed surprised and possibly offended, and Eve stared at Stanley like he was insane, then shrugged and took Astaroth's arm again, and they left. Stanley shuddered with disgust and wiped off his shoulder. He did not like the way that man touched him, nor the look in his eyes, almost like he was his next prey... But Eve left with him. Did it mean she was already a part of his 'harem'? Stanley had a hard time believing it.

The other guests were leaving now, and he noticed Emily alone in the small kitchen, cleaning up. She looked sad and lonely, so he went to her, bringing an empty tray. But as he approached her, he again had that odd feeling about her. She turned around and seemed surprised to see him. And as he looked at her, his vision began to flicker in gray and black, like when he slowed down his heartbeat to make himself invisible, and her image and the apartment flickered before him, alternating between the woman and the room he was in, and the same, solitary woman covered in dust and spider webs in an empty and abandoned apartment with broken furniture, and he thought he heard a word: *'moroi'*. He snapped out of it quickly and shook his head.

"Yes?" she said with a forced smile.

"Oh, I just thought I would help you clean up," he said, handing her the tray.

"You don't have to. Nobody cares about me anyway," she said as she took it.

She turned around and proceeded to wash it in the sink. Stanley did not want to be an ass, person who had actually treated him decently that night, so he rolled up his sleeves and walked over to the sink and picked up a plate and a cloth. He was not exactly an expert in dishwashing, but he tried his best. She stopped what she was doing and observed him for some time, and eventually broke into a smile.

"That's not the way to wash a plate," she said, giggling.

"Really?" he said, turning to her with a smile. "I'm sorry. I grew up in a posh family with maids and as a result I'm completely useless when it comes to cleaning."

His comment made her laugh and she showed him how to use a brush and soap and scrub the dish.

"This is the correct way to do it," she explained.

Emily was not petty nor scheming. She was just lonely, like him, and all she wanted was for someone to pay attention to her. But sadly, everyone present at the meeting that night eclipsed her. She was just ordinary.

"I'm sorry if I was rude earlier. Just a bad habit. That's why my only friends are ghosts," he said.

"You don't have friends?" she asked.

"I do. They're ghosts," he replied, smiling.

"I also don't have friends… not anymore," she said sadly.

There was something endearing about her and the way she was ignored, and now Stanley saw something more in her, something the others did not see, and he almost wanted to spend more time with her. She was not the sort of beauty an artist might want as a model like Eve, but she had the grace, the gentleness of a quiet angel, a natural femininity that stirred something inside him.

"You're beautiful," he said without thinking, and she turned to him, surprised. Her cheeks reddened.

"I... I meant, I'm not a very interesting person, but I can be your friend," he said, catching himself.

Her natural rosy lips parted into a smile, revealing her perfect white teeth.

"Oh, I would love that!" she said.

They proceeded to clean the trays, then the empty glasses, and more dessert plates, all the while chatting, and this time he paid more attention to her. Emily was a city girl with country girl dreams. She, too, came from a posh household, but her fondest early childhood memories were visiting her cousins who lived in the countryside. They taught her the beauty of nature, the names of flowers and trees, and with them everything was simple, unlike with her parents.

"So that's why you decided to open a flower shop?" he asked.

"I suppose so," she said. "City folk can be so complicated; they have to live by strict rules... But flowers don't need to put on a façade. They are themselves, all different but equally beautiful, and they remind us that happiness is found in simplicity. Well, that's where I find happiness at least," she said.

"You're an artist... unlike me," he laughed, and she laughed along with him.

"You're someone who walks around with a shield," she then remarked. "And I wish I could break through that shield someday…"

Silence fell upon them for a moment, but the plate he was holding suddenly slipped from his hands and broke in the sink.

"Oh no, I'm so sorry!" he said, but she laughed again.

"It's nothing, just a broken plate," she said. She moved closer and began to gather the pieces, then took them over to the trash bin.

"So, did your sweetheart like the flowers?" she asked him, and he suddenly remembered their first encounter in her flower shop.

"She did not want them—nor did she want to see me," he said in a cynical voice.

She turned around to face him and lowered her eyes, bringing her hands together as though she were nervous.

"I don't want to keep you here if you don't want to stay," she said. "I appreciate your help, and I would love for you to stay, but I don't want to be annoying…"

"You're not annoying," he assured her. "I was actually having a good time talking with you—and that does not happen with many people, believe me."

She turned hopeful eyes to him, but confidence almost immediately deserted her face again. He was not very good at conversation, and he no longer knew what to say, so he slipped his hands in his pockets and lowered his gaze.

"But you're right, I should probably head back to my hotel. Cornelius—one of my ghosts—is waiting for me," he said.

"Of course," she said.

She quietly walked him back to the door, and he stood on the threshold before her.

"Thank you… for trying to make me comfortable," he said, and he truly meant it.

"Will you come again?" she asked him.

He pursed his lips.

"Of course… I mean, I will try," he said.

She did not suspect the true reasons of his presence, nor did she know or assume what he did for a living, but she smiled anyhow.

"Your sweetheart doesn't deserve you," she said. "You are a very kind man."

He smirked.

"That's not what people usually say about me, but thank you."

He tipped his hat and left, and her eyes lingered on him as he walked down the dark corridor and down the stairs. She then returned inside the apartment, closed the door, and sighed. Stanley had gone and suddenly her entire world seemed so empty and lonely. She had wanted him to stay—so much—but she did not want to scare him away by being too intrusive or assertive. She looked around the cold, dark apartment, of which the sofas, the tables, the furniture were all covered with a light dusting of snow. The wilted flowers in vases all around the room were beginning to rot and fall off their stems. And then she remembered him telling her that she was beautiful. He had said it just like that, because he was a spontaneous young man. It probably didn't mean anything, but still her heart fluttered like a teenager now, and all around her the snow began to melt. A warm, yellow hue filled the apartment like the summer sun she would never see again and all the flowers came back to life. It had been so long since that light, that warmth had come into her world. She walked across the room as in a childhood dream with the sweetness of cotton candy, of daisies, of everything pretty and carefree. She brought her hands to her heart and smiled with joy as she whispered the name of the magician who had suddenly flipped her world upside down: "Stanley…"

Socializing was a pain in the ass, and having 'friends', to Stanley, was very much like having the flu. Like germs, friends dragged you into uncomfortable places and you had to sit around and endure them until they were done with you. But Emily was not such a bad kind of germ, and she understood when he'd had enough socializing and didn't force him to stay. Due to the sudden growth of her circle, she decided to hold weekly meetings, and he attended them only for two reasons: to keep an eye on Astaroth and his activities, and because he did not want Emily to feel left out in her own circle. Hans was a pain and showed up every single time. He always tried to make conversation with Stanley, who ignored him, grunted, and walked away. Eve came occasionally, sometimes with Astaroth. It was unclear whether or not they were having an affair, but she behaved like they were, and as time went by, Stanley's dreams of her crumbled more and more. Something had changed in her. She was no longer the fierce feminist, protector of all women, the mystic, the romantic dreamer he had corresponded with but, quite literally, a bitch. She was always angry, rude to the other attendees, and usually the source of any quarrels that erupted – for Emily's circle was overwhelmingly feminine and the girls formed 'cliques' that seemed to change every other week. There was gossip, criticism, bickering, and arguments quickly flared up. Watching these girls argue about who said what to who about whom gave Stanley headaches, and Hans, who tried to be the peacemaker, sometimes just had to bail out and let the women fight it out amongst themselves. Things were getting out of control, but Astaroth said they would calm down as soon as more men joined the meetings—because apparently, they were the only remedy to these feminine battles royal—and Emily promised that she would try to find new members. Meanwhile, Stanley was not making any progress, whether in his investigation or with Eve, and he couldn't help but think that this change in her was his fault, because of the misunderstanding between them and his failure to resolve it.

"What should I do?" he asked Cornelius one night in their hotel room.

They sat together on the bed in the dark, and Stanley held his head in his hands.

"I don't know. I'm too young to know…" Cornelius said in a small voice.

"That demon already has her… I don't know what to do," Stanley said.

"But what does he want to do with her?" Cornelius asked.

"Use her… traffic her in some way," Stanley said. "But she hates Ernest and Stanley. I don't know how to approach her anymore unless I try going back in time, but we both know how that ended before."

The last time he had traveled through time, hoping to prevent Callie's death, he not only had failed to prevent it, but he had killed and been killed by his own father.

The demonic pocket mirror Belial had given him started blinking on the chair. It was time for Stanley to report to him. He reluctantly got up and picked it up.

"Where and when?" the demon asked him.

"Listen, this is not a good time," Stanley said.

"On the contrary, it sounds like it is," Belial said, and no sooner had he spoken than he appeared before Stanley, scaring him almost to death.

"You know, you could request an appointment," Stanley grunted.

"I did," Belial said, smiling.

That night, he was wearing a formal black tailcoat suit as though he was going out.

"And I told you I didn't want to see you," Stanley said. "I thought you wanted to make me happy. Being nice to me would be a good start."

He sat on the bed and sighed.

"How was I not nice?" the demon asked, curious.

Stanley shook his head and said: "Never mind. Were you going out?"

"I thought I might take you out to a quiet place tonight," Belial said.

"To give you my report? I can do it here," Stanley shrugged.

"To relax," the demon said. "I promised you happiness."

"Well it's not working very well so far," Stanley said.

He got up and grabbed his jacket anyhow. Cornelius also got up, but Belial opened his hands and a children's book appeared in them.

"And this is for the little one," he said, placing it on the bed since he could not see Cornelius. "I apologize, but I must borrow your friend for a few hours."

Cornelius looked up at Stanley, who nodded.

"I can't be any safer than with the King of Hell himself," he said.

He then took the hand Belial was offering him and they disappeared together and reappeared sitting at the small table of a restaurant by the ocean. The air was a lot warmer than in the city they left and filled with the scent of olives and herbs. Stanley looked around him, confused.

"Where are we this time?" he asked.

The demon always took him to random places where his associate would not think of looking for him.

"Parikia, on the Paros island," Belial replied with his usual smile. "Greece," he added before the puzzled face Stanley was making.

"I prefer cold places," Stanley said.

Nevertheless, he took a bite of the meat dish on the plate before him and it was delicious.

"Oh… what's this?" he asked.

"Lamb Kleftiko. I knew you would like it," Belial said, leaning forward.

He picked up one of the fried frog legs in his plate and ate it with delight, then turned his gaze to the docks, where ships awaited the morning to leave, and the dark waves danced under the moonlight. Stanley looked at the people around them. The place was lively, but everyone ignored them, and they all spoke Greek. Being far away from his problems and knowing that they could have a private conversation in a language the people around them could not understand made him feel more at ease. Once again, he had to admit the demon knew a thing or two.

"So, what are we here to talk about?" he asked.

"Anything you want," Belial said.

"Why?" Stanley asked, frowning.

"You're working for me, and I am also working for you," Belial said. "In order to make you happy, I first have to figure you out, and I must admit that understanding your vampire psyche is a challenge for a demon like me."

Stanley smirked.

"I'm also part demon. You're not trying hard enough. So you like frog legs?" he said, gazing with suspicion at the contents of his plate.

"I do. They are my favorite food in this world. Anything else you would like to know about me?" the demon asked with a smile.

"You said you wanted to gather a 'team'... Who are they? Are you working with other vampires?"

"I am a demon overseer, and the order you left oversees vampires and their interactions with humans, but sometimes our two worlds collide. It is inevitable. So, yes, I occasionally work with vampires."

Stanley lifted an eyebrow, then grinned.

"Hopefully they're not like me."

"I'm not sure what you mean..." Belial said, looking puzzled.

"I mean... look at me. I scare people away," Stanley said.

"I'm not afraid of you. On the contrary, I rather like you," Belial said. "You are straightforward, you speak you mind, and your temper is explosive but manageable."

"Is that so rare in your profession?" Stanley asked.

The demon leaned back in his chair and rolled his eyes.

"No demon dares to speak their mind in front of me. As for your peers, they are often aggressive—I sometimes have to physically restrain them before we can even start talking. Working with vampires is what I assume governesses have to deal with when working with toddlers."

Stanley broke into laughter. It was the first time the demon opened up to him and dropped that polite, commercial smile. He was beginning to see what sort of man he was: a very intelligent, sensitive one. As the king of demons, he was probably their 'alpha male' and could beat the crap out of them if he had to, but he was also in touch with his feminine side and knew how to identify his emotions and those of others.

"Am I funny?" Belial said.

"You did have to restrain me. Sorry about that," Stanley said.

"Would you like me to do it again?" Belial asked, with shining eyes.

"Not unless you can transform into a petite, witty brunette with a strong character and a foul mouth," Stanley sighed, and he lowered his sad eyes.

"I cannot," Belial agreed. "So, are the meetings not going well? You don't like them?"

"I like them like I like wearing a dress…"

"Why do you not like them?"

"People are just stupid," Stanley shrugged.

"Everyone has their own insecurities and pain, and I'm sure they bring them along to these meetings. It is what all people do, humans, demons, vampires, not just those in your circle," the demon said.

"Whatever," Stanley said.

He turned his gaze to the waves and the few seagulls hovering above them.

"I feel sorry for Emily, though. She tries so hard to bring everyone together, but they just ignore her," he said.

"Emily? Not Eve?" Belial asked with interest.

"She's sweet but just… ordinary," Stanley said, turning back to him.

"But you said that you heard the word 'moroi' when you had that vision of her," Belial said.

"Yes? Are you on to something?"

"I'm taking notes."

Stanley let out another deep sigh.

"I think I turned Eve into a bitch," he said.

"How so?" the demon asked.

"She's lost her 'shine' somehow… she seems sad and angry all the time. I know it's my fault, but she won't even talk to me.

She called me a patronizing ass and told me to get lost. Perhaps I just didn't know her as well as I thought I did."

"But even in the best of worlds, if you were living together as a couple, you would eventually have discovered that side of her," Belial remarked.

"I don't need a lecture about relationships," Stanley replied. "I know what it's like to live with a woman. Been there, done it. At this point I'm not even trying to mend things between us anymore. I've given up on that. I just want to protect her from Astaroth, but she's always clinging to him."

"And you think she's sleeping with him and you're jealous," Belial said.

"Of course she's sleeping with him," Stanley said.

"Because of her past as a courtesan?"

"What are you trying to say?"

They gazed into each other's eyes for a few seconds, then Belial picked up his glass and took a sip of it.

"Yes, she is sleeping with him," he said.

Stanley pursed his lips and moved his gaze away, knowing his eyes were getting moist.

"You didn't have to tell me. That was just unnecessarily cruel," he whispered.

Then, unable to hold back, he covered his face with his hand to hide the tears coming out of his eyes. Belial put down his fork.

"Why… Why can't I prevent horrible things from happening to those I love? What's the purpose of being so powerful and having swallowed the Time Key?" Stanley whispered, his body shaking softly.

Belial got up and moved his chair beside his. He then sat down and wrapped his arm around his shoulders.

"I'm sorry, Stanley," he said, as though he truly cared. "I don't have a solution yet, but I'm thinking about one."

"You can't find a solution because you're not like us. You've never been human, or vampire, or transgender. How could you save either of us?" Stanley said.

"But, as you said earlier, you were a demon before becoming a vampire, so we are a little alike," Belial said.

Stanley looked into his eyes, and they were filled with compassion.

"I'm not giving up on you – or Eve," Belial said.

"Why?" Stanley asked in disbelief.

"Of course I can't let Astaroth do whatever he intends to do with Eve, but I also want to help two people I see suffering. I want to see your happy ending," the demon said.

"Is that your hobby because you don't have a love life of your own?" Stanley asked, smirking and wiping away his tears, and the demon smiled.

"That's right… ten thousand years old and still single," he joked.

"Well, cheers to that," Stanley said, taking a sip from his glass of wine.

"Cheers!" Belial said, also taking a sip from his.

CHAPTER 11

ADEYEMI SAT ON HIS throne, a glass of blood in his hand, and his yellow eyes that could not see, lost in emptiness. The two thrones by his side were empty. Yvan stood before him, holding a sheet of paper with a list of names.

"Dobromila, from Prague," he said in his deep voice.

"No," Adeyemi said.

"Or her twin brother Bohumil."

"No."

"Hossein, from Persia. Very old and knowledgeable."

"No," Adeyemi said, letting out an exasperated sigh.

Yvan looked disconcerted.

"I have gone through the entire list," he said. "We need to select Aleksandra's replacement."

"Really?" Adeyemi smirked. "I was under the impression that you did not want her seat to be filled."

"Me? Why?" Yvan said, frowning.

Adeyemi rose from his throne and walked past him then stopped, and though he was shorter than him, his presence was so imposing, so powerful, that even Yvan shuddered.

"I think you may be forgetting the very reason why we were both offered seraph positions: to oversee all creatures of the underworld except demons."

Yvan turned around and gazed at him. No, he had not forgotten. To be a part of the Order, one had to be humble and disinterested, for such great power could easily corrupt a weak mind.

A man then walked out of the shadows, clapping his hands. He was a short but muscular sailor with an angelic face, and he was chewing on a piece of barley sugar. He grinned and bowed to them in an exaggerated manner.

"Ah, there you are," Adeyemi said, turning in his general direction. "Any news about the Time Key?"

"I can confirm that it was stolen and has not been found nor replaced yet," the candyman said, and he laughed to himself.

Behind Adeyemi, Yvan gazed at him with a profound sadness. The candyman only briefly turned his gaze to him, then back to Adeyemi.

"If it was stolen, and no one has used it, then we can assume it has been destroyed," Adeyemi said. "I will contact the head of the demons to let him know this was not our doing. We must do everything we can to avoid a war between the two sides."

"Who ever said it was not used?" the candyman said, laughing more.

"Someone used the Time Key?" Adeyemi said, startled.

"Oh… yes!" the candyman said.

"Who?" Adeyemi pressed him.

The candyman's grin widened, and he laughed harder. His eyes then moved to Yvan, and he said: "Who knows?"

Yvan scowled, but Adeyemi ignored him.

"It's alright, just let us know when you have more information," he said.

The candyman bowed again and disappeared, leaving only a trail of smoke behind him.

"Adeyemi, shouldn't we report this to our master?" Yvan asked.

"No, there is no need at this point. This is nothing the Order can't handle," Adeyemi said.

His face appeared confident, but his voice betrayed his angst. They still had no clue who or what murdered Aleksandra, only that she was last seen at a party with a masked young man who matched the description of Stanley, but could just as well have been anybody else. Yvan was sure it was him, and that he had murdered her, and thus tried to flee the country. Adeyemi had doubts, both because the 'bogeyman' was not known to be very social, and also because her death did not benefit him in any way, unless he worked for someone else in parallel. Either way, it was high time for the Order to meet up with the demons and consolidate their peace treaty.

He left Yvan, changed into everyday clothes, and returned to his comfortable apartment in Belgravia, where he sat at his desk. Zahra, the angel who served as his eyes whenever he needed them, entered the room, awaiting his orders as always.

"Anything I can do for you tonight, Master?" she asked.

"I do not need anything, thank you," he said. "Please say your prayers and go to bed."

"Yes, Master," she said, bowing, and she retreated and closed the door.

Adeyemi closed his eyes. He was not born in England, not even in the British Colonial Empire. He was born long before that, in the Oyo Empire, in the year 1703 of the Christian calendar. Captured by enemies, he was sold to whites as a slave and he led a rebellion on the ship supposed to take them to the Americas, but the rebellion was crushed, and his eyes gouged as punishment. It was then, he thought, that his life as a man had truly ended. It was then he understood he would never be free again. He was taken to a place called Virginia. He learned the language of the whites and their religion, and because he was blind, he was spared hard labor in the fields and became the butler of a man who thought himself generous. He was not generous. He had no scruples buying a human being, and he bought slaves as young as five months old. But, without his eyes, Adeyemi saw no possible escape for himself, until he began to *see with his mind.*

It began while he was still human. Pictures came to him, as though he was seeing through others' eyes, and he understood that his mind could latch onto that of certain people—not all—and see through them. And then he saw himself through the eyes of his master. They had dressed him up like white men, with blue breeches and stockings, a fine white shirt and blue justaucorps, and a perfectly curled white wig on his head. They had stolen his identity—every bit of it—and made him their mutt. Filled with rage and having no hope of ever escaping his condition, he entered his master's mind and ordered him to kill him, and so he did. Except he did not die. Adeyemi awakened days later in the dirt, terrified, and had to crawl his way out. Luckily, slaves did not get a coffin or a headstone like the whites, or his escape would have been harder. Like most of his kind, he did not know what he was at first, but he quickly learned. And, in his new form as a moroi vampire, he was not only able to travel through people's minds and use them, but also to subdue the most powerful creatures of the underworld and bend them to his will. He was different from spirituals, who projected themselves outside of their bodies, mind benders, who only created illusions for their victims, mahrts, and other supernatural entities that could interfere with people's thoughts and dreams. Moroi vampires did not require blood to survive; they thirsted for souls, and their ultimate desire was to enter their victim's mind and absorb their very essence. They were gluttons with an endless appetite for souls, and the more he indulged in his obsession, the more his heart shattered. As a human, as a man, he had been shipped across the world and sold like property, but as an undead creature, he infiltrated, corrupted, and assimilated people like his property. He soon reached the point when he could no longer stand himself, and he begged the god he had been taught to pray to deliver him from this nightmare.

It was not God who answered him, but a man in a long white robe. Once a demon, an alp, he had renounced the darkness of his condition and now worked on the other side, the 'good' side, and he had a place there for someone like Adeyemi.

Years had passed, and, ironically, Adeyemi ended up looking after the very people who captured and enslaved him and his people. He tried to be just and fair, and refrain from hating them, for his mission was much greater than the suffering he had experienced as a man. It did not mean he was perfect—no seraph was—but he took pride in knowing that he was better than those who had hurt him. Tough he still felt the urge to feed on souls, he had renounced that path and his addiction. But when the candyman brought them Stanley Suspect, whom he could tell was at least partly moroi, so did his most primal desires resurface, and he had given in once, with Zahra, who he had made his blood mate. Their relationship was a taboo, a conflict of interest. He was no cleaner than the demon he was about to call. But wouldn't God forgive his and Zahra's love if he learned about it?

He picked up the receiver of the telephone on his desk and dialed the operator.

"Please connect me to one, seven, eight, five, two, in France," he said.

"One moment please," the young woman said on the other end of the line.

A man picked up on the other end.

"Luc Baille, attorney at law, how may I help you?" he said in his commercial voice.

"It's me," Adeyemi said.

Silence on the other end.

"We did not kill Beelzebub and Belphegor," Adeyemi said.

"Are you sure about that?" Belial asked in a menacing tone.

"I have no reason to lie to you. I do not want a war between the two sides," Adeyemi stated.

"Really?" Belial said. "I've had a few issues with a certain dark lord illegally crossing the borders and killing my demons in France. What are you going to do about it?"

"We are aware of the matter and he is under investigation."

"In other words, nothing, as usual," Belial said.

"We can only intervene when a crime has been committed," Adeyemi reminded him. "If this dark lord has murdered demons for no reason, he will be prosecuted for violating our peace treaty."

"And what about the major demons that were murdered?" Belial asked.

"Once again, it was not our doing. No one among us has the power to kill a major demon, and certainly not our dark lord."

"Oh, I can think of a few people on your side quite capable of it," Belial replied slyly.

"Are you accusing me?" Adeyemi asked in a dangerous voice.

"No, not you. You don't have it in you," the demon replied.

It sounded like an insult, but coming from him, it also meant that he, too, did not want a war between them.

"I only want to protect peace between our worlds," Adeyemi said, trying to contain himself. "And to prove it, I am willing to collaborate with you to find out who killed Beelzebub and Belphegor."

"Why would I collaborate with a bunch of incompetent, corrupted vampires in white robes who think themselves heavenly creatures because they received a title from the old man?" Belial said. "Open your eyes, Adeyemi. He doesn't care about any of you. You'll never even set foot in Heaven."

"I'm not doing this to go to Heaven. I do it to protect the balance of this world because I know He doesn't—not anymore."

"Well then, at least we agree on something," Belial said before hanging up.

Adeyemi slammed the receiver on the telephone. The old demon was insufferable, but at least he thought he had managed to convey his message to him. Belial talked big, but he was also old and wise, and he knew the head of the seraph would not lie to him, not about such important matters.

He got up and stretched, then walked over to the bedroom and lay beside his Zahra. She was waiting for him and curled up in his arms.

"I'm starved…" he said, breathing in the sweet and pure scent of her long hair.

"Come inside me… inside my mind," she said, caressing his face with her slender hands.

His yellow eyes began to glow, and he pulled her closer.

Yvan traveled back to his castle in the countryside, near Portsmouth. He needed the peace and quiet of his solitary life there, with only the presence of his human manservant, to escape the temptations of London. In his long life, he had found that cities, especially big cities, corrupted people's minds, and it was much easier to remain pure in a remote location, where interactions with others were few and far apart.

The table was set for one in the long dining room of his Medieval castle, and his manservant had left for him a dish of cold meats and a bottle of deer blood, his favorite. The Order permitted creatures of the underworld to feed on what was natural for them, of course, and he was allowed to hunt humans, but he much preferred to stay away from them and was contented with animal blood. It was something that made him feel a little less 'soiled'. He sat at the table and reflected on the days of old, his tormented life as a human, and his even more tormented life as a vampire thereafter. Prayer, sacrifice, abstinence, nothing was able to cure him in the end. He had become what God saw in him: a monster. And if an eternity of devotion to Him, burning witches and soon-to-be vampires and werewolves was not enough, then there was only one thing he could do to change his condition—and Florian's. But the man he had loved, murdered, and transformed without knowing it into his eternal vampire servant, had lost his mind. He would be of no help. Worse, he was getting in his way now.

He was not surprised to see him appear out of thin air at the other end of the dining table. Nothing surprised him anymore with him. The candyman was not capable of teleportation like some demons or becoming invisible like Stanley, rather, he was a master of disguise and cheap magical tricks.

"Good evening," he said.

That night he had adopted the figure of Belphegor once more, as to nag him.

"What do you want?" Yvan asked coldly.

The candyman relaxed in his chair and put his legs up on the table. He began to whistle.

"Nice tapestries," he remarked, gazing at the long tapestries on the walls depicting ancient Viking battle scenes.

"If you have nothing important to tell me, then please leave," Yvan said.

The candyman turned to him and grinned.

"Don't you want to know who killed Belphegor and stole the Time key?" he asked.

Yvan put down his glass of deer blood and glared at him.

"I know you did it. What I don't understand is why," he said. "With the Time Key, I could fix you. I could prevent that accident from ever happening."

The candyman laughed and got up, then he lost his smile. He stared at Yvan coldly.

"Fix me?" he said. "No Yvan, you can't 'fix' me. And you can't fix yourself, because we're not broken. What happened to my face was not an accident, as you like to remember it, but the expression of your hatred of what we are."

Yvan did not answer. The candyman walked slowly over to him, his hands in his pockets and his cruel eyes still fixed on his.

"But you know what? That little gift you left me—your immortality and some of your powers—I quite like it," he then said, leaning over him.

Yvan suddenly moved as to grab him, but the candyman had already vanished. He reappeared in another chair, chewing on a piece of barley sugar.

"Life, death, life, death, just a matter of... How... Hard... I... Crush... You," he sang to himself, raising his arm toward the chandelier. He closed his fist, and the chandelier exploded.

"Get out of here! Now!" Yvan shouted.

He grabbed the bottle of deer blood and hurled it at him, but the candyman once again disappeared, laughing. And Yvan stood there, furious and breathing hard. Florian would never leave him alone, he would continue haunting him for all eternity and prevent him from finding the Time Key. He was sure he had killed at least Belphegor, but he did not know how. A sired vampire like him was not capable of it. There had to be someone else pulling the strings, someone powerful like Adeyemi.

Eve knew she had to return to Paris soon. She could not leave her shop for weeks at a time, and she had lectures scheduled next month. Her life was very busy, as she had wanted it, so why was she spending so much time here, in this small city, letting a demon court her and dote on her? Even she did not know. Perhaps because it was better than nothing. Because, once her herbalist shop closed at night, once Cecile and Florentine left, once the lectures were over, she was alone. She did not need a man—she fared much better without them—but she needed someone she could share her life with, share the laughter, the hopes, and, more often, the sadness and grief that came with eternity. For a few years, Emily had been that person, but she was overwhelming, clingy, and, at times, suffocating. She was also a very lonely person, perhaps more so than Eve, and Eve was sad about their fallout. She had tried to reach out to her, but Emily also had her pride, and for her their friendship was over.

Eve looked down at the silk purse she was holding on her lap as she sat on a bench in the Botanical Garden, a quiet place for a solitary soul like herself at night. Her hands in black lace gloves seemed to belong to someone else. She was petite and slender and she 'passed' better than any of those bitches in Emily's circle, but she still had the same insecurities about her body she'd had all her life. She never let anyone see her completely naked because if she removed her corset, they would see what she was missing to be a true woman. She had come to the meetings at first to see what they were about, but the other girls immediately formed their own clique, rejecting her. And the way they supported each other made her long to be a part of their group, but the more she showed up, the more she was rejected. Charlotte did not like her past as a courtesan, Yvette did not like her attitude, Valerie thought her vain and arrogant, and even Berenice, the quietest among them, avoided her like she was contagious. Apart from them, there was Emily, who still would not talk to her but probably talked about her behind her back, Hans, who now had eyes only for Mischa, and that rude, skinny, always frowning Englishman who seemed bored out of his mind, and like he only ever showed up to see Emily. But Eve did not need any of them. She had Astaroth.

At first, when the demon approached her, she was suspicious of him. She knew very little about his kind, only that they signed pacts with people, and he was honest and upfront about it and the fact that he kept a 'harem'. He even told her how many people were part of it. But he was also a sensitive man who felt rejected among his peers after having transitioned into a man through magic. He truly loved every single transgender person he formed a pact with, only because he knew how lonely they were he could not limit his love to one person. He wanted to give his love to all of them and protect them, since no one else did. He never lied to her. Emily had also been his lover, but they broke up. And now he wanted to add Eve to his 'harem', where she would be loved and cared for. She would be his queen, only she had to share that pedestal with other kings and queens. It was not such a bad proposal. Plus, he could give her the one thing she had always desired: a female body.

It was almost time for her to make up her mind. He had asked her to answer him soon, because he would be busy during the next few weeks with other—demonic—business. Eve sighed and closed her eyes. What did she have to lose, anyway? Her freedom? Astaroth didn't imprison anyone; his lovers were free. He had introduced her to Adriana, whom he had successfully transformed, so she could see the results for herself. Adriana was doing quite well now; she was a popular actress and earned a lot of money. She toured Europe but returned to her 'king' whenever she could. All Eve had to do to be like her was make a pact with Astaroth and agree to be loved only by him for all eternity. He was not the person who could share her life and be there for her every day and night—he was far too busy, between his official function in Hell and his side job as a demonic accountant—he was the man who warmed her heart and body at night, when she felt lonely, but it was more than what she had ever had with men. After over a hundred years of passing from one man's bed to another, from disappointment to disappointment, wasn't it time to settle for something at least? Even if only for those reasons, she ought to settle for someone stable and honest like him, but on top of that, he could make her dreams come true. So why did she still hesitate?

The image of Nicolas came back to her, telling her again there was nothing for her in the world outside his castle, that she would never be anything and that people—normal people—would hate her and hurt her. It was not true. Not only those people hurt her but also those like her. There was no place for her in this world, not in this body. If she refused the transformation offered to her, all she would ever be was Eve, the herbalist, public speaker, occasional courtesan, and whatever other solitary profession she might pursue. Her human friends could never know who she truly was, and she would have to disappear every twenty years to protect her secret.

"You were right, Nicolas, there is no place for me out here except on my lonely pedestal," she whispered.

She suddenly felt invisible arms wrap around her. Not Nicolas' arms—these were the tiny arms of a child. She turned around, surprised, and sensed a ghost child beside her. He appeared to have had curly black hair in his human life, and his clothes were from the last century. He was barely visible to her eyes, if not for the blue halo surrounding him. He hugged her tightly, as though he could feel her pain. She slipped her arm around his shoulders and pulled him closer.

"Are you lost, little one?" she asked him in French, but he looked up to her like he did not understand.

"Are you a foreign little ghost?" she said with a tender smile. "Sei Italiano? English?"

The little ghost nodded to that last one. Who ever knew she would need to know all these languages to speak to a child ghost someday?

"My name is Eve. What's your name?" she asked him.

"Cornelius," he said.

She froze for a second. He couldn't be…

"I came to France to find you!" Cornelius then said, clinging to her even harder.

"Wait… what? Are you Ernest's Cornelius?" she said in shock.

She then remembered that he had dropped off flowers at her shop in Paris, so it made sense that Cornelius would be in France, too.

"Is he here, in Rouen?" she asked, frowning.

Cornelius shook his head and she relaxed.

"Listen, Cornelius…"

"No, you listen to me!" he cried. "The letter you received from him was not true! That's why he came to France, to tell you!"

She sighed and ran her fingers through his curly hair.

"He cried so much when you stopped writing him," the child ghost continued. "He didn't know why you stopped writing him, and then he had a dream and saw the letter. It was not the one he sent you!"

"If he did not write it, then who did?" she asked, frowning.

Emily was the one who had delivered the letter to her, but she was so excited about their romance it could not possibly be her doing. Furthermore, if she had tampered with it, then why sneak into her room to read it? It did not make sense.

"We don't know, but you must believe him! Please!" Cornelius begged her.

"Cornelius..." she said in a soothing voice. "Even if he did not write that letter, we could not have been together."

"Why?" Cornelius asked, his little eyes filling with tears.

Eve lowered her gaze.

"Because... I don't want to be here, in this world, as a vampire, as... me," she whispered.

"Do you mean you want to be human again?" he asked.

She shook her head.

"I just want... to never have been born at all, not in this body," she said. "As long as I'm stuck in it, I can never truly live in this world. I will always be some outcast in the shadows..."

"I don't understand..." Cornelius said, shifting uncomfortably beside her. "Why does it matter?"

"It does, in the world of adults," she said.

A tear rolled down the child ghost's cold little cheeks now, then another.

"Oh Cornelius, I'm sorry. I didn't mean to make you cry..." she said.

She pulled him in her arms and hugged him, and he began to weep loudly—though no human ears could hear him.

"I wanted you to be my mum, and to be happy with my big brother!" he wept like the brokenhearted seven-year-old he was. "Why is it so complicated? You can just love each other and be happy..."

"I'm sorry..." she repeated, but her words could not stop his tears.

In his young mind, he had already pictured the three of them as a family, as the home he perhaps did not have as a human or lost when he died, and the loss of her meant that his dream of a home was destroyed. She, the one he had chosen to be his new mother, was abandoning him, and it broke her heart, too. She never imagined there was a little child out there who hoped to be loved by her. Of course she believed his words—she wanted to believe them—but she was not ready to make peace with Ernest and pick up where they left off. She did not want to open her heart to him again and risk being hurt. He obviously still wanted her, and perhaps she wanted him, but she no longer wanted love, and it would be unfair of her to lead him on.

Stanley walked anxiously across the town center plaza, looking all around him.

"Where did that brat go? I swear, when I find him, I will exorcise him!" he muttered in an angry voice.

Cornelius was being moody that night, and he had escaped him, saying he was going to go find Eve and tell her everything. Luckily, neither of them knew where she was staying while in Rouen. Still, Stanley could not risk him doing something stupid and possibly blowing his cover by telling her more than what she needed to know. Why did he have to be stuck for all eternity with such a brat?

He heard some noise in an alleyway and turned into it. It was a dark passage between houses leading to another street. As a precaution, he made himself invisible. There was someone at the end of the alley, hiding in a door frame. But as he moved closer, he realized there were actually two adults—vampires—and one was biting the other's neck. Strange. But his eyes opened wide with shock when he saw the one leaning against the door, moaning softly as the other—a blond young man—amorously bit him. It was Joseph Stein. Well, apparently he had not gone to the Americas after all, and he had recovered from the loss of his Alice, but what were they doing? It did not look like the blond was killing him. Stanley then remembered how the Order had warned him about biting his peers because it was their way of mating. Great. Did they really have to do it in a public place like this? He turned around, blushing, and walked away.

He made himself visible when he reached the street and mingled with the crowd there. The September weather was nice and shops and cafes remained open late, and many humans, demons, and vampires were out enjoying themselves. Since he had no clue where to even start looking for a ghost who could fly through the walls of houses and might just be hiding in any of them, Stanley decided to kill time by walking around.

A circus was installed on the plaza. Under a large tent, acrobats, jugglers, and clowns were likely performing, and the crowd cheered them loudly. All around the plaza, in cage wagons, were tigers, lions, monkeys, and even an elephant. Stanley had never seen those animals in real life, so he walked around the plaza slowly. Why did he never do such simple things as visiting a circus menagerie, or going to a concert or a theater play? Perhaps because he had spent his childhood locked up at home and it never occurred to him there were things he could do outside. Even now that he had left that human life behind, he did not know how to do anything but work. He did not know how to *have fun*. It made him a little sad, but what could he do about it now? People did not change as adults.

As he was absorbed in his melancholy, he did not hear the light footsteps creeping up behind him.

Ever since that first meeting he attended, or perhaps since he walked into her flower shop, Emily had longed for the sweet magician who played his tricks on her heart. He was guarded and cynical, but underneath the façade she could see what a kind, innocent man he was, and she wanted to see him again and again, and let his cool warmth fill her world and bring it back to life. There was no other woman in the picture and the girls at the meetings preferred the friendly, optimistic Hans to this brooding old young man, so for once she actually had a chance with him. She did not know where the new object of her affection stayed in town, so she had gone out every night, hoping to see him. If he was a 'normal' vampire, unlike her, he had to hunt. So on the nights when she did not get to see him at her meetings, she swept the empty streets and dark alleyways in search of him, and every time she set out with a heart full of hope but came home disappointed. This Stanley was basically invisible—to his kind at least—unless he decided that he wanted to be seen.

But that night, she saw him on the town center plaza. She couldn't believe it at first. She blinked and looked again. It was him. He was standing alone, looking at one of the circus cage wagons, and he did not seem to be enjoying himself. Still, her heart began to race with excitement as she spotted him.

She quietly crept up behind him, her young maiden heart swelling with joy, and she was about to call his name when she heard him mumbling to himself.

"Why did I even come here? For a girl who called me an ass and is sleeping with someone else anyway?" he grunted, and Emily instantly knew who he was talking about.

She lost her smile and all the joy, the hopes that had filled her heart, vanished at once. She had thought there was something between them, but she was wrong again. That blooming love was only blooming in her heart, not his. He was already involved with Eve. It was for her he came to the meetings, and she was the one constantly on his mind. Emily's throat tightened and her eyes filled with tears as she felt her dreams being torn away from her.

"Seems like he didn't like you after all," the voice in her head said in a mocking tone.

She wiped away a tear and turned away.

"Are you really going to give up without a fight?" it whispered.

"How can I fight? I'm not Eve…" she whispered miserably.

"If you always play fair, then you will never win. But do you think he has been fair with you? He lied to you," the voice said.

"You mean I'm not beautiful?" she said, suddenly anxious.

"You're fat and ugly," the voice said. *"You'll never win over Eve with your charms, but this man's heart is weak. Put yourself in danger, show him that you need him, flatter his male ego by letting him rescue you and he will certainly prefer you over a loud, rude woman who doesn't need him."*

"You think so?" she said.

She gazed around her. There were many cage wagons with exotic animals, but one of them was covered up. On the side were painted the words 'The Chimera of Nightmares' and 'Viktor'. Probably some poor circus freak, exploited by his owners, who never even saw a penny of the money they made showing him off. What if she not only set him free, but also used him to her advantage?

The world around her suddenly flipped into her reality. Everything was in slow motion. The colors of people's clothes had faded, and so had the smiles on their faces disappeared. The air was cold, and the sky was no longer clear. A gentle, cold rain was falling all around her. She walked assuredly in this city in ruins among the people with long faces that seemed to roam aimlessly and slipped behind the cage wagon. She peeked inside through the barred door on the back and saw someone like her, except younger. Viktor was probably thirteen or fourteen, a child with lifeless eyes, curled up on a blanket. How sad. He did not even have a jack-in-the-box to entertain him… She lowered her gaze and saw her reflection in a puddle of water by her feet. She was the little girl she always should have been, slender, feminine, sweet, but this world had cut off her beautiful blond hair, and because they all laughed at her, her face was painted like a clown. She raised her left hand and it disappeared in the mist and reappeared beside the man in a tall hat and a striped suit who was talking in slow motion before the sorrowful crowd. It took the key ring fastened to his belt, and now she had the keys.

Viktor stirred and slowly got up as he heard some noise. He looked around his cage and noticed a toy. He did not have toys. Clad only in the torn blue robe his masters made him wear for his act, all he had in this world were a blanket and a pillow. They had even cut off his long hair because it was just too complicated to explain to a crowd how a girl child could transform into such a monster, so they said he was a boy. But he did not mind, because that was how he identified most of the time.

Since he had not seen many toys in his life, he did not know what the red ball rolling toward him might be. He picked it up in his scarred hand and looked at it.

"Do you want to play, Viktor?" a little girl's voice said outside.

A jack-in-the-box head suddenly came out of the red ball, startling him. His lips then parted into a grin, grayish blue fur began to grow on his cheeks, his hands, and his arms, and two horns came out of his forehead. He grabbed the jack-in-the-box head and *ate* it.

"No! Don't eat that!" the girl said.

"I'll eat you too…" he answered.

"Really? Then come and get me…" she replied.

The key ring fell onto the floor of the cage, and Viktor took it.

There was only so much to see of an elephant. It was an elephant. Once again, Stanley did not understand what was so interesting about the animal, except that it, too, looked sad and bored.

"And now, ladies and gentlemen, let me tell you about the most fearsome monster I have ever seen!" a man in a fancy suit told a crowd.

He was presenting a freak show. Stanley walked over to him and listened. It had to be more interesting than watching the poor elephant in his cage.

"This savage child was found by explorers in Russia, deep in the Ural mountains. On a stormy night, a blizzard suddenly came, and a great explorer and his team had no choice but to take shelter in a cave, and what they found there was terrifying. At first, they stepped on bones, and stopped to examine them. They were human remains…"

The crowd held their breath, but not Stanley. So what? They found a mass grave. Big deal.

"The explorers decided to venture further, armed with their rifles," he continued. "In the depths of the cave, they expected to find a bear, but what they found instead defied all the laws of nature. At first, they thought they had found a human child, but as they approached him, his body covered with fur, and he grew the horns of a demon. And suddenly he attacked them with the savagery of a lion, ripping off heads and limbs. It took all the strength of the three remaining men to capture this beast and bring it back to civilization!"

There were cries of surprise and terror among the men and women, but some were also laughing. They did not believe his story, much less in demons. But Stanley's curiosity was piqued.

"Ladies and gentlemen, I present to you... Viktor, the demon child!" the man said, and he pulled the heavy cloth covering the cage wagon behind him, but the wagon was empty and the back door open.

"What?" he said, surprised.

The crowd erupted in laughter and booed him, but a woman suddenly shrieked. Stanley recognized her voice. It was Emily. His eyes then moved to the top of the wagon, where a demon-like creature, all covered in a grayish blue fur, had appeared. His forearms and hands were larger than a human's—more like those of a gorilla—but he otherwise had the proportions of a child of about twelve to fourteen. Because of the horns on his head, Stanley assumed he was a demon, but he had never seen one like him before. The boy let out a loud snarl, and the crowd screamed and scrambled. He then jumped off the wagon and went after Emily.

"Shit! Emily!" Stanley said.

He tried to push his way through the crowd, but they were too numerous and agitated, so he slowed down time and made himself invisible to go after the two of them. He followed them, at a distance first, through dark alleyways between the buildings, but the careless Emily led the creature into an abandoned factory. What was she thinking? That she could hide there? Luckily, he quickly caught up to them and entered the factory. He found Emily standing in a vast room littered with steel beams and rods, nails, and old wooden crates that were falling apart. The dim light from the streetlights outside came in through the dirty, broken windows, creating a gloomy yellow atmosphere, and the air smelled like dust and spilled chemicals. She stood there like a frightened child, looking around her. As he approached her, though, he realized that not only time had slowed down around him—that was his doing—but the reality was also different. Another reality created by this demon? Whatever, he was used to their tricks. He moved in between Emily and the creature before making himself visible again, and only for a split second, instead of the rosy-cheeked, curvy young woman he was used to, he thought he saw the puppet or clown girl who had murdered Aleksandra. But reality and time returned to normal, and Emily was standing before him again. She let out a small cry of surprise and covered her mouth as he appeared, but there was no time to explain things to her. He turned around to face 'Viktor'. But, to his surprise, the boy did not attack. Like a frightened animal, he crouched and backed up against the wall, snarling.

"Stanley! He's dangerous!" Emily said, grabbing his arm.

"Emily, I need you to be quiet and do as I say, and whatever you do, don't look into my eyes," he told her, his eyes focused on the monster. She nodded.

He was not sure what he could do. This demon child had not attacked anyone—yet. Could he really kill a child just for being hairy and snarling? But returning him to his masters seemed just as cruel. He could always flip reality and trap him under one of the heavy wooden crates around them... And then what?

"I just wanted that toy..." Viktor then said in a small voice.

Stanley was surprised to hear him talking. He was not feral at all, just hairy.

His vision was already flickering as he prepared to protect Emily, but it returned to normal as the threat subsided. And as he calmed down, so did Viktor's fur begin to retreat into his skin, and his horns, until he just looked like an ordinary child in rags.

"You're… human?" Stanley said, surprised.

Viktor stared at him with frightened eyes.

"Stanley, he's not human! He's going to hurt us!" Emily whispered by his side.

"No, he's not," Stanley said.

He took a step forward, and the child snarled again.

"You're not in any danger," Stanley told him.

He had more experience talking with ghosts than children, but he was used to dealing with frightened creatures of the underworld. He squatted and reached out to him, but the child seemed even more frightened. He suddenly leapt high above both of them and ran out the door.

"Wait!" Stanley said, but he was already gone.

He would have to let Belial know about him. If anything, he was probably a half-demon or something like that, and his place was not in a cage, but with others like him.

Emily grabbed his arm again and squeezed it.

"Oh, I was so scared!" she said.

He turned to her, only now remembering what he had seen, and he again sensed that same presence around her.

"Emily…" he said.

"Yes?" she said, looking up at him.

"No, it's nothing," he said.

CHAPTER 12

"INTERESTING," BELIAL SAID, SCRATCHING his goatee.

This time, they were sitting in a large teacup on a carousel in some European city. The demon took Stanley to so many places he had lost track of them, only this one was colder than Rouen, so it was probably up north. Norway?

"And then he turned back into a human child and leapt over us and disappeared," Stanley said.

"Of course, a half-demon would be able to do that, and I will send my demons out to find him and assign him to the appropriate coven," Belial said. "I meant the fact that you think you saw Emily as that puppet assassin in some alternate reality."

"But I see all sorts of things in alternate realities, and most of them are not true," Stanley pointed out.

"But some are," Belial said.

Stanley refused to believe that Emily and the assassin were one and the same. Emily was so sweet and… ordinary. He hated himself for thinking that, but there truly was nothing special about her, apart from her being a vampire. She was not unique in her character or tastes, she was rather discreet and did not draw any attention to her. Furthermore, Emily was biologically male, and the assassin was clearly female-bodied.

"Why would Emily kill an archangel? What could an ordinary vampire gain from murdering the people overseeing them? It's not like she might ever be a candidate to join the Order," he said, a frown on his face.

"This is why I believe there is a 'puppet master' behind the murder," Belial said. "Unfortunately, an urgent matter will keep me busy for the next few weeks, so I will not be able to meet up with you. Continue watching Astaroth and do let me know if he looks like he is making a move."

Stanley leaned back and crossed his arms.

"Apart from making a move on my girl, so far, he hasn't done anything. I'm beginning to think this is like that bogus investigation Yvan Thompson asked me to conduct," he said, annoyed.

"It's not," Belial said very seriously. "I've noticed a change in Astaroth's behavior a century or so ago. Demons are not immortal, but we live a very long time, so of course we can change. But documents related to his function started going missing, then objects, like the Time Key—although we now know who stole it and for what purpose—and then a major demon was murdered. I have sometimes wondered whether Astaroth is actually an impostor, someone pretending to be him in order to use his powers."

"The candyman?" Stanley immediately said.

"Unless he is a major demon himself, he could not even unlock the gates of Hell to access the items that went missing," Belial said.

"He didn't have to. Remember how Beelzebub and Belphegor let Callie steal the Time Key and use it to lure me to them?"

"True…"

"What if the candyman worked for Astaroth? Perhaps Astaroth hired him to murder Belphegor and steal the Time Key."

"It wouldn't make sense," Belial said. "If Astaroth is actually an impostor who has successfully taken his place, then why would he steal the Time Key? He is the overseer of the Gate-keeper; he has access to it whenever he wants. Furthermore, if he might benefit from the murder of Beelzebub, the murder of Aleksandra does nothing for him."

Stanley lowered his eyes and reflected for a moment.

"So we have someone—or perhaps a group of people—conspiring against the order of angels and the order of demons at the same time. Who would benefit from both orders being eradicated?" he asked.

"I honestly have no clue. The members of both orders know what would happen if they disappeared," Belial said.

"The end of the world?"

"Of the world you know, yes. I cannot even begin to describe the chaos of a world where there are no boundaries between the world of the living and the world of the dead."

"Like my upside-down reality?" Stanley said, smirking.

"Except you would have no control over it," Belial said.

Pictures of the other alternate reality he had seen around Emily then came back to his mind.

"Is anyone else capable of creating an alternate reality?" he asked.

"A handful of creatures of the underworld," the demon said.

"Any names?"

Belial frowned and scratched his goatee again pensively.

"I would not know. That is not my expertise. I usually rely on Astaroth to identify the most powerful beings in the underworld. We don't care about their existence; we just prefer to know about them in case one of them starts causing trouble."

"So, supposing Astaroth is actually the real Astaroth, if Emily had such powers, wouldn't he be interested in her rather than in spiritual vampires like Eve? I just don't understand," Stanley said.

"Unless his goal is not to upset both worlds," Belial said. "What if... what if there were actually several conspiracies going on at the same time?"

"Oh, several conspiracies... I like it," Stanley said with interest.

"You're not going to like it so much if we can't stop them," Belial said, raising an eyebrow.

"Hey, I'm just your joker card. You're supposed to be the brain," Stanley reminded him.

Belial leaned back and let out a deep sigh.

"I think the brain needs a vacation at this point... But it won't be getting one for a while."

Stanley laughed.

"Well, if you ever want a *real* getaway, I can send you to my upside-down reality," he said.

"Thanks, I'll think about it," the demon said, grinning.

So they were almost back to the beginning, without a clue what Astaroth was doing—or trying to do—but the possibility of another or several other conspiracies going on at the same time. The only new information on the table was that Emily was likely connected to the puppet master and his or her assassin, but she did not seem to know about it. He could try calling Cat again, but would a sìth know what even the King of Hell did not? It was unlikely.

Stanley was tired of being in France. It had been almost a month and he wanted to go home and hide in his house with Cornelius, but Yvan would never let him set foot in England again. He would have to live in exile from now on, in places like this. If he was not sad and angry enough, a new and different sort of melancholy settled in his heart over the loss of the place he called 'home'. Unable to drag his feet up to Emily's apartment for the meeting that night, he sat down on a bench and cradled his head in his hands. He never brought Cornelius to these meetings, just in case Astaroth could see him, but he needed him right now, so much… Since the street was empty and it would still be a long time before anyone else arrived, he let out a few quiet tears, until he smelled someone's lavender cologne very close to him. A gentle hand dropped on his shoulder, startling him, and he looked up, only to find Eve standing by his side. She had crept up on him again without him seeing or even noticing her. Or perhaps he was just distracted that night.

"What's going on?" she asked him with sincere concern.

It was the first time she spoke to him kindly, and it caught him off guard. She was so close to him that he could breathe in her sweet vampire scent under the cologne. It smelled like summertime and games, with musky, exotic floral notes, like she was a creature from some enchanted Paradise. All he wanted was to pull her into his embrace and bury his head in the folds of her dress, but he could, of course, not do such a thing. He did not want to experience her scorn once more. So, he remained there, speechless, fighting the urge to touch her, and more tears rolled down his cheeks. He wiped them away, shook his head, and said: "Nothing."

She sat down on the bench beside him, closer than they had ever been. He was inside her space now, in her aura, and it was warm and benevolent. He could almost see that same green halo forming around her now.

"I'm sorry for the way I talked to you the first time we met; I was just…" she said in a sad voice.

"Legitimately offended, I understand," he said. "I really did come off as a misogynistic, patronizing ass. I should have minded my own business."

"I've been practicing that word, you know," she said with a soft smile. "*Ahse, oahse…*" she then said, trying to replicate his accent, and he laughed.

"It's *arse*," he said.

"*Ahse…*" she repeated, and they laughed together. "Alright, next time I will just say *derriere*."

"*Derr… rr…* Ah, I can't say that one!" he said, and they laughed even more.

"You look like you're carrying the weight of the entire world on your shoulders," she then said in a soft voice. "Would you like to share some of that burden with me?"

He lost his smile and pursed his lips.

"I'm afraid I cannot, for your own safety, but I appreciate your concern."

She moved her gaze to the tall building before them, in which Emily was probably preparing snacks for everyone. There was light in her apartment. She was working hard behind the scenes, as usual, and she would be ignored.

"I came early, hoping to talk with Emily and make things right again, but now I don't feel so brave," Eve said.

"Make things right?"

"We used to be close friends. It was so good to have a friend who resembled me. But I was not able to protect our friendship."

"Did you have an argument?"

"She was becoming suffocating—or so I thought," she said. "I've lived alone for so long in a world that thinks of me as a monster… perhaps I forgot how to deal with having real people in my life."

Her eyes welled up with tears as she spoke, but she drew in a deep breath and held them back.

"I'm rather solitary myself, so I can understand," he said.

Silent minutes passed, and Stanley did not want their conversation to end—ever. But he did not know what to say anymore. Then they spoke at the same time: "If you want..."

"Go ahead," Eve said, but because she had caught him off guard, he knew he was going to stutter.

"I... I..." he stammered.

He closed his eyes and tried to focus on his speech again.

"Do you suffer from asthma?" she asked.

"N-No... I stutter... Just a moment," he said.

He drew in a deep breath.

"I'm alright now," he said.

"Is that why you hold your breath a little before saying each sentence? Because you stutter?" she asked.

"I suppose so. I never noticed," he said. "It doesn't happen too often anymore, but if you startle me, it might."

"Then I will try not to surprise you," she said, smiling.

This could not be real, it had to be a dream. Not only was Stanley sitting next to Eve, but she was being kind to him, like she was as his pen friend. Or perhaps this was the Eve he knew coming back to life. He refused to believe it was because of him, it had to be something else, but still he was grateful even for these few priceless minutes spent with her.

He felt something warming up in his chest and moving, and he remembered the rose Cat had placed inside him in his dream. Was it real, after all? If it was, it wanted to come out now, but he did not want it to, so he covered his chest with his hands.

"By the way, what was your name? I'm sorry, I've met so many new people lately, I may have forgotten," she said.

"My name is Stanley," he said, turning to her with a polite smile.

His chest grew cold again. He was just a stranger to her, whose name she did not even remember.

"And I'm…" she said, but he cut her: "Eve."

She stared into his eyes, surprised, then broke into a faint smile.

"Stanley… I will remember your name this time."

"Hopefully in a good way," he said.

A small red ball then came rolling down the street, seemingly out of nowhere, and hit Eve's foot.

"Oh! What's this?" she said.

She was about to pick it up, but Stanley caught her hand.

"Don't touch it," he said in a whisper.

"Why?" she asked, but as she gazed into his eyes, she saw the fear and danger in them.

"Eve, I want you to get up slowly, and I will put a stone against the ball as you remove your foot from it. Then I need you to get inside that building. Go straight to Emily's apartment and make sure she's alright," he said, looking around them.

"What? Is she in danger?" she whispered.

"I hope not," he said.

They both slowly got up and Stanley grabbed a stone and slipped it against the red ball, where Eve's foot had been. She removed her foot, also looking around them, but she could see no one. With gestures of his hands, he told her to get inside quickly, and he watched her until she entered the building. Then, he switched into his invisible mode, both to protect himself and to see the unseen. He scouted the area again: no one. But the breeze carried to him the scent of candy. The candyman? This was not his operating method…

A child then came running down the street. He appeared to be an ordinary—human—middle-class child, and he wore one of the white and blue sailor suits popular for children in those days. He was the one who brought with him the scent of candy.

He picked up the ball, laughing, and ran back to wherever he came from without ever seeing Stanley.

Perhaps it was nothing after all, just a child who had lost his toy… alone… after dark. Stanley frowned and looked around him again. Was this a warning that someone was watching him and Eve? He made himself visible again and was about to enter the building himself when he thought he saw Emily from the corner of his eye, standing behind a lamppost.

"Emily?" he said, but no one answered.

He shrugged and went inside and up to her apartment. She immediately opened the door when he knocked and let him in. Eve was sitting alone in the dining room and looking sad again. Apparently Emily and she still weren't on speaking terms.

"Stanley! You're early!" Emily said happily.

"I just came to see if I could help out," he said pleasantly. "Why don't you let me take care of – whatever you were doing—and you go and keep Eve company?"

She lost her smile at once.

"I'd rather you help me in the kitchen, if you don't mind," she said.

"Of course."

He was not sure how his clumsy self could help her, but he could not force her to speak to Eve if she did not want to, so he followed her into the kitchen and helped her set out glasses for wine and many varieties of vampire-friendly and demon-friendly snacks she had prepared with love, and that people would devour without ever thanking her.

"Emily… thank you for your hard work," he told her as she finished putting together the last tray, and she smiled and blushed.

Guests began to flock in a few minutes later—new faces and old ones—and some of the new girls even made conversation with Eve. *Good. No battle royal tonight*, Stanley thought. But he realized he had grown fond of these meetings, even if he did not like most of the people. They were like a family, with all their differences and disagreements, but they still showed up and put up with each other because they had something in common.

Hans showed up, rosy-cheeked and excited, and Mischa, his counterpart, followed him inside. Hans was definitely in love, Stanley could tell, but Mischa's expression remained mostly the same as usual, except for an occasional smile now and then. Good. At least Stanley no longer had to worry about that pretty boy making another move on his girl.

He retreated to his usual corner and leaned against the wall, his arms crossed, until he sensed the presence of another one like him—a necromancer. *Oh shit*, he thought. He was hoping for a quiet evening for once. But if this one was like his father, then this would end up in a duel and probably with the stranger's death.

Emily opened the door and a blond boy in his twenties with a freckled face walked in. He wore an expensive and perfectly tailored gray pinstripe suit with a blue vest and a charcoal gray tie. He looked like he owned a wardrobe full of luxury brands but had rather plain taste himself and did not know how to make his tie match the rest of his outfit. His hair was wet and messy, as though he thought his good looks spared him the use of a comb after bathing. *Prick*, Stanley thought. But the one who walked in after him made him nervous. It was *him* again, Joseph Stein, the necromancer. With his curly black hair and big, intense black eyes, he still had the romantic face of a twenty-something, but Stanley knew he was much older than that. The pretty boy he came in with was the one Stanley had seen sucking on his neck in the streets the other night.

They were obviously mates, and, in their bizarre dynamic, the powerful necromancer completely yielded to his young mate. Joseph was not exactly dominant everyday life, but Stanley had caught a glimpse of his other, sadistic side, that could manifest when provoked. Did the boy with him know what he was getting himself into? But it was not what bothered Stanley—after all, they were adults and could suck on whoever's neck they wanted. It was the fact that another necromancer could be happy.

As he had expected, Joseph immediately noticed him in his corner and seemed worried, perhaps even frightened, but the blond by his side, who apparently had no clue what happened when two necromancers met, dragged him to Stanley.

"Hi, my name is Andre," he said cheerfully, stretching out his hand to Stanley, who stared at him, surprised and annoyed at the same time.

By his side, Joseph looked like he wanted to run and hide, and Stanley wanted to run away from both of them. There would be no duel tonight, as neither of them was feeling confrontational.

"That's Stanley, he's always like that," someone said.

Of course, the insufferable Hans had to jump in. Stanley had had enough and walked away, leaving the lovey-doveys with the goody-goody so they could all be friends in their pink fairy floss world while he moped alone about the misery of his life, thank you very much. He sat on a sofa and let out an exasperated sigh. He watched his love at a distance, who sat near Hans, the newcomers, and a few other faces Stanley knew. They all introduced themselves and their existential angst to the others. Nobody ever asked Stanley about his angst—not like he wanted to share it with anyone, anyway.

"And I was thrown out of home by my father at sixteen for wearing a dress," , the shapeshifter, said. "Well, not only was I transforming into a woman, but after I died and was reborn, I could also transform into a cat. A cute little cat."

Joseph and his partner laughed.

"My name is Andre, and I was born in America, in Tennessee, about eighty-five years ago," the pretty boy then said. "I ran away from my parents' farm to live as my true self but died soon afterwards. Then I awakened as a vampire and decided to pursue my dream career as a ballet dancer. I know other dances as well. Joe and I actually met when he came to one of my performances in New York."

Stanley cringed. He hated ballet and found it stupid. Wasn't there anything more interesting to do as a vampire than hop around on a stage in tights?

"So how long have you two been together?" Hans asked them.

"A few weeks," Andre said, while Joseph said: "Twenty-six days."

They turned and gazed at each other with starry eyes, one thinking how cute the other was, counting the days since they got together, and the other finding his mate's vagueness absolutely endearing through the rose-colored lens of love.

Those two won't last, Stanley thought, smirking. They were obviously on their honeymoon, spending someone's money in France—probably Joseph's—but they had very little in common, and when they came down from the heights of infatuation, they would probably end up hating each other.

"You two are just too cute!" Hans commented.

But because he liked to remain the center of attention and the pretty boy dancer Andre was almost stealing his crowd, he then proceeded to show off his knowledge of medical science.

He had even brought medical journals talking about transgender people and new surgeries some were attempting, and he passed them on to the lovey-dovey couple. The pair, who had no financial concerns, seemed very excited at the prospect.

Eve, who had been sitting there with her arms crossed and an angry look on her face, finally asked Joseph the question on everyone's mind: why had he joined their circle? He seemed puzzled, perhaps even frightened by her question. Mischa, usually a quiet member of the circle, then took Joseph's side and defended his presence as the partner of a transgender person, to which Eve replied that the intersex vampire was not really one of them either. Hans naturally intervened, and Stanley, who was as bored as usual, leaned forward, anticipating a fight. But Eve simply got up and left them. She walked over to him and sat heavily on the sofa, saying: "These goody-goodies are too much for me!"

Stanley was delighted. He would gladly have talked to her about anything in the world just to be near her and hear her sweet voice, but the fear of stuttering once again resurfaced in him. He cleared his throat.

"Which one? Doctor know-it-all, dapper boy, or his lovestruck Romeo?" he asked leaning over to her.

"Dapper boy is the most annoying one," she said.

"Right? Blond hair, angel face, millionaire lover all smitten over him, sucking on each other's necks in the streets… He makes me want to puke," he said, grimacing.

"On the streets? There are hotel rooms for that!" she said with a disgusted face, and they turned to each other and laughed.

"You're always so quiet… why do you come and just stay away from everyone?" she then asked, gazing at him intensely. He lowered his eyes and began to wring his hands nervously.

"I… uh…"

She returned her gaze to the other attendees and let out a soft sigh.

"Am I a horrible person?" she asked.

"Not at all. What makes you think that?" he asked.

"As I get older, I find it more and more difficult to get along with anyone," she said. "I don't hate Mischa, but I am a little upset that Hans would choose someone like them over me. And Joseph and Andre flaunting their love just make me jealous."

"Why?" he asked. "You wouldn't want someone like Hans or Andre anyway, right?"

"Of course, I just… envy them. I don't think I can ever be in love again," she said sadly.

"Have you ever been in love?" he dared to ask.

She closed her eyes, visibly pained.

"You heard them. I used to be a courtesan. Men paid me to love them. But there were two men I loved—or at least thought I loved. Both of them broke my heart," she said.

Stanley's chest felt tight. He knew he was probably the second one.

"Anyway, hopefully this will be my last night enduring this," she said.

"Your last night?" he said, suddenly worried.

She turned to him with shining eyes.

"Tonight, I will make a pact with Astaroth."

"What kind of pact?"

"He's going to transform me into a real woman."

Stanley stared at her, stunned. Of course he wanted her to have the body of her dreams and be happy, but he did not trust that a demon could give it to her—not for free.

Astaroth arrived a little late, and Stanley overheard him talking to Andre and the others about this fabulous transformation he offered, and several were interested. It all seemed very legitimate, and he offered his services like any other demon would. It was not a crime in their world. What his admirers did not know was that there was always a hidden clause with demons, something that was to their advantage. But what did he get by transforming transgender creatures of the underworld? His own loyal army? Belial could probably raise an army of demons ten times the size any of his enemies could. There was nothing Stanley could do, so he got up and took his hat.

"Are you leaving already?" Eve asked, turning curious eyes to him.

"I need some fresh air," he politely replied.

Trying not to draw too much attention, he quickly made for the door and left the meeting.

CHAPTER 13

STANLEY STEPPED OUT OF the apartment building and slipped his hands in his pockets. That night, the air was just a little colder, and he could already sense the coming of autumn. Was it all going to end like this, with Eve choosing Astaroth? But he heard footsteps behind him and turned around. She had followed him.

"Eve…" he said as she walked up to him.

"I also needed some fresh air," she said, but she did not look like all she wanted was a midnight stroll through the streets of Rouen. There was insecurity in her eyes—the insecurity of someone who was about to step into a new life and leave the old one behind.

"So, what was that thing earlier?" she asked as she started to walk beside him.

"Oh, that? It was nothing after all," he said.

His heart was racing again, because this short walk would probably be his last chance to talk to her and dissuade her from binding herself to the demon forever.

"You sure have amazing reflexes," she remarked. "Like a spy."

"I needed them in my former profession," he said.

"And what was that profession?"

He pursed his lips.

"Shall we walk through the graveyard? I like graveyards," he offered instead, and she smiled.

"Yes, I love graveyards and crypts," she said, and then she laughed to herself.

"What?" he asked.

"Hans once offered to walk me home, and I took him to a graveyard. He did not like it, or perhaps it was my sense of humor. Who knows?"

"What did you say?"

"I made a joke about penises," she said.

Stanley tried hard to suppress his laughter, but he couldn't.

"What?" she said.

"The poor, prim and proper Hans… It must have been too much for his virgin ears!" he said, and they laughed together again.

"I don't really know. I'm one of the people who would rather not have one…" she then said with a sigh.

"We aren't defined by what's between our legs. It's all here," Stanley said, pointing to his head. "Besides, I have a bigger one than Hans – mentally."

"Really? How big?" she asked, amused.

"Oh, the biggest one you've ever seen," he assured her, and she laughed again.

"Stanley, you really are… special," she said, and the way her cheeks turned slightly rosy when she talked to him was so endearing, he just wanted to grab her and kiss her right then and there.

They turned right and headed to the local graveyard. It was quiet at this hour, except for a few ghosts lingering near their graves or chatting with each other. Stanley tipped his hat politely as they walked by.

"Can you see them?" she asked, surprised.

"You can too?" he said.

"Not all of them, but I can sometimes see the aura of spirits," she said with some sadness. "Do you believe in magical creatures, too?"

"I do, and I have seen them," he said. "I'm a necromancer vampire."

"Really? I used to have a friend who was a paranormal investigator. He could also see ghosts," she then said, and she lowered her eyes.

Oh, why couldn't she guess what he was trying to tell her?

"So, when you make this pact with Astaroth, what does he obtain in exchange?" he asked, changing subjects.

"My eternal love," she said, and her voice did not carry any of the excitement of a young woman about to exchange eternal vows with a man.

"Do you love him?" he asked, and she shrugged.

"He seems to love me more than any other man I've had in my life."

"Demons are not monogamous. I heard they keep 'harems'," he warned her.

"I know. He was upfront about everything. He is a king with many kings and queens, and I, too, will become one of his queens," she said.

"I understand your desire to have the body of your dreams, but…" he tried to say, but she interrupted him.

"But you're not me."

They stopped and gazed into each other's eyes.

"Stanley, I appreciate your concern for me, but I am a grown-up woman," she said. "I've been arrested and beaten up for just existing. I've been everyone's fetish, their dirty little secret, away from their wives. Perhaps I don't love Astaroth… so what? Love has only made me miserable. I want more from this life; I want to be myself at last. And entering an uncommitted relationship with a demon to obtain it is what I want to do."

He lowered his gaze and took her hand.

"Please, Eve, listen to me. There is something I need to tell you."

"Yes?" she said.

Now was the only chance he would ever get to tell her about his feelings for her and the true reason for his presence here.

"I… I didn't come to France as a tourist," he said.

He looked into her eyes again and she seemed perfectly confused. But she let him hold her hand like a friend and she had not unleashed her powers on him. It was a good sign.

"I came to see you," he said.

"Are you… a fan of mine?" she asked, more and more confused.

"No, Eve, I'm… Ernest."

The look on her face went from confusion to shock to anger. She tried to remove her hand from his, but he wouldn't let her go.

"Please, you must listen to me," he begged her. "The letter you received was not from me, someone tampered with it!"

"Oh, right, like the other letters were not from you, 'Ernest' – or is it Stanley?" she said, furious.

She snatched her hand away from him.

"It's Stanley, and I did lie about my name, but not the rest. I just couldn't tell you what I did for a living!" he said.

"So you were never a paranormal investigator, and all the dreams I told you about and the tarot readings, all that was for nothing?"

"No! I truly was a paranormal investigator when I first wrote you!" he said.

She began to walk away, not wanting to hear anymore, but he followed her.

"It's just... My real name is Stanley Suspect, and it makes people laugh, so I thought Ernest would be better," he said. "And I was a paranormal investigator, then I started working as a hitman and I killed my own father, and he killed me, and I became a vampire!"

"You ought to stop now, because your story is only getting worse and worse," she said angrily.

"But it's the truth!" he said.

Since she would not listen, he grabbed her arm and made her stop.

"Eve, I came all the way to France to tell you that... that I love you! And you would be making a terrible mistake if you make a pact with a demon tonight," he said.

He did not know what to do anymore. It seemed like the more he said, the worse he made things. The thought of going back in time and starting this conversation over crossed his mind, but he was not able to focus enough to even attempt it. She gazed into his eyes and her eyes were like dangerous black flames now.

"You 'love' me?" she said. "You didn't even trust me enough to tell me your name! And now you want me to trust you and not make a pact with Astaroth? Why should I?"

"Because I made a pact with a demon, and she tricked me," he said. "And I had to make a pact with another, and he sent me here to observe you—not as a spy, but..."

She freed herself from his grip and took two steps back. Her body began to glow with a green halo again, and her ethereal form came out and shrieked loudly. Stanley took a step back.

"Eve, please..." he begged her.

"I've heard enough, Stanley, Ernest, or whoever you are!" she shouted. "You're nothing but a sick, lying stalker!"

"No, I would never…" he said.

"Get out of here! Now!" she shouted, and her spirit lunged at him.

He slowed down time and made himself invisible to avoid it. She seemed startled and looked around her. But, as she could no longer see him, she brought her spirit back inside her body and began to cry. The thought that he still mattered enough to her to make her cry warmed his heart, but watching her suffer was unbearable. He had broken her heart twice now. He wanted to reappear and console her, to get down on his knees before her and tell her again that he loved her, but she would probably not listen, so he retreated, and she ran away into the night.

He walked back to his hotel with a heavy heart and waited until he was in his room and had closed the door to let out the tears he had been holding back. He leaned back against the door and let himself fall to the ground, having not even the strength to stand anymore. Cornelius immediately came out of the wall and went to him.

"Stanley! What happened?" he cried in a panic.

But Stanley only grabbed him and squeezed him in his arms as he cried his heart out. Cornelius had no idea why he was crying, but still he wrapped his tiny arms around him, and when most of the tears had come out, Stanley let go of him and wiped his eyes.

"Did something happen with Eve?" Cornelius asked in a small voice.

He sat on the floor beside him, ready to console him with his ghostly hugs if he still needed it.

"She's decided… she's decided to make a pact with Astaroth," he said. "He will give her the body of her dreams, and in exchange, she must love him forever. I've lost her, Cornelius."

"But how can someone force themselves to love someone else forever?" Cornelius asked.

"Oh, the demon doesn't care whether she loves him or not. I'm sure he gets something else out of that pact. If only I knew what, I could have warned her, but I don't… I failed, Cornelius."

Cornelius lowered his eyes.

"The other day, I tried talking to her, and she could see me and hear me," he said. "I tried telling her that someone had changed the letter Ernest sent her and that she should talk to him, but she didn't want to. She said she was so sad in this body that, no matter what, she could not have been happy with Ernest…"

"We could have been… I would have loved her so much. I would have done everything in my power to make her every dream come true…" Stanley said, wiping away more tears. "But she's gone. She told me she was going to make that pact with Astaroth tonight. There's nothing I can do anymore… nothing."

"Why couldn't you just tell her the truth?" Cornelius asked him. "If you just told her that you loved her, then wouldn't she be happy? And if she was happy, she wouldn't have to force herself to love someone she doesn't love."

"It's not that simple, Cornelius, and I did try telling her, but she would not even listen," Stanley said.

He felt the rose moving in his chest again, and this time he let it come out. It appeared before them and he held it between his hands for a moment, then let it go, and it vanished.

"What was that?" Cornelius asked.

"The rose Cat gave me for my journey… It was useless after all," Stanley said. "Like my love for Eve. Everything was useless."

"Well, there is something you could do…" Cornelius said in a small voice.

"Cornelius…" Stanley said in a reproachful tone. He knew what he had in mind.

"But it wouldn't just be for you. If you reverse time and prevent this argument from happening, then Eve would not have to cry," Cornelius said.

"But I haven't really mastered the Time Key that well… what if I get sent back to the Middle Ages?" Stanley said, turning to him.

"You wouldn't. It would just be like rewinding a pocket watch a little," Cornelius said.

Stanley gazed at the darkness around him. Perhaps Cornelius was right. If he could not win Eve's heart or prevent her from making mistakes, at least he could spare her the anger and sadness of finding out who he was, and perhaps they could be friends again. He would just never tell her the truth.

"Alright," he said. "But take my hands. I don't want to do this alone."

"I'm ready!" Cornelius said with a smile.

He took his friend's hands and Stanley closed his eyes. Like when he used time travel to protect himself from the sunlight, he focused on turning back time just a little. He pictured the pocket watch in his mind and the hour hand rotating backward until it reached an hour and a half, then he ordered it to stop. He opened his eyes and he was again in Emily's dining room, sitting beside Eve.

"Anyway, hopefully this will be my last night enduring this," she said.

It had worked. He had returned to the exact point in time he wanted, and she was not angry. Perhaps swallowing the Time Key was not such a curse after all. But Cornelius was not with him and he wondered if he had been sent back in time with him, and if so, where.

"Your last night?" he said.

She turned to him again with shining eyes.

"Tonight, I'm making a pact with Astaroth."

"What… kind of pact?" he asked her slowly.

"He's going to transform me into a real woman," she said.

Stanley stared at her, wondering if there was anything else he could tell her to prevent her from making this awful mistake. His heart was racing. He could not afford to lose her again.

"Demons always ask for something in exchange," he told her.

She lowered her eyes.

"I know. I will become a part of his 'harem'… forever."

Stanley boldly took her hand.

"Eve, I can't explain why, but you need to trust me. Don't make a pact with a demon," he said.

She removed her hand from his, looking surprised and uncomfortable.

"Well, trusting every other kind of creature has not done me any good so far," she whispered. "For many years, I loved a werewolf. He said he wanted to 'protect me' from everyone and everything, but I only ended up becoming his prisoner. And he was just the first of a series of bad men in my life…"

"And that's it? You're going to give up on all men because you think they're bad, and go with a demon probably just as bad as them? What if he turned out to be abusive? You would end up stuck with him like a wife in an unhappy marriage," he insisted.

She looked surprised again. Eve was a strong and independent woman, but she was romantic at heart. Stanley knew she was sleeping with the demon, but he had not imagined the possibility of her having feelings for him. His heart sank again.

"I was in love with a demon, too," he whispered, lowering his eyes.

"You?" she said.

He nodded.

"A succubus. Her name was Callie. I fell head over heels for her and did terrible things, thinking they were all for her. But she never even loved me. Her heart belonged to another all along."

"I… I don't know what to say," Eve said.

"I probably shouldn't talk about my past, it's rather sordid," he said, turning back to her. "But I truly care about you and I don't want you to make the same mistake I made."

"Stanley, I appreciate your concern, but we don't even know each other…" she said. "I promise you I will consider your advice as a friend, but I still want to make that pact with Astaroth."

"Eve, please don't. There has to be another way to give you the body of your dreams. Hans said there were surgeries nowadays…" he said.

"We're both vampires, Stanley. If a surgeon cuts us the wrong way, we might turn into ashes. I want what Astaroth is offering me, whatever the price I have to pay to get it," she said, rising from her seat.

Stanley watched her, feeling his heart sink more and more as she drifted further and further from his reach. And then he felt the rose moving inside his chest again. He reached inside his jacket and it was there, in his pocket. He pulled it out and gazed at it: it was a beautiful red rose in full bloom, like his love for her, and a golden thread was wrapped around the stem and tied in a bow.

"Wait, Eve!" he said, getting up.

She turned back to him, and he handed her the rose. She looked surprised.

"A good luck charm, since you've made up your mind," he said, forcing himself into a smile.

She, too, smiled, and took it, then gazed into his eyes intensely.

"Are you…" she started.

"Yes?"

"Are you also a magician?" she asked after a moment of hesitation.

"No, just someone who cares about you," he said.

"Thank you," she said, before walking away.

She had made up her mind. She was going to go down the same path as him and nothing he could say would stop her. He watched her go to Astaroth, who had just arrived, a smile on her lips, and the demon took her hand and kissed it. They then sat together on a sofa and were joined by others. Stanley had had enough, so he quietly got up and made for the door—or not. Joseph and Andre had also decided to leave early and the old necromancer was standing awkwardly by the door while Andre talked with Emily. He seemed extremely uncomfortable around feminine energy and like he could not wait to get out. Seriously? Stanley had never seen anyone so powerful and shy at the same time. Besides, if he was women, why did he love Alice and then Andre, who was also technically female-bodied? Either way, he needed to get out and running into him was inevitable. So be it.

He approached him slowly, his hands slipped in his pockets as usual, and the old vampire turned to him with a disconcerted look. That night, they were equally powerful, but there was not any more reason for them to fight now than there was when the Order sent Stanley to investigate him.

"Too much feminine energy?" he said to engage him.

"Uh, yes," Joseph said, blushing slightly. "I'm uncomfortable among women, especially dominant ones."

Stanley could relate. There was a lot of dominant feminine energy in the room.

"Don't mind Eve. She's just a strong and independent woman," he told him.

Joseph lowered his eyes sadly, and for the first time Stanley thought he saw another side of him. He had not, as Stanley thought, only come to the meeting for his love, but because he was questioning something about himself, and he had not found the answer he was looking for.

"Are you a man or a woman?" Stanley asked him, before realizing how awkward a question it might be.

Joseph turned to him with curious eyes.

"I mean… how do you see yourself? I guess that's all that really matters, not how we see you," Stanley said.

"I know it might sound stupid, but I don't really know what I am… How do you see me?" Joseph asked him, still uncomfortable.

Stanley had not expected that question. How was he to know who Joseph was? He shrugged.

"You have an androgynous aura about you," he said, and his answer actually seemed to make the old vampire happy.

"And you do write romance novel better than women," Stanley added.

"How do you know I'm a writer?" Joseph asked, surprised.

"We met once. You don't remember?" Stanley said.

Joseph scowled as though he struggled to remember him. Well, why would he? No one remembered Stanley. He was invisible even when he was visible.

"At a bookstore several years ago," he said to help his memory.

"Oh, you're that guy, the one with the child ghost! How could I forget? But you're a…" Joseph suddenly said.

"Yes, I'm that guy, just a little paler now," Stanley said, smirking.

"I'm Joseph Stein in real life, but everyone calls me Joe," the old vampire then said.

He extended his hand to his younger counterpart with a warm smile, but Stanley hesitated. He could sense a lot of similarities between them—perhaps as necromancers—but Stanley was also a demon. Why did Joe want to shake his hand? Did he read minds through skin contact or have some other special ability?

Stanley finally cautiously took his hand and shook it. Not a good idea. He did not know what happened when other necromancers shook hands, but he felt a sudden rush of adrenaline through this simple touch that awakened his violent side, but also… attraction. Now he wanted to suck Joe's dark soul right out of his body and *devour* it. Gross. Disgusting. If Joe experienced the same sort of feelings, he was able to disguise them so well Stanley never would have known. He was trying to be friendly, and it was in their interest, both of them, to not suck each other's souls out of their bodies.

"So, were you already a vampire when we first met?" Stanley asked him, trying to make peaceful conversation.

"Yes," Joe replied. "I am over fifteen hundred years old."

That certainly explained how much self-control he was capable of. Stanley wished he could say the same.

"Let's be friends," Joe offered.

Stanley stared at him. His offer sounded genuine, but the young necromancer's mind suddenly filled with images of his father, when he found him in the attic, and how they killed each other. Necromancers did not let each other live, and now, as he stood before someone exactly like him again, Stanley understood why. Two such powerful beings could not coexist in the same space, it was simply impossible.

"Necromancers can't be 'friends'," he said, before leaving the apartment, and Joe watched him walk away sadly.

Eve did not notice Stanley leaving the meeting, but after some time, she realized he was gone. Now that she thought about it, he never stayed very long. He stood or sat alone in a corner, then left. Perhaps their short conversation was too much for him.

"Astaroth, where is Stanley?" she asked, leaning over to her soon-to-be eternal love.

She rolled the rose between her hands slowly.

"Who?" Astaroth asked her.

"Stanley… the one who always stands in a corner," she said.

"I have no idea," he said. "Is there a problem?"

"No, I guess not," she said, lowering her eyes.

The rose she was holding lost a petal. It fell softly into the folds of her dress. It was nothing, just a small rose petal given to her by a stranger who was nothing to her, but a stranger who cared enough about her to warn her about what she was getting herself into. He was not very old in vampire years. She could tell he was much younger than her. They had a few things in common, but the fact his experience with a demon had been a bad one did not mean that hers also had to be. An odd feeling gripped her chest now, something in between regret and anger, and she did not know why. She then noticed the golden thread around the rose's stem—the same one that led her to the masked man in her dream, whom she once believed was Ernest. She had forgotten that dream; it was so long ago, but now the height, the appearance and the eyes of the masked stranger, his voice, and the fact he spoke English, all reminded her of Stanley. How strange. She suddenly got up, but Astaroth caught her hand—not firmly, but just enough to demonstrate his superior strength.

"Where are you going? We have plans tonight," he told her.

"I know, I… I just have to check on something," she said.

He let go of her hand and she walked over to the door that had remained open as some other guests were leaving. She peeked into the hallway but Stanley was not there.

"Is everything alright?" Emily suddenly asked behind her.

They had not really spoken since that incident and the mood between them was still tense, but as a proper hostess, Emily checked on all her guests regularly.

Eve hesitated, still holding the rose, and Emily noticed it.

"That's a lovely rose. Did Astaroth give it to you?" she asked with a polite smile that seemed to hide some jealousy.

"Oh, no, Stanley actually gave it to me. I was looking for him. Did he leave?" Eve asked.

Emily lost her smile, and Eve thought she could even see anger surge in her black eyes.

"Why would Stanley give you a rose?" she asked coldly.

Eve suddenly realized that Emily liked Stanley, and she did not want to stir up any more trouble between them.

"It's not what you think. I don't know why he gave it to me. He probably just wanted to get rid of it," she said.

"Then give it to me," Emily ordered her.

Eve stared at her for a moment, confused. By any and all standards, it was a strange demand. But Emily did not even wait for her response; her hand reached for the rose, but her fingers touched one of the thorns on the stem.

"Ouch!" she cried, quickly removing her hand.

Eve took advantage of the situation to slip the flower into her purse. She took Emily's hand and checked her fingers.

"Are you alright? Did you hurt your finger?" she asked.

"It's nothing. I guess I should just mind my own business," Emily said.

She lowered her gaze and left Eve to return to the kitchen, but Eve followed her.

"Emily…" she said softly behind her former friend as she began to put dirty trays in the sink. Emily did not answer.

"I've been meaning to tell you… I'm sorry about what happened. I was just very upset that night. I was heartbroken," she insisted, and Emily finally turned around with a sorrowful look.

"You have everything I want," she said.

"That's not true and you know it," Eve said. "I don't have your talent. I can make dresses following a pattern, but I can't embroider as well as you."

"But all the men love you."

"As a fetish. Do you want to be someone's fetish?"

The two women gazed at each other quietly again, but Emily finally broke into a sad smile.

"I would just be happy if the man I like wanted me, even as a fetish. But he doesn't look at me in that way. He doesn't look at me at all," she confessed.

Eve smiled and took her hand again.

"So you have found someone! Would you tell me about him, as a friend?" she said.

"Are we friends again?" Emily asked in a small voice.

"Of course," Eve said.

She drew her into her arms and hugged her. Emily then pulled away from her and smiled.

"I like Stanley," she said. "So please leave him to me."

Eve gazed at her again, puzzled, but smiled politely.

"There is nothing between Stanley and me," she promised her.

Mischa had retreated to a corner of the room and observed the other guests at a distance. Eve was right, they were not like them. Mischa was neither a 'he' nor a 'she', they were intersex and did not identify with one gender or another. They were not transitioning, and if they were ever arrested for crossdressing, their anatomy was so ambiguous that no one could exactly tell whether they were male or female. They were different, even from this group of people. Everyone present clearly knew whether they were a man or a woman, but Mischa did not. They wore their brown hair long and tied in a ponytail, and men's clothes because it was convenient, but they were not trying to be a man or a woman. Perhaps they would never find anyone like them in this world. With a deep sigh, they set down their drink and left the meeting.

The streets of Rouen were deserted at this hour of the night, and it was a much safer city than Paris, where Mischa lived. Here, they could safely walk down the street, thinking, and just making sure to avoid vampire hunters. They had noticed a sprawling population of demons, but they usually did not interact with vampires. Mischa knew of their world because, in their great solitude, one night, they met an incubus and followed him back to his apartment. It was a strange, physically rewarding but emotionally taxing night. The young man was very sweet and had no problem with Mischa's body, but they were not 'in love', though Mischa was not sure exactly what that entailed. It was strictly a pleasurable arrangement—the sort demons were good at—and it left Mischa with bittersweet memories. Then, they met Madame de Sangue, who invited them to a meeting. There was a circle of transgender individuals who met in Paris and other cities around Europe. Mischa's family were Russian aristocrats, and they had moved to France before they were born. Because they traveled a lot, Mischa spoke several languages, but because they were born different, they did not socialize very much and had no friends. Madame de Sangue assured them they would make friends if they joined the circle, so they came, and they indeed made a friend, a German named Hans. Being intersex and not having had a loving relationship with their parents, who wanted them to be a girl and forced them to behave accordingly, Mischa could better relate to the transgender men in the circle. Like them, they were only able to live as themselves after they died and awakened again as a vampire. But they did not see Mischa as one of them. Even Hans did not, and yet he still made it a point to never leave them alone at the meetings. Mischa had come to like him, so much so that they attended the meetings only for him now. But now that Hans had found new friends in Andre and Joe, there was, once again, no place for Mischa. Perhaps it was not such a bad thing. Being different from everyone else gave Mischa a sort of freedom other people would never know. After all, an outsider everywhere was not forced to live up to anyone's standards. They smiled at the thought of it. But someone followed them. They could hear their brisk footsteps on the paved street, so they turned around and were surprised to see Hans trying to catch up to them.

Well-groomed but practical in his comfortable pinstripe suit, Hans had the looks of what he was when he died: an average, upper middle-class university student. A little shorter than Mischa, he was blond of hair with a youthful, oval face, and some natural facial hair on his chin and sideburns. The young man smiled as he caught up with Mischa.

"Why did you leave so suddenly and without saying anything?" he asked, trying to catch his breath.

"You were busy," they said.

"Not too busy for you," he joked.

Mischa shrugged and kept on walking.

"Did I say something wrong?" he asked.

"You heard Eve. She was right. People like me and Joseph don't really belong in that circle."

"Who says? I didn't see a set of written rules regarding who can and cannot be a part of it," he said.

"I'm not like you—any of you," they reminded him.

"Is anyone like anyone else in this world?" he asked.

"You are like them."

Hans grew silent and slipped his hands in his pockets.

"Where are you going?" Mischa asked him, feeling uncomfortable now.

Once again, they had ruined the mood with their negativity. It was inevitable. Everyone ended up hating Mischa, and the more they tried to interact with people, the worse it got. That was why they were always alone. They did not understand people, nor did they see any point in learning their social cues, so people perceived them as rude and standoffish. But Hans was trying to hang on.

"I… I just thought I might walk you back to your place," he said in an uncertain voice.

"Why? I'm not in need of your protection," Mischa said, and this time Hans stopped.

They also stopped and turned to him. For the first time, Hans had lost his usual smile and they could even see sorrow in his black eyes.

"I'm… sorry," he said before turning around and walking away.

Mischa watched him for some time, as many different emotions rushed through them, emotions they had never felt before. Were they friends? Had they just killed their friendship? Would Hans never again look into their eyes with excitement and talk to them about his passion for medical science? Would he prefer to be with Joe and Andre? Mischa did not want to let him go. A strange, new pain grew in their chest at the idea of no longer having him in their life, but they were not sure what it meant. Something was cracking inside them, like a mirror about to shatter. Were they hiding behind that mirror, that cold façade all this time because it was easier than facing the world and the negative feelings they risked if they became close to someone?

Hans was no stranger to rejection; it was basically the story of his life. Rejected and opposed by his parents for affirming his identity as a man, heartbroken by Margarete, the childhood friend he secretly loved, when she decided to marry, he was then turned down from medical school when, as the good, innocent boy he was, he applied under his legal name, Hannah Dietrich. He was told 'women required special permission from a board member' to be accepted, so he decided to go stealth and applied again as 'Hans Dietrich', and, to his surprise, he was admitted, and nobody tried to verify his identity. He thought his dreams were finally about to come true, but his life took a different turn as he became a vampire.

In the vampire world, biological sex, gender identity, and sexuality did not matter very much. Dominance and power did, and Hans was neither strong nor dominant. He had retained his friendly nature and did not want to fight in their stupid games of power. With time, he had learned to identify the most aggressive vampires, like Stanley and Eve, and he tried to befriend them before any confrontation occurred, but he had failed with both of them. Stanley never liked him, and while he originally thought he might be attracted to Eve, he quickly realized that she was not his type at all, and now she resented him for it. But what was he supposed to do? Lead her on just so he could say he had courted someone in his lonely life? It would not be fair to her. And how could he even pretend to like her when Mischa came into his world a few weeks later? From the moment Mischa had walked into the room, Hans had felt something new, a great, powerful attraction that surpassed everything else, even his puppy love for Margarete. Mischa was not 'normal'. They were not like anyone else, but something in their vision of the world, in their occasional smile, in their loneliness, reminded him of himself and he wanted to connect with them on a deeper level. It took a long time for him to get Mischa to finally open up a little to him, and he realized they were basically a neglected child who was left to raise themselves by their busy parents. The only life they knew was as an outcast, and despite being obviously very lonely, they did not quite grasp how to step out of that loneliness. But, he thought, he was helping them, one step at a time, one friendly outing in a café at a time. And the usually quiet Mischa had a lot to say when encouraged. They not only liked photography, but they understood art as another world in itself, one in which everything was possible, in which they could exist as themselves. As for Hans, he did not think he had ever felt so happy in his human or undead life as he had in the last few weeks. He awakened in the evening excited. He was restless, thinking about the next time he would get to see his mysterious love, and when those meeting nights came, he felt like his heart was flying high in the sky—flying with Mischa.

But the androgynous beauty had just shot it down with cold arrows and now he was falling again. Just when he thought they were finally becoming closer, they had reminded him, in their usual cold way, that they were just two strangers. Mischa did not *need* him like he now needed them...

Love was a strange sickness that propelled one's hopes and dreams up to the moon and stars and only made the return to reality harsher. As a medical science scholar, he knew that infatuation produced in the body the same chemical reaction as drugs and he was wary of such short-lived feelings, but that feeling did not go away. He needed that stupid chemical reaction in his body to end now, but it just wouldn't.

As he walked, his thoughts grew darker and darker. His death and awakening as a vampire had been particularly traumatic and since then, he often suffered from melancholy, paranoia, and intrusive thoughts, for which he self-medicated with morphia and cocaine as needed. He socialized intensely to avoid those thoughts, but the lack of consistent people in his new life eventually always brought him back to his lonely apartment where he would shoot up some cocaine to escape everything. But drugs did not heal heartache. He was spiraling downward, and fast. Suddenly, the memories of all his past failures were resurfacing, and he felt all his courage deserting him. He was a handsome, smiling young man on the outside, but inside he was a monster, a chimera stuck between life and death in a reality more horrific than his wildest dreams. 'Hans' was dead, and yet another Hans was very much alive and walking down the dark streets of Rouen, one that no one in this world would remember because all those who knew him in the human world were dead. No, he was not alone, he had friends. He drew in a deep breath and tried to bring forth the image of the new friends he had made, Joe and Andre. But he was alone. Not alone. Alone... He was so lost in his spiraling thoughts he barely heard the voice calling out to him.

"Wait!"

It was Mischa. The object of his love had followed him and caught up to him in an alleyway between two streets. Hans stopped and turned around, and they gazed at each other in the shadows.

"Yes?" Hans said in an unemotional voice.

"Why aren't you smiling anymore?" Mischa asked.

Hans wondered whether they were rude or just clueless. Had they not just coldly rejected him? He tried to force himself to smile.

"I'm smiling now," he politely responded.

Mischa seemed confused.

"You changed all of a sudden," they said. "I don't understand all these things. You need to explain them to me. Tell me what you are feeling right now."

Hans lowered his eyes.

"What I am feeling right now? Heartache, I suppose..." he muttered, his hands still in his pockets.

"Why?"

He turned puzzled eyes to Mischa and finally realized that they were not playing any games with him; they only needed more explanations about others' feelings.

"Because I like you and I guess you don't feel the same," he said.

"Why do you think I don't feel the same?" Mischa asked, more and more confused. "We were just walking, and I said I didn't need protection - which is true since I am obviously stronger than you, so why would you protect me? But you suddenly walked away as though when you said you wanted to walk with me you meant something else than walking and I… I just don't understand all these things."

The beautiful being stood before him, nervously clenching their fists and pursing their lips. They were truly distraught, and so was Hans. He knew how practical Mischa was, but he had assumed they at least knew the meaning of such things as a man offering to escort them home. But since Mischa was neither man nor woman, it probably was a rather confusing move on his part, and now he understood how even more confusing his sudden departure might have seemed. There was only one way to be with Mischa: honest and straightforward. So, he gathered his courage.

"I like you Mischa," he said again. "I think about you all the time and if I could, I would spend every minute with you. And I don't think it's just a temporary chemical reaction in my body. I think it's a lot more."

Mischa's black eyes filled with emotions they had no words for.

"When you walked away, I felt something 'breaking' inside me, and I think only you can fix it," they replied in a soft voice. "I'm not sure how, but only you can do it."

Hans understood, and his heart filled with hope and joy again. Gone were the dark thoughts and doubts, and now a great inner sun was rising inside him. Those stupid chemicals… He moved closer and took their hand. Mischa's fingers tightened around his, but their eyes remained unsure.

"Does this feel any better?" Hans asked with a tender smile.

"Yes…" Mischa said. "But I feel other things too."

"What do you feel?" Hans asked in a quivering voice.

They gazed into each other's eyes quietly as Mischa tried to make sense of their own feelings, and Hans held his breath. He did not want to let go of the hand he was holding – never again.

But Mischa surprised him by moving forward and kissing him. It was his first kiss. It was awkward, trembling, but beautiful. Their lips parted and they gazed into each other's eyes again, and Hans was quite sure his eyes shone as brightly as Mischa's.

"This is what I feel like doing with you," Mischa whispered.

"I heard it's better if you hold your partner when doing it," Hans said, blushing.

With hesitant moves, Mischa slipped their arms around his waist. Hans smiled and embraced them, laying his head against their shoulder, and he could hear Mischa's heart beating as fast as his. Their arms tightened around him.

"I feel… fragile all of a sudden. Perhaps I do need your protection after all," they whispered with their eyes closed.

"We can be fragile with each other… and also protect each other," Hans whispered.

Mischa did not know how to identify their own feelings very well, but what they described was the longing and desire associated with romantic love, and that was enough for Hans. They were two odd souls that had come across each other by chance, and found each other, and now all the darkness in his world seemed to vanish at once.

"Do you still want to walk me back to my hotel?" Mischa asked him softly.

"Absolutely," Hans replied.

Eve and Astaroth returned to his apartment that night after the meeting. Astaroth was a major demon, and they apparently earned high wages—that or they could make money appear out of thin air—for he owned several luxury apartments around Europe - even one in Venice. So when Eve left her shop in Paris to come to Rouen for a weekend, she stayed with him—just like she used to live for a few days at a time with her lovers when she was a coquette. Her throat suddenly felt tight as she crossed the threshold of the apartment and was reminded of her years as a courtesan. She reached into her purse, searching for the rose Stanley had given her, but she could not find it. It may have fallen out when they got into a cab under the pouring rain. An even stronger sense of regret filled her now, and Astaroth noticed it. After closing the door and taking her purse and hat, he came to her and cupped her face with his long and slender fingers, those who had been so good to her.

"What is it, my dear? You look so sad since we left Emily's place," he said, looking into her eyes.

"I…" she started, then sighed.

She walked over to the sofa and sat down.

"I'm just feeling very lonely tonight, that's all," she said.

He came to sit beside her and wrapped his arm around her shoulders.

"Have I not been giving you enough attention?" he asked her in a hot whisper. "You know you are my shining star, my precious diamond…"

"And…?" she asked, turning to him.

He frowned.

"And what?"

"Are we in love? Is that why we are making a pact?" she asked, looking into his eyes, and he seemed hurt, but not in the way Nicolas always seemed hurt around her, more like his pride was hurt.

"Are you in love with me?" she asked him again.

"The purpose of our pact is to seal our love and give you the body of your dreams," he reminded her.

"Nicolas wanted to make me his countess," she said, observing his reaction. Her words amused him.

"Well, I am not a count, but I am part of the Evil Trinity. I should think I am a little higher in rank than your count," he said.

"The Evil Trinity? Who are the two others?" she asked. He did not seem to like that question as much.

"Belial and Beelzebub, but Beelzebub has been murdered. Her position is currently vacant," he said.

"I see," she said. "But I cannot help but wonder why you chose me. Surely you don't form pacts with strangers or people not worth it."

He smiled again and rose and went to pour them two glasses of wine.

"You are absolutely right," he said. "I am interested in you for other reasons."

"What reasons?" she asked, taking the glass he handed her.

He sat beside her again, loosened his tie, and unbuttoned the top of his shirt.

"Of course I can transform any random human or creature of the underworld, but it should not be free for all," he said. "It should be a privilege reserved to very special people, like you. You are a spiritual vampire. Do you know what that means?"

"No," she said.

"It means your spirit has the ability to leave your body and can attack others – including their spirits. You are very powerful."

"And? Joseph Stein is very powerful too," she remarked.

"I don't like Joe, he has been courted by other demons," he said.

"What do you mean?"

"Well, of course I don't know for sure, but he is very old, and I am sure many a demon would like to transform him into a demon, too."

"So, this is not only about transforming me into a real woman, you also intend to make me a demon?" she said.

"Nothing will be done without your consent," he assured her. "But I would love to see you someday fill in Beelzebub's seat and be my equal."

He grinned and for the first time she thought she saw his true nature. It was something very subtle, a cat-like sort of detachment mixed with interest. He did not see her as just another member of his 'harem', but something like a consort. And, once again, the voice of the Fae resounded in her mind: *"Run!"*

She put down her empty glass on the table before her, feeling suddenly dizzy.

"Sorry, I'm not feeling very well. Can I just rest tonight?" she asked.

"Of course," she heard him say, and those were the last words she heard before collapsing in his arms.

CHAPTER 14

EVE KNEW SHE WAS dreaming when she opened her eyes and found herself in the ruins of the old abbey where she had once found the book left by her ancestors, for the sun had not quite set yet and its last rays were not burning her alive. She touched the skin of her face and rose and looked around her. She stood in between collapsed walls and rubble, dressed in her peasant dress and clogs, and she was human again. And beyond the walls of the abbey were tall walls of flames, but she did not fear them. She felt very peaceful somehow.

"Did I die again? Is this Hell? Or my version of Heaven?" she heard herself ask aloud.

"Eve," an unknown voice suddenly said behind her.

She turned around and recognized the stranger clad in a long crimson cloak.

"Aurelia?" she asked slowly.

Aurelia nodded and walked over to her and hugged her.

"My great descendant! I see you at last!" she said.

"But... I've already seen you in my dreams," Eve said, not understanding.

Aurelia reached up to her face and caressed her cheek with the same gentleness as her mother would.

"Of course you have. You are by far the most talented witch in our lineage," she said with a proud smile.

"A witch? Me?" Eve said.

Aurelia nodded again.

"Because you have more than just our craft. You have vampire blood!"

"I'm not sure that is a good thing. I am dead, you know that, right?" Eve said, smiling sadly.

"On the contrary, you survived," Aurelia said. "Come with me."

They sat together on a large stone and Aurelia gazed at her great descendant again, and her eyes were filled with pride and love.

"I used astral projection to meet you in your dreams," she said. "I needed to tell you who you are."

"Who am I?" Eve asked, confused now.

"Our clan, the Escobars, is one of the extremely powerful supernatural females," Aurelia explained. "We are all descendants of the original moroi, the first undead being. And as his blood spread throughout his children and grandchildren, so did they become different sorts of undead creatures. The most commonly known to people in this part of the world is the strigoi, the blood-sucking vampire, but moroi means much more than just drinking blood. We are those whose life has reached another form in between the world of the living and the dead. We are almost as gods and goddesses, ageless and practically immortal after we die in our human form, and that is why the forces of God hate us."

"So we're not actually monsters, but just the natural evolution of some humans?" Eve asked.

"Yes," Aurelia said. "Unfortunately, some of us have chosen to live in self-hatred and work for God, like Yvan the Inquisitor."

"Yvan the Inquisitor?"

"Yvan Thompson," Aurelia said. "He is a very old strigoi who has vowed to eliminate all those with powers equal or superior to his—supposedly in the name of God. He has been hunting the women of the Escobar clan, for the undead ones have fostered their living daughters and taught them immensely powerful craft. We know of the spells to seal a demon or release it, or even kill at a distance."

"I don't understand. I thought we were not monsters?" Eve said.

"We are not," Aurelia assured her. "These ancient spells were stolen by our ancestors from the most powerful demons and angels of the ancient world, and without them, they ceased to reign over humans and humans to fear them. We stole them so they would remain in the hands of pure-hearted women, who vowed never to use them."

"But why not just destroy all traces of them? Wouldn't it be the simplest way to protect the world?" Eve asked.

"Because, though we hate to think about it, the time may come when one of us will have to use them to restore the balance of this world," Aurelia said. "I have been chased across Spain by powerful demons. I know someday I will awaken to my true nature as a moroi, but that day has not come yet. So I fled to France, hoping I would be safe here, but now the inquisitors are after me."

Eve gazed at her sadly. She couldn't bear to tell her she would burn at the stake before ever awakening as a vampire.

"You look so sad, my child," Aurelia said, and then she understood and lowered her gaze.

"Aurelia…" Eve said.

"I see. I suppose I will never awaken," Aurelia said.

"You don't have to die. You must run away!" Eve said, taking her hand.

"It's alright, dear," Aurelia said. "If I run away, another inquisitor will come after me. They have vowed not to let a single one of us live. But you are here, in my dreams. It means my daughter survived and had a daughter and a granddaughter."

"Yes, there are many, many generations after you, but I'm afraid your craft was all but forgotten, except for a few tinctures and herbal teas," Eve said.

They smiled at each other. Aurelia's features were sharper, squarer than Maryse's, and if Eve had been born in a female body, they could have looked like twins.

"It was not forgotten. You memorized it all," Aurelia said with confidence.

"I did?"

"Look around us," Aurelia said.

Eve had not realized it, but while they were talking, the sun set in the distance and the flames crept closer, and now all around them on the walls she could see ancient words and formulas in glowing green letters. She was looking at them through the eyes of the Fae, and no one else could see them. And, indeed, she remembered seeing them before and memorizing them. The Fae was now the book of shadows containing the Escobar witches' knowledge.

Aurelia took both her hands and squeezed them.

"My child, I am being called back now," she said with some fear.

"Aurelia! No!" Eve said.

"I traveled to you from my prison cell. I am to be executed at dawn. I was hoping to escape somehow, but now I know that I must face my destiny and you will avenge me," Aurelia said, as tears welled up in her eyes.

"I will save you! Take me with you!" Eve begged her, clinging to her desperately, but Aurelia shook her head.

"You are beautiful, my child," she said, before vanishing, and so did Eve awaken from her dream.

She opened her eyes in a bedroom, but not the one in his Astaroth's Rouen apartment. This was another one she had never seen before. It was a vast suite with golden door and window frames and beautiful purple wallpaper with modern and fashionable oriental patterns. The eighteenth-century ceiling was painted with little cupids and demons running naked around Aphrodite emerging from the ocean. The furniture was also a mix of eighteenth and nineteenth century. It was tasteful, old, but modern at the same time. She lay in a bed fit for a queen, in a thin, white silk nightgown. She immediately sat up in the bed and covered herself with the blankets. Her corset had been removed and she never removed it. She needed it as her shield.

"Astaroth!" she cried in a panic.

After only a few seconds, he walked into the room, wearing only a purple bathrobe as though he had been bathing, or…

"Where are we? What did we do?" she asked him.

Of course he was her lover, or she his, but he had never done anything to her without her knowledge, and he knew her boundaries. Her corset was not to be removed under any circumstance and she did not want to be seen without it.

He smiled, walked over to her, and sat on the side of the bed.

"I just thought I would surprise you with a romantic vacation in Vienna for our union—and your transformation," he said, taking her hand and kissing it. "How do you like it, my princess?"

"I… I like it, but I need my corset. Where is it?" she asked, trying to regain her composure.

She wondered what they had done and why she did not remember any of it. She only remembered feeling dizzy after drinking some wine. Had he drugged her? It seemed unlike him, who was always so protective of her and attentive to her needs.

"Eve, darling, you are perfect with or without your corset," he assured her with a smile.

"That's not the problem. I want my corset! I told you never to remove it!" she said, agitated.

"Well, you have a walk-in closet full of new dresses—and corsets," he said, gesturing to two large doors.

She got up slowly and walked over to them, and as she opened them, she discovered the wardrobe of a queen or an empress. There were ball gowns and opera gowns, spring, summer, autumn, and winter dresses, in every color and pattern, and all the accessories that went with them, and she was sure the Empress Elisabeth of Austria herself did not own so many. She did not think herself a vain woman, but the sight of all these magnificent dresses certainly distracted her from her angst. She turned to the demon again, surprised.

"Are these all mine?"

He nodded, a doting smile on his lips.

"A wedding gift—for my special fiancée," he said.

He liked to refer to their future pact as a sort of marriage, but it was not really like she was marrying a man—more like she was becoming a part of a sultan's harem. But she would be his favorite. He had made it clear, and while he may dote on the others too, she knew she would have more than them.

Having forgotten about her discomfort now, she walked slowly through this enchanted forest of dresses and shoes and touched them, feeling the softness of the fabrics against her fingers. She had had beautiful gowns in her courtesan days, but none like these.

"I think a ball gown would be appropriate for tonight, since you are to become Cinderella," Astaroth suggested.

Indeed, they were already supposed to proceed with the transformation the night before – or whenever she last was in Rouen. But he had waited until she was rested and feeling better.

As her fingers brushed upon the shimmering fabric of a red ball gown embroidered with silver threads and diamonds she suddenly heard Aurelia's voice through the Fae: *"A spell to seal a demon..."*

She stopped and a sudden fear gripped her. She was the last of the Escobar witches, and possibly the only living—or rather undead—being who knew all the most powerful spells of the ancient world. Astaroth did not know, of course, but what if others found out? Once she made a pact with him, she would belong to him and so would her knowledge if he chose to use it. But no demon would want to seal himself away unless he was mad.

"What's wrong, my darling?" Astaroth asked in his smooth voice.

He joined her and looked at the dresses with her.

"I think this one is a perfect choice. You will look just like a rose in full bloom," he commented about her choice gown.

"Astaroth... will I be safe with you after we make this pact? Will you always protect me?" she asked him.

"Do you want to be protected? I thought you enjoyed being free and independent, that is why I let you have your shop and pursue your hobbies," he said tenderly.

She smiled.

"Of course I don't want to give up any of the things I like. I meant, in the demon world, if I end up becoming one—will my life be in danger?"

He caressed her hair softly and kissed her forehead.

"It is a dangerous world, but there is only one demon above me: Belial, and he will not let anyone harm you, I promise," he said.

"Belial? Is he the one who transformed you into a man?" she asked.

"Yes," he said. "You see, you will be protected by men, but gentle ones. I hope that won't be too much pressure for an independent woman like you."

"No, of course not," she said, smiling.

In the end, perhaps all she wanted was to feel like a real woman and surrender her safety to a kind man so she could focus on being herself and not always be a warrior.

"I will let you get dressed. Meet me in the dining room when you are ready and I will transform you," he said, kissing her hand one last time, and then he left her.

She took the dress and found the corset and petticoats she needed. Then, among the dozens of pieces of jewelry stored in elegant antique boxes, she picked out the diamond necklace and earrings she wanted to wear for what would be like a new birthday. This was her last night in this horrible body. The nightmare of over a hundred years was finally going to be over, and if she had to make some compromises for it to end, then so be it. But as she did her makeup in front of the mirror, the image of Cornelius the child ghost somehow came back to her. The poor, lonely child, stuck in this form for hundreds of years, had come to see her as a new mother through the letters she exchanged with Ernest. She remembered how he cried when she told him she could not be his mother and it still broke her heart. How she would have wanted to be his mother... And then she remembered Stanley. Nobody knew him in the vampire circles. He was a stranger Emily had come across in her shop in Paris and randomly invited. He seemed rather moody, but her short conversations with him had been more entertaining than any she'd had with the other girls or Hans, and she might even go as far as saying that she liked him. Perhaps they could still be friends. Or would he still want to after she was no longer transgender like him? Could she still attend the meetings at all?

"Darling, are you ready?" Astaroth called out to her from the dining room.

"Almost!" she said.

She shook her head. This night was all about her and her new life, and she was going to seize happiness now, as it was offered to her.

With reaffirmed confidence, she got up and walked proudly out of the closet and into the dining room where her prince awaited her. He smiled as he saw her. He, too, had dressed up like this was truly their wedding, in a luxurious purple and white uniform inspired by the Austrian Empire's army. He offered her his hand and she took it.

"Tonight, we shall make a pact binding us for all eternity, and then I will transform you into a woman. We have already discussed the terms of this pact. Do you agree to it?" he asked her again.

"I do," she said with a bright smile. "So, how do we make this pact?"

"It must be sealed with a kiss," he said.

"I'm ready," she said.

She closed her eyes and felt his lips come down upon her bare shoulder. He lay there a long, soft kiss that left her skin tingling, and as he did, images flashed through her mind: flames, Hell, witches, a moonlit sky, a forest with dozens of green lights rising from the ground. She felt the Fae curl up inside her like an angry animal. She wanted to come out and protect her from this intrusion upon her body, but Eve would not let her, not tonight. When Astaroth removed his lips and she opened her eyes, she still felt like herself. Nothing had changed, except that Astaroth seemed a little taller.

"You… You didn't do anything to me!" she said, and then she stopped.

Her voice was unrecognizable, and it came out so easily in such a high pitch. She turned to a large, hanging mirror on the wall and walked slowly toward it, and the woman she saw inside it still had her features, but they were just a little smoother and rounder. She was definitely shorter and the breasts in her corset were real. A small mark on her skin was the only sign that she had formed a pact with a demon. She looked down at her cleavage, then felt the now flat space between her legs, then turned back to Astaroth.

"I can't believe it! Is this me?" she shouted with the excitement of a child.

"It is you, my Cinderella. You have become a true princess," he told her with a smile.

Unable to contain her joy, she began to swirl around the room in her dress, her eyes falling briefly upon the paintings and the furniture all around her, and all she could think about was her new life and all the things she would do now.

"Shall we go out to celebrate your transformation?" Astaroth said, offering her his arm.

"Yes!" she said, proudly taking it.

And so he took her out that night to try out her new body. They went to the opera and then to a masquerade ball, and as they danced together and she gazed into his eyes under the mask, she became convinced that he was the man she had seen in a dream, so long ago, the one whose destiny was tied to hers by a golden thread. So what if her new prince was a demon? He was a sweet one after all, who loved her, and how could she not love him after all he had done for her?

After the shows and the dances, he took her back to their suite in the early hours of the morning and made love to her—like a man to a woman—and she felt herself falling more and more in love with him. And as she fell asleep in his arms—without her corset this time—she felt happier than she had ever been in her life. But the honeymoon did not last as long as she had expected it.

The awakening came very suddenly, after only seven nights. Astaroth was so proud of his new 'princess' he wanted to show her off to everyone, starting with the members of Emily's circle. So she was presented like royalty to this small court of admirers in the demon's apartment . All the girls were there, and so were Hans and Andre without his paramour, Joe. *Good riddance*, she thought. Two goody-goodies were enough. But, unlike the girls, Hans and Andre only seemed to have come out of curiosity, not because they wanted the same transformation. The young Andre was especially suspicious of demons, though Eve could not understand why. Emily and the other girls had nothing but praise for her new body, and she bowed to everyone like a princess, a princess' perfect smile on her lips, but she was sad not to see Stanley there. Had he come, she could have shown him that everything was alright after all. She sighed and was about to get herself a drink when Astaroth came up beside her.

"You ought to go talk to Andre," he discreetly told her.

"Andre? Why? I don't like him," she said, sipping on her glass of champagne.

"Because I want him to join my harem next," he said.

"Then why don't you go talk to him yourself?" she said.

He dropped his large hand on her shoulder.

"I told you that I want you to go talk to him," he said, and for the first time, his voice was cold, almost menacing. She turned to him slowly and looked into his eyes.

She did not want to obey him, but now the urge to do as he said was almost irresistible. She put down her glass and walked over to Andre like a puppet in the hands of her master, and he watched her at a distance.

The rest of the evening went by like a dream—one she was not a part of. She saw herself as though from outside her body, making polite conversation with Andre and Hans and a few others, smiling, laughing. She was Cinderella, but the fairy godmother had not warned her that her prince would turn her into his puppet.

The guests eventually left, and she sat quietly by the window, thinking about what had just happened. Astaroth put away the empty glasses and trays for his demonic servants to clean the next day and slammed a cabinet door shut to get her attention. She turned to him, startled.

"Why are you not happy?" he asked her in the same cold voice he had earlier.

"I am happy…" she said softly.

"Then why won't you simply do what I tell you? I just want you to make friends with Andre. How hard is it?" he said.

"But we don't even like each other. We have nothing in common."

"Call him," he said, and it sounded like an order.

"What?"

"He and Joe are staying in a hotel not far from here. They have the telephone in their room. Call him and invite him over tomorrow night," he said, turning to her.

She frowned and rose from her chair.

"No," she said. "You call him yourself. I don't care who else you want to give your 'love' to, but don't involve me."

"You're a mouthy woman," he said, irritated.

"It took you that long to realize it? I thought you knew me," she said.

He let out an exasperated sigh and walked over to her and grabbed her arm.

"You will do as I say!" he said, and this time his grip was so strong it could almost break her arm.

Again, she heard the Fae telling her: *"Use the spell!"*

Indeed, she had forgotten she had it. Was this what Stanley had tried to warn her about? Did he know Astaroth was an abusive man in private, or did he just guess? And how come she did not? But she would not be abused by a man—never again.

With a loud shriek, she suddenly let out the Fae and it pushed the demon away. He fell onto a chair and broke it. But before she could even begin to recite the spell she had memorized, Astaroth said: "You shall not use your mouth against me!"

Eve tried to say the words again and again, but not a sound would come out of her lips. She brought her hands to her throat, horrified. Astaroth got up, an evil grin on his lips.

"I knew it all along. You are the one who knows the sealing spell," he said.

He walked over to her and she backed up against the wall, the Fae between them.

"Make that thing return inside your body," he ordered, and again, without her consent or understanding, the Fae retreated inside her. She was left alone with him and helpless since she could not utter a word against him.

"What are you going to do to me?" she asked, her body shaking both with anger and fear, but he came to her and caressed her face softly.

"I'm asking you again: please call Andre and invite him over," he said.

"Why? What will you do to him?"

"You will help me convince him to make a pact with me."

Eve held her breath. No, she could not do that to Andre, even if she disliked him. He was like her, a member of a vulnerable minority who had no one but each other to stay safe. And when the danger came from another member of the same community, it was even more deadly.

"Astaroth… Are you really transgender?" she asked him in a whisper.

"I am," he said, and his eyes softened somehow. "All the things you and Andre have been through; I have also been through them in the demonic world."

He let go of her and walked over to the window, his black eyes losing themselves in the night and the city lights outside.

"I was born a lesser female demon. I was nobody," he said. "My kind does not even look human. We are short and blue-skinned, and we steal the bodies of our prey. Of course, we are hated in the demon world and often killed, so as soon as we can walk, we start stealing human bodies to go unnoticed. Only we can tell another body thief when we see one. The majority of us choose a prey of the sex we were assigned at birth in our covens, but I always stole male bodies. Because of the reproductive issues this could pose—imagine a female of my kind seeking me out as a male to impregnate herself and finding out that she cannot because, even in another's body, I remain an egg-carrying demon—transgender body thieves like me are outcasts. But I decided I would not only be a man, but a male demon, and why not one of the most powerful? So, I stole a major demon's body."

He turned to her with shining eyes, and she stared at him in shock.

"I am transgender… but I am not Astaroth," he said.

Something inside Eve wanted to yield to him, to go to him and embrace him. After all, they were the same, except she was lucky enough to grow up in a safe home and he was not. But it was not her compassion he wanted; his heart had turned cold over the years.

"There is nothing in this world more important than power," he continued. "I did not only choose you because I wanted you in my harem. I chose you because you are immensely powerful and I intend to make you a major demon. Together, we can recruit Andre, and with him, we will finally have enough combined power to seal Belial or disable him long enough that I can infiltrate his body. We will create a new, unsurpassed Evil Trinity and reign over this world that hurt us."

"Andre? What are his powers?" she asked, surprised.

The annoying pretty boy seemed rather weak to her.

"He is a spiritual, like you, except he does not cast spells," he said. "I will need his powers to physically disable Belial and remove his soul from his body. You will then seal him away forever and I will take over his body."

"If this spell is so powerful, I'm sure he knows it too," she said, frowning. "He might use it on you first once he figures out your plans."

"And you will protect me," he said.

She slowly walked over to him and gazed into his eyes.

"Astaroth, I understand what you have been through and why you want to do this, but you can't use me and Andre as puppets. We are like you."

He removed his gaze from hers and it turned utterly cold.

"No, you are not like me. You have a circle of friends who accept you. I will never have that. I am alone and I must survive in this dangerous world by all means," he said.

Eve lowered her eyes. Her heart was torn now between the desire to free Astaroth from this inner prison he had created for himself and show him that he could be happy among them without killing anyone else, and the mission Aurelia had entrusted her. She had passed on to her the magic of the Escobar witches because she was pure-hearted and would use it only to protect this world, not to seal away the third member of the Evil Trinity so that Astaroth could take his place. If she agreed to it, what would he ask of her next?

The demon turned to her again and grabbed her wrist, not as firmly as he had before, but firmly enough that she could not free herself from his grip.

"Call Andre," he said once more.

"No," she said, turning to him. "I refuse. I can't do that to him. We are not your puppets."

"Is that your last word?" he asked as his eyes turned fierce.

"Yes," she said. "And I will not seal away Belial."

"Fine," he said, and he dropped his other hand on her head.

She closed her eyes, shaking, as she thought he was going to kill her, but what he did was perhaps worse than that. In just a few seconds, she felt her dress becoming looser around her chest and tighter around her waist. The laces in her corset ripped as her body changed again.

"No! No! Please!" she said, but it was too late.

He removed his hand, and she was back in her old body again. She stared at him in utter shock. Of course, since he was like her, he knew what would hurt her the most, and this was her punishment for refusing to obey him.

"I was willing to make you my queen, to put you on a pedestal above all others, but you turned it down. Blame yourself," he said.

She stared at him angrily, breathing heavily. The Fae wanted to come out now and tear him apart, but she couldn't bring it out, nor say anything against him.

"Now go to the bedroom and take off your clothes. You might as well make yourself useful in some way," he said.

She did not answer.

"What's that look for? You only do it for money and I gave you dresses and jewelry. Now be a good girl and do what you do best. Go to the bedroom and take off your clothes."

There was no way to describe the horror, the utter disgust he inspired her now, but worse even was the fact that her body began to move on its own and walk toward the bedroom like a puppet. She was his puppet now. She had done this to herself, and no one knew, no one would come to save her.

Eve was like a bird in a cage again, and she had let herself be captured, and when she awakened the next evening, she thought she was back in Nicolas' castle in Gevaudan. But she was not. She was in Rouen, lying in Astaroth's bed, feeling frightened and soiled. She heard Astaroth stirring behind her and did not move, not even when he leaned over her and kissed her cheek.

"Are you in a better disposition now, my love?" he asked her, and his whisper was like that of a snake. How could she have fallen for such a monster? But her instinct told her that she ought to lie—at least until he left her alone—or he could hurt her even more.

She suddenly burst into tears.

"Oh, what is it, my dear? Has my princess had a nightmare?" he asked, as though he was truly concerned about her.

"You don't love me at all…" she sobbed, curling up into a ball.

"But I do love you. You are the most precious princess in my harem," he assured her. "You just need to learn my rules now, and when you obey them, you will be rewarded."

Rewarded with some cheap magical trick to make her look the way she wanted for a few days? She did not want illusions anymore; she would rather trust an actual licensed surgeon than a demon. Perhaps she should have listened to what Hans had to say. But what hurt her the most was the idea that someone like Astaroth could turn against those like him, who shared the same suffering. Why?

"You don't believe me, but I will show you how good I can be to you. I'm not your enemy," he said.

She had heard that before… from her pimp, Madame de Guigne. She rolled over and looked into his eyes.

"Buy me a new dress," she said coldly. "I can't visit Andre in my old dress that no longer fits my body."

His lips parted into a smile, and he began to laugh.

"Is that what my darling wants? I can easily make that happen," he said. "How about you go shopping tonight? Put it all on my account. I must go to the office and get some work done, or Belial will scold me."

He slowly got out of bed and stretched out naked in front of her. Not only did he have no shame in abusing her, but he seemed proud of himself. The feelings of disgust he now inspired her were such that she wanted to throw up. But she would get her revenge. She couldn't here and now. She needed to think about her safety first, but she would return and do to him what he did to her. When she finally managed to let the Fae out again, she would show him no mercy.

Unaware of her plans, he slowly walked over to the closet and opened the doors. There, he dressed in a classic charcoal gray suit and tie before leaving. Eve did not waste a second. She immediately got out of bed, picked up her clothes that lay scattered on the floor, and dressed in haste. Her entire body was shaking. She had done this once already, with the help of the Fae. Now she had to do it again alone. But she had educated thousands of abused women and told them exactly what to do to get away from their abusers. She knows what to do, only it was harder alone and without her powers.

She left the apartment building and walked hastily down the dark streets until she found a dress shop. There, she purchased a black dress, complete with a hat and gloves, and a new partial wig that looked nothing like her usual hairstyle. She changed into the dress and put on the wig, then, using her pocket mirror, she fixed her makeup, accentuating the black eyeliner around her eyes—that was to make her feel stronger. She then told the shopkeeper to discard her old clothes and left, and headed to her next stop: the post office. She did not have a plan; she was making it up as she walked down the street, feeling her strength grow and grow. It was not over yet. She was an Escobar witch, not some nobody.

Filled with Aurelia's confidence and Maryse's rebellious spirit, she entered the post office and went into a public telephone booth. There, she sat down and browsed through the telephone book, searching for a certain phone number. There was only one person who might help her now—two actually, but she did not know where Stanley was staying—so another demon it would be. She found two phone numbers listed for the address of Astaroth's office, both matched with human-sounding names. Luc Baille, attorney at law, and Kadir Aslan, accountant. At least they were easy to identify, she thought. She dialed the operator and asked to be connected with the first number. The telephone rang a few times and a man whose voice she had never heard before picked up the receiver on the other end and said: "Luc Baille, attorney at law, how may I help you?"

She sighed with relief.

"Hello?" he said.

"B–Belial…" she tried saying, but the words only came out in the softest whisper.

"Who is it?" he asked, his voice very serious.

"Has Astaroth arrived yet?" she whispered.

"No, he is late," he said. "I can write down a message if you would like."

"No!" she said in a panic. "He… He must not…"

Again, she could not say anything about him.

"Could you be Eve, by any chance?" Belial suddenly asked.

She stopped breathing. Did he know? Was he in on it all? If so, why would he let Astaroth do this to her?

"Eve," he then said in a low voice. "I can hear in your voice that something is not right. I need you to tell me what happened, please."

"I… I can't!" she said.

Her body violently shook with fear now, as though the shadow of Astaroth was always over her, as though he could hear her every word. Could he? She did not know.

"Stay where you are. I will come to you," Belial said.

"No! Please!" she said in a panicked whisper.

Tears began to roll down her cheeks.

"Eve, I know something is going on, but I don't know what. Right now, you are the only person with that knowledge. If you are not safe, please tell me where you are and what happened so I can help you," he insisted.

"I… can't speak…" she said, struggling, and this time he understood.

"Did he put a spell on you? Have you made a pact with him?"

She let out a soft sound and began to cry. Belial remained silent for a moment, then said, "You must leave the city, tonight. Get on the first train and go somewhere safe, somewhere he will not know of. Just tell me where you think you might be going, and I will find you."

She listened to him quietly, unable to think of a place where she might go, and then she remembered Montpellier and Nicolas' abandoned castle. No one knew where to find it except the locals. It was very far from Rouen and she would not make it overnight, but she could get a head start.

"Castelcombe Castle, in Gevaudan," she said.

"I will remember it. Go now. I will keep him busy in the office," he said.

"Why… why are you helping me? You understand what I'm trying to tell you, right?" she said softly.

"That he has hired you and made a pact with you to kill me? Yes, I understand that," he said. "But something made you change your mind and warn me, therefore I trust you, and I want you to trust me. I am the King of the Evil Trinity and Hell, but I, too, have to abide by the laws of our realm. And to arrest a criminal, I need proof and witnesses. You are my only witness, so stay alive, please."

"I can hardly stay alive when I am already dead," she said with a faint smile.

She heard him smile on the other end.

"I will protect you. I am a friend," he assured her. "Stay safe."

He then hung up the phone and she understood that Astaroth had probably arrived at the office. She needed to get to the train station now.

CHAPTER 15

BELIAL WAS FURIOUS. HE had been trying to call Stanley on the magical pocket mirror he entrusted him for days and nights, but the moody young man was not answering. And now Astaroth had made a pact with Eve. Why didn't Stanley warn him? Either he was the most pathetic spy ever, or he was moping alone somewhere while his sweetheart was being stolen by another, regardless of the threat it posed both to her and the entire underworld. The young man was seriously the most difficult vampire Belial had ever dealt with, and when he found him, he would hang him upside down in the caves of Hell. No, Stanley probably wouldn't care about that... He would force him to attend salons and socialize for the rest of his undead life instead. That would be worse for him.

As he was pondering what to do with his disobedient 'joker card', the door to the building opened and closed: Astaroth had arrived. Belial let out a deep sigh and walked out of his office to meet him in the hallway.

"Good evening," he said casually.

"Good evening," Astaroth said as he removed his coat and hat.

He walked past Belial and up to his office, and Belial followed him.

"Yes?" he said, as he went over to his desk.

He sat down and Belial also took a seat and smiled pleasantly.

"Am I supposed to guess what is on your mind?" Astaroth asked.

"Maybe," Belial replied with a smile.

Astaroth arranged the files on his desk and pulled out a folder he intended to work on that night.

"How are things progressing with the seraphim?" he asked.

"Do you mean about the Dark Lord of England trying to start a war with me or the investigation of the murder of Beelzebub and the theft of the Time Key?" Belial asked in return.

"Both?" Astaroth said.

He did not have a sense of humor like his boss, and only enjoyed conversation with people who flattered him. Those who did not bored him like this one.

Belial sighed and scratched his goatee pensively.

"There sure is never a dull moment in the life of a major demon," he said.

"Indeed," Astaroth said.

Since this was going to be a long conversation, or rather a monologue from his boss, who apparently wanted to vent, the demon simply began to work on his accounting while vaguely listening to him. But Belial simply sat there and observed him. It was unusual. Astaroth lifted his gaze.

"I am confident that we can defend the country with our demonic armies, both in terms of numbers and power," Belial said.

"Good," Astaroth replied.

"But we know where that threat comes from. A simple dark lord. There are other enemies more powerful than dark lords—some powerful enough to murder a major demon like Beelzebub."

"You know my opinion. Adeyemi did it," Astaroth shrugged.

"Except he didn't, I am sure of it," Belial said.

"You're not always right," Astaroth remarked.

"Thanks, I know that," Belial replied with polite annoyance.

"Shall I begin reviewing applications for Beelzebub's seat? I have a great candidate in mind," Astaroth then said casually.

"That seat is reserved for Joe," Belial replied, testing his reaction. Astaroth was not happy about it.

"Joe has no intention of becoming a demon. I'm sure he has been propositioned in the past and he has obviously refused. My candidate is not only powerful enough, but also willing," he insisted.

"And who might that be?"

"Eve."

Belial cringed.

"Not her. She's too impulsive. Also, you know that, to avoid any conflict of interest, I would have to transform her into a demon, and you would lose your pact with her."

He noticed how the pen Astaroth was holding trembled slightly in his hand. He was trying to contain his anger. But now Belial had him cornered: he knew he would not be able to use Eve to get rid of him—not legally, at least.

"I am still the King of Hell," he reminded him.

"And I am just an accountant," Astaroth said, pretending like he knew his place.

Belial laughed.

"You are still in charge of Time," he said. "Has a new Time Key been manufactured yet?"

Astaroth gazed at him and smirked.

"A new one cannot be manufactured as long as the old one still exists, and it has been used recently in this city. Any ideas who it might be?"

Shit. Stanley had used it. Belial would have to have a serious conversation with him about the dangers of using it. It was not some wish-granting token, but one of the pillars of the creation of this world that materialized in different forms as it evolved over time. By swallowing it, Stanley had become the Time Key.

"Your guess is as good as mine," he said, shrugging. "Speaking of time, you're often leaving early or arriving late these days."

Astaroth scowled.

"I am not on hourly wages. I am paid monthly and always complete my hours," he remarked.

"Indeed, you are paid monthly," Belial agreed. "I heard you were giving a party last night."

"That is correct. Eve and I were celebrating our union."

"Congratulations," Belial said. "But I heard there was more than that… I heard something about a transformation."

"I have no idea what you're talking about," Astaroth said. "I am curious who you heard it from…"

"A depressed alcoholic whose muse happened to be at your party."

"Ah. Joe then," Astaroth said, unimpressed. "We all have our preferences. I collect transgender people, and you collect…"

He made gestures with his empty hands like he did not know what Belial's preferences were.

"Hot-tempered brunettes," Belial answered him. "But I think I am liking necromancers more and more."

Astaroth grinned.

"Are you thinking of adding Joe to your harem? He does not look very appetizing. Besides, don't you prefer women?"

"Most of the time, but I can make exceptions," Belial said. "Joe is shy like a virgin, and I quite like his dark necromancer eyes. But he only came to my place for drinks and emotional comfort last night. He doesn't trust demons."

He sighed and pensively looked at a painting on the wall.

"Oh, well then, I have another necromancer for you. He might be a little more difficult than Joe though," Astaroth said.

"Really? Who?"

"I believe his name was Stanley," Astaroth said.

"Never heard of him. Is he transgender?" Belial asked.

"Yes."

"And you don't want him? I'm surprised. Or could it be that you like very specific transgender people in your harem?"

Astaroth put down his files and stared at him.

"He smells like woodfire smoke. He has belonged to some-one else before, but I didn't see a mark on him," he said. "Either way, I don't like damaged goods," he then added with a grimace.

"Interesting," Belial said. "I wonder who he has belonged to and how he got out of that pact."

"I don't care enough to investigate him. My next spouse will be Andre," Astaroth said, unconcerned.

"Oh, Andre. You're ambitious. Do you think Joe will let you have him?"

"He let him come to my party alone last night," Astaroth remarked.

"Well, good luck with him," Belial said with a smile.

"Anything else you need? Shall I bring out teacups and cook-ies, or can I get to work now?" Astaroth then asked, annoyed.

"No, nothing," Belial said.

He got up and left his coworker, having a clearer idea of what was going on. Astaroth had recruited Eve with the long-term plan of making her take Beelzebub's place, and now he had his eyes set on Andre. Andre was also a spiritual vampire, though his abilities appeared to be most-ly defensive, but he had a fatal flaw: he could not fight without his Joe. The newly mated pair were inseparable to the point they physically suffered from being apart, and yet Astaroth had already managed to convince Andre to come to his party alone the night before. Belial was quite surprised when a depressed Joe showed up at his door to cry on his shoulder and drink his gin. He had hoped that, by introducing Stanley into Emily's circle, he and Joe would become friends and that Joe and Andre's relationship would become healthier, but that had not happened. In fact, he had not delivered to Stanley anything he had promised him. No wonder the boy would not talk to him: he had completely failed him and more than anything else, more than his throne being threatened even. He hated losing a challenge. He sat down heavily at his desk and took his head in his hands, wondering what to do next. And then a new thought struck him, so simple and evident he had never considered it before: Eve, Stanley, Joe, and Andre were all vampires. They were not demons like himself, and perhaps they acted and reacted in accordance with different instincts than demons. They always spoke about dominance and blood masters, but that did not mean much to the King of Hell. He picked up the telephone and dialed the demonic archives.

"Yes, this is Belial. I need everything you have about vampires: their anatomy, their lifestyle and hunting habits, their social structure, their psychology," he said. "Yes, the sooner the better."

He hung up the phone, and no sooner had he done it than a bat flew in through the unused chimney. He observed it as it flew around the room, and then it shifted mid-air into a beautiful woman. She landed on the ground with the grace of a cat and stood before him. Unlike most women in the underworld, who liked to show off their charms, this one wore ancient warrior clothes in the Hun fashion, complete with a short saber and a knife. Her black hair was shaved on the sides and long and braided on top. Definitely not your ordinary female. He noticed the mark of the demon Mammon boldly displayed on her breast.

"Mammon's pupil?" he asked. He had heard of her but never met her before.

She bowed her head slightly, not like a woman, but like a proud warrior.

"My name is Sorana, from the ancient kingdom of Dacia, where vampires originated. I am a strigoi, shapeshifter, and also librarian and curator of the demonic archives," she said. "I was told you wanted to know about vampires."

"Do librarians need weapons these days?" he asked, lifting an eyebrow.

"Manuscripts and scrolls sometimes went missing. That was before I took over the position," she told him with a grin.

He smiled.

"Sorana… please have a seat, for this might be a long conversation," he said, gesturing to her to sit down. "I need to know everything about vampires: strigoi, moroi, shapeshifters…"

She smiled and sat down with him.

Joe turned to Andre with a smile, and his love smiled at him in return. He then signed the document on the table and handed it to the man before him, who read it.

"Alright, you'll have the mansion for a month. Are you sure you're not staying longer?" he asked.

"We might. We're still deciding on our next move. I will let you know if we are renewing the lease. The only thing I ask is that you communicate directly with my bank for the rent. I am very busy and cannot be disturbed during the daytime," Joe told him with a polite smile.

"Not a problem," the man said, getting up.

He was the estate manager for a wealthy family who had decided to rent out one of their mansions in Rouen, and since the couple would be staying there for at least a few more weeks, they decided to rent it. For Andre, who only earned money occasionally as a dancer, it was a dream home, with a large dining and ball room and dozens of windows, a living room, a drawing room, a parlor, a game room, a smoking lounge, an office, a kitchen, a gymnasium because the owners were sports enthusiasts, a solarium, two bathrooms with indoor plumbing, and five bedrooms upstairs. It was already furnished, and they were allowed to add their own furniture but not to change the wallpaper, which was brand new. For Joe, who had lived over fifteen hundred years and had loads of money stashed in various banks across Europe from thousands of years working as a musician, bard, poet, author, playwright, and inheriting the estates of his friends who did not make it to eternity, it was just another rental in another city. The Roman Empire, the Middle Ages, the Renaissance, France, Spain, Italy, Greece, Egypt, the Ottoman Empire, the Silk Road, Russia… Joe had traveled for hundreds of years from court to court and theater to theater, playing songs or writing poetry for some distant, idolized lady he would never lay hands on in real life. He had many friends in the intellectual vampire circles and was known as the timid, funny one who could always be talked into drinking himself silly, but few could claim to be his close friends, and among those few, most had eventually died. After living through one tragedy after another, he settled for a quiet, secluded life, until his publisher introduced him to an energetic but somewhat reclusive young writer named Alice. She became his pen friend for over forty years, and he wanted to believe they were in love, but he would never know. Afraid to tell her about his true form and nature, he let her believe he was just a shy old man, and he watched her home on her last night, waiting underneath her window, until someone blew out the candles and he knew she had gone. His heart had died that night, and his brief encounter with another young woman who died on the very night they met only confirmed to him that he should never fall in love. And then he met Andre.

He never knew of—or perhaps did not know how to identi-fy—his attraction to men before the blond angel came dancing into his life on a Broadway stage in New York. Andre Schnei-der, a young vampire dancer with blue eyes, crashed upon his heart like a golden shockwave, making him feel happy and sad at the same time, hopeful, restless, longing, craving, and needing again for the first time in centuries. And it was quite the same for the impetuous angel, who immediately began following him around everywhere. It took them a long time to finally open up about their feelings for each other, simply because they did not really have a road map for the sort of relationship they wanted, but in the end this raging passion was too much to contain inside, and they had become lovers and blood mates, and since then Joe's life had been like a brand-new dream, one he had never experienced before. But now Andre was already drifting away from him, making new friends like himself, and Joe felt like he could not be a part of it all. When he heard about Emily's circle, he was excited to go there with his love, but Eve's comments reminded him that, indeed, he was an outsider there. While he did not think of himself as transgender like Andre, he had always liked more feminine clothing when men's fashion permitted it, and he had always secretly wanted to try on a dress and be doted on by a man. But Emily's circle was clearly for people who were out and open about their identity. They knew exactly who they were, and he did not, and he did not feel like there was a place or a circle for people like him, who were still trying to figure themselves out after over a thousand years.

"You look troubled. Is everything alright?" Andre asked him after the estate manager gave them the keys and took his leave.

"Yes, I'm absolutely fine," Joe said. "So how do you like your European honeymoon, my angel?" he asked, drawing him into his arms.

Andre smiled brightly and kissed him. He was so handsome and pure in his gray pinstripe suit and tie, and Joe—who had technically become a vampire at a younger age than him – felt old and ugly in his boring black suit.

"I love it! France is so beautiful!" Andre said. "Can we see Germany next?"

He was lonely, Joe knew it. They had exchanged blood vows very quickly, after knowing each other only for a few weeks, and one night the demon Belial showed up out of nowhere and offered them to come to France with him, where their combined powers might be needed. Young as he was, Andre immediately agreed to follow him and simply thought of this as a romantic honeymoon with his love, during which they may have to fight a few undead creatures, nothing more. But now he clearly felt lost and alone in this country, of which he did not understand the language and customs while his love did.

But the young one hated showing any weakness, so he made it a point to act overly excited about all of it.

"Of course, we can go to Germany. We both have German origins, after all," Joe said with a smile. "We can also see Italy, Spain, Austria, but I can't take you to England as there is still a bounty on my head there."

"Seriously? Just for publishing a scandalous book? British people are so hoity-toity…" Andre said, rolling his eyes, and Joe laughed.

"Only the vampires," he said.

"Oh, by the way, I'm going to see Hans tonight," Andre suddenly said, and Joe lost his smile.

He knew he ought to be happy about the fact Andre was socializing and making friends here; it was a good thing, but inside he was possessive and jealous. Terribly so.

"But weren't you with him last night already?"

"Yes, we went to that party, but tonight we just want to be among boys."

Joe pursed his lips and removed his arms from him. Of course, when Andre talked about 'boys', he meant himself, Hans, and possibly Stanley. Not Joe. He was in a separate category. He socialized with men and liked drinking and playing cards, but with them, he often felt like he was playing a role. He preferred deep conversation with women, but he had an inexplicable shyness when it came to being physically close to them, and, after going to Emily's meeting, he had realized his shyness extended to transgender women as well. So, he could physically not be around the people he had the most fun with.

"You can come along if you want," Andre added in a voice that sounded like he did not really want him to.

Joe knew he was probably overthinking this, but even this slight loss of interest in him he sensed in Andre seemed like their love was already crumbling. Having observed his friends' relationships over the centuries, he knew that growing apart was normal, but his heart did not know that. He wanted his and Andre's hearts and bodies to be fused together day and night, forever, he wanted to possess him down to the very depths of his soul, to exist through him. Now that he had awakened to what love meant to him, he could never return to what he was before. Perhaps it was a necromancer thing.

"That's alright," he said with a polite smile. "I think I will just go shopping. I've been wanting to try out new hobbies."

"Music?" Andre said.

"Uh…" Joe said, uncomfortable.

"Joe…" Andre said.

"What?"

"You have that look again, like every time you're not telling me something. What is it?" Andre said.

"I don't have any look," Joe said, retreating from him.

"Joe…"

The old vampire walked over to the window and gazed at the peaceful night sky. Humans never guessed what a dangerous world they lived in and what creatures dwelled in the shadows and murdered each other. Creatures like him. But Andre came and pressed himself against his back, his slender but strong arms wrapped around his waist. And then he said the words Joe needed to hear: "I need you, my Joe."

He turned around and embraced him, burying his head in his shoulder and breathing in his scent like he could never get enough of it.

"Do I still have all your love?" he asked in a whisper.

Andre pulled away to look into his sorrowful black eyes.

"I could never love anyone like I love you," the blond said, his blue eyes shining brightly. "You I loved before I met you didn't really see me as a man, and you know how unhappy I was with them. I was like a small voice in this world, always trying to say something, but no one ever listened."

A certain sadness flashed through his eyes, and he lowered them.

"I'm still… very young and ignorant. I'm very small in this world compared to you," he added.

"No, Andre, no," Joe immediately said, cupping his face with his hands. "You are my Icarus, my angel, the sunshine that lights up my dark world. I am absolutely helpless without you…"

Andre looked again and gave him one of his sweet, romantic kisses. Joe closed his eyes with pleasure, savoring the taste of his tongue like the nectar of love. Their lips parted, and he opened his dreamy eyes to him.

"I'm addicted to you…" Andre whispered. "But I'm afraid my love will constrain you and crush you. That's why I'm trying to spend time with Hans."

Joe wanted to be constrained, he wanted to lose himself entirely in him, but he also knew it was not healthy. At least, knowing that Andre still felt the same about him reassured him.

"You can constrain me…" he whispered against his lips. "I want you to tie me up and have your way with me."

Andre had that naughty smile again and bit his lip.

"How about we try that tomorrow night?"

"Deal," Joe said, and they kissed again.

The clock struck eight o'clock, and Andre was supposed to meet with Hans at nine. So, he quickly slipped on his jacket and hat, kissed his love one last time, and headed out. Joe watched him leave and let out a deep sigh.

This was also part of life as an undead creature. You had a lot of time to be around your friends when they were around, but then everyone went their own way, and you did not see them again sometimes for centuries. So Andre needed to enjoy Hans' company right now, before he moved on to some other destination, and Joe had no reason to be jealous because he was the one who would always be with Andre.

Shortly after his muse left, Joe grabbed his coat and hat and also left to roam the streets of Rouen in search of inspiration. Knowing he had Andre's unconditional support, whatever he chose to wear or to do, was empowering. He was not ready to step into the world of transgender women yet and try on a dress, but there was something discreet and easy he had wanted to try out for a long time: embroidery. So, he went to a lady's boutique and stepped inside. But the moment he entered this very feminine shop filled with dresses, combs and mirrors, knitting and embroidery supplies, and, worse, women, he immediately felt shy again.

"Can I help you?" a grimacing young woman at the counter asked him like he had walked into the wrong shop.

"I… Uh…" he said, shrinking underneath his hat and blushing, but a familiar voice called out to him.

"Oh, hello Joe!"

It was Emily, who was shopping for pretty things for her flower shop in Paris. She walked over to him, a smile on her lips. He took a step back and tipped his hat.

"Good evening," he said.

"Were you looking for a gift for a friend?" she asked. "I can help you. What kind of lady is she?"

Joe lowered his gaze and pursed his lips.

"No… Uh… It's not for a friend. You know, I think I came to the wrong place."

He turned around and left the shop and began to walk down the street, his hands in his pockets. His cold body was sweating and his heart racing. No, he was not ready to do this, not alone. He needed Andre to hold his hand, even for this first, tiny step toward feeling comfortable with himself. How stupid. How utterly stupid. A grown-up man – over a thousand years old – like him, unable to buy a simple embroidery kit in a shop full of women. How much more pathetic did one get?

He soon heard Emily's quick, light footsteps behind him and turned around.

"Why did you leave so abruptly?" she asked him.

He felt more at ease with her alone, away from that crowded shop, not enough to look into her eyes, but enough to have a conversation with her.

"I apologize. I was just feeling uncomfortable."

"Do you often feel uncomfortable? I certainly do," she said.

She started walking beside him. He did not mind her company. She had always been polite and welcoming with them.

"Yes, in fact, I can't think of a place where I do feel comfortable except at home with Andre," he said, gazing straight ahead.

"I'm sorry I didn't notice. What a terrible hostess I am. I should have made sure you were at ease."

"No, you did," he assured her.

"But you didn't come to Eve's coming out party after her transformation, and you're alone again tonight," she said, turning to him.

Joe was not very tall, even by European standards, and she was a little shorter than him. But what he liked about her was the darkness she seemed to hide underneath all her floral dresses and smiles. He could tell that, like him, she was a very lonely person.

"I just feel like it's not quite the circle for me, that's all. I don't know if there is a circle for people like me," he said sadly.

"My circle is for people like you, too. Please, come again," she said.

She suddenly took his arm, and he quickly moved away from her. She stared at him, surprised and confused.

"I… I'm sorry. I have problems touching people. Women especially," he said, keeping his eyes on the ground.

"Oh, I did not know. It sure seems like I'm doing everything wrong with you…" she whispered sadly.

"You aren't, it's just… me," he said, trying to regain his composure.

She gazed at him with compassion.

"You are so much like Stanley. You should try to be his friend; he is very lonely."

"Oh, I don't think so. He would probably prefer to be friends with Eve," he said, and her demeanor suddenly changed.

"Why are you saying that?" she asked in a cold voice.

"Saying what?" he asked, puzzled.

She pursed her lips and balled her fists as though she were trying to contain her anger.

"Eve, Eve, it's always all about Eve—the beautiful, strong, independent Eve who has it all: a political career, money, handsome men! No one cares about the short, fat Emily with her stupid flower shop!" she said, and tears began to roll down her cheeks. "Even Stanley… why does she have to steal Stanley from me?" she said in a choked voice.

"Oh Emily… No, I did not mean anything like that!" Joe said in a panic.

Gathering his courage, he stepped closer to her. He suddenly felt the late summer air turning cold and moist around them as though it was about to rain.

"You need to go now. It's not safe," she told him in a voice that sounded like a warning.

"Why? It's just a passing squall," he said, but she shook her head, turned around, and ran away.

"Emily!" he called out, but she never turned around.

Joe felt terrible now for mentioning Stanley and Eve. After all, he did not know anything about them; Hans was the one who said Stanley liked her. He had not realized that, perhaps, there was actually something going on between Stanley and Emily. It made sense that two solitary and awkward people like them should become close. He hoped he had not ruined things between them.

The cold breeze seemed to leave with Emily, and now the warm late summer air blew on his cheeks again, but he felt cold inside, so cold.

He walked alone for a long time, then decided he wanted to be in a quiet place. The graveyard would not do; it was full of spirits always wanting to make conversation with a necromancer like him, so he found a lonely bench on the Seine River banks and sat down, and only then did he allow himself to let out the tears he had been holding back all this time. If men had to be strong, tough, and never show their feelings, then he was not much of a man. He cried often when he was alone—probably more than his female friends. He was not normal.

Stanley watched Belial's mirror glowing softly on the dresser in the hotel room where he stayed. He watched it glow on and off for several nights, unable to move from his bed. Eve was lost—lost to him at least – and nothing he had tried to save her had worked. It was not the first time he lost someone he loved, so why was he like this, he, the cold hitman they called the 'bogeyman'? Because he'd had enough of everything and everyone.

"Stanley… you should at least go hunting," Cornelius said in a small voice beside him.

The child ghost watched over him like an angel, as always, and he was grateful for his presence by his side. He knew if he left him alone he might do something crazy, and until now he had considered it crazy, but now he was not so sure.

"I feel… strange," he muttered.

"Because you're hungry," Cornelius said.

No, it was not only that. He did not only want to hunt a pretty young woman and feed on her blood, he wanted to hurt someone, to control someone's mind and watch them suffer as he killed them. He wanted to do something *evil*.

"I'm a monster," he whispered.

"No, you're not. You're my best friend," Cornelius said, wrapping his arms around him.

Stanley closed his eyes. He did not want to make Cornelius sad by doing terrible things in front of him. With great effort, he rolled over and sat up in the bed. He watched his reflection in the tall, cracked mirror across the room, and the disheveled Stanley he saw looked more like a revenant than an undead creature.

"I look dreadful, don't I?" he said, smirking.

"Well, you're always pale nowadays, but you do look a lot paler than usual," Cornelius said.

"I guess I should go hunting," Stanley said.

"I'll come with you," Cornelius immediately said.

"No, you know I don't want you to watch me when I feed."

"Why? Humans eat chicken and beef. Vampires eat humans. It's only natural for you," the child ghost said.

"Still, I would prefer to do it alone. You were once human. It could be traumatic for you to see me eating one of your kind," Stanley said, getting up.

Cornelius did not understand the meaning of the word 'traumatic', but he knew that his undead big brother looked out for him, as adults were supposed to look out for children, so he nodded.

Stanley barely got himself dressed and didn't even bother to comb his hair before he left his room and began to roam the streets in search of a prey. There were many women out with their husbands and families on summer nights, but he needed to find one who was alone. He eventually picked the daughter of a baker walking home alone and proceeded as usual when he hunted. He followed her into a dark alleyway and approached her, hypnotizing her with the purple hue in his flickering eyes. Then, he gave her the 'prince's kiss' and slowly drank her blood until she took her last breath. But when he was done with her, rather than leaving her dead body intact on the pavement, he picked up a glass shard on the ground. Mechanically, moved by some darker instinct, he cut open her blouse and began to carve into the skin of her chest. He was not hurting her—she was already dead—but he wanted to ravage her, to scar her, to tear her apart in such a horrible way everyone would know what a monster he was inside. Her hot blood splattered on his jacket and his face, but still he continued until he had disfigured her so badly she was unrecognizable. Then, he quietly rose and gazed at the scene of his crime until he could not stand himself anymore. He removed his jacket and wiped his face off with it, then threw it away and began to run.

He ran for a long time, unsure whether he was visible or invisible to humans. He was losing his mind. He had already been on the verge of madness since childhood, after the murders of his twin sister and his mother, but living with Cornelius, and later William, and even his father's ghosts, had provided him the stability he needed. And now he no longer had it he felt himself slipping more and more into this dark hole that had been waiting all his life to engulf him, to swallow him whole.

"Cornelius!" he cried out in despair as he ran, tears pouring down his cheeks.

He needed to get back to his hotel room to pick him up and then leave this city and everything behind. But long before he ever got there, as he was running down the banks of the Seine River, he found Joe. The old vampire was sitting on a bench, a sad look in his eyes, and he, too, looked like he had been crying. He noticed Stanley before the young vampire ever reached him and rose from the bench. Stanley stopped in his tracks and gazed at him, breathing hard.

"Joe?" he whispered.

The two necromancers stared at each other in the darkness, and both felt as though the world around them had disappeared. They were two creatures of darkness, alone in their worlds, and now these worlds were colliding and there was no one to restrain either of them.

"Stanley? What happened? There's blood on your shirt…" Joe said.

He took a step toward him, but Stanley took a step back, closed his eyes and shook his head.

"Stay where you are," he warned him. "If you come any closer, I might hurt you."

"Why Stanley? Why would you hurt me?" the sweet Joe asked. He felt the same surge of adrenaline as Stanley, but he was determined not to fight him, and he knew Stanley was also resisting the urge.

"I'm a monster," Stanley said, keeping his eyes closed. "I kill people, Joe! I kill them because I *like* it! That's why… that's why I shouldn't be in this world!"

"Stanley…!"

"Don't come near me, and don't look into my eyes…" Stanley repeated, but the old vampire was stubborn and kept inching closer to him. He darted off, but Joe gave chase, and he was quick. Dammit.

"Stanley, please come back! Don't do something stupid!" Joe cried.

Of course, he was very old and had probably come across many vampires who'd had enough of their lives and decided to end things. Well, it was not really like many things could still kill Stanley, except perhaps a silver stake or fire. Fire. Of course he could do that. He made himself invisible so the old man could not follow him, but he had underestimated him.

"You think I can't find you just because you disappear from my vampire eyes?" Joe said, and as he ran, his body morphed into a black mass with two glowing red eyes. It moved within the same dimension as Stanley did when he made himself invisible, and it was a lot faster than him now. Still, he made it to his destination first: the old matchstick factory on the banks of the river. Since invisibility was useless, he returned to his normal form. He slipped inside through a broken window and knocked over a few things to slow down the old man. Then, he went on to the storage room where he knew he would find chemicals and closed the door and locked it. There were many large glass bottles with yellowed labels on them. Potassium chlorate, sulfuric acid, sugar, gum… whatever. Stanley just knocked them all over to see what would happen, and as the chemicals and the sugar mixed on the floor, they instantly ignited, creating spectacular purplish flames. Stanley watched the flames with morbid delight. He wanted them to ravage his body now, like he had ravaged that girl's body. He wanted to experience as much pain as he possibly could when he ended it all. But Joe suddenly broke down the door and burst into the room in his vampire form.

"Stanley! Are you crazy? We need to get out of here, now!" he shouted.

Stanley turned to him with angry and vicious eyes. The flames formed a wall between them now that could not be crossed. Joe tried to protect himself with his arms.

"I told you not to come near me. Now you get to die with me," Stanley told him coldly.

"Stanley, you're having a crisis. This is not you!" Joe pleaded. "Come to me, I will protect you!"

Protect him? Why would anyone protect someone like him? There was only darkness inside him. He slipped his hands in his pockets and waited for the flames to engulf him. Joe shook his head.

"I hate to do this, but you're leaving me no choice," he said.

This time, he closed his eyes and morphed again, and the black mass he had become flew up in the air, above the flames, and headed toward Stanley. A challenge? The young one smirked and stretched out his hand.

"You wanna play? I, too, have a few tricks up my sleeve," he said.

He turned his hand in a clockwise motion as the black mass hit his forehead, pressing onto it as though it could enter his mind. Stanley growled and resisted. The room around them became dark, and the walls disappeared, but the floor and the fire were not flipping upside down as Stanley had expected. Instead, black thorn bushes emerged from the floor, breaking through the tiles, and oxygen became so scarce the flames began to retreat until the fire died out completely. The air turned as cold as winter and filled with the putrid stench of mold and rotting flesh. It was suffocating, terrifying, and yet very familiar to someone like Stanley.

"Welcome to my upside-down reality," Stanley heard Joe's vicious voice whispering directly into his mind.

He closed his eyes, unable to prevent the old vampire from penetrating him, and it was the most frightening experience Stanley had ever had. He was not just being violated physically, it was his mind, his deepest, darkest thoughts the perverted necromancer was digging into. He saw his old home, Cornelius, Giselle, his nightmares, he saw and felt his anguish, growing up in a female body, every intimate detail of it. He saw his love for Callie and his grief after losing her... everything. Worse even was the feeling that the old necromancer enjoyed it in a voyeuristic, perverted way. It was how Joe controlled and terrorized his prey.

"No! Stop! Please!" Stanley shouted at the top of his lungs, and the black mass immediately retreated.

He let himself fall backward, exhausted from this mental battle, and two strong arms caught him and closed around him in a tight embrace.

"I'm sorry Stanley. I had to," Joe whispered in his ear in a genuinely remorseful voice.

Stanley curled up in a ball and burst into tears, and Joe covered him with his body, rocking him softly like a child. Being cradled like this by the very one who had just violated him was the most horrible feeling, and yet, somehow, Stanley had wanted him to go that far. He had wanted someone—anyone - to find him in the darkness and reach out to him because he was no longer capable of saving himself.

"I want to die... I want to die!" he repeated.

"I know," Joe said softly, still rocking him. "But I want you to live. I need you to exist in this world."

"Why?" Stanley sobbed.

"Because no one can understand the darkness in me like you can," Joe said. "You think you're a monster? You think you can kill savagely and for no other reason than your own satisfaction? I can do much worse than that, and I have. I hunt bad men, criminals. I terrify them first, then I torture and kill them in the same way they tortured others. I return the pain and suffering tenfold, but not because I want to be a hero. I *need* to hurt and kill, and the only outlet I found was to kill terrible people. I collect the screams of my victims and keep them inside me like tokens, and I will keep your screams too. You belong to me now. A piece of me will always remain in your mind, watching you."

His voice was no longer that of the shy, sweet man Stanley had observed, but that of a sadistic killer like himself, and yet he was also Joe. That very thought made him stop crying. He rolled over and gazed into Joe's deep and sorrowful black eyes.

"It's not so bad. If you're always inside my mind, then perhaps you can stop me from doing stupid things," he said, and Joe broke into a smile.

"I never again want to see you like I saw you tonight," he told him, this time in a tender voice. "If you feel anxious, angry, or scared, call out to me in your mind and I will hear you. Your cries for help will never again go unheard."

Stanley's eyes filled with tears again and he buried his face in Joe's shirt. The old vampire pulled him tighter in his arms and continued rocking him until all those dark and dangerous feelings left his young body.

CHAPTER 16

"So, you killed your sister and your mother with your eyes?" Joe said.

Stanley nodded. They sat quietly against the wall of the old factory now that the fire had been put out and the storms in Stanley's mind had passed.

"And then I forgot…" Stanley said. "I grew up, my father tried to ship me off to the funny farm, I escape and lived on my own for a while, until I met a succubus. I fell in love like an idiot, followed her all the way to Edinburgh and sold my soul to a demon for her. Well, she would never have done the same for me. She never loved me - not one minute of the few months we spent together! When I found out the truth and the trap she had dragged me into, I wanted to kill her, but the candyman got to her first. But I swallowed the Time Key and teleported back to my old home where I ran into my father. As it turned out, he was a necromancer too, and we did what necromancers do: we killed each other. Except he had already died once and I hadn't. So I turned him into ashes and awakened like this."

He gazed at his trembling hands. Thinking he was cold, Joe removed his jacket and dropped it around his shoulders. Stanley turned to him and smiled sadly.

"But the worst part was returning home and finding out that William had already crossed over… without me. I had promised him…"

He wiped away a tear and Joe dropped his arm on his shoulder like a kind brother.

"I never wanted to kill anyone… but by the time I was five, it was already too late," Stanley whispered. "Every time I kill, even to feed, something breaks inside me, but I just can't resist the urge."

"Stanley," Joe said, "you need to understand that we are vampires—necromancers. As vampires, we must feed, and as necromancers, the desire for violence is in our nature. It doesn't make it morally right, nor does it excuse senseless murder. You think of yourself as some dangerous serial killer, but you're not. You had no idea what you were doing as a child, and the fear you developed of being looked at proves that you did not want to kill your mother and your sister. And then you were tricked into becoming a hitman by the demons and the angels."

"I could have chosen death instead," Stanley said. "And that girl I cut up…"

"If you were a sadistic murderer, then why not do it while she was alive?" Joe said.

"What?"

"You killed her first. Your purpose was not to inflict pain upon her. I think you were calling out for help, for someone to stop what you couldn't."

"Maybe," Stanley admitted.

"My first murder was my brother-in-law, after he beat my sister to death. I made my niece and nephew orphans," Joe said softly, his eyes lost in the shadows around them.

"Couldn't you turn him in to the police?" Stanley asked.

Joe shook his head.

"There was no 'police'. This was in the fourth century, in a small Jewish village. Domestic violence was never discussed, and men never accused. People preferred to believe it was always the woman's fault," he said sadly.

"I hope you hurt him then," Stanley said.

"I put him in a fire head first, and I listened to his desperate screams until he died. I'm not proud of it, but that's the sort of man—of monster I am," Joe said. "And then I killed my brother Caleb, who also turned out to be a necromancer. He kidnapped me; I had no choice. But my friends got in the way and died too, and I learned than my father had died of grief. I killed all of them…"

Stanley rested his head on his shoulder, and Joe rested his head on his.

"This was all after you awakened as a vampire. You didn't tell me how you died," Stanley said.

"Suicide," Joe said slowly.

"What happened?" Stanley asked.

"As a child, I was mocked and attacked for being different and seeing spirits. My father thought I was possessed and tried to exorcise the 'demon' out of me through prayer and beatings. Everyone hated me. I thought this world did not need me, so I tried to end my life. But the world—or God perhaps—decided that I was not to die but to live eternally instead."

"If you knew you were going to meet Andre someday, would you still have wanted to die?" Stanley asked him.

"I don't know… I don't know if my twenty-three-year-would have had the courage to live on fifteen hundred years to find his soulmate. But I found solace, friendships, and love in my undead life. Even though I lost many friends, I can truly say that my life as a vampire has been better than my life as a human."

"Do you think my life will ever be happy?" Stanley asked, closing his eyes.

"We'll never know if you end it now. I don't know what happens to us when we die. The only thing I know is that all possibilities disappear. For instance, if I had not followed you tonight, I would have lost the possibility of being your friend," Joe said.

"You're too old and wise for me. I have no arguments to contradict you," Stanley said, smirking.

"Would you like to come over to our place? We're renting a mansion in town for a month. Stay with us for some time and let us be your friends. You need friends," Joe said.

"Thanks, but I ought to return to my hotel room. Cornelius is probably worried about me," Stanley said with a sigh.

"Alright, I'll walk you there," Joe said.

He got up and offered Stanley his hand. The young one took it and let Joe lift him up. Damn, he was physically strong, too. A good thing he had absolutely no intention of challenging him to a real duel.

They left the factory together and walked slowly down the street, chatting like old friends. It was the first time Stanley got to talk with someone exactly like him, who lived in the same dark world of necromancers. He noticed how they even walked in the same way, their hands in their pockets, and with Joe's jacket on, surrounded by his sweet, rose–like vampire scent, he felt peaceful.

"So you were looking for embroidery needles? What's so exciting about that?" he asked.

"I just like all the little things… you know, how the threads make a heart shape or a little flower," Joe said, trying to picture with his hands what he lacked the vocabulary for, and Stanley laughed.

"I think you mean 'stitches'."

"Stitches, exactly," Joe said. "But I was too embarrassed to buy a kit in the end."

"I'll get you one if you want. I don't care. I've worked in women's boutiques before," Stanley said.

"Oh, would you help me?" Joe asked, hopefully.

"Of course," Stanley said. "It's the least I can do after you stopped me from setting a whole block on fire."

Joe smiled at him, and Stanley smiled in return.

"I don't know what you did to me in that factory, but I feel better. Thank you," he said.

"Sometimes a festering wound needs to be reopened in order to heal," Joe said, moving his gaze away. "And sometimes meeting someone worse than yourself can make you feel better."

"You're not worse than me," Stanley said, smirking.

"I am," Joe said.

Stanley suddenly grabbed his arm and they came to a halt on the plaza near the train station. The plaza, surrounded with theaters and *café-concerts*, was always busy at that time in the evening, especially in the summer, but he sensed that presence again nearby.

"What is it?" Joe asked him, frowning.

"I don't know, but we could be in danger," Stanley said, moving his gaze around them.

A slender figure suddenly pushed through the crowd and threw itself in Joe's arms.

"Andre!" he said, surprised. "I thought you were with Hans?"

Andre turned his worried eyes to him, and for the first time Stanley realized that, unlike most vampires, they were blue with purple hues. They had never changed when he did. And that was not the only thing he noticed about him. Close to him like this, he could see a blue halo around his body similar to the green one he sometimes saw around Eve's body.

"I was, but I had an odd feeling, so I was heading back home to check on you..." Andre said, cupping his love's face nervously. "Are you alright? Where's your jacket?"

He then turned to Stanley and his eyes narrowed as he saw him wearing it. He eyed the other necromancer from head to toe, easily spotting the bloodstains on his shirt. Stanley pulled the jacket over them and moved his gaze away.

"What happened? What did you do?" Andre asked him.

"You'll read about it tomorrow in the newspapers, I guess," Stanley said.

"He was just feeding and... things got a little messy," Joe tried to explain.

Andre looked angry and hurt that Joe would cover up for him. He pulled his love aside to talk to him, but Stanley could hear their every word.

"I thought there was some sort of vampire police here in France?" he said.

"Yes, the Freemasons are a police force comprising both humans and vampires who oversee our peaceful cohabitation with humans, and they condemn senseless murder and unnecessary cruelty when we feed," Joe said. "But it's not what you think. The girl was already dead."

"What did he do?" Andre asked again.

Joe sighed and looked away.

"Joe, if he is dangerous and could expose our kind with senseless acts, we need to turn him in to the Freemasons!" Andre insisted.

"You won't have to. I'll turn myself in," Stanley intervened.

"No, you won't," Joe said.

"Why? Why shouldn't he?" Andre said angrily.

"That's right, Joe, why wouldn't I?" Stanley said, gazing into his deep black eyes.

But a fast-moving shadow behind him caught his eye.

"Eve?" he said, frowning.

Without thinking, he pushed them aside and began to chase her. Joe and Andre followed. The woman Stanley had seen was Eve. He had no doubt about it. He could sense the strong yet peaceful aura that surrounded her, but she was dressed in black and seemed to be running from someone. He caught up to her inside the train station. She almost jumped when he caught her arm and quickly moved away, terrified.

"Eve, it's me!" he said, backing away slightly.

Joe and Andre then arrived, wondering what was going on.

"Eve?" Andre said as he gazed at her. "What happened to you?"

She turned away from them as to hide her face. It was no longer the one Andre had seen at the party. A great sense of shame filled her now, mostly over how stupid she had been to believe Astaroth and his lies.

"What do you mean 'what happened'?" Joe asked, turning to Andre.

"I thought Astaroth had transformed you. I saw you..." Andre told Eve.

She turned back to them with tear-filled eyes, her entire body trembling.

"It's all over, I guess. I'm not Cinderella anymore," she said. "I'm sorry, I should have listened to your advice," she then told Stanley, who stepped forward and gently took her hand.

"Eve... did he hurt you?" he asked her.

The spell the demon put on her would not let her tell them what had happened, so she pursed her lips and lowered her gaze. Quiet tears rolled down her cheeks, and Stanley wanted nothing more than to embrace her now and protect her.

"I have to go," she said.

"Where to?" Stanley asked.

"I can't tell you. I can't tell anyone," she said.

But as she was about to leave them, all the lights in the train station began to dim at once and a cold breeze blew upon their faces.

"A power outage?" Joe said, looking around them.

"One that also turns people into scarecrows?" Andre said.

All the people in the crowd were collapsing one after another, and as they hit the ground, inside their clothes, in place of their bodies were rotting bales of hay and sunflowers and daisies, as though they had only been scarecrows all along.

As the lights went out, a blueish light settled on the empty train station, and the air was so cold frost began to form on the trains and the platforms. Joe, Andre, Stanley, and Eve were the only living beings left.

"What's going on?" Eve asked, terrified.

The three men immediately surrounded her to protect her.

"I've never seen anything like this before…" Andre said.

"Be careful. We are inside someone else's alternate reality," Stanley warned them.

"Who?" Joe asked.

"I don't know her name, but she is deadly," Stanley said.

"Let's try to make it back to the doors," Andre suggested.

So they moved slowly, surrounding Eve, until a loud noise startled them.

"Watch out!" Joe cried as he saw the giant wheel of a locomotive rolling in their direction.

It was followed by several others, and soon they were coming at them from all directions, crushing the rotting bodies of the scarecrows with crunching sounds. The group had no choice but to scatter. Joe and Andre rushed to the revolving doors leading out of the station's great entrance hall, but before they could reach them the floor before them was seemingly sliced in half and the wall, the windows, the doors, everything toppled into the darkness like a stack of cards.

"Stanley! Eve!" Joe shouted when he realized they were not following them.

"I could use some help here!" Stanley said, who was struggling to dodge the giant wheels. "Cornelius!" he cried out, but his ghost was not anywhere near and could probably not even hear him from another dimension. He could not even focus long enough to slow down time.

"Wait for me! I'm coming!" Andre called out to him. "Joe, you follow me in your other form!" he then said, turning to Joe, who nodded. This was not their first battle together, and they knew how to coordinate their powers now. Letting out a loud and angry cry, Andre let his ethereal form out of his body, and it came out as a blue giant with oversized fists that wrapped around him. It brought its fists in front of Andre, who dashed forward, crashing through the wheels one after another. Meanwhile, Joe adopted his other form and slid on the ground behind him until they reached Stanley.

"Holy shit! Andre!" Stanley said, astounded.

"Stay behind me! The Bouncer will protect us!" Andre ordered, as he positioned himself in front of him and Joe appeared behind him.

As for Eve, she had no choice but to climb into one of the trains. Once inside, she began to run through the slippery, frost-covered rows of seats, in which more rotting scarecrows were seated. But another wheel crashed inside the wagon and gave chase. She let out a cry and ran faster. This could not be

Astaroth's doing. Belial was supposed to keep him busy. If not him, then who would be trying to kill her?

She moved to another wagon, dropping her hat in her escape, and she noticed a man standing at the other end. He was dressed like a ticket controller and seemed rather pale, but he was not made of hay like all the other people. He stood still at the other end of the aisle, seemingly waiting for her. She stopped, having only a second to decide what to do. She was stuck. So she gathered her strength to let out the Fae, but before she could do anything, the man's head suddenly popped out like a jack-in-the-box. She fell to the ground screaming, and he got on all fours and pinned her to the ground.

"Stanley!" she cried out desperately.

The trio was stuck in a corner of the great entrance hall now, and giant locomotive wheels kept coming out of seemingly nowhere and crashing into Andre's Bouncer, but the young man was weakening.

"Joe, Stanley, I need you two to come up with a plan and quickly!" he said.

"We're in another dimension. I can't summon any ghosts or control them," Joe said, anxiously.

They suddenly heard Eve's cry in the distance.

"Eve!" Stanley cried, and, without thinking, he ran out in the middle of the wheels.

He needed to slow down his heartbeat to make himself invisible and slow down time, but he was far too agitated, and his heart was racing furiously. Eve was in danger and he knew exactly who he was facing, and what she could do to her.

"Stanley! Don't!" he heard Joe cry, but he could not stop him.

"Die! Disappear! Whatever you are!" Stanley shouted, his vision flickering in red and black.

A giant wheel then struck him, and he lost consciousness.

Eve opened her eyes in a place she had not seen in a long time, but she instantly recognized it. It was the small bedroom she shared with Faustine, above her shop in Montpellier. The air in the room was cold, as usual, because they never lit a fire at night unless one of them was sick. The room was filled with the stench of rotting plants or flowers, and Eve noticed vases all around the room, all containing wilted flowers. They were on every shelf, every table and chair, every flat surface. It was odd, but she did not pay any further attention to it. She rolled over on the bed to Faustine, who was lying beside her, except she was not asleep. She lay on her side, her open eyes fixed on Eve and her skin pale. She was dead.

Eve shrieked and got out of the bed. She gazed at Faustine's body for some time, stunned, then threw the door open and ran down the stairs and out of the shop, but when she crossed the threshold, she did not find herself in the streets of Montpellier but in the great hall in Nicolas' castle. She shook her head in disbelief. This could not be real, it had to be a dream. But if so, how did she get out of it?

"Eve…" she heard Nicolas' deep voice coming from the top of the stairs.

She immediately darted off to a side staircase and climbed it in haste, reaching the second floor, then ran down the corridor to the door she knew led down to the kitchen, from which she could find her way out. But as she reached it, she heard his heavy footsteps right behind the door and ran toward the upper levels instead.

"Eve…" she heard Nicolas's voice again, and it sent shivers down her spine.

He knew she had run away from him and this time he would not forgive her. But there was another voice echoing along with his, a deep voice too but one that did not belong to a male.

She had heard it before. Stanley's? It spoke a language she did not understand, but she thought it bid her to go up to the attic.

"Stanley?" she whispered, utterly confused, but the footsteps behind her were getting louder, so she made for the attic, whatever would happen to her there.

In the train station, Emily gazed sadly at the woman who lay on the ground before her, her arms stretched out and tied to the train tracks. She lay the rotten sunflower she had been holding on her breast. Eve looked like a lifeless doll, helpless in Emily's world of desolation, but there was still too much life, too much anger and passion inside her. Emily did not have such things as 'life' and 'passion' inside her. Perhaps that was why neither Astaroth nor Stanley wanted her. No one wanted her; she was invisible. No one but the voice who always talked to her.

"You ought to have her long hair," it said in her head.

Emily hesitated, then sighed.

"But her hair is black. It would not suit my complexion," she said.

"Emily…" it whispered.

Emily then turned back to the train stopped half a mile away, near the platforms.

"My, I almost forgot it is time to serve my guests tea and snacks," she said.

She walked slowly back to the train, humming to herself, and climbed into one of the wagons. There, her three guests awaited her, strapped to their seats with thick leather belts and asleep. Scattered on the headrests of all the other seats and the floor were wigs made from the luscious blond hair she had collected from her victims over the years, as she waited for her own hair to grow back—the hair that was stolen from her. She turned her gaze to Andre. Too bad his blond hair was so short, it would be of no use to her. She shrugged and went to the table she had set up in the middle of the aisle. On it were slices of stale bread, along with rotting flowers and a knife. Still humming to herself, she began to chop up the flowers and place them between two slices of bread.

Stanley was the first to open his eyes. He looked around him, dizzy and confused. They were still in the alternate reality, but the woman standing in the wagon with them was not the puppet girl he had expected to see, but…

"Emily?" he said.

She turned around and smiled.

Joe and Andre then opened their eyes, and Andre let out a soft cry as he realized they were trapped. Emily then turned to them, a frown on her brow.

"Emily? What happened? Where are we and what did you do to us?" Andre asked, tugging at the straps around his wrists on the armrests. "Are those… real people's hair?" he then asked.

"Of course they are. I wouldn't wear cheap wigs," she said.

Andre turned to Joe, who did not seem so frightened, and the quick glance they exchanged let him know that he had a plan.

"Emily, why did you bring us here?" Joe asked her calmly.

He noticed Stanley's eyes flickering, but with a glance let him know not to use his powers now.

"Why, for tea, of course," she replied. "You all leave before the end of the meetings; you never stay and have tea with me."

"I'm sorry Eve," Stanley intervened. "I'm the one who always leaves first. Let them go, and I will have tea with you."

She turned to him with shining eyes and smiled.

"Why not have tea all together instead?" she said.

"But we're not all here. We can't have tea without Eve. Where is she?" Joe asked.

Emily lost her smile and returned to the preparation of her sandwiches.

"Eve is a bad friend. She steals everyone from me," she said.

The air inside the wagon was getting colder, and a dense fog formed outside the windows.

Emily suddenly spun around with a sandwich platter and walked over to Stanley.

"There you go, my dear. I made some sandwiches just for you," she said.

"I can't eat them, Emily," he replied.

Joe and Andre tensed.

"But I made them for you," she said, growing irritated.

"Emily, this is not food. It's rotten flowers," Stanley said.

Joe had come across many sick individuals in his long undead life and contradicting them when they were in a position of power over you was not the right method. But, perhaps because of her affection for Stanley, it did not seem to trigger Emily, on the contrary. She returned to the table with her tray and set it on it.

"You're right," she said, and they all let out a sigh of relief.

"Emily, please release us so we can all have tea together," Joe said, but she was not listening to him.

"Emily… what were you thinking?" the voice said in her head. *"Stanley is a vampire; he feeds on blood."*

"Oh, how silly of me," she said to herself. "Stanley is a vampire, he needs blood."

She placed her left hand on the table and took the knife. She was about to slice off her finger when Stanley and Joe both shouted: "Stop!"

She turned her head to Stanley, looking confused.

"Emily, come here," he said, and she obeyed him.

"Joe, what do we do?" Andre whispered to his companion.

Both of them could break out of their straps, Andre using the Bouncer and Joe his other form, but they first needed to find out where Eve was and what Emily had done to her.

"I don't know," Joe said. "We're in her world and it obeys her rules, and we don't know what those rules are."

"Yes, Stanley?" Emily said with a smile.

"Emily, you didn't bring us here to have tea, I know it," he said, looking into her eyes. "Is it because you are lonely? I know how you feel, and I'm sorry if I made things worse."

She lost her smile and pursed her lips.

"You gave Eve a rose," she said. "Why didn't you give me a rose?"

"Because roses are not your flowers. You are like the summer sunshine. Daisies and sunflowers suit you better," he replied with a smile.

"Really?" she said. "Were you going to give me flowers?"

"I will give you more than flowers if you release us and take us to Eve. I will give you a kiss," he promised.

Her eyes filled with hope for a second, then the voice told her: *"It's a lie."*

"You're lying," she said.

"I don't love you. I never have. You're just an empty puppet," the voice said.

"You don't love me, you never have. I'm just a puppet for you!" she told Stanley.

"A puppet? How?" he said, tugging at his straps now.

"Andre, get ready," Joe whispered to his partner.

"You did this to me," Emily said.

Her image flickered before them, and suddenly her skin and clothes melted like ice in the sun, and in her place was the puppet assassin Stanley had encountered in London.

"Stanley!" Joe shouted.

He immediately changed forms and slipped out of his seat while Andre broke out of his by bringing out the Bouncer. Stanley let his heartbeat accelerate to the maximum and, with a loud cry, broke out of his straps as well. Emily turned to him, surprised, and Joe reappeared behind her and grabbed her into a tight headlock, but she laughed and liquefied to escape him.

"Do you like to play? I do too!" her now childlike voice resounded all around them. "Let's play 'railroad tracks'!"

"Shit! Eve is somewhere on the tracks!" Stanley said.

The wagon suddenly jolted and they heard the locomotive whistle. The train they were in was moving.

"Let's get to the locomotive and stop it!" Joe said.

They rushed across the wagon and into the next, and in this one, the seats were filled with mannequins dressed like travelers. The moment the trio entered, their heads all popped out like jack-in-the-boxes, and red balls rolled on the floor toward them.

"Dammit! We don't have time for this!" Stanley said.

He let his heartbeat quicken again and his vision flicker in red and black, and let out a loud shriek, and all of the mannequins and balls exploded at once.

"Clear! Let's go!" he said, and Joe and Andre followed him.

They finally reached the locomotive and pulled on the heavy brake, all three of them together, but it seemed stuck.

"Pull! Harder!" Stanley said.

"We're trying!" Joe said.

But even with his physical strength, far superior to that of the younger vampires, it would not budge. They pulled and pulled until the handle finally broke in their hands.

"Shit!" Andre said. "What do we do now?"

"Joe, Andre, I'm going to slow down time and find Eve. I need you two to stop the train by whatever means!" Stanley said.

He leaned out the locomotive's door: the train was not going too fast yet, so he jumped off and rolled on the ground. Then, he immediately got back up on his feet and slowed down time and rushed ahead to find Eve.

"Well, we're going to need some muscle. Are you ready?" Joe told Andre.

"Ready!" Andre said.

They each climbed out on one side of the locomotive and Andre brought out the Bouncer. Then, they descended at the same time until their feet touched the tracks and pushed back the locomotive with all their strength. It was too heavy, even for two powerful vampires like themselves. They were being pushed down the tracks, their feet digging a trench in the ground and shattering the sleepers between the tracks.

"It's not working!" Andre cried.

"We just need to slow it down until Stanley gets to Eve!" Joe said. "Push!"

He let out a loud cry and released all his power, creating a dark sphere around the two of them, and the train finally began to slow down.

Meanwhile, down the tracks, Stanley finally spotted Eve. He immediately broke the leather straps tying her to the tracks and pulled her out of the train's way.

"Andre! Joe! I've got her!" he shouted.

"Andre, let go, now!" Joe told his mate, and both darted to the sides and let the locomotive and the wagons it was pulling go by. They then all gathered around Eve, who remained unconscious.

"Eve! Wake up, please!" Stanley repeated, patting her cheeks softly, but she did not seem to hear him. They heard Emily's voice instead, echoing around them again.

"A princess cannot wake up without a prince's kiss. But Eve's prince does not want to kiss her. He wants to kill her…"

"What is she talking about?" Andre whispered.

"I don't know…" Joe said. "We are in an alternate reality, so perhaps Eve is too."

"An alternate reality inside Emily's alternate reality?" Stanley said.

"So who is this 'prince' who wants to kill her? Astaroth?" Andre asked.

"She never loved Astaroth," Stanley said, shaking his head. "I think I know who he is. She often spoke about an abusive man she loved for many years, a werewolf, but he died over a century ago."

"So Eve is stuck in a past reality… How do we get there?" Joe said, frowning.

"And how do we do it while Emily is trying to kill us?" Andre said.

"We were all hit by those wheels, but they did not crush us or kill us. I don't think she is trying to kill us…" Joe said.

"Then what?" Andre asked.

"She wants us to save her," Stanley said. "I encountered her once before in her childlike form. She was an assassin sent to kill an archangel. Someone is manipulating her and making her do those things."

"You've seen her alternate form before? What is she capable of?" Andre asked him.

"I'm not sure," Stanley said. "She attacks mainly with toys and mist or ice. The air is always cold around her and living things wither and rot away."

"I know what she is then. She is an elemental," Joe said.

"An elemental?"

"They are extremely powerful vampires, like us necro-mancers," Joe explained. "They can control various elements, and I think hers is air in all its forms."

"Then why is her world one of winter?" Andre asked.

"Winter is not an element in itself," Joe said. "Emily is an air elemental, and her world is one of winter because her heart lives in an eternal winter. My world is quite similar to hers, it's always cold."

"There is one thing I don't understand," Stanley said. "If this is a world of sadness for her, how come she appears in it in the form of a little girl—one with the body that would make her happy?"

"Perhaps she feels like that is what was stolen from her at an early age. What happened in her past?" Joe asked.

Stanley remembered her telling the members of her circle once, but he did not remember what she told them. How terrible of him. Like everyone else, he had not paid much attention to her and to her suffering. He was part of the problem.

"This is everyone's fault, but especially mine," he said. "All Emily ever wanted was for someone to notice her, and no one ever did. I can't even remember what she told us about her past."

His eyes filled with tears at the thought of the pain he had caused her every time he ignored her, left her meetings early like he was bored, and forgot every word she told him. How hard would it have been to spend a little time with her and listen to her? Joe placed a friendly hand on his shoulder.

"It's not always easy for those who want to be approached to let themselves be approached, just like it can be difficult for two people to come together even when they desire it," he said. "I can try to enter Eve's mind and save her, and then we can save Emily."

"No, you must not," Stanley told him firmly. "I don't know what Astaroth did to Eve, but she was traumatized, and now she's probably facing older trauma as well. The last thing she needs is a stranger penetrating her mind and seeing it."

"I know, and I really don't want to do it, but what else can we do? We can't face Emily while trying to protect an unconscious friend," Joe said, troubled.

"Yes, actually, we can," Andre intervened. "I too have trauma from the past, and I would not let a stranger into my mind, only someone I deeply trusted. We all have trauma, and so does Emily. She has cracked the door open for us, but not all of us can enter her mind – she won't allow it."

"I think she will allow me," Stanley said.

"So, what is your plan? You think you can find her in here?" Joe said.

"I have to," Stanley said.

He turned his sad gaze to the woman he was holding in his arms, the one he loved so much, even if she would never be his. He took her hand and kissed it.

"Eve, I know you can't hear me, but… I love you," he whispered to her.

Joe and Andre gazed at him with surprise.

"I'm sorry for not being the prince you were waiting for. But I am the one who will fight for you no matter what. So please, be strong. You must save yourself from this dream," he told her, before gently handing her over to Andre.

"Please, protect her with your blue… thing," he said.

"Don't worry, I've got this," Andre told him with a smile.

Stanley got up and Joe was about to follow him, but he gestured to him to stay there.

"I need Andre to protect Eve, and I need you to protect Andre."

"But Emily is an elemental. I don't know the extent of your abilities, but elementals are as powerful as necromancers," Joe warned him.

"And I am the same as Emily. I'm that invisible guy nobody remembers, even when I am visible," Stanley told him with a sad smile.

"I'm sorry…" Joe said, lowering his gaze.

"We're all capable of hurting others… and also caring for them," Stanley said. "Only a few hours ago, I thought I had hit rock bottom and lost all hope. But here I am now, with friends who care about me. Let me go find Emily before she reaches that rock bottom."

Joe nodded and let him go.

Stanley walked back to the platform, and from there to the great hall of the frozen train station. Everything was eerily quiet. Too bad he had thrown away his jacket and the token from Cat. He really could have used a cat guide right now.

"Emily, where are you?" he said in a loud voice. "You haven't sent me any wheels or jack-in-the-boxes yet. I'm starting to get bored!"

"I'm sorry, I have more toys we can play with," her distant, childish voice answered.

He mentally noted the direction it was coming from. Around the great hall were a series of shops and waiting rooms over two stories. She was somewhere upstairs.

"So what are we playing next?" he asked her.

"Do you want to play dodgeball?" she replied, giggling.

"I thought we already played that with the locomotive wheels," he said, walking in the direction of her voice. "How about a game of chess instead?"

"I don't like chess… How about hide-and-seek?" she said.

He finally reached the stairs leading up to the second floor. Unlike the great hall, it was pitch black upstairs. But darkness was nothing to someone like him. He got into his black and red hyper-vision mode and climbed the stairs slowly.

"I'm coming Emily, are you ready?" he said.

"Not quite yet!" she replied playfully.

"Alright, I will count to ten, and after that I will find you," he said.

"No, you won't!" she replied.

He heard her laughter moving away from him in the shadows. He was still inside the train station, and he could see the floor and walls with his hyper-vision. He had never been in this part of the station, but it looked a lot like a labyrinth. Almost all the shops were the same size, with identical windows and facades. It would be hard to find her if she was hiding in one of them. But her voice seemed too distant to be coming from them… unless she was actually somewhere else.

"One," he counted as he walked. "Two."

He passed hat shops and tie shops, a few gift shops, and a toy store. He stopped in front of it.

"Three. Are you ready now?" he said.

"Not yet!" she said.

She was not in the toy store. Of course not. Emily owned a flower shop. He ran back to the flower shop he had just passed and entered it. Like the rest of the floor, it was pitch black, but he noticed a small, blue glowing door at the base of the counter, just like one Alice might have found in the Wonderland. It would have been too small for an ordinary adult man. Luckily, Stanley was born in the wrong body, and a skinny one too, so he opened the door and crawled inside. It led to a blue tunnel of which the walls, the floor and ceiling were all made of china dolls with glowing red eyes. Great. One of Stanley's phobias. He drew in a deep breath and focused on getting out of the tunnel, but all their little eyes on him sent him back to a time in his childhood when he experienced terrible fears and had no one to reassure him.

"If you try anything, I'll blow your porcelain heads to smithereens!" he warned the evil little things in a whisper, and perhaps they heard him for not one of them dared to move.

He eventually emerged from the tunnel in what appeared to be a crime scene. He was standing in the bedroom of a wealthy home, with elegant furniture and floral wallpaper on the walls. The room was dark and cold. Two bodies lay on the bed covered in their own blood, a hatchet on the bloody sheets beside them. The woman had been scalped. From their features, he could tell they were Emily's parents. She had murdered them. He gazed at them without any emotion.

"It's not fair. You didn't count to ten," he heard her say right behind him.

He spun around and she was facing him in her child form, dressed only in a light white summer dress, and her face painted like a sad clown. The joints of her arms and legs were like a puppet's, and he could almost see the invisible threads tied to her. He was suddenly reminded of his own alternate reality, the one in which Callie and Cornelius were his wife and child, but as puppets. So the puppet master was not only inside her mind but also in his.

"You shouldn't have seen this. Now I have to kill you," she said.

It was difficult to read her face under the makeup she wore, but he could hear sadness in her voice. She suddenly raised her right hand and long, black, twisted claws grew out of her fingers. Her hand then disappeared and reappeared out of thin air right beside him, but he caught it before it could reach him, and held her gaze.

"Why do we have to fight, when we are the same?" he asked her in a sad voice.

She stared into his eyes, and he could see in her eyes the will to fight quickly subside. The claws retreated inside her fingers and she brought her hand back to her own body.

"Why are we the same?" she asked in a fragile voice.

"I also killed my parents and my sister," he said.

"You did? Why?" she asked.

"I don't know," he said. "But I know that, like me, you never wanted to do this, right?"

She seemed to be struggling now.

"He made me… you made me…" she said, as though she was about to cry.

"Who made you?" he asked.

He took a step forward until they were only inches apart but kept his hands to his sides as to not frighten her.

"The voice… it's like yours," she said, trembling.

"But it wasn't me. Do you know who is talking to you? What's his name?"

"S…Stan…" she started, but she suddenly brought her hands to her throat. Someone was choking her.

"Emily!" he shouted, grabbing her arms.

"Don't touch me!" she warned him.

"I have to!" he said.

Though she struggled and resisted him, he felt his way around her head and found the invisible threads and broke them. She fell to the ground and he kneeled beside her.

"There, he can't hurt you anymore," he told her.

"Oh, you think so?" another voice echoed around them.

Stanley looked around him, confused. Whoever had just spoken had the exact same voice as him, pitch and all. Emily then vanished from his arms.

"Emily!" he cried, panicked.

"You want the girl? I hope you find her before she dies…" the voice said, followed by its vicious laughter.

Another glowing blue door appeared on the other side of the room. A sign on it read: 'Emily's story'. Stanley cautiously got up, and then he heard Joe's voice directly in his mind.

"Stanley, are you still doing alright?"

"Yes, I'm fine. Could you please not use my mind as a telephone?" Stanley told him.

"Sorry, I was very worried," Joe said in a small voice.

Stanley smirked.

"Are you all doing alright?" he asked.

"Let's see… Apart from a rotten sunflower storm and a few vampire-eating scarecrows roaming along the platforms, we're alright," Joe joked.

"Vampire-eating scarecrows?" Stanley repeated.

"They tried gnawing at us, except they didn't have teeth. Andre and I took care of them."

"Nice."

"And where are you?"

"I'm not sure, but it's not just us and Emily. The puppet master who controls her is in this dimension too," Stanley said.

"Puppet master?" Joe said.

"Yes. Now please get out of my head. I need to focus."

"Sure."

Stanley drew in his breath and walked over to the door and opened it. Whatever was behind, he had to go deeper into Emily's mind to find her.

CHAPTER 17

EVE FINALLY REACHED THE attic and pushed the door open and immediately covered herself with her arms. A dim blue light, like that of a cloudy day, was coming in through the tall, broken windows, and the air was icy. But it was not real sunlight, for it did not burn her alive. She immediately closed the door and moved a dresser in front of it—as though it could save her from a vengeful werewolf.

"Eve... I know where you are," she heard Nicolas' voice again, and then his heavy footsteps in the winding stone staircase.

She looked around her, terrified. There was nowhere to escape, except through the windows. And then what? Could she jump to the ground? As a vampire, would she survive the fall? Even in a dream, she could still experience pain. What did princesses usually do to escape monsters? Some used their long hair... She looked around her again. Her hair was not long enough to do anything, but there were multiple crates filled with old servants' dresses. She ran over to them and began to tear them up and tie them into a rope.

A loud knock and jolt against the door startled her.

"Eve... open the door," Nicolas ordered.

Hearing his voice again so close to her almost froze her with fear. Of all her abusers, he was not the one who had hurt her the most physically, but he was the one who had scarred her forever inside, because she had loved him—so much. She had placed all her trust in him as her protector, and he had turned into the greatest source of danger for her.

"Eve... fight!" she heard the Fae tell her.

She shook her head and her eyes welled up with tears. She could not fight Nicolas, the man she knew had loved her so much, to the point of letting himself be killed when she escaped him. The only man, perhaps, who had ever truly loved her.

He kicked the door again, harder this time. He was going to break it down in a matter of seconds, she knew it. So, even if she did not have enough of her makeshift rope, she tied it to one of the angled beams of the low ceiling and got out the window and began to let herself down the stone wall of the castle. She then heard the door burst open, and soon Nicolas's terrible, werewolf face appeared at the window.

"You cannot escape me!" he snarled, and he began to pull her back up.

"No! No!" she cried.

She was still too high above the ground not to hurt herself, but she had no choice now. So, she let go of the rope and fell to the ground. She felt the bones in her legs shatter as they hit the dirt and shrieked in pain. But vampire wounds—and bones—healed quickly. In just a few seconds, her bones were back together—not quite like they had been before, but sturdy enough that she could stand on her two legs. The wounds still throbbing with pain, she limped her way to the castle's gates. But ahead of them was not the forest of the Gevaudan mountains she knew so well; a thick forest of thorns and swamps had replaced it. It surrounded the castle. Had she not been through it before, the last time she escaped him? She was sure she had, except it was somewhere else in the forest. A magical swampland that moved across the forest? Either way, she had to get across it, so she ran into it, ignoring the pain, and immediately her feet sunk into the mud knee-high. She removed her boots and stockings to move faster in the mud and tore off her dress knee-high so it would not weigh her down so much.

"I won't stop! I mustn't!" she repeated to herself.

Her mother, Faustine, and all her ancestors had taught her to be a strong, independent woman. She would not let a man kill her—not even in a dream.

"Eve, look inside you," the strange voice she had heard before and that was not the Fae suddenly said.

"What? Who are you? Stanley?" she said, looking around her as she made it deeper into the swamps.

The thorns and trees now almost completely shielded her from the dim, blue sunlight, but she had no fear of the darkness. She was a vampire, after all; darkness was her realm.

She felt something stir inside her chest and it began to glow with a soft red light. She stopped for a second, and suddenly the rose Stanley had given her emerged from it. What could she possibly do with a rose now? But everything had a meaning in dreams, so she took it and marched on.

"You know my name," the voice said.

"You sure sound like someone I know, but that doesn't mean I'm going to trust you," she responded. "Get out of my head! I don't need anyone's help!"

"Eve, I'm only here to protect you. These men want to hurt you," the voice said.

"What men?" Eve said, coming to a halt.

"Eve, what are you doing? Were you trying to betray me?" Astaroth's deep voice said to her right, and she turned around, terrified.

He was standing there, in the swamp, clad in his purple and green suit, his arms crossed and a triumphant grin on his lips.

Eve immediately darted off to her left but only found herself facing another man, a shorter, blond one in a crimson suit. His eyes were a piercing green color and he did not appear to be a vampire.

"My apologies," he said with a condescending smile. "My tongue slipped and I told Astaroth where you were headed."

She recognized Belial's voice—the man who was supposed to protect her. They surrounded her, and now Nicolas was approaching her too. He had fully transformed into a were-wolf, and the only human thing about him was his torn, red justaucorps.

"Fight!" the Fae told her.

"Come to me, I will protect you," the other voice told her.

She shook her head and began to run again to escape them. How many more men would she have to escape? All those who abused her? This nightmare had to end somehow, but she did not know how to make it end. She knew how to protect other women from the violence of men, but when it came to herself, she had failed miserably.

She ran for long minutes, tripping, falling, and tearing her dress more at times.

"That's it, come to me," the voice guided her, and because she had no better idea, she followed it, until she came to solid ground again and emerged into a small clearing with a little house. It was a lovely cottage, lost in the middle of the forest, and around it in the grass was a bucket of rainwater, the frame of an old cart, and a spinster wheel. Above the front door, bundles of dried herbs were hanging, as well as garlic. Eve smiled. An old woman probably lived there—a superstitious one. Had this happened in real life, Eve would have thought

about protecting her from her pursuers, but this was a dream, and her thoughts were not as clear, so she imagined she would be safe inside the little home and ran to it.

"Open the door and you'll be safe," the mysterious voice urged her, and she obeyed it. But no sooner had she pushed the door open than she found herself in her childhood home again, at a time when her father ruled over her and her mother like a king, except, this time, she was playing the role of her mother and protecting her young self.

"What do you think you're doing, you stupid woman?" her father yelled in her face. "That child is a boy and his name is Paul! So take that stupid dress off him and put him to work!"

"No!" she firmly replied.

Behind her, her five-year-old self trembled with fear in the beautiful Cinderella dress her mother had made her.

"You little bitch!" he said, grabbing her by the throat.

He threw her to the ground and punched her repeatedly, her face, her arms, her belly, he spared no part of her body, and she curled up into a ball like Maryse used to and covered her face with her hands, crying. She could hear her child self crying as well, and all she could think of was how to get the two of them out of that house. But to go where? Who in the village would protect them? No one.

"Uh oh, it looks like you've only returned to the beginning," the voice said in a mocking tone.

Now she was sure it was not Stanley but someone trying to trick her by using his voice, so she would no longer listen to it.

Her father kicked and punched her until he was satisfied, then he walked heavily over to the pantry and grabbed a bottle of strong wine to quench his alcoholic thirst. Eve remembered her father being violent to her and her mother, but she had forgotten how savage he could be, and how he terrified both of them. What could a woman and child, bound to a violent man by law, do to escape him? In a society where the Church told its followers every Sunday that women should obey their husbands, and when even the Bible detailed how a man was allowed to beat his wife if she misbehaved, what could they do? They were helpless. Helpless. She hated that word. Had she not fought for all these years so that women could finally be considered independent human beings with rights, and not the possessions of men? She turned her desperate gaze to her child self, who looked up to her for protection and had no one else, but she no longer had the strength to fight. The barely mended bones of her legs still hurt her, and her body was sore everywhere. She could feel blood pouring down the side of her right eye, where her father had punched her.

"Why... why are you putting me through this? Haven't you had enough?" she whispered to whoever was controlling her mind in such a cruel way.

"Shut up, you bitch!" her father shouted, and he knocked her in the back of the head with the wine bottle he was holding.

"Poor Eve... so fragile and alone. I wonder what all these men are going to do to you..." the voice said.

She looked up and saw Astaroth's shadow leaning against the glass of the small window behind her child self, and Nicolas' deep, low snarl resounded behind the front door. He began throwing himself against it and scratching it. They were going to get inside and kill her – all of them. Nothing and no one could save her now. She closed her eyes and waited, ready to accept her fate this time. She had fought as hard as she could, but in the end, she had lost.

But, just as she was giving up the last of her hope, she felt something lukewarm on her hand, like a kiss, and she clearly heard Stanley's voice. His words were unclear, but the pitch, the tone, and the manner of speech were his. She thought she heard the words 'I love you'. She opened her eyes and saw the red rose on the floor beside her, brushing against her hand, and it glowed again in a soft red hue. A great warmth now swept across her body, and she felt the presence of her mother, Faustine, Aurelia, and all her female ancestors. She felt their love and protection. It was not over yet; she still had the Fae, a supernatural gift handed down to her by generations of women, and she also had the gift of a stranger who cared about her. Gathering her strength, she crawled back onto her hands and knees, and eventually managed to stand up just as Nicolas broke down the door. He and Astaroth came in and stood before her. Then, slowly, they fused together into a giant werewolf covered in thick, black fur. Each of its paws was as large as Eve's head, and its mouth was big enough to swallow her whole. It crouched before her.

"What a terrible monster lives inside your head…" the mischievous voice said this time. *"I wonder what he will do to you. Will he rape you and then skin you alive? Will he devour you, one limb after another, as you cry out for help?"*

"Wouldn't you like to know?" Eve retorted, powering up.

The one who had created this and visibly intended to scare her by using her greatest fears against her seemed puzzled by her response and did not answer.

The monster was ready to attack her, but so was she. So, as it lunged at her, she released the Fae upon it. With a loud and piercing ethereal shriek, it grabbed the monster's head and dug its long claws into it. The monster snarled and fell to the ground with the Fae, and Eve suddenly remembered the words of the demon sealing spell. She opened her mouth, and as she spoke, they came out of the Fae's mouth instead: "Ovilus

Ocidoe Mabya Unah, Seve Deu Amakhna, Diez Deoi Avilis, Lehtyoht Livyoht Ocida!"

Because the monster contained a demon within him perhaps, he let go of the Fae and let out a loud cry before exploding. Eve covered herself as the beast's blood splattered all over her, and then she turned to her child self to see if she was alright, but she had disappeared. The Fae floated back to her, awaiting her bidding. She was alone now in her old home and safe, but still stuck inside that dream. She heard the sound of hands clapping around her.

"Bravo, Mademoiselle," the voice said. *"You have defeated your demons, but why are you still stuck here? I wonder..."*

"Because you're keeping me here. What do you want from me?" she replied in an angry voice.

There was no fear, no weakness left inside her, and she was ready to face whoever was pulling the strings behind this nightmare. But the mysterious voice did not answer her. Too bad. She did not need it to get out of here. There was another spell she remembered now, one to lift the veils of illusion and reveal the truth. So, still clenching the rose in her hand, she recited it: "Varieh Amarya Selphea Unah, Drivai Seve Hemsallah, Drivai Seve Miravis, Leptu Ocida!"

Like the last time, the words did not come out in her voice, but in that of the Fae, and instantly the house, the walls around her, the forest, everything collapsed like a deck of cards. None of it was ever real, she already knew that, but also now she could see they were nothing more than a child's drawings on giant sheets of paper. And when all of them had fallen, she stood in an attic – not the one from Nicolas' castle, but a modern one. To her left was a tall, dusty mirror leaning against the wall. In front of her was a small table with what appeared to be the tools used to perform an exorcism. On the floor was a Ouija board and some old, discarded china dolls, and to her right was some-one. She turned to the shadows and could barely distinguish two pale, skinny hands, and a shape. She could not tell whether the person was a man or a woman, nor what they were wearing, but the size of the hands matched that of an older child or young adult, and they appeared to be sitting on a pile of old toys. A toy ring was on their slender finger. The moment she turned her gaze in their direction, she heard the voice that had been haunting her shriek.

"Get out!" it hissed, and Eve suddenly opened her eyes in Andre's arms.

"What... what happened?" she asked.

"Are you awake now?" Andre gently asked her.

She sat up and looked around her. She was with Andre and Joe, in one of the wagons in the train station. They were still stuck in that alternate reality. Joe looked anxiously out the window of the wagon, on the lookout for more monsters or traps.

"Where is Stanley?" she asked, sitting up on the seat.

"This alternate world was created by Emily," Joe said, turning back to them.

"Emily? But how? Why?" she said, confused.

"We thought she was jealous of you and Stanley, but he thinks it is something else," Andre explained.

"Well, whatever it is, now I know how to get us out of here. I remembered the spell in my dream," she said.

"We can't do anything now. We must wait for Stanley's signal," Joe said.

"Why?"

"Because he thinks Emily is being manipulated by some-one. He calls him the 'puppet master'."

"The puppet master? Yes... I found him in my dream somehow, and that's when he kicked me out of it," she said.

"You found him? Did you see his face?" Andre asked.

"No, but his voice was very similar to Stanley's."

"So you think Stanley could be the puppet master?" Joe said, frowning.

"I don't know. I heard both their voices on separate occasions in my dream. The pitch was the same, but not the way they spoke," she said. "Stanley always holds his breath for a split second before speaking because he knows he might stutter. This one did not have any problems speaking."

"Perhaps this puppet master can impersonate people, but never quite perfectly?" Andre suggested.

"I agree," Eve said. "But I didn't fall for it and I found him. He didn't like that."

"Then he will certainly try to punish you," Joe said.

"Let him try. I've got a few more spells ready for him," Eve said.

Joe and Andre both noticed how her demeanor had changed, and how much stronger she seemed now. Whatever monsters she had faced in her dream, she had vanquished them on her own, like Stanley said.

"Stanley was right to trust you. He never doubted that you could save yourself," Joe told her with a smile.

"Stanley?" she said, surprised.

"You seem to know each other very well," Joe said, and Eve stared at him.

"Speaking of him, how will we know when he is ready for us to intervene?" Andre asked Joe.

"Or when he stupidly dies?" Eve said.

"I am in contact with him through his mind. It is part of my abilities as a necromancer—and no, I am not the puppet master, I promise," Joe said.

"You look too sweet to be that sort of monster," Eve said. "So at this point, we're all on standby?"

"Right," Andre said.

She sighed and rested her head in her hands, and then she remembered the rose. Was it truly magical or just a part of her dream? She no longer had her purse with her, but she reached into , just to see if anything would happen, and her fingers touched something. She pulled it out and it was the same rose, except the golden thread was missing from it. Her eyes opened wide as she realized the meaning of it, what she had missed all along.

"We need to go find Stanley, now," she said, rising to her feet at once.

"But he said…" Joe started.

"I can't explain how, but I know Stanley and I are connected by this magical rose and the golden thread that used to be tied to its stem," she told them. "Stay here if you want. I'm going to find him."

She walked across the wagon to the door and kicked it open. Now this puppet master had really pissed her off, and she was not going to let him take the lives of Stanley and Emily. Joe and Andre scrambled behind her.

"Eve wait!" Andre cried.

"We're coming with you!" Joe said.

She turned to them and smirked.

"Are you two afraid of the dark? Because we're going deep into the darkness," she said.

"Oh, I think we can handle that," Andre replied with a grin.

He brought out the Bouncer as they were sure to encounter a few monsters along the way, and they got out of the train and rushed over to the great hall. There, Eve quickly spotted the golden thread tied to the railing of the stairs leading up to the second level.

"It's my turn to save you, Stanley," she whispered.

Stanley stood in the darkness before three doors, all identical. Above them was a sign with the question 'Where was Emily born?'. The sign on the first door read 'Paris', the one on the second door read 'Rouen', and the one on the third door read 'Reims'. Stanley frowned. He had no idea where she was born. Had she ever even told him? His first guess would of course be Rouen, since she owned an apartment there, but she also owned a flower shop in Paris. He racked his brain. She had probably mentioned it when she introduced herself to the members of her circle. He tried to replay the scene in his mind as best he could, and then he remembered her saying it, but it was not one of these names. It sounded something like 'Chamicy' or 'Chantely'.

"Chamity? No, that's not it," he said. "Puppet master… you want to play, but you're not playing fair!"

He heard the voice of the puppet master laughing.

"Why am I not playing fair?" it said. *"You have eyes."*

"I can't choose any of these doors because none of them are correct," Stanley said.

"One of them is. It's only a matter of how you look at it," the voice said in response.

Stanley smirked. Yes, he had definitely been in this one's alternate world before, or the puppet master in his, he was sure of it. So he walked to the first door and flipped the sign. On the back of it was the word 'Chartres'. Not that one. He flipped the second one and it said 'Giverny'. Possible. He then flipped the third one and read the word aloud: "Chantilly". That was definitely the one. He grinned and pushed the door open. It led to another dark place. In the center of it, under a bright spotlight like the stage of a theater, was Emily, sitting on a bed. She was very much younger—perhaps thirteen or fourteen—and slenderer. This was long before she awakened as a vampire and her beautiful eyes were the color of the summer sky. Her curly blond hair was not nearly as long as he had seen it on her, but it was pulled back into a tiny bun she seemed very proud of, and she wore a white polka dot dress that most certainly belonged to a bigger woman, her mother perhaps. He then heard the sound of a door opening and a woman screaming something in French. Emily got up, terrified, and then she and the bed vanished. Three doors appeared in front of Stanley, with the question: 'What happens next?'

Stanley did not have the answer, but as he read the suggestions on the signs on the doors, he suddenly remembered. She had been sent to a correctional home for boys. How could he have forgotten something that had obviously shaped so much of her life? He assuredly walked over to the door bearing the sign 'Correctional home' and pushed it open.

In the next scene, she was sitting on a dirty floor beside a bunk bed. Her beautiful curls had been shaved off. She was wearing a worn-out brown shirt and pants, like a prisoner, and she was crying. Four strong arms, also clad in the same brown shirts, suddenly came out of the darkness, grabbed her arms, and dragged her away from Stanley's sight.

"Emily!" he cried out, but he could no longer see her.

She had never told them what happened to her in the correctional home, but, judging from her cries, it was not hard to guess. Stanley balled his fists.

"Enough!" he shouted. "Take me to Emily now!"

The voice laughed again.

"How can you claim you want to save a girl you don't even know?" it said.

"I know her enough!"

"Really? Then can you answer the next question?"

Three doors appeared once again, and this time the question was 'Who was Emily's first love?'. Stanley did not know, and he was sure Emily had not shared that information with anyone at the meeting. There were three names to choose from: 'Robert', 'Eric', and 'Sylvain', and beneath each of them was a yellowed photograph tenderly framed by a young woman in love. Having no clue what type of man Emily liked, Stanley went to each of them and observed them carefully. All three of them were reasonably handsome, although he was not into men. Robert was apparently an officer, Sylvain a sailor, and Eric looked more like an unskilled worker, perhaps a laborer or someone who worked in a factory. He had the kindest face of the three of them, and a small, dried daisy had been slipped in the frame—perhaps the first gift the young man gave the young woman in love. This one had to be Emily's. Stanley opened the door, and this time he found himself standing on the edge of a cliff in the darkness. Beneath him was a sort of bloody stew in which floated a multitude of blond hair scalps and women's bodies, as well as the ones of Eric and Emily's parents. Before him was a rope bridge, and in the middle, standing perfectly still with her bare feet on the strings, was Emily's child form. She looked down and seemed terrified. Behind her, in the distance, Stanley could see the shape of someone sitting on a throne, probably the puppet master.

"Good job," he said, clapping his hands.

Stanley ignored him and held out his hand to Emily.

"Emily! Come to me! I will save you!" he cried.

She turned her frightened eyes to him.

"It's a lie," the puppet master said.

"Don't listen to him, Emily!" Stanley said. "Why would I come all this way if not to save you?"

"He's a hitman. He just wants to kill you," the puppet master told her.

Emily looked back at him, then turned to Stanley again.

"Is it true?" she said in a small, fragile voice.

"I was a hitman, but not anymore," Stanley said, lowering his eyes. "Emily, please come to me!"

She looked down once more at the bloody stream underneath her. The level was rising quickly. She turned back to him with moist eyes.

"I can't. Every time I become close to someone, he makes me kill them!" she said, clinging to the ropes on either side of her.

The rope bridge rocked as she moved. This was not good. Stanley did not know what could happen to her if she drowned in her dream, but he did not want to find out.

"Alright, stay there, I will come to you!" he said.

He was not afraid of heights, but he had never been on a rope bridge before. He cautiously grabbed the ropes on either side and descended slowly onto it. It was not too difficult. The bridge rocked a few times, but he finally made it to Emily.

"Emily, come," he told her with a warm smile.

He reached for her hand, but the moment he touched it, his skin began to freeze.

"Stanley, no!" she begged him. "You will lose your hand if you touch me!"

He smiled.

"I'm not afraid of you—nor of losing a hand for you. Besides, I'm a demon and a vampire. It will probably grow back," he joked.

She took his hand, and the cold crept up his arm, but still he would not let go. They made their way slowly back to the cliff, and he climbed onto it, but before she could, the bridge suddenly vanished.

"Emily!" he cried.

She almost fell, but he held on to her as tightly as his frozen fingers could. He lay on the ground and grabbed her with his other hand as well.

"Stanley! You must let go! You'll lose your arms!" she cried, desperate.

Tears streamed down her cold cheeks, washing away the clown face to reveal her gentle, youthful features.

"I'm sorry Emily. I'm sorry for everything I didn't see, for every time I didn't listen," he told her. "But I can't let go of you. I'm going to save you!"

"Why? I'm not important. You're in love with Eve," she said, gazing into his eyes.

He had no answer for her and his hands were losing their grip. She shook her head sadly.

"In the end, I was nothing to anyone..." she whispered.

She was beginning to let go of his hand.

"No! No! No!" he cried.

But suddenly another pair of arms grabbed Emily's, and another. The first was Eve's, and the second Joe's. Two giant blue arms then reached down and grabbed Emily by the waist. Andre was there too, with his Bouncer, and the Fae floated above all of them as to protect them.

"H-How did you get here?" Stanley said, surprised.

"I'll tell you later," Eve said. "Emily! Please let us help you!"

Her and Joe's hands were also frozen now, but they did not let go, and neither did Stanley.

"What are you doing? You should let go of me!" Emily pleaded, crying. "I don't deserve to live. Look at all this blood... it's from all the people I killed!"

"Oh, don't be such a silly goose. We've all killed people. We're vampires," Eve told her.

"But I'm cold inside. I am the winter... you will freeze if you touch me," Emily said.

"Emily, it's only a passing squall," Joe told her with a friendly smile.

"We're all terrible people. This world has broken all of us in some way, but here we are, all together," Stanley told her. "Remember why you created that circle: so that we could all protect each other in this cruel world that won't."

"We're like a family—your family," Eve told her.

"Eve, we need that spell of yours, now," Andre said. "I'm trying to pull her up, but something else is pulling her down!"

Stanley noticed how high the level of the bloody stream was getting, and the waters were moving up in intermittent waves now. One of them hit Emily's legs and they broke off like icicles. She cried out in pain.

"Emily! Let us pull you up!" Stanley shouted, panicked.

"I can't! I'm not strong enough!" she said.

Eve powered up the Fae and turned to the puppet master in the distance.

"We're not afraid of you. We're stronger than you think," she warned him.

"No, you're not," he answered with confidence.

Eve could still not see his face, but she could tell he was smiling in the shadows. But she would not let him win and take Emily from them. She opened her mouth and through the Fae shouted: "Varieh Amarya Selphea Unah, Drivai Seve Hemsallah, Drivai Seve Miravis, Leptu Ocida!"

The cliff and the bloody stream instantly disappeared, along with the puppet master, and all five of them fell. Joe and Andre hit the floor first and rolled. Eve bounced against a brick wall and fell onto her hands and knees, and Emily and Stanley fell through the glass of the window of a shop. They were back in the real world, in the train station, in a part of the second floor closed to the public.

"Are we back?" Eve asked.

The Fae had returned inside her.

"I think so," Andre said, as he helped Joe up.

Stanley pushed himself up over Emily. She had resumed her vampire form and her legs were alright, but a large piece of glass had pierced her chest and she was bleeding profusely. Around the wound, her skin was melting away and turning into ashes.

"Emily! No!" he cried.

He tried to remove the piece of glass, but his hands were still frozen. Emily smiled and shook her head.

"Sometimes you just can't win," she whispered. "But I'm glad you all came... just for me."

"Emily!" Eve cried as she rushed over to her side and took her hand with her frozen fingers.

"Eve... are we still friends?" Emily asked her.

"Yes, we will always be friends! You are as dear to me as Faustine!" Eve said, crying.

Stanley once again wanted to turn back time to save Emily, but how far should he go? When did the puppet master start manipulating her? He realized the limitations of the Time Key, and that he could simply never turn back time enough to save everyone.

"Stanley, I have something to ask you," Emily then said, turning to him.

Joe and Andre also came and kneeled beside her.

"What is it?" Stanley asked her, as tears also rolled down his cheeks.

"Would you kiss me… on the forehead? You promised me. I know I'm not a princess, but you were my prince," she whispered, her eyes also welling up with tears.

"I'm not a prince," he whispered, but he leaned forward and, instead of kissing her forehead, he kissed her lips softly. She smiled through her tears and gazed into his eyes, and her black eyes were the last thing he saw of her before her entire body dissolved into ashes. All four of them then saw her soul leaving her body in its childlike, girl form, except her face was no longer painted like a sad clown and she was no longer a puppet. She smiled at them and vanished into the darkness, and Stanley let himself fall among her ashes, heartbroken. By his side, Eve covered her face and wept loudly, and Andre wrapped his arms around her, while Joe pulled out a handkerchief and covered his face with it. They had lost this battle, and it had cost them an irreplaceable life. Even though Emily thought she was so small and invisible, and no matter what she had done in the past, she had brought them all together and touched their hearts in a way no one else ever would.

CHAPTER 18

STANLEY SAT ON A sofa in the dining room of Joe and Andre's new home, his head hanging low. By his side, Cornelius sat, leaning against him. On another sofa, Joe finished a bottle of gin, his sleeves rolled up and his dark gaze lost in the dancing flames in the chimney. Though the mansion had electricity, they had not turned on any lights other than the fire. They couldn't. He and Andre had not even had a chance to move in and enjoy their first love nest before a new tragedy struck. He was used to grieving the loss of a friend or a loved one, but this loss was somehow crueler than all the others. They were so close to saving Emily… so close.

Having no willpower or desire to do anything after what happened the night before, and because Eve was still in danger, they all returned to Joe's mansion and Joe, who knew Belial, called him. Astaroth knew that Joe did not trust demons, especially him, so he would not dare to come here looking for Eve. Furthermore, she had not exactly been friends with him or Andre before that night, so he would have no reason to assume she would be with them. Belial, who appeared to be busy with something else, had not told Joe what he intended to do yet, so they decided to rest for the night—those who could—then figure out their next move. They installed Eve in a room without mirrors because demons could use them to travel, and Andre made the arrangements to have his and Joe's belongings delivered from the hotel where they had been staying. Stanley did not have any belongings, and now he no longer had the magical feather given to him by Cat, either. Andre came down the large, carpeted staircase leading to the entrance hall and dining room. He walked over to them and quietly took the bottle of gin from Joe's hands.

"Andre..." Joe protested in a whisper.

"Come with me," Andre whispered.

Joe got up and followed him to the drawing room, and Andre closed the door.

"I just called Hans and Mischa in Paris. They were devastated," he said.

Joe nodded and pursed his lips.

"Any news from Belial?" Andre asked him.

"No, and I was not able to explain to him what had happened," Joe said.

He walked over to a cabinet and pulled out another bottle.

"That's enough, Joe," Andre gently told him.

"Why? Can't I even drink after losing yet another friend? I spend all my undead life burying friends," Joe said in a dark voice.

"Not when you have living friends who need your support," Andre said. "Let's go back to Stanley."

"I don't think it matters to him who is there or not," Joe said.

He put away the bottle anyhow.

"It does, and it would matter to Emily," Andre said. "Do you think this is how she would want us to celebrate her life? By sitting in the dark and drinking away our sadness?"

Joe smirked.

"Emily's life will never be celebrated. I don't think many people will even remember her name," he said in a cynical voice.

Andre hated when Joe drank and became like this. He was aware of his drinking problems, but he had been drinking a lot less since they got together and he had hoped it would become a thing of the past. People thought they were living the dream—a newly mated couple spending their honeymoon in France—but it was darkness that had brought them together. Joe was a depressed alcoholic, and Andre was the sort of man who always hid his own sadness behind a smile and a positive attitude. He had to be everyone's hero and save the day. That night, he, too, wanted to drink and forget everything with Joe, but someone had to stand strong and support all of them, and it had to be him.

"Do what you want, then. But I will celebrate her life," he said.

He was about to leave the room, but Joe caught his arm and pulled him to him, then dropped his head onto his shoulder and burst into tears. Andre slipped his arms around him in a tight embrace.

"I'm sorry Andre, I just can't deal with this alone. Not again," Joe said softly.

"You're not alone," Andre said, running his fingers through his thick black curls. "And it's alright if you cry in front of Stanley. He doesn't expect you to be stronger than him. We're all in this together."

Stanley sat silently, gazing at the flames, and replaying the last twenty-four hours in his mind, wondering how far he should go back in time, and what he could have done to prevent this from happening. Perhaps he could have visited Emily rather than go feed, perhaps he could go back and stalk her until he found out who the puppet master was and killed him. A dark desire, darker than any other before, rose inside him. He would find the puppet master and not only kill him—he would torture him to death for what he did to Emily...

He looked down to his hands still clutching the small hand-kerchief in which he had gathered some of Emily's ashes. Andre had taken away his soiled clothes and given him one of Joe's black morning suits to wear because he had nothing black in his wardrobe. Joe had broader shoulders than Stanley and the suit was too big, but it was comforting.

"Stanley..." Cornelius said softly.

"Not now," Stanley said.

The child ghost did not know Emily, but he understood the grief of adults and, right now, he did not know where to go. So he left the sofa and flew over to the drawing room where Joe and Andre had retreated. He flew in through the wall and found them embracing each other and crying, and he, too, burst into tears.

"Cornelius!" Joe said, surprised.

"Stanley is sad, and everyone is crying, and I... I..." Cornelius sobbed.

Joe left Andre and picked up the child ghost in his arms. He sat down in a chair with him and rocked him softly. Andre came to sit on the arm of the chair with them. As a spiritual, like Eve, he could sense the aura of Cornelius rather than actually see him, but Joe could clearly see him.

"We're all very sad because we lost a dear friend," Joe explained to Cornelius. "But it will get better, I promise. Stanley will get better soon."

Joe's scent and voice were especially soothing to ghosts, and he tended to attract them like a magnet. And while Cornelius perceived Stanley as his big brother, he felt like a tiny child again with Joe and wanted him as a parent figure, like Eve. So he curled up against him and closed his eyes.

"Stanley is always sad. I don't know if he will get better…" he whispered.

"We will help him," Joe promised.

Eve awakened around seven that night. Frightened by this unknown room at first, she soon remembered where she was and why. She sat up on the bed and looked around her. The bedroom was completely dark. She had slept in her black dress because Joe and Andre did not have any clothes she could wear, and her hair was probably a mess. She slowly got up and opened the door. The corridor was silent. She remembered there were two bathrooms on this floor and walked over to one of them. There were no candles because the home had electricity, so she switched on the bright light and gazed at her face in the mirror. She looked more like a witch than ever, with all the black eye makeup running down her cheeks and her tangled hair.

"Look at me, Emily," she joked, before bursting into tears.

She walked over to the faucet and washed her face, washing away both the makeup and the tears, then she combed her hair as best she could and let it fall loosely over her shoulders. Her perfect iron curls were gone now; only uneven waves remained. At least she was already wearing mourning clothes and did not have to worry about that. She noticed an empty vial near the sink and picked it up and slipped it inside her pocket, then left the room.

She went downstairs to the dining room and found Stanley alone in the dark, staring at the flames in the chimney. The young man had been only a stranger to her until last night, but now everything was different. She walked over to him and sat by his side.

"You're awake…" she said.

He lifted his gaze and turned to her, only then realizing how close to him she was sitting.

"I couldn't sleep," he said.

She noticed the handkerchief he was holding and pulled the vial out of her pocket.

"Why don't you put her ashes in this? It will be better than a handkerchief," she said softly.

He did not answer, so she took the handkerchief from his hands and helped him pour the ashes into the small glass vial and close the lid. They held the vial together for some time, then Stanley slipped it inside his breast pocket.

"Emily loved you," Eve then whispered, lowering her gaze.

"And I didn't even pay attention to her. What a horrible man I am..." he whispered.

Eve shook her head.

"Among all of us, you are the one who paid the most attention to her. None of us would have understood how much she was suffering. We would probably have reacted like vampires do when they are attacked. We would have killed her."

"No, I don't think you would have," Stanley said. "Neither would those two goody-goodies."

Eve unwillingly smiled.

"But how did you find me?" Stanley asked.

"I followed the golden thread, just like in our dreams... Ernest," she said, turning to him.

Stanley froze. How and when had she realized who he was, and why had she not said anything?

"I... I can explain everything!" he said, panicked.

"Go ahead," she said, removing her gaze from his.

"If I do, will you hate me?"

"It will depend on your explanation."

He lowered his head and sighed.

"I didn't mean to lie to you, I just thought… I didn't want to sound like a lunatic when I wrote you the first time. Stanley isn't my birth name, obviously, but my legal surname is Suspect. Stanley Suspect… it sounded stupid, so I signed the letter 'Ernest' instead," he said nervously. "And then I saw you in person in Edinburgh when I was still human. That's how I knew you were transgender. It was not obvious, just a feeling I had. Something about you touched me so deeply that night that I could never stop thinking about you. A group of men tried to burn down the theater, and you saved everyone, but you wouldn't remember me, of course. I know I should have told you the truth about who I was and what I did, but I was afraid you would hate me…"

"Why? What did you do?" she asked softly.

"I found out I was a murderer since my childhood, and I simply followed the same path as an adult," he explained. "I became a demon and worked as a hitman of the underworld. I was a cold-blooded killer for a living, but I quit that life."

"I see," she said, bringing her hands together on her lap.

"I didn't lie in my letters about my feelings for you, it was all true," he continued. "But someone intercepted one of my letters to you and changed it. I couldn't understand why you stopped writing me. I was heartbroken, until I had a dream and a magical creature showed me what happened and gave me the rose for you. But I also saw you were in danger and decided to leave everything and go to France to protect you. That was when I got captured by my former employers and, when I escaped, I ran into Belial, who hired me to spy on you and Astaroth. That's the whole truth. I came for you, but I was also supposed to watch you. I tried telling you once, but you got so angry I had no choice but to turn back time and not tell you. But every time I use the Time Key, someone dies…"

"The Time Key…" she said.

"It's some kind of ancient artifact. When it came into my possession, it had the shape of a pocket watch. I swallowed it out of spite after I found out my lover Callie had only been playing games with me and intended to go back in time to be with the man she actually loved all along."

"That sounds like something you might do," she said, smiling to herself.

He turned to her and waited to hear what she had to say, but she left the conversation there and got up.

"Eve…" he said.

She turned to him, and he could not read the expression in her eyes. Was it anger? Sadness? Disappointment?

"Are you angry? Please tell me the truth…" he said in a soft voice.

"I don't know, Stanley," she said, before walking away.

A loud knock on the front door startled all of them. Joe and Andre came out of the drawing room with Cornelius and gestured to Eve to retreat in the office until they knew who it was, and so she did.

Andre opened the door. It was Belial. He stood under the rain, dressed in a black suit and hat, a briefcase tucked underneath his arm.

"Good evening. What a storm out there!" he said, tipping his hat.

He walked inside and removed his coat and hat as though he owned the place and hung them on a coat rack.

"What took you so long?" Joe asked him, frowning.

"An arrest warrant and an uncooperative criminal," Belial said.

"Fair enough. And do we get a briefing on what Astaroth was involved in, or is it classified information?" Joe asked.

"I promise you will all get a briefing later about the reasons why I brought you together. Where is my witness?" Belial said in response.

Joe rolled his eyes with irritation.

"In the office," Andre said, closing the front door. "Eve, you can come out, it's Belial," he then said.

Belial noticed Stanley on the sofa and pointed his finger at him.

"You, I need to talk to you in a minute," he said in a somewhat angry voice, and Stanley sighed.

Really? He was going to scold him now for not keeping in touch with him after what just happened?

Eve cautiously opened the office's door.

"Are you Belial?" she asked in a suspicious voice.

"Pleasure to meet you, Mademoiselle," the demon said, extending his hand to her, but she would not shake it.

"Where is Astaroth?" she asked instead.

"Let us talk privately for a moment," he offered.

She let him inside and closed the door.

"You'd better not try anything," she warned him. "I blew up Astaroth in that alternate reality. I'm sure I can do the same with you here and now."

He smiled.

"I'm glad to see you have recovered your spirit, and no, I do not wish to sample your powers tonight. I'd rather talk peacefully," he said.

"Then talk. I'm listening," she said, crossing her arms.

"Because I now have enough evidence to prove Astaroth's intent to conspire against me, I was able to use the article 422 of the Demonic Constitution to issue an arrest warrant against him and have him taken to Hell and incarcerated. Of course, it did not go smoothly and I had to hire some muscle, but you are safe now, I promise. I will, however, need a deposition from you in order to formally prosecute him."

A cold chill went down her spine. Even if he was prosecuted, as long as he lived, he might return looking for her. He would never forgive her for testifying against him. But she could not live in fear all her undead life. She no longer wanted to.

"I want to testify against him, but I made a pact with him and he ordered me not to use my mouth against him," she said.

"I see. It was clever of him, since you know the only spell that could seal a major demon," Belial said with a grin.

"If you know, then why are you trying to help me? I could seal you away and take your place," she said with a frown.

"I don't think you would want my job," he replied, still smiling. "Mostly paperwork, no personal life…"

She finally broke into a smile.

"So, how do we do this?"

"Do you think you could perhaps put in writing what you cannot tell me?" he said, turning serious.

"I could try," she said.

He invited her to sit at the desk and switched on the desk lamp. He then pulled out some forms from his briefcase and a pen.

"Please write only using this magical pen. It belongs to me, so no one will be able to read what you wrote until I reveal it. I will keep it sealed away until the trial date," he said.

She took the pen and the paper.

"I don't know the rules in the world of demons… What can you prosecute him for?" she then asked, looking up to him.

"Demons do have a code of conduct," Belial explained. "Such things as senseless murder and torture are not permitted outside of the execution of a contract. A demonic pact is also meant to benefit both parties, even if they do not benefit equally from it, and while bending the truth in order to obtain a pact is permissible, using my name in vain is not. I have heard from several sources now that Astaroth has been claiming that I transformed him into a man. That is not true, and no demon has the power to permanently alter anyone's body."

"I know… He told me how he got his body," she said. "Belial, why would a transgender individual prey on others like him? Of all people, why would he choose to hurt us?"

"I do not know," Belial said. "I only know that there are such individuals in all circles. I am not familiar with transgender circles, but I have seen homosexual men calling for the arrest and prosecution of their peers. Sometimes their anger is fueled by a specific person, or something that was said or done. Cruelty is unfortunately a part of this world."

"But does that mean we should respond with similar cruelty?" she asked him, and he could see the sincerity in her eyes.

"Eve, I know you have been close to Astaroth, and you may understand his motives better than I do, but he has hurt and abused you. He has also conspired with you and probably others to murder me. It is my job to prosecute and sentence him in accordance with his crimes, nothing more, nothing less."

"I understand," she said. She took the pen and gazed at the blank sheet of paper. "Belial, do you think there will ever be a world in which people like Stanley, Andre and I can live as ourselves without facing persecution?" she asked, looking up at him.

"Most certainly," he said. "But it will be through the progress of medical science, not the work of demons. No demon can permanently transform your body into anything else than a demon, and that transformation would only affect the vampire side of you. If you would like, however, I can research all the latest medical treatments and find out what options are available to you here and now," he offered.

She sighed.

"Unless you can change my genitalia and give me a baby, I don't know what can be done," she said.

"I cannot change your genitalia; however, you can be a mother right now. I was told there is a child ghost in the other room who would love to have a mother again," he told her with a smile, and she also smiled.

"Thank you. You are a good friend to us," she said.

"It's my pleasure. Now, if you don't mind, I do need to go talk to Stanley. I will return in a few minutes," he then said, getting up.

"Is he in trouble?" she asked, worried.

"I'm afraid he is," Belial said. "But you needn't worry about it. He is a grown-up man and he can handle the consequences of his own actions."

"Of course," she said.

He left the room and found Stanley waiting for him in the entrance of the mansion, his arms crossed. He could sense the child ghost with him.

"Shall we go into the parlor—just the two of us?" Belial said.

"I'm ready," Stanley said. "Cornelius, why don't you go with Joe and Andre?" he then asked Cornelius, who nodded and flew back to the dining room, where the couple sat on the sofa in front of the fireplace.

Stanley followed Belial into the parlor and the demon switched on the lights. They sat down together and he pulled out a thick notebook from his briefcase and placed it on the table. He opened it at a certain page then slipped it to Stanley. The young man quietly took it and began to read:

'September twentieth, 1890, Rouen, district two,

Stanley attends a meeting and leaves with Eve. They have an argument. Eve makes a pact with Astaroth. Stanley encounters Joseph and challenges him to a duel. Joseph is killed.'

And, superimposed over the letters, was another note, with a different narrative:

'September twentieth, 1890, Rouen, district two,

Stanley attends a meeting and befriends Joseph. Eve leaves with Astaroth and decides to wait before making a pact with him.'

Underneath both, barely visible, was a third narrative:

'September twentieth, 1890, Rouen, district two,

Stanley attends a meeting and befriends Joseph. Joseph leaves with Andre, who considers making a pact with Astaroth. They have an argument. Andre goes to Astaroth.'

Belial pulled the notebook back to him slowly.

"As you can see, young man, every time you use the Time Key, history gets rewritten slightly differently," he said. "There is a balance between life and death in this world, and if someone who was supposed to die is saved, another person must die. If something bad was meant to happen and you change it, another bad thing will happen somewhere down the line."

"So if I hadn't gone back in time, I could have killed Joe, and Andre could have been the one to make a pact with Astaroth?" Stanley said, shocked.

"And a million other possibilities," Belial said.

"So there is a timeline in which Emily does not die..."

"Stanley..."

"Please, tell me! Tell me what I have to do to save her!" Stanley said, leaning over to him.

"No!" Belial suddenly shouted, getting out of his seat. "Are you stupid, Stanley, or do you just lack common sense? Do you not understand what I just showed you?"

Stanley looked up at him and did not answer. He had never seen the demon angry, let alone so angry.

"This notebook comes from the Time department. It is so dangerous that only I and one other person are allowed to access it, and I would not have looked at it without serious reasons," Belial said. "Every time some idiot like you finds a way to travel through time, not only his or her destiny changes but also that of all the people even remotely connected to them. That is why we just cannot let people rewrite history to their liking. Do you understand that?"

"I do," Stanley said in a low voice.

The demon leaned over the table with a menacing air.

"Now that you have swallowed the Time Key, *you* have become the Time Key, and that means that if someone conspiring against me—and you can imagine how many demons and angels are—finds this notebook and sees whose destiny keeps changing, they would immediately know who possesses the Time Key and how they could use it. So, what should I do with you?"

Stanley lowered his eyes sadly.

"I suppose killing me would be the best option," he said. "You might as well. Nothing changed for me after all. I never became happy and I don't think I will ever be..."

Belial sighed and sat down again. He brought his hands together on the table.

"I apologize. I should not raise my voice like that when I am the one who did not keep my promises to you," he said.

"Belial, please tell me just one thing. Is there any timeline in which Emily lives?" Stanley asked him in a choked voice.

Belial sighed again.

"No," he said. "In all the timelines I checked, Emily dies before the end of the year except, in most of them, she never becomes close to you, Joe, or Andre, and her friendship with Eve is never mended. It is my understanding that all four of you tried to save her last night, so I assume those two things changed in the current timeline."

"Thank you," Stanley said.

A new warmth filled his heart, knowing that, at least, this timeline had been a little better for Emily.

"I'm sorry for your losses, and that I could not prevent them," Belial said softly.

"Can I take a vacation?" Stanley asked in a small voice. "Now that our contract is over and Astaroth is in jail…"

"Our contract is not over. It's a pact, Stanley, you can't back out of it. Furthermore, I have not yet fixed the situation between you and Eve," the demon said.

"I don't think she wants it to be fixed," Stanley said. "I told her everything…"

"And what did she say?"

"I asked her if she was angry. She said she didn't know."

"Well, that's not…" Belial started, but Stanley cut him: "No!"

He rose from his chair and kicked it, except now with his vampire and demonic strength, it crashed against the wall and shattered. Oops. He would have to reimburse Joe and Andre.

"Stanley…" Belial said, also getting up.

"I don't want your help anymore! I just want you to leave me alone!" Stanley suddenly shouted, before leaving the room.

"Stanley, where are you going?" Belial said, rushing after him.

"I don't know… Vienna, Berlin, wherever!" Stanley grunted.

He opened the front door and slammed it so hard behind him the frosted glass part with beautiful mosaics shattered. Eve ran out of the office, frightened, and Joe, Andre, and Cornelius soon arrived, too.

"What happened? Where is Stanley going?" Eve asked.

"He said to Vienna or Berlin," Belial said, looking angry.

"Vienna?" Joe said, confused. "Did you two have an argument?"

"Don't worry, I will reimburse the furniture and the door," Belial promised. "I think he just needs to be left alone right now."

From his conversation with Sorana, he had learned that vampires in general and necromancers especially were solitary and prone to outbursts of anger, and best left alone when angry. They were always suspicious of others and their motives, and only trusted a handful of people selected by them for whatever type of connection they felt with them.

"No!" Eve suddenly shouted, and she, too, ran out the door into the pouring rain.

And vampire women were unpredictable. Belial had forgotten that one.

"We have to find him before he does something stupid!" Joe said.

"I don't think that is his intention. He just wants to be left alone…" Belial repeated.

"Well, friends don't just leave each other alone in a time of crisis. What world do you live in?" Andre said. "Come on, let's go!"

He grabbed two umbrellas and threw his coat and hat to Belial.

"Where to?" Belial asked, putting them on.

"To the train station, of course! Do you think he can fly to Vienna?" Andre said.

Belial rolled his eyes, but followed them, certain that he was right and they were wrong. After all, he had known Stanley for longer than they did and, through their pact, he was his personal protégé.

Only after he had been walking in the rain for several minutes did Stanley notice he had forgotten Cornelius. He could not leave the city without him. But he needed to be away from that house and all the people in it, at least for the rest of the night. Perhaps he could go to the train station and wait for him there. Yes, Cornelius would soon come looking for him. It was not that far away from Joe and Andre's place.

The romantic city looked very different that night, under the rain. It was as though even the sky wanted to cry with them for the loss of Emily. Stanley wiped away a tear. He had come all the way to France, leaving a comfortable, well-paid job with the Order to save Eve, and in the end, he had accomplished almost nothing. Eve was not like Callie, and his love for her never seemed to fade, no matter what happened between them. But now that she knew everything, he could not bear to face her. It was too painful. After their breakup, she had moved on to other men, and fought her own battles. She was long over him, but he would never be over her. He felt his knees weakening underneath him as he walked down the nearly flooded streets, his skinny body soaked from head to toe. He allowed himself to cry at last, as the rain would hide his tears from the few passersby who might see him. How he wished the rain could wash away his body and his soul and cleanse him from within...

The sound of light footsteps running behind him on the wet pavement did not even catch his attention until a familiar voice called out his name: "Stanley!"

He stopped and turned around. It was Eve. She stood under the rain, soaked like him in her black dress, and breathless.

He had never seen her like this, her hair undone, her make-up gone, and her eyes so fragile and vulnerable. She was the young girl from his dreams again, who sat like Cinderella by the hearth, waiting for a prince, but instead only ever came across monsters. That small light of hope had never quite left her, and he felt like if he turned around now, it might. But he had to go, he was suffering too much.

"Eve?" he said.

She threw her hands up in the air.

"So that's it? You're leaving us?" she said.

"Yes."

"You... you can't!"

"Why?" he said in a trembling voice. "Eve, you don't understand the pain I have caused everyone—including you. Everything would have been better if I hadn't played with time, but I was a stupid, arrogant fool. I thought I could make things right for me, for us, and instead I made things worse, and lives were lost because of me. Emily died in the way she did because of my intervention."

"Lives are lost every day, Stanley. You can't save everyone," she said. "If Emily was still alive, a hundred other people would still have died yesterday in this city alone. Some of them might have been your friends. You can't run away from death forever, and you can't run away from me!"

But he wanted to, and not only because of the guilt he carried. Hearts were strange things that made you think you desired something more than anything in the world, and when it was finally there, before your eyes, they made you hesitate to seize it because the result may or may not be what you had dreamed of. He still loved Eve with all his heart, but now the prospect of having that dreaded conversation with her—about them, and whether or not they should pursue the romantic relationship they had started at a distance—terrified him.

"Eve, please go home. You will be better off without me," he said, shaking his head.

He turned around, but she grabbed his arm and forced him to look at her. Damn, she was one strong woman. She could probably rip his arm off and beat him with it if he pissed her off.

"No! I'm not going home until we settle this!" she said, and he realized that she, too, was crying. Seeing tears well up in her beautiful eyes broke his heart, and even more so if he was responsible for them.

"Why are you crying?" he asked in a small voice.

"Because you just threw all this information at me, and… and now you're leaving!" she said, trying to find her words.

"I told you what I wanted you to know, that's all," he said.

"And you won't even hear what I have to say?" she said in disbelief.

He gazed at her intensely, still wanting to escape her but emotionally unable to do so.

"I… When I realized who you were, of course I was angry," she said, looking into his eyes, then away, then into his eyes again. "And then I felt embarrassed and stupid because, all this time, you were watching me and I didn't know who you were. You heard the girls talk about my past as a courtesan, you knew about my relationship with Astaroth. But, most of all, I felt like I had lost you again… Because I, too, was a liar and I didn't want you to know all those things about me. I knew after you heard them there was no way we could ever return to what we were before!"

"What made you think that?" he asked. "I don't care what you did in the past. It doesn't change anything for me."

"Then why…?"

He hesitated and lowered his eyes.

"Stanley, what does your heart desire? Because I know what mine does," she said, moving closer until he could not escape her piercing eyes.

There was no escaping her. She would not let go of him because she had made up her mind. What they had was not broken, only cracked, and the love they felt for each other had already filled those cracks. All she was asking him now was to acknowledge it.

"My heart still desires you… only you," he whispered in a trembling voice. "But I'm not a good man, I'm…"

She did not let him finish his sentence and kissed him instead. He closed his eyes and pulled her into a tight embrace. They both had a past, but she had chosen him, and now he knew he had also made the right choice with her, because she loved him regardless of what he had done, and there was no greater feeling in this world. Their lips parted and she gazed into his eyes and smiled.

"I'm not a good girl either," she said.

"Well, I prefer bad girls anyway," he replied, and they laughed together and kissed again.

So this was how their fairy tale ended, under the pouring rain in the streets of a small French city. He never would have imagined it that way, but now that she was in his arms, he knew he wanted to keep her there forever. They were so absorbed in each other they barely noticed someone holding an umbrella over their heads. Joe had arrived first and, quiet as always, he sheltered them from the rain, looking away as to protect their privacy but still peeking now and then, taking mental notes for his next novel. By his side, Cornelius stared at the two of them, wondering why they were playing kissy kissy under the rain when they could do it indoors. A few paces away, Andre and Belial walked briskly under an umbrella of their own.

"Did I miss something? I thought they were not on speaking terms," Belial said, confused, as he saw them.

"You know what your problem is? You think too much like an attorney. You should read Joe's novels. They always end like this," Andre told him with a smile.

Indeed, the demon thought he would have to check them out—for his work, of course.

Because Emily's only wish in her human and undead life was to exist and be remembered, they all agreed that she needed a grave in her name. Of course, there was no body or death certificate, but Joe had friends who ran an undertaker business in the city and one of them knew how to pull strings, so a place in a graveyard was found and a headstone ordered in her memory, and they decided they would have a small chest with her picture in place of a casket, and fill it with flowers, notes, or objects dear to them they wanted her to have, wherever she was now. Joe had taken care of everything and paid for it. Eve had traveled to Paris to close down Emily's shop and gather some of her items she wanted to keep with her, and Andre had kept himself busy preparing the funeral and letting out his anger against a punching bag in the gymnasium. Stanley, who still blamed himself for what had happened, had preferred to hide in the dark. But now the day he dreaded had come, and he had to face it.

"Stanley, Eve, it's time to get up," Andre said in a disheartened voice as he knocked on the door to their room.

Stanley pulled Eve closer. They were not mates yet, but right now they did not want to spend their nights alone, so they slept beside each other, fully dressed. And though their friends already considered them a couple, both of them felt like it would be wrong to call themselves so, not so soon after Emily's death.

"Stanley, we must go," Eve told him softly. She did not want to go to their friend's funeral any more than he did.

"I don't think I can," he whispered.

"We must," she said. "Do you remember our promise to celebrate her life?"

Eve got up first and helped him up. She then left him to go clean up in the bathroom and fix her hair somewhat. He also got up and arranged his black suit and gazed at the bowtie Joe had given him. It was black but seemed inappropriate, so he went over to Joe and Andre's room and knocked on the door. Joe opened it, looking as tired and weary as him. Stanley smirked.

"Look at us. We both look like a mess," he said.

"I guess so," Joe said sadly. "Did you need something from me?"

"Do you have another tie? Something not so... festive?" Stanley said, showing him his black bowtie.

"Of course," Joe said.

He walked over to his closet and came out with several other black ties, then picked one and tied it around Stanley's neck.

"I guess this is the night we say goodbye to her..." Stanley said, grabbing his hand when he was done.

Joe shook his head and smiled.

"No, Stanley, this is the night when we make her dreams come true," he said.

Stanley also smiled at him. Eve then walked out of the bathroom. She had put on her hat and covered her face with a black veil, and she wore her brown shawl around her shoulders.

"This is not too much, is it?" she said softly.

"No, it's what most people would wear," Stanley assured her.

He offered her his arm and they went downstairs, where Andre and Belial awaited them, both dressed in sober black suits. Cornelius immediately jumped into Joe's arms. He wanted to be carried that night.

"The carriage is ready," Belial said. "Our friends from the funeral home will be waiting at the graveyard."

They stepped outside and all got inside a small carriage and rode over to the graveyard. The sky was clear that night and the air was getting colder; the summer had come to an end and the world was quietly preparing to fall asleep during the cold season.

They arrived at the graveyard, where three vampires and a human awaited them. They were the people from the funeral home. Among them, Stanley recognized the short woman with black hair and a faded pink dress: she was the owner of the other funeral business in London. Perhaps she had moved here. They had prepared a simple, rounded headstone with a flower bouquet engraved on it and the name 'Emilienne "Emily" Martin'.

"Well, I will go first," Andre said, knowing that if he did not, no one would.

He kneeled by the small chest and place a folded note and a daisy beside Emily's picture.

Joe then went to the chest and placed a small notebook he had filled with poetry for her inside.

When her turn came, Eve went to the chest and sat for a long time beside it in the grass, gazing at her friend's picture.

"Emily… I brought something special for you," she said, removing her shawl. "This is not my mother's magical shawl, but I made it just the same. Faustine once told me that my mother had given me the gift of love so that I could give it to others and make it multiply. But I was not able to give it to you who so deserved it…"

She wiped away the tears rolling down her cheeks. Stanley joined her and kneeled beside her as she neatly folded the scarf and placed it in the box. He then drew a small flower bouquet from his breast pocket. It was a little late in the year, but he had found some daisies – Emily's favorite flowers—and purchased them the night before.

"Emily, I don't have a letter or poems or even a shawl to give you, but I will keep your ashes with me, forever," he whispered, and as he gazed at her picture, he thought he saw her smiling at him.

When all were ready, the men from the funeral home closed the chest and lowered it into the grave they had dug, then filled it with dirt. Emily's friends watched them until they were done, unable to walk away or say goodbye. Just as they were finishing, small white flakes began to fall from the sky, spiraling slowly down to them.

"Snow? In September?" Joe said, surprised.

Stanley opened the palm of his hand and caught one of the small flakes. It was not snow, but a flower petal. It could have been brought by the wind, but there were no trees in full bloom at this time of the year.

"Emily…" he whispered, and Eve leaned against him and let out the rest of her tears.

"I need to go home… to Montpellier and the mountains," she whispered.

He pulled her closer and closed his eyes.

"Let's go there together," he said.

CHAPTER 19

"So all this time we were on your 'team' and you just didn't feel like you needed to tell us?" Joe said, his arms crossed.

Across the table, Belial leaned forward, his hands together. After Astaroth's arrest, he had finally decided to gather them and explain to them why they all knew him but not of each other working with him, and Joe did not trust him. Andre was surprised, Stanley indifferent.

"The whole point of having secret agents is that they are secret, Joe," Belial pointed out. "I did not lie to any of you. I brought you and Andre back to France from the Americas because of the actual threat posed by a dark lord, and I brought Stanley to you because I knew you would befriend him, and that I might need all of you to help in the capture of Astaroth."

"We're both necromancers. You were taking chances," Joe said. "What if he had challenged me to a duel instead?"

Belial smiled.

"The two of you lived in the same neighborhood in London for years, literally a few blocks from each other, and it never happened," he said.

"What about me? I made a pact with Astaroth. I'm not on your 'team'," Eve said. "Unless you want to offer me another pact."

"The only way to cancel a pact with one demon is to make another with a demon equal to or above them in the hierarchy. That means, if you wanted to be free from your pact, you would have to make one with me, but I know you do not want that," he said.

"Indeed."

"But you still want her to work for you," Joe said.

"I hope she will, but I cannot force her," Belial replied. He then turned to all of them. "I still have not been able to solve the mystery of Beelzebub's murder, and now we are apparently facing a very powerful being who can impersonate others. He or she has decided to impersonate Stanley, which means you might all be targets. So our work together is not over."

"Couldn't it be the candyman though?" Andre said. "Stanley says he can steal anyone's face."

"Possibly. We still don't know exactly what his basic powers are, and the way he tried to murder Emily - through long-distance strangulation—is one of his operating methods," Belial said. "However, if he was capable of creating an alternate reality, then why did he never use it with Stanley?"

"It's not him," Stanley said, a frown on his face. "And the puppet master does not create an alternate reality. Rather, he appears in the alternate realities of powerful creatures of the underworld and uses their fears and weaknesses to control them. He seems to enjoy hurting and terrifying them before killing them."

Belial listened, intrigued, then wrote down a few names in a small notebook.

"Any ideas who it might be?" Joe asked.

"No, but *what* he might be, yes," Belial said. "I have done some research about your kind and learned there are two kinds of 'vampires': the strigoi, purely a bloodsucker, not very powerful, and the moroi, who may also drink blood to survive but have primarily psychic abilities. Andre and Eve are spirituals, and Joe and Stanley are necromancers who can talk to the dead and create alternate realities to trap their victims like spiders. All of you are moroi, and so is the puppet master.

"Moroi... yes, I've heard that word before, in Emily's world," Stanley said.

"And so have I, but where...?" Joe wondered.

"Could it be from a certain Sorana?" Belial said with a grin.

"You know her?" Joe said, his eyes opening wide.

"Is she a friend?" Andre asked him.

"She's a necromancer and we never killed each other," Joe said, uncomfortable. "I met her over a thousand years ago. She was from the old kingdom of Dacia, now called Transylvania, and a part of the Austro-Hungarian Empire."

"Precisely," Belial said.

"So, what? The puppet master is a moroi like us? That doesn't really help us," Stanley said.

"Indeed," Belial said, "So, here is what I have at the moment."

He clapped his hands and the diagram he had previously shown Stanley appeared on the table before them.

"My three prime suspects regarding the murder of Beelzebub are the seraphim Adeyemi Ojo, Yvan Thompson, and Astaroth," he explained. "Only Yvan Thompson, known to hate demons with a passion, has an apparent motive, but he lacks the power and is not known to work with others. Adeyemi Ojo has the power but no motive and has even offered his full cooperation in my investigation."

"He could be trying to cover up his tracks," Stanley remarked.

"True," Belial said. "Then, Astaroth himself would have no motive to murder the third member of the Evil Trinity, especially one below him in terms of power, unless he is not Astaroth but a body thief, as Eve believes. He is, however, adamant that he is Astaroth and I was not able to find any substantial proof that he is not."

"He's lying," Eve immediately said.

"And I believe you, however, I must proceed with caution," Belial told her. "There has to be proof of his true identity, and I will find it."

"So, what about the puppet master?" Stanley asked.

"What we have so far are only two of his victims and his operating method," Belial said. "Aleksandra was a seraph, a water elemental and shapeshifter. Emily held no important position, but was an air elemental. I went around my list of suspects once more, and though Yvan Thompson was not said to be very fond of Aleksandra, there would be no point in him eliminating the third in line to the seraph throne when he is already second. As for Emily, she has no connection to any of them. So my investigation is stalled. At this point, I am open to all your suggestions."

All exchanged glances.

"We don't have any," Joe said.

Eve got up and walked across the small, crowded parlor. Stanley knew she was not well yet and wanted to go home to the south of France, but Belial was concerned about letting the group separate.

"I need some air," she finally said, and she left the room.

Stanley got up and followed her.

"Eve..." he said in a low voice as he joined her in the corridor.

"I know that demon wants us to be safe, and I understand that the puppet master is very dangerous, but... I just need a break from all of this," she whispered. "I need to go back to Montpellier, to Faustine's old store, to see the mountains again…"

"Then let's go," he said.

"Stanley… you always side with me," she said.

"Do you not want me to?"

She sighed.

"Why don't you go rest for now? I will deal with Belial," he offered.

"I suppose I should…"

He smiled.

"We're in a luxury mansion with electricity and indoor plumbing. Might as well enjoy a hot bath, right? I think Joe even has some scented oils hidden somewhere in the bathroom," he said, making her laugh, then she lost her smile.

"Stanley…"

"Yes?"

She seemed to hesitate, then shook her head.

"No, nothing."

She left him and went upstairs to take a bath, and he watched her leave. Joe, Andre, and Belial then emerged from the parlor and Belial grabbed his coat and hat.

"Keep in touch with me regularly," he said, before taking his leave.

Andre stretched.

"I'm stiff, I'm going to work out," he said. "Joe?"

"Darling, you know I don't like sweating," Joe said.

"That's not what you say in bed…" Andre replied, making his lover blush.

Stanley rolled his eyes. Those two were still too much for him.

"I'll be in the library then, I'm also not a fan of sports," he said.

Apart from a gymnasium with all the latest equipment, the mansion had a full library—some of the books belonging to the landlord, and some to Joe and Andre. Stanley seated himself in a chair and pulled a cigarette case out of his breast pocket. He knew he was a guest in this home and the goody-goody Andre, who was into healthy vampire living and sports – whatever that meant - did not want anyone smoking or drinking around him, but he was dying for a smoke right now.

"Cornelius?" he called out, but the child ghost did not answer. He was probably taking a nap in the wall somewhere. He was never very interested in adult conversations.

Stanley shrugged and was about to light his cigarette when Joe walked in.

"Oh, Stanley, please…" he started, and Stanley cut him: "I know, I know."

He got up and was about to head outside.

"I meant: can I have one too?" Joe said with an accomplice grin.

Stanley smiled in return and followed him out in the backyard—a small patch of grass with a few benches and a table. They sat together around the table and lit themselves a cigarette. The nights were getting cold, and the city was quieter now. Stanley turned his gaze to the starlit sky. It looked as lonely as he felt right now in this world, even surrounded by new friends. Whether as a human or a vampire, his life would always be marked by grief and loneliness.

"So, Andre, the sports enthusiast, won't let you smoke and drink? How do you deal with that?" Stanley asked casually.

Joe lowered his eyes.

"He loves me and wants me to be around for a long time. And I love him and want to be with him," he said.

"Sorry, I didn't mean to judge your relationship," Stanley said.

"I used to be an alcoholic… Even now, I would kill for a drink," Joe admitted, sucking on his cigarette nervously, and Stanley noticed his trembling hands.

He gazed at him quietly and realized just how much effort the old, depressed vampire put into keeping up with his new-found love. He still thought they were polar opposites and had no clue what brought them together, but after all, to each their own.

"Are you going to leave us?" Joe suddenly asked, turning his black eyes on him.

"What makes you think that?" Stanley said, shrugging. "We have to protect this city and perhaps the entire world from chaos with all these demonic and angelic conspiracies…"

"But what do you want to do?" Joe asked.

He knew him quite well already and understood that he was unpredictable and not always true to his word. Stanley turned back to him and smiled sadly.

"I have a feeling that if I just go on a whim, you will follow me," he said. "We're necromancers. Even if we are friends, we like to know where the other necromancers are and what they are doing. We watch each other like predators."

"You're wrong," Joe said, lighting himself another cigarette. "You still haven't helped me buy an embroidery kit."

Stanley smiled and laughed softly.

"True."

Joe smiled in return, and he had that look in his eyes again—that perverted look.

"And I need to know how your romance with Eve will evolve for my next book. It's prime material," he added.

Stanley raised an eyebrow.

"Is that your thing? Thinking about what others do in bed?"

"It is," Joe said.

"Are you a voyeur?"

"With years and years of experience."

Stanley chuckled.

"You'll be disappointed. Nothing is happening between us."

"Why?" Joe asked, turning serious. "Because of Emily?"

Stanley did not answer and moved his gaze away.

"Did you love her?" Joe asked him.

Stanley brought his fingers to his chest and felt the shape of the small vial containing her ashes in his pocket. It was his new token, which he would never part with.

"Stanley, you don't have to force yourself to love Emily because she loved you. And you don't have to hold back from loving Eve because of her," Joe told him.

"I'm not forcing myself to do anything, nor am I holding back," Stanley replied.

"Then… what?" Joe said.

"I think I did love Emily, or I could have loved her, but not as much as Eve. Eve is a great woman, a public speaker, someone women admire. Emily and I were just ordinary people—invisible people in a crowd. My heart belongs to Eve, but I don't think I could ever forget Emily, and now I feel guilty toward both of them…" Stanley admitted in a small voice, but Joe was not overly concerned about it. He offered him another cigarette and Stanley took it.

"Thank goodness your heart still works. I was getting worried," he said.

"What?" Stanley said, surprised.

"It's normal to fall in love, and sometimes with more than one person at a time," Joe explained. "How you decide to live these loves is up to you, but in your present situation, only one of the women you love is still alive—in our world. Don't let that love drift away because of another that can no longer be lived. Being with Eve here and now is not like betraying your feelings for Emily."

"Are you saying I should just forget Emily?" Stanley asked him.

"No, just acknowledge your feelings for her and be ready to move forward with Eve."

"Like you did after losing Alice?"

"How do you know about her?" Joe asked, frowning, but he quickly figured it out. "It was you, wasn't it? The one who visited my room in London? And you followed me to Alice's grave..."

"Nothing personal, one of the seraphim sent me to investigate you," Stanley said, appraising his reaction, but Joe simply shrugged.

"I suppose it was old Yvan Thompson. He really needs to find himself a hobby," he said with a sigh. "Alice was a pen friend; we never met in person. I couldn't possibly tell her I was a vampire, and I can't touch women or be close to them. I don't know why. But still I believe—or I want to believe—that we loved each other over the forty years or so we corresponded. It took me over a decade to move on after she died. I spent my sleepless days and nights living in the memory of her, worshipping the letters she left me, crying, drinking a lot... I never realized that I was digging a grave and just burying myself in it until I met Andre."

"And how did Andre change that?"

"I eventually moved to Paris with my friends, who introduced me to another human, Elise. She died that very night in a fire. It was not an accident. She was murdered," Joe said, lowering his eyes.

"I'm sorry…" Stanley said.

"So, I decided to cross the Atlantic with friends and go somewhere—anywhere but here," Joe continued. "But I brought my depression to New York with me and even my friends could not cheer me up. I drank more and more and became darker and darker."

Stanley leaned closer, intrigued.

"One night, my friends dragged me to a performance and Andre bumped into me in the street," Joe said. "It was love at first sight, for me at least. He had someone already. When I saw him dancing on the stage, it was like the skies had opened up and Icarus himself had descended into my world. I was restless, jealous, longing… I had never felt that way before with any of the women I loved. Also, I didn't know know he was transgender, so I had to question my preferences."

"So, how did you end up together?" Stanley asked.

"Andre and his sweetheart broke up soon after and he started following me around," Joe said, smiling to himself. "Andre wants to see the best in everyone. I still don't know what he sees in me, but, little by little, his warmth and his light began to fill my world. But of course, I'm a necromancer, so you can guess things were not all smooth and easy. Gang wars, another necromancer, a duel, both of us almost died, and then Belial showed up and said he needed some muscle back in France and I just happen to be one of the most powerful vampires alive, so here I am…"

"Goodness, Joe… That sounds like an amazing romantic thriller! Why don't you write about that?" Stanley said.

"It's a lot more fun writing about other people's lives," Joe pointed out, making him laugh.

"But I'm curious about one thing... Andre is female bodied. Do you not have any problem being 'close' to him?" Stanley asked, as the old vampire intrigued him more and more.

Joe seemed to reflect on it for a moment, then said: "I don't know. I think I react to how I perceive people rather than what their body looks like. I would never have known Andre was transgender if he hadn't told me. I'm not clueless—well, maybe I am—but I've met a lot of people in this world and not all men look masculine or have deep voices. When I met you, I also never suspected anything. I have been deeply in love with women and those feelings were genuine, but I didn't love them like a man loves a woman, and I didn't behave like a man toward them. Perhaps that's why most of them rejected me or lost interest. I like to feel like a damsel in distress with Andre... He is my knight in shing armor."

He covered his reddening cheeks with his hands like a young girl in love, and Stanley raised an eyebrow.

"So, you love women like a woman and men like a man?" he asked, puzzled.

"Something like that," Joe said. "I've stopped trying to figure myself out a long time ago because I just can't."

"I suppose it would be awfully rude of me to ask you *how* you are intimate with Andre..." Stanley said.

Joe burst into laughter.

"But you want to know, right?"

"Please?" Stanley asked with a grin.

"If I tell you, will I get all the details of your passionate love with Eve?" Joe asked, back to his voyeur self.

"Probably not," Stanley said, laughing.

"Stanley..." Joe said, pouting.

"But kissing her was like... tasting Eden's forbidden fruit," Stanley said.

Joe immediately pulled out a notebook and pencil from his breast pocket and jotted it down.

"Eden... fantastic!" he said. "What more?"

Stanley lost his smile and turned somber.

"And nothing more," he said sadly. "Our situation is very different from yours and Andre's. We started corresponding several years ago, just like that. We had never met in person. The tone of our letters became increasingly romantic, and then someone—probably Astaroth—tampered with one of the letters I sent her, and she stopped writing me. So, I decided to come to France for her. She didn't know me since I always wrote her under a fake name, but she figured it out eventually, and here we are now... It feels awkward. Where do we start up again?"

"I see," Joe said. "But I'm sure she feels the same, and it's going to be awkward until you both have an open-hearted conversation about it."

"That's not my forte," Stanley remarked.

Joe reached across the table and took his hand. They held hands now, as friends, but also as a way to communicate strength to each other. Perhaps it was a necromancer thing.

"I know how you feel. Eve is a very strong woman, and she is also very much older than you, so you're afraid things may not work out, but I'm not worried for you two," Joe said. "You have what matters the most: that burning flame that never quite died."

Stanley smiled at him.

"Thanks, Joe."

"And when you do get some 'action', please make sure to report to me," the old vampire added, making Stanley laugh again. He sure was persistent in his quest for steamy details about his friends' lives. Who ever knew the pervert hidden behind those romantic black eyes?

Stanley returned to the room he shared with Eve and found her already laying in the bed. She had changed into a long-sleeved nightgown and the whole room smelled like floral soap and herbs. Thinking she was asleep, Stanley closed the door quietly behind him and removed his shoes and jacket and tie. She rolled over in the bed and gazed at him in the dark. Her long black hair was still somewhat damp after bathing and she wore no makeup. He preferred her natural, like this, but he also understood why she wanted to wear makeup.

"Did I wake you up?" he whispered.

"No, I was not sleeping," she said. "Come here."

She parted the blankets so he could slip underneath them, but he hesitated.

"Stanley, at some point we need to be able to sleep like normal people, like a couple," she said.

"Of course," he said.

He got underneath the blankets with her and gazed into her eyes. They were alone in the quiet room, and Cornelius had been asked not to barge into the rooms shared by adults now, or he might see something he did not want to.

"Eve, I have something to tell you…" he said, taking her hand.

"Yes?"

He hesitated and drew in his breath.

"What is it?" she asked.

But, not finding the words, he grew silent instead.

"Stanley…" she then said, lowering her gaze. "I feel guilty… because of Emily. She was in love with you."

"I know," he said. "But even if she had lived, and no matter how much I liked her, my heart was already taken. It belonged to you."

She smiled sadly.

"Knowing that you liked her somehow makes me feel better. She deserved to be loved."

"But we also have to live in the present," he said. "If vampires do live almost eternally, then we will lose many more friends along the way. We might even lose each other."

"I don't want to think about that," she said, closing her eyes. "I just want to be with you, right here and now."

"That's also what I want," he said, pulling her closer.

"Do you still love me like you said in your letters?" she asked in a fragile voice.

His heart was racing again. There was so much he wanted to tell her, so much he needed to tell her.

"I love you…" he whispered, "With all my heart, my soul, my life. I love you like I've never loved anyone before. You're not a fetish for me. There is just something in you that lights a fire inside me every time I see you, every time you speak. I want to become one with you, in every way…"

Her cheeks reddened slightly as she listened to his impassioned words.

"But if you don't…" he started.

"I do…" she cut him. She turned her shining black eyes up to him. "Even before you gave me the rose and I realized you were Ernest, I felt attracted to you. I didn't want to, because I didn't want to fall for yet another man who might break my heart. But I felt good with you, like we had known each other from a past life… I've been with men who liked men and men who fetishized transgender women, but no man, ever, liked me for who I am, until I met you."

Stanley brought her hand to his lips and kissed it softly.

"Why are you only kissing my hand when we both want more?" she whispered.

He felt his cheeks blushing, too.

"I… I'm afraid I don't know what to do… or how to do it, you know, with a transgender woman. I don't have any accessories…" he admitted, embarrassed.

She laughed and moved closer.

"Well, how about I teach you about my body and you teach me about yours?"

He nodded.

"Treat my body like a woman's," she instructed him.

He shifted under the sheets as the heat grew in his body. What he felt for her was very different from his young, naïve feelings for Callie. He had loved Callie because she was the embodiment of all his desires, but he loved Eve because she filled the holes life had burnt through his heart and healed them with her magic. He did not only want to make love to her, but to become one in body and soul, to fuse with her until they formed just one eternal entity, and it was exciting yet frightening.

Moving his hand slowly up her nightgown, he caressed the bare skin of her neck. She rolled onto her back and stretched out her arms, gazing into his eyes with longing.

"Touch my breasts," she said in a languid voice, and so he slipped his hand into her nightgown and began to caress her chest, paying particular attention to her nipples. She closed her eyes and breathed in deeply.

With gentle fingers, he unlaced the front of her nightgown down to her belly, and moved over her. His lips came down on her quivering skin and he breathed in her sweet scent. Her hips shifted underneath him, and he could feel a bulge forming between her legs. With his tongue, he slowly trailed up her belly, her torso, and up to her neck, savoring the skin he now wanted to bite. It was an urge even more powerful than sexual desire, somewhat similar to what he had felt when he first met

Joe, but much stronger with Eve. But he remembered what it meant in their world and tried to hold back.

He suddenly felt her fingers creeping up his shirt and unbuttoning it. He moved back slightly, and she continued, and when she was done, her fingers caressed his binder underneath. He removed his shirt completely and proceeded to unfasten the binder for her.

"You don't have to remove it," she told him in a whisper.

He shook his head.

"You're not wearing your corset. I also don't want to hide anything from you. I just would prefer if you don't touch my chest."

She nodded.

"I will make sure not to."

He smiled. Callie always pretended that she respected his boundaries and his identity, but deep down, he knew that she only considered him as crossdressing woman. That was why, in his upside-down reality, she picked his female-bodied self over the male-bodied. Not being a man in her eyes frustrated him, and he hoped that it would be different with Eve. He removed his binder and exposed his bare chest to his love and she gazed at him tenderly.

"Do you see me as a man now? Please tell me the truth," he told her in a whisper.

She sat up, slipped her hand behind his neck, and kissed his lips.

"You are absolutely a man," she then said, smiling, and he also grinned.

Her hands then began to unfasten his trousers, and he let her proceed and remove them, as well as his underwear.

"Are you going to look at my body too?" she then asked.

He felt nervous again, and hesitated. She had not given him all the details, but he knew that she had been sexually abused by Astaroth. But if she was asking him to take off her clothes now, then it meant that she wanted it. He was not forcing her in any way. She lowered her eyes.

"Please, undress me," she bid him.

So, he slowly pulled down her nightgown and helped her remove it. She would not look into his eyes until he was done, and he could sense her discomfort, so he brought his hand to her cheek and caressed it.

"You know I will never force you or hurt you," he reminded her, and she nodded, then looked into his eyes.

"Do you still see me as a woman? I have a penis…" she said, unsure.

Though she had extensive sexual experience, he could tell that all of her partners had disrespected her body and her identity. She was romantic and dreamed of a magical love, but all she ever got were bits and pieces of love she had to pay for with sex, so she had detached herself from it for many years. And now she was faced with the possibility of her adolescent dreams finally coming true. She felt just as frightened as Stanley did.

"It's not a penis, just a large clit," he said, and she laughed softly.

He wrapped his arms around her and lay her back down on the bed and looked into her eyes. They were closer than ever like this, skin against skin, their hearts beating fast.

"Are you nervous?" she asked.

"Me? Not at all," he said, smirking, and she laughed again. "Liar."

"You think I'm lying? Let me show you," he said, diving into her neck and kissing it as his hands caressed her torso and her sides.

His fingers found her nipples again and teased him as he kissed her, passionately this time, and she moaned softly and shifted underneath him. She grabbed his fingers and guided them to her bottom parts. He understood her demand and began to stroke them. She rolled her head back and moaned again. But he was uncomfortably aroused himself and he, too, needed to feel pleasure with her. So, he moved his leg between hers and began to rub himself against her leg while still stroking her. She slipped her fingers in between his legs and also began to stroke him. He came instantly and let out a soft cry as she teased his sensitive spot. He had not measured just how aroused he was. The heat between their bodies was intense now, even if their blood was cold. She moved forward and kissed his lips harder, parting them with her tongue and pushing it deep into his throat. His thoughts were a mess now, and he rubbed himself harder against her hand as his tongue hungrily sought hers. He came again, wetting her leg, and stroked her harder. Her bulge hardened more and more under his strokes, and she pulled him closer and kissed him fiercely until she, too, reached her climax. She looked into his eyes as her body still shook from the waves of pleasure, and her eyes were gentle and vulnerable. In that moment, he knew that she was his, that he had imprinted on her heart and soul so deeply nothing could ever erase him. He, the invisible nobody, was suddenly somebody, and the new warmth that filled his heart almost made him cry. He smiled and kissed her, and gazed into her eyes again as though he could never get enough of them.

"We're… dirty now," she finally said, and he grinned.

"I guess we are," he said.

She laughed and pulled him closer.

"Thank you… for respecting me. It means more than you can imagine," she whispered in his ear.

"I love you, Eve," he told her again. "And I want to show you my love in every way, by respecting you, by loving your body in the way you like, by protecting you… I hate the fact that other men couldn't do those basic things for you."

"I don't want to think about them anymore," she said. "I want to feel loved, free, and happy with you only."

"Then what shall I do next to make you happy, my love?" he asked, smiling.

"Well, I can think of a few things," she said with a naughty grin, and so she showed him the many other ways he could pleasure her that night.

The next evening, Stanley was the first to come downstairs. Eve was getting ready to go out with him for the first time as a couple, and it filled his heart with pride and joy. This was the beginning of a new life for both of them—not quite the happiness he had imagined, but still happiness. Belial had not failed him after all. Now he and Eve were reunited, and he had even made new friends. His life was not so lonely and dark anymore, and he no longer had any desire to use the Time Key. He gazed at the fireplace and the fire still burning inside it. Though Cornelius was given a room of his own, he was asleep on the sofa, a book in his hands, and, though he did not need it, Joe had covered him with a blanket to make him feel at home. Perhaps they could furnish his new bedroom with books and toys during their temporary stay, Stanley thought. He would submit the idea to his friends. Speaking of them, it was unusual for Joe and Andre not to be up already—neither of them were late sleepers. He checked the kitchen and the office, but did not see them. He then heard a noise in the gymnasium on the other

side of the mansion. It was right beside the solarium, which the
vampires only used at night, of course.

As he walked slowly down the corridor, his hands in his
pockets, he thought he heard heavy breathing and panting
sounds. *Seriously?* he thought. The sounds became louder as
he got to the gymnasium, and they were accompanied by loud
thumping. Stanley grimaced. Who knew they liked it rough?

"Are you getting there yet?" he heard Joe ask casually.

"Not quite…" Andre said, panting heavily.

"But you've been going at it for an hour, darling," Joe said.

"I can't… stop… until I'm spent," Andre replied.

Stanley's eyes widened. What on earth were they doing
in there and why was Andre the only one not 'spent' yet? It
had to be some very acrobatic fetish. He wondered whether
he should go back upstairs discreetly, but now a sort of sick
curiosity crept inside him. He was not particularly interested in
what two men did together, but he wondered what Andre and
Joe did. So, he quietly peeked inside the gymnasium and saw
Andre there, in black tights, ballet pointes, and a loose-fitting
white balloon-sleeve shirt. He was practicing his dance moves
and a new aerial and landing heavily on the ground. Stanley
did not understand anything about ballet, but he could see the
technique and precision required, and what Andre was doing.
He was in control of every muscle in his body, of every move
he made, like a king in his own world, but he was dancing for
the king of his world, Joe, who sat at a table in the solarium,
sipping on a cup of tea and gazing at him like a dazzled damsel.
Every few seconds, the pair exchange lovey-dovey glances that
made Stanley roll his eyes.

"Oh, good evening Stanley," Joe said, finally noticing him.
"Would you like a cup of tea?"

Stanley grunted.

"You two were so loud, I thought you were doing something else," he said.

"Like what?" Andre said, coming to them.

He shook his sweaty hair and grabbed a towel to wipe off his face. Stanley, who did not care to sample his bodily fluids, moved away.

"Could you please keep your sweat to yourself?" he said, annoyed.

"Why? Sweating is healthy. You should work out, too," Andre said with a smile.

"No thanks," Stanley said, but Andre leaned over to him as though he was scrutinizing his face.

"What?" Stanley said, blushing.

"Someone's cheeks are awfully fresh and rosy tonight. I wonder what happened?" the naughty blond said.

"Did something happen?" Joe immediately asked, attentive.

"What? No!" Stanley said, blushing even more.

He hated having friends after all, especially when they were so nosy about his intimate life.

"A fresh, rosy complexion, shining eyes… It must have been a pretty intense night of lovemaking," Joe remarked. "Did she put up a fight? Did you seduce her?"

"Joe!" Stanley protested.

"Aren't you going to tell us? Come on!" Andre said playfully.

"No! Mind your own business, dapper boy!" Stanley said, pushing him away, but Andre laughed and pushed him right back. Stanley then took his towel and proceeded to chase him until they were both pushing and swatting each other with the towel. Eve joined the small group and sat beside Joe, who moved his chair away slightly as he always did around women.

"What exactly are they doing?" she asked.

"Letting out some steam," Joe replied. "Tea?"

"Yes, please."

He poured her a cup of tea and she took a sip of it, then gazed around the solarium and the gymnasium as he eyed her with shining eyes.

"Do you also work out?" she asked.

"I don't like sweating," he politely replied.

They sat awkwardly together for a few minutes before Eve broke the silence.

"Joe, I meant to apologize…"

"Huh? For what?" he asked, surprised.

"For not being very friendly with you the first time we met. I was so bitter and unhappy back then," she said, lowering her eyes.

"You don't need to apologize," he said. "I can tell whether people actually hate me or are just unhappy with their lives, and I never felt like you hated me."

"But I told Stanley I did," she said, turning back to him with guilty eyes, and he laughed.

"I'm a famous author of sultry romance; many people love me and just as many hate me," he said. "But I'm glad we are friends now, and I'm hoping you can teach me how to embroider."

"Embroidery? Yes, I can teach you," she said, smiling, and he smiled in return.

"Love looks beautiful on you. It gives you a brand-new glow," he remarked, and she blushed slightly.

"So, now that we are officially friends, you must tell me what happened last night," he then said. "Does Stanley need some coaching? I can recommend toys…"

Eve laughed.

"I think we can manage," she said.

She had never met anyone quite like Joe and Andre before, and, despite her original reaction to them, they had welcomed her with open arms and treated her and Stanley as their close friends. And they did not want anything from them in return but their friendship, and perhaps some sultry anecdotes for Joe, which he would not get.

The poor Joe sighed and turned back to his love and watched him play with her love. The recent events had been tragic, but some light had come out of it. The smiles on Stanley and Eve's faces made him happy, and he hoped nothing would come to shatter this happiness.

Cornelius, who had awakened, flew into the solarium through the walls and immediately claimed Eve's lap, saying: "Mummy!"

"Oh, you scared me sweetie!" she said, laughing, as she scooped him up in her arms.

He curled up against her and let out a contented sigh.

"Will you and Stanley read me another book tonight?" he then asked.

"I will tell you fairy tales you have never heard before, tales from a faraway land of mountains and magic!" she promised him.

"Really? Did you also learn them from a book?" he asked, turning his big black eyes to her and she smiled lovingly.

"No, they are from *Maman*—my mummy," she said. "A long time ago, when I was a little girl, she gave me the gift of love so that I could go out into the world and give it to special people like you and Stanley."

"Is your *Maman* still alive or is she a ghost like me?" Cornelius asked.

"Well, I don't know. She had to leave this world, but I think a part of her lives inside me," she told him. "And I know she is watching over her new grandson now."

Cornelius smiled with delight and hugged her. She closed her eyes and held his little ethereal body against her heart. She never thought she could be a mother someday, and yet she also had a child to love now. Joe gazed at them quietly, smiling, but the telephone suddenly rang, startling Eve.

"Don't worry, it's probably nothing. I'll get it," he said, getting up.

He went to the office to pick up the call. It was Belial.

"Good evening. What's going on?" he asked pleasantly.

"Joe, where are Stanley and Eve?" the demon immediately asked in a serious voice.

"Right here, at home, why?" Joe said.

"And they both spent the day there?"

"Of course. Vampires cannot go out in the sunlight. We sleep during the day."

Belial did not respond.

"Did something happen?" Joe asked, suddenly worried.

"Some stupid kids managed to find a real book of spells and summon Astaroth back into this realm," the demon said.

"I'm not sure I understand…" Joe said.

"Some of our most powerful spells were stolen by humans a long time ago—witches like Eve's ancestors," Belial explained. "We eliminated all those we could find and burned all their books and scrolls. But some witches managed to conceal these spells with a magical formula in the blank pages of a book that was passed down from mother to daughter for generations—and I believe that would be the book Eve once found and discarded."

"I still don't…"

"Well, that book mysteriously reappeared right here in Rouen, on the shelves of a public library, of all places," Belial continued. "It was placed there intentionally by someone who wanted humans to find it—and they did. A group of wannabe sorcerers. The book's pages were filled with silly, made-up formulas humans think we use, but they somehow managed to summon Astaroth from his prison in Hell."

"But I thought no one could open the gates of Hell except major demons," Joe said, frowning.

"Exactly. No one, and I mean it," Belial said. "There is no way the book's seal could have been lifted unless a major demon or a witch like Eve was present with them in the same room."

"It wasn't Eve. She didn't leave the mansion," Joe assured him. "Could it be any other demon?"

"I don't think it was," Belial said. "Major demons can open the gates of Hell, but our magic leaves a trail. I know who goes in and out of Hell, and no one crossed the void between worlds last night."

"Belial, I'm getting very nervous. Can you please stop this gibberish and tell me who you think did it?" Joe said, agitated.

"Someone who can lift the veil between worlds and dimensions. Someone who seems to be nowhere in our reality but also in everyone's alternative realities…"

"The puppet master…" Joe whispered. "So, he is also a witch?"

"Or a necromancer."

Joe's hands began to shake. Indeed, some necromancers could infiltrate other's minds and the worlds they dwelled in, but he had never heard of one who could use that form to travel to other dimensions, such as Hell. Unless that necromancer had become a demon…

"It's not Stanley!" he immediately said. "He was in Emily's world with us, and we all saw the puppet master—at least his shape in the shadows."

"Calm down. I don't think Stanley is the puppet master," Belial said. "But he may be someone with a very similar path as Stanley. I know only of two other necromancers who became demons and are still alive: Mammon and Sorana, and both are absolutely loyal to me. But there could be others. After all, I only came across Stanley after another demon had secretly recruited him."

"Please don't tell me we're going to have to fight another necromancer…" Joe said.

"I don't know, Joe. I'm still investigating," Belial said. "For now, do not take your eyes off Stanley or Eve, not even for a second. Even if it wasn't her, Astaroth is on the run now and she might be in danger."

"I understand."

Joe put down the receiver and gazed at his trembling hands. As necromancers, he and Stanley were among the most powerful undead creatures and only needed to fear their own kind or major demons. But they were friends now, and they had Eve with them who, if she was not a demon, combined the magic of witches with the supernatural being she carried within, and was probably as powerful as a major demon.

CHAPTER 20

THE OLD CARRIAGE STOPPED in front of the heavy iron gates surrounding what appeared to be a Medieval castle in ruins. The coachman looked around him, lifted his hat, and scratched his head. He did not recognize this place, neither did he know it even existed. When his client said he was going to Deaulme Castle right outside of Portsmouth, he assumed he had made a mistake and meant Portchester Castle. But as they traveled down the muddy roads in the middle of the night, his client told him to turn down a narrow path into the woods. He wondered whether the man had bandit accomplices waiting for him in the dark to rob him, but the mysterious man seemed a lot wealthier than he, the humble coachman.

"I-Is this the place, sir?" he asked aloud.

"It's here," the man's deep voice said inside the carriage.

The coachman pulled on the brakes and got down to help the man out. At least he had promised to pay him good money for this little adventure in the dark—whatever he intended to do in those ruins. He opened the door and the tall gentleman with a tan and smooth, long black hair, stepped out. He was one of those elegant dandies, the sort who could spend a fortune on a daring green suit with a matching hat and a purple tie. He closed his eyes and breathed in the night air, seemingly enjoying the smells of mud and manure left by the horses on the path.

"The British countryside… what a lovely place!" he said.

The coachman raised an eyebrow.

"Better watch your footsteps, sir. You wouldn't want to soil your shoes," he warned him.

"I will be careful," the stranger promised, as he pulled out his fat wallet. "Oh, and before you leave, you might want to check the left rear wheel. It's making noise."

"Oh, thanks. I will check it," the man said.

He went around the carriage and the traveler put away his wallet, and pulled out a carpet bag, from which he grabbed a large leather apron. He removed his jacket and hat, rolled up his sleeves, and put on the apron, then went around the carriage.

A single scream echoed throughout the forest, and the horses became agitated and started stomping their feet as they heard the sounds of a beast feeding behind them and smelled fresh blood. They pulled and tugged at the carriage so hard the brakes eventually broke, and it started moving in the mud. But before it could go anywhere, the stranger came back around the carriage. He calmly discarded his bloody apron and wiped the corners of his mouth with a handkerchief. He then put on his jacket and hat, took his canvas bag, and detached the horses. The two mares, terrified, immediately ran off. The man smiled and pushed the gates open. He walked leisurely down what was left of the path leading up to the castle, stepping over thorns and fallen branches, and avoiding those still on the small trees and shrubs, until he reached the old ruins. There, he went around and knocked on the back door. After a good ten minutes, an old human opened the door.

"May I help you?" he lazily asked, as though the man's peculiar appearance did not surprise him. Though he was human, he wore butler clothing from the last century and did not seem to know what year it was.

"I am here to see Lord Yvan Thompson," the stranger politely told him.

The old butler sighed.

"And who shall I announce?"

"Astaroth, Great Duke of Hell," the traveler said with a smile.

"This way please," the old man said.

He took the demon up a series of winding stone stairways and into a great hall in which the walls were decorated with tapestries representing Norman conquests and battles. At the end of the hall, sitting on an antique wooden throne, was the man he had met on a train as he fled France, except he had traded his modern black suit for what appeared to be his favorite fashion—a seventeenth century wine-colored justaucorps and breeches with an abundance of lace.

"His Grace Astaroth, Great Duke of Hell," the butler announced, before excusing himself.

Yvan cringed. He hated demons, but sometimes people in his position had to make unspeakable deals to protect this world from vermin.

Astaroth walked over to him with a grin on his lips and bowed slightly before him. They were almost of equal rank in their respective worlds. Yvan rose from his seat.

"Astaroth... Will you be staying for dinner?" he asked.

"I had a snack on the way," Astaroth replied. "Shall we sit down and talk?"

Yvan pursed his lips and threw a glance over his shoulder. Adeyemi was getting suspicious of him and was likely to send someone or *something* to spy on him. But the great hall was empty apart from the two of them.

"We can talk here," he said, turning back to Astaroth. "I suppose you have very important information for me, which you could not disclose when we first met."

"Indeed," Astaroth said. "You and I have many things in common."

Yvan scoffed.

"You have some nerve… What would I have in common with a demon?"

Astaroth put his travel bag down and began to pace across the hall slowly, pretending to admire the tapestries.

"I heard you lost someone several centuries ago," he said. "I just happened to find that someone and make a pact with him."

Yvan's eyes opened wide with terror.

"What… You did this to him?" he said, furious.

He balled his fists and began to power up. A great, white halo formed around his body and his skin tone slowly changed from white to red. His long, smooth black hair began to lift in the air as he prepared to attack, but Astaroth waved his hand in a friendly gesture.

"There is no need to fight here and now, my friend," he said. "I saved a dying man, stuck in the middle of his transformation into a vampire. Nasty wounds. Not repairable. So I gave him some of my essence instead and gave him the ability to steal someone else's appearance, even if only temporarily."

Yvan drew in a deep breath and tried to control his anger. After all, he was the one who had killed Florian and destroyed him mentally. This demon had only saved him. His skin returned to its normal tone and the halo around him disappeared.

"Tell me the truth… Does Florian also work for you?" he asked.

"The candyman works for himself, did you not know that?" Astaroth replied. "But it is a long story."

"I'm listening," Yvan said.

"You see, it all started with Beelzebub, the third member of the Evil Trinity, wanting a certain demon candidate. And to get him, she ordered Belphegor, the Gatekeeper of Time, to break our laws and let a succubus 'borrow' the Time Key and use it. This, of course, was bound to draw the attention of someone like the candyman. Once the key had been returned to Belphegor, he murdered him and stole it. He passed it along to an accomplice, but he, too, got murdered and our special demon candidate stole it. Beelzebub, who had then already obtained his allegiance and made a pact with him, never knew he was in possession of the Time Key, until he used it and vanished."

Yvan sat down in his throne, an angry look on his face.

"Continue," he said.

Astaroth casually walked over to him and seated himself on the armrest of the wooden throne, crossing his legs.

"It did not take very long for Beelzebub's precious new recruit to betray her, and a little bird told me that the candyman even found him a job on the other side…"

He turned to Yvan who stared at him, horrified.

"Stanley… Suspect?"

Astaroth nodded.

"But Stanley is disloyal by nature, so he betrayed you too, and now he works for our side again."

"For you?" Yvan said.

"No, for Lucifer himself."

Yvan covered his face with his hand. This was bad—very bad. It was simply too easy for these hitmen to cross from one side to the other, gathering extremely sensitive information along the way. They were both double agents and had fooled everyone.

"But if Florian wanted the Time Key, why did he not steal it from Stanley?" he asked.

"That's the best part of the story…" Astaroth replied. "The Time Key somehow fused with his body. In essence, he *is* now the Time Key."

Yvan shook his head in disbelief.

"So, did Stanley or the candyman murder Aleksandra?" he asked.

"Neither," Astaroth said, getting up. He turned around to face him. "I told you the best part of the story, but I left out the most frightening one. There is someone else out there, someone with the powers of a major demon, and whose sole intent is to destroy this world. He has Stanley's talent, the candyman's insanity, and Adeyemi's mind control abilities."

"Then we must involve Lucifer and…" Yvan said.

"No. The crazy man up there will not hear of this, and neither will Lucifer," Astaroth said, losing his smile. "Lucifer is weak-minded, he has spent too much time among humans and is incapable of making the right decisions for this world."

"But isn't he your liege?"

Astaroth's eyes turned dark and cruel.

"I'm tired of being only a 'part' of the Evil Trinity," he said. "In the end, only one will reign over Hell, and that one will be me."

Yvan stared at him in shock.

"You… You killed Beelzebub?"

Astaroth nodded.

"I did, and I am going to steal Lucifer's body, but for this, I need your help."

"Why? This is none of my business," Yvan said.

"But it is your business," Astaroth said. "In order to carry out my plans, I need two spiritual vampires' help, and they will not cooperate unless we capture their mates and hold them hostage. But, if these mates get killed by our new enemy or the candyman in his quest for the Time Key, then my plans fail, and you also fail to protect this world."

"So, in order to save this world, we only need to find out who this new menace is and capture vampires?" Yvan said. "What would my role in all of this be? You are powerful enough to capture vampires."

Astaroth smirked.

"I need you to watch Adeyemi, and also tell me all you know about the Escobar witches."

Yvan suddenly remembered Aurelia Escobar's prophecy and shuddered.

"Escobar... impossible!" he whispered. "I killed the last of them!"

"Eve Chauvin is her direct descendant," Astaroth said. "The little bitch tattled on my plans and had me arrested, but someone helped me escape... by giving a group of humans access to one of the forbidden spells known only by major demons and seraphim."

Yvan's blood almost froze.

"You think... Adeyemi is the one trying to destroy the world?" he said in a trembling voice.

"I do not know, and I am not close enough to him to find out. This is why I need your help," Astaroth said.

Yvan covered his face again. He had spent all his mortal and undead life fighting against evil, only to now find out it had potentially infiltrated even the seraphim order. And now the only way for him to save this world was to make a pact with a demon who wanted nothing less than to take over Hell. God would never forgive him.

"I will help you," he finally said, turning back to the demon. "I have only one personal request."

"I am sure I can accommodate it. What do you want?"

Yvan's eyes filled with tears.

"Once this is all over, please let me use the Time Key so I can save Florian—even if it means living forever without him. I'd rather he had a chance to live his life as a human and die than live like he does now."

Astaroth frowned. He did not like the idea, but if that was all it took to secure him a seraph as his ally, then he could bend the rules for him.

"Alright, you will be allowed to use it once, and solely for that purpose," he said. "So, do we have a deal?"

Yvan rose and stood before him.

"Yes, we do," he said.

"You know how us demons seal contracts," Astaroth then said with a grin.

Yvan glared at him, his body trembling slightly. Yes, he knew, and he also had a fairly clear idea of what this one would ask for—he could read it in his eyes.

"You cannot place your mark on me," he stated coldly.

Astaroth's grin widened. He moved up close to him until Yvan could feel his sweet demonic breath upon his lips. They were almost of equal height, and this demon purposely assumed an attractive form – attractive enough to corrupt even his senses. The demon's long, slender fingers moved up to his face, then traced its contours down to his neck. Yvan's body stiffened as the tempting fingers slowly went down the fabric of his justaucorps until they reached his breeches. He closed his eyes and drew in a deep breath.

"Poor Yvan…" Astaroth whispered in a sultry voice. "It's hard enough spending a human lifespan denying yourself what you desire most, but to spend all eternity pretending to be somebody else must be excruciating."

"I am not pretending to be somebody else," Yvan said, opening his angry eyes.

They fixed on the demon's, who seemed to particularly enjoy the situation.

"If I cannot place my mark on you, how about inside you?" he whispered, and Yvan's entire body shuddered with the terrible delight of imagining oneself giving in to sin.

"That is not what God..." he tried to say, but the demon's lips suddenly fell upon his, silencing him. He tried to struggle, but the demon caught both his wrists in a marvelously tight grip. With a defeated moan, Yvan closed his eyes and let the man kiss him until he was done, until his tongue begged for more, until he felt like his body might just catch fire right there and then if he did not give in to him. Astaroth moved back slightly and grinned with satisfaction.

Yvan opened his eyes again and asked: "Are we done now?"

The demon chuckled softly.

"Silly, that was just an appetizer. You know exactly how I am going to put my mark on you. But I need you to agree to it first."

He still held his hands in a firm grip, and Yvan did not want him to let go. Anger, disgust, as well as desire rushed through his entire body now. He had been down the path to Hell with Florian already, and it was indeed paved with temptation, but to go down that path with a demon this time...

"Say it," Astaroth bid him, knowing he had already won this game of power.

"My chambers are upstairs," Yvan finally said in a whisper. "I have shackles and whips..."

The demon's eyes shone with interest.

"Well then, we'd better head up there," he said.

CHAPTER 21

FLORIAN STOOD ALONE AT the bottom of the dark staircase leading up to the attic. It was an old, wooden staircase—the sort that creaked underneath one's footsteps. All over the gray walls that had not been repainted in years were large brown water stains and clusters of black mold, and the air smelled of mildew. The door to his right, the one leading to the other rooms, suddenly shut and the attic door opened a crack. Long threads of blood began pouring down the walls and the stairs until they reached his feet. He grinned and began to chew on a piece of barley sugar as he climbed the stairs, and then he pushed the attic's door open – a dusty attic, pretty ordinary apart from a set of ritual objects on a small altar and a Ouija board on the floor. The door slammed shut behind him, and he slowly turned to the figure sitting in the shadows, on a pile of discarded toys, and tipped his hat.

"Good evening," he said. "Nice place, really. It could use a little dusting."

That night he wore his preferred appearance, that of a young student with overgrown, curly brown hair, and an air of innocence. He was dressed in a brown suit with a red bowtie.

"Welcome," the other replied in the shadows.

"I thought I was coming to a party," the candyman then said with a mischievous grin. "But where are all the guests?"

The other raised his left hand and dozens of spirits emerged from the wall. There were men, women, children, soldiers, all dressed in the fashion of the time period in which they died.

"Right here," he said. "How did you make it up to the attic? Have you no fear of anything?"

The candyman broke into laughter and pulled out another piece of barley sugar.

"Of course I do. I'm terrified of running out of these," he said, showing him the candy, and the one in the shadows grinned.

"Ah, I should have known," he said. "But now you have found me, I must kill you."

The ghosts all moved closer to the candyman, who shrugged.

"You can't kill me, because I am an anomaly. I'm not even supposed to exist."

"Is that why you are so desperately trying to find the Time Key?"

The candyman laughed again.

"No," he said. "I am trying to destroy the Time Key. The man who did this to me wants to go back in time to prevent it from happening, but I want it to happen. I want him to remember it and suffer for all eternity!"

"Then we have something in common," the other said.

"Everyone has something in common with you, when you look hard enough," the candyman said. "Let us work together."

"I don't work 'with' anyone. I make them work for me," the other responded.

"That's unfortunate. I guess I shall have to work alone then," the candyman said.

He was about to turn around and leave the attic, but the ghosts moved in front of him.

"I didn't say you could leave, did I?" the one in the shadows suddenly said in a dangerous voice. He rose from his position and slipped his hands in the pockets of his brown and black cutaway morning suit.

The candyman turned back to him and grinned.

"Is fear your thing? I can be afraid if you want me to. I can beg on my knees too," he joked.

"I don't need that. I need a new puppet," the other said. "Become my puppet and I will give you what you desire."

"Oh, shall I call you 'Master' too?" the candyman said, laughing to himself.

"You're insane," the other said, "but you can be useful to me."

He stepped out of the shadows and presented him his hand. His middle finger bore a toy ring, as though he were the king of some fantasy childhood realm.

"Do they not make gold rings in London?" the candyman asked him.

"We're not in London, you nincompoop. We're in Transylvania," the other replied.

"My apologies," the candyman said. "This world is so strange, I often forget what reality I am in."

He kneeled and kissed the toy ring that was presented to him.

"There is no such thing as reality—everything in this world can be flipped upside down any time," the other replied with a grin.

"That is the best way to enjoy it… I am the candyman, and you are?" Florian said, looking up at the familiar face.

"Stanislav," the other responded.

About the Author

JC COMPTON IS A non-binary author with an international background, being born in France and now living in the USA. They have a degree in East Asian Studies and are particularly passionate about Japan and China. Their multicultural experiences and friendships are reflected in the diversity of their characters and the worlds they create.

"If you want to reach the sky, aim even higher" could be their life motto.

JC writes diverse LGBTQIA+ fantasy, sci-fi, and paranormal romance stories, and is the author of the self-published series Undertakers Inc. They hope to bring readers exciting, empowering, fun, and creative stories where the LGBTQIA characters are the lead and their friends of all backgrounds and orientations are also represented.

Excellent LGBTQ+ fiction by unique, wonderful authors.
Thrillers
Mystery
Romance
Young Adult
& More

Join our mailing list here for news, offers and free books!

Visit our website for more Spectrum Books
www.spectrum-books.com

Or find us on Instagram
@spectrumbookpublisher

www.ingramcontent.com/pod-product-compliance
Lightning Source LLC
Chambersburg PA
CBHW051510250626
47156CB00001B/36